The Wish List

The Wish List

GABI STEVENS

paranormal romance
A TOM DOHERTY ASSOCIATES BOOK
NEW YORK

THE WISH LIST

A Tor Book
Published by Tom Doherty Associates, LLC
175 Fifth Avenue
New York, NY 10010

www.tor-forge.com

Tor® is a registered trademark of Tom Doherty Associates, LLC.

ISBN 978-0-7653-6503-3

First Edition: May 2010

Printed in the United States of America

0 9 8 7 6 5 4 3 2 1

To Bob, who always, always says the right things (except when he doesn't). You are my hero.

ACKNOWLEDGMENTS

As usual, I couldn't have made it through this book without the help and encouragement of Barbara Simmons, Molly Evans, and Shelley Wimmer. Ladies, you provide more strength than you know.

A final read from Lydia Parks made all the difference in the world. Thank you for taking time out of your (unbelievably) busy life and giving me your input and your friendship.

Alessandra Anderson has always believed in me and has helped me so much with the fantasy elements. And she's introduced me to so many wonderful authors and stories. Of course, I know where she lives, so she's easy to track down. Baby girl, you have no idea how important, beautiful, and spectacular you are.

And while I speak a few languages, French is not one of them, so I thank Hannah Rabinowitz for her input. Hannah, next time I call you for help, don't panic.

I also want to thank Marlene Stringer for being an extraordinary agent, Heather Osborn for making my book stronger, and Melissa Frain for all her help too. The professional side of this business is much easier with women like you in my corner.

In addition, although I have never met the woman, I'd like to thank J. K. Rowling for making the world believe in magic again.

The Wish List

1

HOW TO BE A FAIRY GODMOTHER:

•

Never Reveal Yourself to Your Charges.

SAN DIEGO, CALIFORNIA

THE AUNTS HAD summoned her.

Their cryptic message had left her alternately curious and worried. Why were they so adamant to see her? Something about a job and "it's time."

Kristin Montgomery parked her Camry in front of the bungalow in Mission Beach and locked the door. As usual she'd found a great parking spot. She shouldn't have. Parking in the crowded streets of the little beach community should have been a bear, yet a space always waited for her whenever she came to visit the aunts.

Kristin inhaled deeply. The ocean breeze played with her hair, and the fresh sea air contained a tang that always smelled of adventure to her.

Today the smell of adventure was even more powerful.

Don't be ridiculous, Kristin. She turned up the walk. Deep pink bougainvillea bushes lined the path to the door. The house seemed normal from the outside, still as charming and quaint as the day her aunts moved in when she was a teenager. The cottage was some seventy years old and had a value of over seven hundred thousand dollars. Only in San Diego could a tiny box with a postage stamp yard be worth so much.

The three old women weren't really her aunts, and they couldn't really summon her, but Kristin loved them. But why had they sent for her?

She rang the doorbell, then tried the door. As usual, it swung right open. "Haven't I told you it's not safe to keep your door unlocked?"

Chaos greeted her. Suitcases, bags, and a huge trunk yawned in the living room in front of her. Clothes draped over the sides, maps and papers filled the pockets, and a lone shoe sat in one bag while its mate lay on the floor.

Aunt Rose walked out of the study, her arms filled with a jumble of clothes. "Oh, tosh, dear. No one would harm us." She brushed a kiss against Kristin's cheek. "It's good to see you again, love."

Kristin eyed the tiny white-haired woman. "Do you need any help?"

"Nonsense. I'm not carrying bricks." Rose placed the top three items into the first suitcase and the rest into the second.

Kristin followed Rose. "Are you moving?"

Aunt Lily entered the room. "Don't be silly, dear. We'll explain in a moment." Tall and lithe, Lily clutched a large bottle of sunscreen and towels draped over her arms. Her iron gray hair sported three pairs of sunglasses and two hats sitting at a jaunty angle.

"Planning an outing to the beach?" Kristin raised her brows.

"One does not take suitcases to the beach, dear," said

Lily. With a tilt of her head, she deposited the sundry items into the nearest open suitcase, then arranged them in an orderly fashion.

"So what's going on?"

"It's the Time of Transition," said Rose with a bright smile.

"Transition?" Kristin wrinkled her forehead.

Hyacinth, the aunt who completed the trio, strode into the room with brochures, pamphlets, and other papers sticking out of a purple folder. "You haven't told her yet, have you? You didn't start before I was here, did you?" Her short silver hair bounced on her scalp as she shook her head scoldingly at Rose.

"Of course not, Hyacinth. We wouldn't do that to you." Rose lifted her shoulders in an endearing shrug. "We're a team."

"But you're here now." Lily moved to Kristin and took her hands. Rose and Hyacinth gathered around her as well. They exchanged glances with one another, as if sharing a conspiratorial secret. Lily said, "We're not really your aunts, dear."

Kristin stifled a laugh. "I know that."

Hyacinth burbled out a puff of air. "And as much as I hate to admit it, we're getting old." She lifted a finger as Kristin's mouth opened to protest. "It's true. We've gotten slow and that's a problem."

"But it's the Time of Transition, so we can celebrate," said Rose. "Our tenure has come to an end."

"Excuse me?" Kristin eyed the three old women. What were they talking about?

"Your turn to take over, dear," said Rose. She turned to her companions. "What time does the taxi arrive?"

"Thirty minutes," said Hyacinth. "Damn, we'll never be ready."

"Of course we will, and watch your language. It just doesn't suit us to curse," said Lily.

"None of our charges can hear me," said Hyacinth.

"Kristin can," said Rose.

"She hardly counts. She's one of us now." Hyacinth examined the suitcases. "We'd be better off if we combine some of these. We might not be able to handle so many bags."

"You may be right, Hyacinth." A rare frown touched Rose's face, but an instant later it dissolved into her customary smile. "If we need more room, we can always buy more suitcases."

"Or zap up a couple," Hyacinth said.

"Maybe not. Our powers will be in flux and our wands might act up," Lily said.

Kristin held up her hands. "Hold it. Wands?"

"Yes, dear. Wands. But we can't be sure how reliable they'll be." Lily reached into a bag and transferred its contents to another case. "Still, we should take fewer suitcases. Definitely."

"Wait." Kristin waved her hands until the aunts looked at her. "Let's start over. First, where are you going?"

"On a world cruise, dear," said Rose, combining the contents of two bags. "It's been so long since we've traveled."

"For a vacation anyway," Hyacinth added. "It's our retirement gift to ourselves."

"Retirement?" As far as Kristin knew, the aunts had never held jobs. She always thought it odd that they seemed well-off despite no visible evidence of income, but she never considered it her business to ask. "Retirement from what?"

"Why, being fairy godmothers." Hyacinth closed one

now-full suitcase. "It's the Time of Transition. Time for us to step down."

Uh-huh. Fairy godmothers. Kristin drew a deep breath. "You're joking, right?"

"We wouldn't joke about such a serious matter," said Rose. "Now where did I put my brush?"

"Here it is." Lily handed it to Rose. "'Fairy godmother' is such an inaccurate term. Really we're more like liaisons, but people seem to understand 'fairy godmother' better. I'm sure your arbiter will explain."

"Arbiter?" Kristin's brows drew together.

"The person appointed by the Council to oversee your transition." Hyacinth closed another suitcase. "Sometimes they can be a pain in the—"

"Hyacinth," Lily said sharply. "Anyway, I'm sure your arbiter will be fine."

Kristin scrutinized the aunts. They had never shown signs of delusion before. "When was the last time you had a physical? A complete examination? Maybe you should postpone your trip and make sure you're healthy enough to go. You've admitted you're old."

"She doesn't believe us." A bright laugh tinkled from Rose's throat.

"I blame the modern world," said Lily with a sigh. "No one believes anymore."

"Some still do." Hyacinth cocked her head at Kristin.

"Well, naturally Kristin does," said Lily. "She is Arcani."

"Arcani?" Kristin's voice rose in pitch.

"A member of the magical world," Rose said.

"Look, Aunties, I love you, but I don't believe—"

"Do you remember your seventh birthday?" said Lily.

"Sure. I begged my parents for a pony. I didn't get one."

"Of course you didn't get one. We aren't irresponsible." Hyacinth snorted at the thought. "You didn't get that pony because you couldn't have cared for it. Your parents didn't have the money to board it, and you certainly couldn't have kept it in your backyard."

"But that's what I wished for."

"You wanted a pony so badly. Your every wish on every star was for that pony." Lily sighed at the memory. "Every dandelion you blew, every time you went through a tunnel, every wishbone you broke, you spent that prayer on your pony."

Kristin wrinkled her brow. "How do you know that?"

"Just because we didn't get you a pony doesn't mean we weren't listening," said Rose with a smile. "That was the year we sent you Mr. Pickles."

Kristin's jaw dropped. Mr. Pickles had been her cat and the best companion she'd ever had. The animal had been the friendliest creature on the planet. She wore him draped around her neck as a child, used him as a confidant when she was a teenager. Her heart had broken when she had to leave him with her family when she went off to college. But Mr. Pickles had waited for her, and during every break and vacation, the animal gave her the emotional support she needed as she took her first tentative steps into adulthood. She would have sworn more than once in their many years together that the cat understood English. Mr. Pickles had died last year, a well-loved and dearly missed friend.

"Mr. Pickles." Hyacinth chuckled. "I always thought it was a ridiculous name, but he liked it."

Her knees weak, Kristin plopped onto the sofa. "What do you mean, 'he liked it'?"

"You don't think we'd send you an ordinary cat, do you? Cats can be so contrary, but Mr. Pickles was special." Lily patted Kristin's shoulder.

This was absurd. Kristin calmed herself. "Look, you can't be serious about all this."

"Why not?" said Lily.

"Because . . . because . . ."

"Now you're just being stubborn." Hyacinth sat beside Kristin and hooked her arm around Kristin's shoulders. "We've been watching over you for years."

"But there're no such things as fairy godmothers." Kristin rubbed her forehead.

"Nonsense, dear. We're standing in front of you," said Lily.

"We're really quite famous," added Hyacinth.

Rose nodded. "You studied the Brothers Grimm."

"Well, yes, but—"

"They were great historians. They wrote about us. Well, not *us*, but our predecessors."

"And now our time is up. The Time of Transition is here." Lily crossed to an antique armoire. She opened the doors and pulled out a slender case that looked as if it could have held a flute. "You must choose."

Lily opened the case. Inside lay three slender batons. Gnarled, yet with a smooth patina, each switch glowed with its own colors—yellow, red, and black. Ornate handles of beautiful filigree work wound up the bases. The gold that encased the yellow wood held gems in a classical design; the green verdigris of the red wand looked like vines twisting up a stalk; the stark geometric designs of silver contrasted sharply against the black wood of the third. Kristin picked up the red wand. It tingled in her hand and warmed her palm.

"Well done," said Rose, clapping her hands.

"That one is like mine," said Lily. "Magic with a good dose of reality. It suits you."

"How can it suit me? I'm a CPA." Kristin's sense of frustration grew.

"You chose it." Rose shrugged and spread her hands.

Kristin drew in a deep breath. "Aunties, you can't think—"

"Admit it. There's a part of you right now that's hoping we're right." Hyacinth crossed her arms over her chest.

And in that mix of emotions that swirled through Kristin—the shock, the disbelief, the exasperation—there *was* a spark of hope, a wish that it all was true. "Fine, but that doesn't mean I'm magical."

"Arcani, dear. Sorry to hurry you, but we're running out of time here." Lily pushed the case back into the armoire and then closed a third suitcase. "Your apartment lease is up in a week."

"How did you—" Kristin interrupted her own question. They knew. Somehow they knew.

"You can move in here," Rose said as she closed the trunk. "We won't be here for months, we need someone to care for the house, and you love it. Besides, this house knows magic. The test will go smoother here."

"What test?" asked Kristin, feeling more overwhelmed by the minute.

"The Time of Transition is a testing period to see if you are capable and worthy of the job. Your arbiter has the final say." Hyacinth tightened the straps on the trunk. "But we have faith in you."

Kristin tried to form an argument, but no words sufficed. She had to say something. "Aunties, I don't have powers. Not a twinge, not a hint. Logic, sure, but magic? I don't even have luck."

The three ladies stopped, looked at her, and burst out laughing.

"Well, of course you do," said Lily. "The gifts of a fairy godmother don't come into bloom until the age of twenty-seven. Three times three times three. Quite the magic number. Your birthday was only last week."

"Even then, it takes years to come into the powers fully." Hyacinth sat on the trunk. "It took me a decade."

"A decade?" Kristin stared at the three women. "Just how old are you?"

"Ninety-seven," said Hyacinth. "It's been a great journey, but I'm ready to rest."

"I stopped counting at eighty," said Rose. "It just isn't polite to celebrate birthdays and expect presents after that."

"Seventy years is long enough at any job. Now we have time to take our little vacation, and then see where the Magic needs us," Lily said.

Questions whirled in Kristin's head. Ninety-seven? Wands? Magic? She shook her head. Impossible.

"I know this is a lot, dear," said Lily, patting Kristin's arm. "But one of your tests is adaptability. We weren't allowed to prepare you."

"This is insane." The words burst from her lips. "You actually believe you are fairy godmothers and I'm next in line."

"Ooh, that attitude won't help you." Rose shook her finger at Kristin. "You've lots to learn in the next few weeks."

From the street a car honked. Hyacinth poked the

curtains apart and looked out. "Taxi's here. I'll tell him we need help." Hyacinth bustled from the room.

Kristin stood. "Look, I'd love to house-sit for you while you're gone, but—"

"Excellent. That's the first step." Rose hugged her. "You'll see. The right person was chosen."

Lily gathered her purse, fished through the massive depths, and pulled out a set of keys. "Here you go, but you don't need to bother with locking the house. No one harms the fairy godmothers."

As the keys hit Kristin's palm, their sharp edges proved how little they had been used.

Rose wrinkled her nose. "There was that one time . . ."

"No need to frighten the child," Lily said "That episode occurred sixty years ago. Old news. We took care of it then, and nothing has happened since. No one will harm her."

Hyacinth returned with a Filipino cabdriver who grinned at each of them. "Benito has come to help us with our luggage."

"Ladies, it is my pleasure." The smiling man grabbed two of the suitcases and lifted them. "I'll be back for the trunk."

Hyacinth nodded in appreciation. "Remember when Benito was a boy and we—"

"No time, dear," said Lily. She turned to Kristin. "You'll find a list of rules and tips in the printer by the computer."

" 'How to Be a Fairy Godmother.' The title was my idea," said Rose with a self-satisfied smile. "I know how much you like rules and lists."

"I recommend practicing here at home first before you go out on the street. You'll do great, kid. You've got the spirit, the gift, and the brains," said Hyacinth. She hugged Kristin, wiped her eyes with the back of her hand, then cleared her throat. "I'd better go help Benito before he hurts his back again." Hefting a satchel, Hyacinth left the room.

Rose took out a handkerchief and dabbed at her eyes. "Hyacinth never did like to show her emotions. I envy you. Just starting out. It will be wonderful. Remember: Refer to the rules. They will help you. I wish your parents could have lived to see this." Crying in earnest now, Rose grabbed her purse and hurried out of the room.

Her parents? She was the only child of an older couple who had prided themselves on their common sense. They wouldn't have believed any more than she did.

Benito returned with a dolly and hoisted the trunk onto it. "I hope you don't mind me using this. I found it by the front door."

"That's why I put it there," said Lily with a smile. She waited until the cabdriver had left, then cupped Kristin's cheek. "You parents would've been so proud of you."

Kristin had to try one last time. "Aunt Lily, please. You can't—"

Lily shook her head. "Don't start off with negativity." Then her expression changed to a look of sympathy. "I know it's hard. It was easier in my day. We believed so much more than they do today. But you'll be fine. We'll pop in to check on you in a couple of weeks." Lily kissed Kristin's cheek.

Pop in? From a world cruise?

Benito came back and lifted the last bag. "This it?"

"Yes, thank you, Benito. You're a good man."

The cabdriver blushed. "Just doing my job." He left the room again.

"This is your home now," Lily said. "Take your time, and try not to let logic get too much in the way of your instincts. Good-bye, dear, dear Kristin."

Lily followed the cabby outside. For a moment Kristin stared after her. Then she heard the door to the cab close, and she ran to the doorway. The three aunts waved at her through the car's windows as the taxi pulled away from the house.

Kristin looked down at her hands. She still held the keys and the red wand.

Right. A wand.

She turned slowly, walked back into the cottage, and flopped onto the sofa again. She tossed the keys onto her purse, and then placed the baton on the coffee table and stared at it.

The burnished wood glowed in the sunlight, and the green metal encasing it looked almost alive. She picked it up again. The handle molded to her palm as if it were made for her. A thrill shot through her. Maybe . . .

Pulling her bottom lip between her teeth, she swished the wand.

Nothing. No colorful sparks, no flowers popping out of the end, no triple-scoop hot fudge sundae on the table in front of her.

Kristin laughed at herself. The aunts could be allowed their fantasies. Their delusions were harmless. If they wanted to believe they were nearly one hundred and fairy godmothers, that was fine. They would hurt no one with their stories. The wands were pretty pieces of art, no doubt. Not magic, but pieces of fantasy art. She'd store this red one safely beside its sisters in the case. She opened the door of the armoire.

The case was not there.

With a frown, she laid the wand on the shelf and checked the other spaces. Nothing. Hmmm. She must have been mistaken when she saw Aunt Lily return the case to the armoire. Well, she'd find it later.

In the meantime, the house was hers to use, and she'd enjoy living here. The small but beautiful garden, the sea air, the interesting neighborhood—she had always liked it here. She might as well see what her aunts had left her to read. "How to Be a Fairy Godmother." Entertainment, pure and simple, and probably good for a few chuckles.

She walked to the study where the computer was hooked up. Top-of-the-line machine. She hadn't realized the aunts were so savvy. Kristin reached for the printer, then stopped.

No papers lay in the output tray. The printer was empty.

2

HOW TO BE A FAIRY GODMOTHER:

•

Always Keep Your Wand Handy.

SHE SHOULD HAVE known.

No instructions rested in the printer's out tray, no sheets in the feeder tray, no papers at all. She was an idiot to have believed there might have been. Chagrin seeped through her.

No sense brooding about it. On the bright side, her short-term housing problem was solved. She had been dreading signing another lease on her fleabag apartment.

Her brow furrowed. Her lease expired in a week. She had taken this week as vacation for the move. But by now all the preliminary work should have been done. By now she should have compiled a list of suitable places, visited them, and narrowed down her choices. Why hadn't she? Inaction was most unlike her. Had some part of her known she'd have this house?

She snorted. *Don't be stupid.* She didn't believe in

psychic powers, ESP, magic, or fairy godmothers. A CPA lived for numbers and rules, not intuition and premonitions. She calmed down. The aunts' house was here and she needed a place to live. A convenient solution, and practical as well. Although *she* would keep the front door locked.

Twenty minutes later, she parked her car in front of her apartment building (and she wasn't going to think about how she found another parking spot directly by the door). Excitement bubbled through her. She was finally moving out of this place with its warren-like hallways and rarely functioning safety features. Kristin walked toward the building door and pulled out her key in case the security door was actually working today.

"What the hell do you think you're doing?"

She whirled around, and her throat closed in fear. A hulking brute of a man stood beside her, glaring at her. In the next instant, his fist shot out. Screaming, she cringed and braced herself for the blow.

It never came.

"Stop that noise."

Startled silent, she stared at him. His hand was behind her back, and he was practically growling at her. He cast his gaze skyward. "God, Aldous, what did you get me into?"

The man's scowl almost made her scream again, but instead she wrinkled up her forehead. "Are you going to hit me?"

"What the hell are you talking about? I don't hit women." He held out his hand. "What were you thinking?"

Clutched in his fist was the red wand. Startled, she looked up at him. "Where did you get that?"

He shook it at her. "It was following you. Why didn't you stow it?"

"What are you talking about?"

"Your wand. It was following you. Do you *want* to be seen?"

"Seen? What the hell are you talking about?" She stared at the wand in his hand, and then looked into his eyes.

And froze.

A burnished copper gaze blazed back at her, its fire summoning images of Vulcan's forge. Black hair shadowed his brow, and an aquiline nose guided the burning gaze into hers. Her breath rushed out of her.

Wow. What a face.

Wow. What an angry face.

He glowered at her. "Take this thing." He thrust the wand at her.

She took it. "Who are you and how did you get this wand?"

He closed his eyes as if seeking patience. "I didn't get the wand; it followed you. That's why you either stow it or carry it with you." He reached into his jacket's inner pocket and brandished a long white willow stalk wrapped in gold and inlaid with ebony. "Like this."

"Oh my God, you think you're a fairy godmother . . . er, godfather too?"

"Very funny." He squinted at her with a mixture of disbelief and disdain. "I am a wizard, not a fairy."

"Oh, well, pardon me." She didn't care how lovely he was to look at; she wasn't about to hang around with some delusional man. "Thanks for your help. I'll be seeing you." *Not.*

She slipped her key into the lock and opened the security door. As she pulled it open, the handle jerked from her hand, and the door slammed shut, reverberating with a loud crash. "Hey, you can't—"

"I haven't finished with you yet." The "wizard" was pointing his wand at the door.

"Did you do that?" She faced him, anger riding high in her blood. How dare he bang the door shut. Then she noticed how far her head tilted back to look into his gaze. Her eyes widened. God, the man was tall. He towered over her. She swallowed hard.

"Now you look terrified." He sighed and pinched the bridge of his nose.

"Should I be?"

"No." He drew his hand down his face.

"And I'm supposed to trust you?" Panic rose in her throat. "I don't know who you are—"

"Ritter. Tennyson Ritter. I'm your arbiter."

"The guy who's supposed to test me?"

"Judge you, observe you, decide whether you pass or fail."

"Thanks, but I'll pass. I mean on the test thing."

He let out an angry breath. "And you're Kristin Montgomery, who lives at Seven Thousand Beadnell Way, Apartment Two C."

She hated the Internet. Any creep could get all kinds of information.

"Don't pretend you don't know—" He stopped and peered at her, his eyes widening. "Good God, you're a Rare One."

"A 'Rare One'?"

"You're not from an Arcani family, are you?"

"Uh, no. I'm American."

He groaned. "Great. What else could go wrong on this job?"

"Job?" Resentment flashed through her. "Look, Mr. Wizard—"

"Ritter."

"Whatever. I don't know what you're talking about. And I sure as hell don't trust you." Kristin scrunched her eyes closed for an instant, then opened them. She placed her best problem-client smile on her face and thrust out her hand. "Thank you so much, Mr. Ritter. Have a nice day."

"You don't get it, do you? I'm stuck with you. I'm your arbiter until this is done, which from what I'm seeing will thankfully not be too long." He flicked his wand, and the entry door opened in front of her. By itself.

A cold anxiety gripped her stomach as her breath rushed out of her. She stared at the door and then at the keys in her hand. "How did you—"

"Please tell me you're not that dense." He sheathed his wand, grabbed her arm, and guided her through the door.

She pulled back. "I will scream if you don't let go of me."

"I'm *not* going to hurt you." His voice crackled with impatience, but he released her arm and started down the hallway. "And put your wand away."

She glanced down at the wand and shoved it in her purse. "Where are you going?"

"Your apartment. I assume that's where you were headed." He strode down the hallway.

The off-yellow paint glowed sickly in the bad lighting of the few cheap Santa Fe–style sconces. He walked past several apartments as if he knew exactly where he was going, which alarmed her. He didn't look like a stalker, but how would she know? As they passed yet another door, one of her neighbors, Mrs. Fernandez, poked her head out of her apartment.

"Good afternoon, Kristin," said the woman. She held a bag of trash that was suspiciously half-empty.

The wand jabbed her through the purse. She tightened her grasp on it. "Hello, Mrs. Fernandez. How are you today?"

"Can't complain too much. My son is coming to dinner tonight." The hint in her voice was one Kristin was familiar with. Then Mrs. Fernandez's eyes narrowed. "Is this your boyfriend?"

"No," said Kristin a little too eagerly. "He's . . . uh . . . my . . ."

"Tutor. Tennyson Ritter. Pleased to meet you." He held his hand out to the older woman and smiled.

His face transformed. Kristin nearly gasped. Gone was the scowl, and in its place radiated an expression of warmth and comfort.

Mrs. Fernandez giggled, sounding like a schoolgirl with a crush. "I didn't realize you were taking classes. What are you studying?"

"Italian," he said.

"Business," she said at the same time.

He glared at her, then reached for the trash bag. "Can I take that for you? Save you the trip?"

Kristin nearly choked. This man couldn't be the same troll she'd met outside. He was charming and polite, gentlemanly and caring, and . . . gorgeous.

"Thank you, Tennyson," said Mrs. Fernandez, handing over the bag.

He took it as if she had granted him a favor. "My pleasure." He gave a little bow of his head.

"Don't forget about dinner, Kristin dear," said Mrs. Fernandez in a singsong voice.

"I'm afraid she can't make it. She has too much studying to do. I'm a terrible slave driver," Tennyson said.

Mrs. Fernandez patted his arm. "I understand. You young people have so much going on. Perhaps next time." She slipped back into her apartment.

Kristin stared at him. He had saved her from hurting the woman's feelings, but how had he turned on the personality so easily?

"Are you going to stand there gaping or shall we get on with this?" He continued down the hallway and stopped two doors down, her front door.

Jerk. "I'm not going to just let you in—"

"These locks couldn't keep me out." He took the key from her hand and shoved it into the lock. "Besides, I told you I'm not here to hurt you."

It was her turn to scowl. She stepped into her apartment. If she was fast enough . . .

He pushed inside behind her and deposited the small bag of trash into her kitchen garbage can.

She glanced around. What could she use as a weapon?

"Quit looking like a scared rabbit." He gave her a look of disgust. "I'm not going to hurt you."

"How am I supposed to know that?"

"Because I told you. I'm your arbiter."

"Right. Because I'm a fairy godmother."

"You got it." He examined the apartment. His lip curled. "You chose this furniture?"

"How do you do that?" she asked, totally irritated.

"Do what?"

"Turn off the charm. Mrs. Fernandez was ready to adopt you, but with me you're cranky and bad tempered."

"I like Groundlings. *You* are an inconvenience."

She ignored the insult. "What is a 'Groundling'?"

"It's what we call non-magical humans. They're firmly rooted on the earth. No fantasy, so 'Groundling.'"

"What do you mean, 'no fantasy'? They create stories, music, and—"

"If you're going to argue with me every time I try to explain something, we're not going to have an easy time together."

"No one asked you to hang out with me."

"Yes, they did. I'm supposed to supervise your transition."

She stewed over that answer for a moment. "Then answer me this, Mr. Supervisor. Why did the wand jump in my purse when I first saw Mrs. Fernandez?"

"First, I am not your Supervisor. I am your arbiter. Second, she must've had a wish."

"Yeah, for me to marry her son." Kristin grabbed a box out of the hall closet and started throwing things into it.

"Are you dating him?"

"Of course not. It's just wishful thinking on her part." She tossed a winter coat that was by no means necessary in San Diego into the box.

He eyed her actions askance. "What are we doing here?"

"Packing." Kristin threw a shoe into the box and rummaged around on the floor for its mate. "I'm moving."

"Let me help." He drew out his wand and passed it over the room as he mumbled a few words she thought sounded like Latin. A moment later boxes and bags lined the walls. The room otherwise was empty. Completely. Including the furniture.

Her knees failed and she jellied to the floor. She couldn't explain what she'd just seen, or rather what she didn't see, or rather what she thought she didn't see. God, she couldn't even explain her lack of understanding. But her apartment was empty. "How . . . how . . . how . . . ?" She drew in a ragged breath. "The furniture is not mine."

"Thank God. I was wondering about your taste. But you could've told me before I packed." He swished his wand again. The sofa, tables, and chairs reappeared, and the boxes numbered fewer.

Without the support of the wall behind her back, she'd have been a puddle on the floor. Until now she had dismissed the claims of her aunts as ravings, harmless delusions. The incident with the door could have been a gust of wind and this guy's statements the rantings of a weirdo. But now . . . ?

How did a CPA reconcile magic with her world? It wasn't possible. Magic was a myth, a fable, a fairy tale. Ha! Fairy tale. Poor choice of words. Because if it was true, *she* was a fairy godmother. . . .

"Are you okay?" Tennyson leaned over her. His brows angled together over his eyes in an expression of concern. "You look pale."

Sudden anger flooded her. "No, I am not okay. Everything I've known to be true no longer is, and suddenly I find out that I'm . . . I'm some sort of magical freak with powers that I don't even know how to use or summon or if I even have them. I get thrown into something I don't understand and am not sure I want to understand, and instead of sympathy, all I get is some wiseass grouch who gives me grief. How the hell am I supposed to go to work now?" She swung her wand. "Am I supposed to do people's taxes with this?"

Tennyson ducked. "Hey, don't wave that thing around."

"What? I'll take somebody's eye out?" She pointed it straight at him and rose from the floor. "I don't even know what I'm capable of. Maybe I'll turn you into a newt." She stepped toward him, aiming the wand at his heart.

"I'd fail you for sure if you did." But he backed up a step.

"Ah, but it would be an accident. I don't know what I'm doing." She thrust the wand forward.

He jumped back. "Cut it out."

"Come on, you great wizard. How much harm can I do? You have your own wand. *En garde*." She flicked the wand up.

Heat surged in her palm. Red sparks burst from the end of her wand and zipped into the light fixture over the dining table. She yelped. The crash of shattering glass resonated in the room as the light fractured into thousands of shards.

She dropped the wand as if it burned in her hand. "Oh God." Tears welled up in her eyes, and her lips trembled.

Tennyson waved his wand over the mess. *"Intactus."*

The glass pieces flew out of the carpeting and fused together. A moment later the fixture hung unbroken from the ceiling again.

Through her watery gaze, she recognized the steely set of his features. Anger oozed off him in waves. Then she was blind, for the tears started in earnest. She waited for him to yell at her.

And waited.

She sniffed, wiped her cheeks with the backs of her hands, and blinked her vision clear. His expression was transformed. The angry lines had vanished and a look of sympathy had replaced them.

He picked up her wand and pressed it into her hand. "Lesson number one: don't use your wand in anger." His voice was gentle.

She gulped, and the tears started anew. Horror at her lack of control and an overwhelming sense of ineptness swamped her. Chaos threatened at the edge of reason, and a sense of loss filled her. Her normal life was dead, and she was mourning its passing.

Several moments went by before she grew aware that her arms were around his neck and she sobbed into his collar. He held her in a comforting embrace, offering her support. The damp warmth at his neck—her tears, his heat—mixed with the crisp, slightly menthol scent of his soap and his shaving cream. He wore no cologne. Just the inviting, musky, clean smell of a man.

Her awareness shifted again, and she realized his arms held her as gently as a butterfly, yet she knew if she collapsed she'd never hit the floor. He was so much bigger than she. The top of her head nestled under his jaw, and his shoulders seemed broad enough to carry any burden she might place on them. So why didn't she feel the slightest bit of fear?

She wasn't one to run from her problems, but the temptation to stay in his arms enticed her. He'd keep her safe and teach her and help her—

What was she thinking? She didn't know him at all.

Okay, she could probably say he wasn't a serial killer . . . she hoped . . . but beyond that she couldn't swear to any aspect of his personality. Except that he had been kind to a hysterical woman.

She hiccupped softly, then pushed away. "Sorry. I didn't mean to cry on you. You don't happen to have a tissue, do you? Mine seem to be . . ." She pointed to the boxes along the wall.

He waved his wand and a box flew out of the nearest carton.

"How did you . . . never mind. Thanks." She blew her nose, and collected herself. Now that her crying had stopped, embarrassment swept through her. One side of her mouth rose in a grimace of regret as she saw the sodden lump that now passed as the collar of his twill shirt. "Your shirt. I'll have it cleaned for you." Her chest shuddered as she inhaled.

"Don't worry about it." He tapped his wand against the cloth, and the shirt appeared freshly pressed and stainless.

"Right, I forgot." She stared at the wand that lay still in her palm and retrieved it. "Do you have a textbook that covers the use of this thing?"

He raised an eyebrow. "A textbook?"

"Or a class I can take? I have a lot of learning to do."

He scrutinized her for a moment; then he nodded slightly, and a reluctant smile of approval curved his lips. "A grimoire. Magic is personal, but there are spells you can learn. Mostly you find your own way, but I'll see what I can find."

"Thank you." She walked around the apartment. Her closet stood empty, her things were packed, and the ugly furniture that remained belonged to the building. "Well, moving is going to be easier than I thought."

"You won't miss Mrs. Fernandez?" he asked with a wry arch to his brow.

"She's sweet, but her matchmaking efforts were beginning to annoy me." She grabbed a carton, headed for the door, then stopped. She eyed him. "Can you hocus-pocus all this to my new place?"

"I could, but what would you learn from that?" He leaned against the wall and crossed his arms over his chest. "You need to use your magic."

"But you packed it all for me."

"Ah, but that was a different lesson you needed to learn." His voice held a hint of criticism, and lines of smugness crinkled his mouth.

The troll was back. And to think that, moments ago, she had thought him almost human. "In that case, here." She shoved the box at his chest.

"Hey." His arms flew forward as he caught the box and clasped it against himself.

She grabbed another carton. "I'll move the old-fashioned way because I'm not willing to fry my stuff for a lesson." She pushed past him into the hallway, ignoring his cry of outrage. A satisfied smirk of her own curled her lips.

She might not know magic yet, but she could handle trolls like Tennyson Ritter.

3

HOW TO BE A FAIRY GODMOTHER:

Trust Your Instincts.

MANUAL LABOR. GROUNDLINGS believed it good for the soul, but Tennyson thought it highly overrated. His jacket lay discarded inside the bungalow, and his shirt was going to need another pass with his wand before it regained its crisp, freshly ironed look. He fingered the wand in his back pocket, tempted to use it to transfer this load into the house. Then he remembered the woman inside who insisted on moving the hard way. What insanity had seized him when he offered to help? Oh yes. He was her arbiter and had to get to know her. He just hadn't expected that getting to know Miss Kristin Montgomery would cost so much sweat equity. True, magic had its cost as well, but a moving spell was elementary. He could do one without a rise in his heart rate. Unlike lugging boxes. With a disgruntled grumble, he hefted another box from her car and carried it up the path.

Kristin brushed against him as she headed to the car for another load. The scent of coconuts and jasmine, a bright, clean smell, wafted from her hair. He inhaled deeply, but she had already passed him. Just as well. He wouldn't want to be caught sniffing her.

Hauling the box into the small living room, he eyed the cottage. It reeked of femininity. Lacy antimacassars on the sofas and chairs, the Meissen figurines, the crystal and porcelain vases—God, it was as if he had walked into an antique store. He didn't know why he was surprised. The fairy godmothers had had nearly a hundred years to collect the frills and gewgaws of three women.

A strange tapping caught his attention. Probably the dishwasher or something. A house this old needed constant repairs. Still he could understand the appeal of the cottage. Small, pleasant, and comfortable, it spoke of a simpler time when life was less about the things one had and more about what was truly important. Of course, he would change the decor in a heartbeat.

Kristin entered the room and placed a carton on the floor. "That's the last box for this trip. I'm heading back for more. Are you coming?"

"No." A thrill of horror went through him. "While I enjoy a good sweat as much as the next man, I prefer it while engaged in other, more entertaining activities."

A hint of red crept into her cheeks. "I don't think so."

His lip tilted up in one corner. "I was speaking of playing rugby, not offering an invitation."

The red deepened. Her green eyes blazed, and the color in her face brought out new highlights in her auburn hair. Her chin lifted a notch. "As if."

That's it, sunshine; you tell me. Show me your verve. His grin widened. Several strands had escaped the sloppy ponytail she had pulled onto the back of her head and danced around her chin. Without thinking, he reached forward and tucked one behind her ear. The hair slipped like satin between his fingers.

Her green gaze delved into his own, and then she stepped back. "Yes, well, thank you for your help."

He frowned. The wispy silkiness of her hair lingered on his fingertips. Trying to get rid of the sensation, he rubbed his fingers together. The strange tapping reached his ear again. "Just remember I'm not a handyman."

"Why would I think you're a handyman?" Letting out a puff of air, she shook her keys. "Now if you'd leave, I can get the rest of my stuff."

"This is stupid." He grabbed his wand from his pocket. *"Requiro."*

A moment later, boxes filled the small room.

Kristin glared at him. "You could've done that earlier and saved us some work."

He jabbed his finger at her. "I was trying to get *you* to use *your* magic."

"I don't *have* magic," she said between clenched teeth.

"You're Arcani. Of course you have magic. You're just too stubborn to use it."

"You keep using that word. Arcani. What is it?"

"The name for the humans of the magical world." He shoved his wand into his pocket. "And if you don't start showing me what you can do, you're going to fail this test."

"You could just save some time and fail me now."

She didn't flinch. His exasperation had met equal tenacity.

Once again that tapping reached his ears and was riding on his nerves. "What is that noise?"

She listened for a moment, then went to the armoire and opened the door. Her wand flew out and hovered near her.

The tapping had stopped.

"Why did you shut it in there?" he asked.

"It was in the way." She caught the wand in her hand. "I didn't need it flying around me while I was working."

"Why didn't you . . ." Understanding dawned. "You don't know what to do with it."

"How could I?" Her voice crackled with impatience.

She was right. A brief twinge of remorse trickled through him. She really had no way to know. Showing her how to stow her wand wouldn't break the rules. Much. "There are three ways to store your wand. One, carry it with you." As a demonstration, he tucked his into his back pocket.

"Because that's so convenient with what I'm wearing." She twirled like a model on a runway. She was right. Her shorts didn't have pockets, and even if they did, the way they molded against her cute butt left little room for a wand.

He swallowed hard and tore his gaze from her rear end. He forced his voice into a strict businesslike tone. "Option two: put the wand into its case."

"I don't have one," she said in a like timbre.

"Then you use the third option: releasing it to its plane."

She stared at him without comprehension.

"Wands have a home, if you will. Some other dimension where they wait until you need them. But magic requires energy, so to release the wand costs an Arcani some of his strength. Not much, but if you need to use your wand a lot, keeping it near is better than sending it away." He pulled out his wand from his pocket. He held it up for her to see, then addressed it. "Sanctum."

His wand disappeared.

She jerked back slightly. "I don't think I'll ever get used to seeing that." She drew in a deep breath. "How do you get it back?"

"Call it."

"I have to give it a name?"

He laughed. "No. Just concentrate." He opened his palm and a moment later his wand reappeared in his hand. "Now you try. And concentrate."

Despite the dubious look she shot him, she focused on her wand. "Sanctum."

The wand disappeared. She shook her hand as if she had just received a static shock. Surprise and disbelief widened her eyes. Her mouth parted a little.

"Now bring it back."

She stared at her palm so hard her brows drew together. A second passed, then another, pink infused her complexion, and her nose scrunched up. "Come back, wand," she mouthed.

The wand rematerialized. With a whoop of triumph, she curled her hand around it, and she blew out the breath she had been holding.

"Maybe you *should* give it a name. Might make it easier to call next time."

Her look of triumph fled, replaced by that guarded

veneer she had worn since he had packed up her apartment. Damn it. He felt churlish for destroying the moment for her. Perhaps Aldous had been right. He had spent so much time studying the *Lagabóc* he was forgetting how to deal with people. "I shouldn't have—"

"I've got a lot to unpack." She placed the wand back in the armoire and closed the door. The tapping recommenced. "Maybe you should give me a little more time to get used to . . . things."

"Fine. I'll be back tomorrow."

"Fine."

"Fine." He pivoted, grabbed his jacket off the back of the couch, and stomped through the front door. A little time would be a good thing. A little time to gather his wits and to learn to control his reactions around her. A little time to recover his coolness. Wasn't that why they had given him this assignment? His renowned coolness?

What was it about her that threw off his equilibrium? He hadn't been this impatient since he was a child. Maybe he should ask the Council to assign someone else to Kristin. Then he could return to his research, a job more important than babysitting a Rare One who was too afraid to even pick up her wand.

Since he had the rest of the day off, so to speak, he could go to the Academy and continue his reading of the *Lagabóc*. Chapters of notes waited for his analysis. He had only been halfway through the book's secrets when the Council had summoned him to take on this job.

Aldous had nominated Tennyson for the task. He knew Aldous wanted to groom him for the Council because Aldous worried about the makeup of the body.

They had spent many nights over a beer discussing the egotistical and self-aggrandizing members who had somehow been chosen to govern this part of the Arcani world. But while he appreciated and agreed with Aldous's concerns, Tennyson didn't believe he was ready to abandon the academic life and take on the role of a politician. No, he'd sooner spend his time studying the intricacies of Merlin's logic and the hidden secrets of the *Lagabóc*.

Yes, that's what he would do. Work on the book. And forget about Kristin for a day.

And her blazing green eyes and silken curls.

KRISTIN OPENED THE lid on the next box and grimaced at the pile of books inside. She needed a break. Leaving the unpacking for later, she went into the bright yellow kitchen and explored its contents. With a squeal of delight, she found a Tupperware container filled with cookies and a note. As she bit into a cookie, she read:

Dear Kristin,

I hope these chocolate chip cookies help ease your transition to your new home. I made them just the way you like them—without chocolate chips. I suppose that means I can't call them chocolate chip cookies, can I? Never mind. We'll think of a good name for them when I return.

All my best,
Aunt Rose

Kristin popped the last bit of the chocolate-chipless cookie into her mouth as she finished reading. Aunt

Rose may have shoved Kristin into a world she wasn't ready for, but the woman sure could bake.

Or maybe she used magic.

On that thought, Kristin grabbed another cookie and returned to the living room. Ignoring the many boxes that still waited, she opened the armoire and removed the rosewood wand. It lay warm and smooth in her palm as if patiently awaiting instructions.

She examined it. That Tennyson troll had told her she had magic. But how did she use this thing? She pointed it at a book and said, "Come."

Nothing happened.

Of course nothing happened. She might now believe in magic, but that still didn't give her the capability to perform more than the disappearing wand trick.

She tried again. Concentrating until her brow furrowed, she stared at the book. Adopting a somber voice, she commanded, "Come."

"You'll never get it to move that way," said a small, tinkling voice at her shoulder.

Kristin yelped, dropped the wand, and whirled to see who was speaking.

Fluttering at eye level flew a beautiful, tiny woman. *Oh my God, a fairy.* A real live fairy was flying beside her. A perfect little woman with translucent sky blue wings. Flying around her. With wings. Well, duh, with wings—she was flying. And laughing.

Kristin frowned. "It wasn't that funny."

"Yes, it was," said the pixie, wiping her eyes. Her expression grew serious. She pointed her minuscule wand at the book and in an uncanny imitation, albeit a few octaves higher, said, "Come."

The book lay unmoving, and the fairy rolled with laughter again.

"Thanks a lot." Kristin let out a puff of exasperation and flopped into a chair. The fairy might be beautiful, but she was irritating as well. "I'm happy you find this so amusing."

"I'm sorry, but you're terrible at this." The sprite landed on the arm of the chair, still grinning. "You must be a new one. We've been wondering who would be chosen. I'm Calliope, but my friends call me Callie."

"Nice to meet you, I think. I'm Kristin."

Peering at her, Callie walked up and down the arm of the chair. "You don't seem to be a prime candidate to me."

"That gives me so much confidence," said Kristin.

"Didn't mean it as an insult, but, really, you can't even get a book to come to you. Even if you just came into your powers—" The fairy stopped short. "Hold it. You're a Halfling, right? Was your mother the human or your father?"

"Both."

"But that's impossible unless . . ." The pixie's mouth dropped open. "You're a Rare One."

"So I've been told."

"Wow. I've never met one before. They're really . . . rare. Wait 'til the others hear about this." Callie flew off the edge of the chair and started for the window.

"Wait," cried Kristin. She jumped up from the chair.

The pixie circled back and hovered in front of Kristin's face.

"Could you help me?"

The fairy's eyes opened wide. "Me?"

"Please? I don't know anything, and, well, you're a fairy. Maybe you could teach me something?" *Anything.* A condescending sprite was a better teacher than a troll. Kristin gave the magical being her best puppy-dog look.

The fairy smiled brightly and bowed her head. "I'd be honored."

Kristin picked up her wand and watched the fairy expectantly.

The fairy pointed at the book and said, "*Vení.*"

The book lifted gently from the shelf and floated to Kristin's waiting hands.

"Now you try." With a wave of her wand, the fairy sent the book back to its shelf. "It isn't that hard. You have to want the book to come to you, and you have to believe."

"Like in *Peter Pan*?"

"Ugh. Don't mention that awful book again. One of us revealed herself to that horrid J. M. Barrie, and what did he do? Betrayed our secrets to the world. You can't trust Groundlings. That's why we have rules." Callie pointed at the book. "Now you try."

Kristin eyed the book. *I can do this.* She pointed the wand. *I am magical.* She focused on the book. *I am the next fairy godmother. I am . . . Arcani. "Vení."*

For a second nothing happened. Then the book rose a quarter inch off the shelf and wobbled forward through the air. Kristin held her breath. Had the book been human, its flight would have resembled the first steps of a toddler. Half the distance to the chair, the book dropped to the ground as Kristin expelled her breath.

She dropped into the chair again. "That was awesome." Her arms hung at her sides. "But I'm so tired."

"You should be." Callie gave her a grin of approval. "You've never done magic before. You're out of shape."

"Out of shape? I exercise four to five times a week." Except these past two weeks because she had been . . . busy. Oh, hell, she hadn't wanted to go.

"Wrong kind of muscle," said Callie. "Don't worry; it gets easier."

Kristin expelled a breath. "Why couldn't I make the book fly before you helped?"

"Did you believe it would?"

Chagrin flooded her. "No."

"Well, there you go. The magic is an extension of you. How do you expect it to work if you don't believe?" Callie fluttered up to Kristin's eye level.

"What's '*vení*'?"

"It means 'come' in Latin. Imperative mood." Callie's voice had the inflection of a schoolmarm, until Callie giggled.

"Great. Now I'll have to learn Latin in addition to using a wand." Kristin grimaced.

"No, you don't." Impatience curled Callie's lip. "I already told you magic comes from you. It's a very personal thing. You use whatever works. For some of the simpler spells, a common word has come down through the years because, well, we all used to speak Latin, didn't we?"

The idea that the Arcani had a history seemed odd, but if she thought about it logically, it made sense.

Callie shrugged. "And you don't always need words. We all use different techniques."

Nerves bunched up in a hot ball in her stomach. There was no organized method she could follow? She had to make things up and feel her way? There was no instruction book? She lived her life by neat columns and numbers that added up to the proper amounts. Improvisation was *not* acceptable. Kristin looked around for a pad of paper and a pen. "I need to take notes."

"Don't worry. Rare Ones have a lot of power. You'll catch on. I'll come by again to see how you're doing."

"Thanks. Do you think you could—"

But the sprite darted out of the window before Kristin could ask anything else.

"Great." Kristin eyed the book on the carpet. "I have great powers, and all I can do is drop a book on the floor."

Ineptitude flooded her. She didn't want to be a Rare One. She was never good at not being good at things. Even in school, every subject had to come easily for her, and if it didn't, she would force herself to study until she was competent. And the few times she couldn't learn her way out of incompetence, she quit. Like art. She sucked at art. But this. This was her worst nightmare. And textbooks didn't even exist to try to learn from.

"Oh, vanish," she said, pointing the wand at the book. The book shimmered on the floor, then disappeared. "No, wait. I didn't mean it. Unvanish. Oh, hell. I hope that book wasn't important."

A knock sounded at the front door.

No. No more. I don't think I can handle any more magic today, she groused. But she pushed herself out of her chair, shut the wand back into the armoire, and crossed to the front door.

She opened it to find a distinguished-looking man standing on the stoop. His black hair had a hint of gray at the temples, and his suit reeked of money. If anything, being a CPA had taught her to recognize wealth. The crisp collar of his shirt couldn't be the product of any bargain store rack, and his tie probably cost more than her entire wardrobe. Okay, hyperbole, but it was silk and, if she wasn't mistaken, hand dyed.

"Forgive me," he said in a rich timbre with a slight foreign accent. "I am looking for Rose, Hyacinth, and Lily."

"My aunts. I'm sorry. You've just missed them." She peered past him to the black BMW at the curb. A man with aviator glasses waited outside the car. He had a driver?

"Ah, a pity. When are you expecting them back?"

"I don't really know. They left this morning on a world cruise."

"Impossible."

Out of the corner of her eye, she saw the driver step toward the house, and then a burst of fiery heat slammed into her, followed by a wall of cold that gripped her heart. She shuddered and stumbled back. The sensation stopped as suddenly as it started, leaving her feeling slightly nauseated. She looked at the chauffeur who stood unmoving by the car again.

"Are you okay?" The man's hand grabbed her elbow to steady her.

"I . . . I . . . I think I am. I just got dizzy for a moment." She rubbed her forehead.

"Maybe you should sit down." He led her into the house to the first chair he saw. "Can I get you water?"

"Yes . . . that is, no . . . I mean, who are you?"

The man smiled. "Forgive me. I am Lucas Reynard. And you are . . . ?"

"Kristin Montgomery. You know my aunts?"

"We've known one another for years. I was hoping to catch your aunts before they left."

Something in his tone made her squint at him. "Are you a . . . a . . . fairy?"

Lucas laughed. "Do you have any idea how that would sound to a Groundling?"

She blushed. "Sorry. I'm just so new to this whole magic thing."

His eyebrows arched. "New?" He peered at her. "Ahh, that is why you are here. You are the new godmother, *n'est-ce pas*?"

"Yes, and I'm really bad at it. So far." She let out a puff of air in exasperation.

He tilted his head. "Time of Transition, right?"

"You know about it?"

"A little." He smiled at her, and Kristin's face flamed anew at his scrutiny. "Now, the water. Where is the kitchen?"

"I'll get it."

She tried to stand, but he shook his head. "You need to sit. Tell me the way."

She pointed toward the kitchen. He disappeared and was back in less than a minute with a glass.

He pulled out a wand from his inner coat pocket. Holding the glass in his palm, he gave a little swirl of the wand tip, and water spilled into the glass. "Here. Drink this."

"So you're a wizard?"

"Sorcerer. Now drink."

"Thanks." She took a long swallow. The icy fluid soothed and tingled as it slid down her throat. She inhaled sharply. "That was not tap water."

He looked shocked. "Good heavens, no. It's from a source in the Pyrenees. Known only to myself and a few shepherds."

She drank deeply again. "You could give Evian a run for its money with this."

"And spoil the joy of such a secret? Never." He clasped his hand to his chest in a dramatic gesture.

She laughed at his antics.

"Am I rightly assuming you feel better?"

"Much, thank you." She downed the rest of the water and was quite sorry to see the glass empty in her hand. "So what's the difference between a sorcerer and a wizard?"

"A sorcerer gets his power from the earth. Wizards can create their own magic, but at a cost to themselves. We harness our magic from nature."

"The source of the water." She nodded toward the empty glass in her hand.

"Exactly. Now my turn for a question. You seem to know very little considering you're a godmother."

"That is not a question."

"You're quite right, so here it is. Are you a Rare One?"

Kristin scrunched her eyes shut. "I'm beginning to hate that term."

"So you are?"

"Yes. I had no idea magic even existed before today."

Lucas let out a low whistle. "This must be quite a day then."

"You're telling me. Hey, maybe you can help me." She retrieved her wand. "I just made a book disappear and I have no idea how to get it back."

He pressed his lips together as if preventing a chuckle. He cleared his throat. "What was the title?"

She thought for a moment, then shook her head. "I

don't know. It was just a book on that shelf." She pointed with her wand. The remaining books fell off the bookcase. "Oops."

Lucas did laugh then. "I apologize. Now let me see. Not having the title makes it a little more difficult, but . . ." He focused and pointed his wand at the coffee table. *"Liber."*

The book reappeared on the table.

"Thank you." She grinned, and Lucas answered with his own smile.

He was rather attractive when he smiled. Suave, and dashing. That was the word for him. "Dashing." If she hadn't seen Tennyson earlier—

Why on earth was she comparing Lucas to the troll?

"Is something wrong?" asked Lucas.

She realized she was frowning. "No, I'm sorry. I'm just overwhelmed with everything." She waved her hand over the boxes that still needed unpacking. "And I just moved in."

"May I help you unpack?" He raised his wand.

"No," she said quickly. "No, I need to do it myself. I'm particular that way."

"I understand," he said with another smile. "I'll take my leave then. But may I call on you some other time? For coffee perhaps?"

"I'd like that," she said. "And thanks again for your help."

"It was my pleasure, demoiselle."

They walked to the door, where he took her hand and kissed the back of it. "Good day, Kristin Montgomery."

She felt almost like a princess. "Good-bye, Lucas."

As she closed the door behind him, a rush of satisfaction filled her. The troll might be exasperating, but her last two visitors proved not all Arcani were.

Not bad for a day when her world turned upside down.

4

HOW TO BE A FAIRY GODMOTHER:

Practice Brings Comfort and Comfort Brings Ease.

WHAT WERE THE odds of having a peaceful day?

Kristin snorted. After yesterday, she didn't think she'd ever have a peaceful day again. She had cried more, yelled more, and pouted more than she had in the past year. All in one day. Late in the evening, after unpacking boxes and organizing their contents, she had finally crawled into bed. This morning she awoke late. It was Sunday, she had nowhere she had to be, and she needed a day of rest to synthesize all that had happened yesterday. Wizards and fairies and wands, oh my.

Kristin pulled the first volume of the *Grimm's Fairy Tales* from its new position on the shelves and sat down in an overstuffed armchair. Her heritage was English, she lived in Southern California, but for some reason she had studied German until she was fluent.

Now she believed she understood why. Aunt Rose had said Jacob and Wilhelm were great historians, and if one wanted information, it was best to go to the source. Flipping to the story of "Dornröschen," known as "The Sleeping Beauty" in English, Kristin settled in for a good read. She loved all the tales, even the terrifying ones.

But as she read of the magic spells and the curse placed on the beautiful young woman, Kristin's mind drifted. The tales contained so many stories of tests, of tasks, of trials. Would this Time of Transition be as difficult as the tests were in the stories she loved?

"I see you're reading the masters," Tennyson said.

Book flying, Kristin sprang out of the chair and whirled around. Tennyson grinned at her.

"How did you get in here?"

"The front door."

"It was locked. Did you consider knocking?"

"For a moment, then I decided not to bother." He shrugged and retrieved the book from the floor. "You really ought to take better care of your books. You can damage the spine by throwing them across the room."

"What do you want?"

"I *want* to work on my research, but that choice was taken from me when I became *your* arbiter. Come on. Let's go."

She eyed him for a moment but made no move. "I'm not going anywhere. I have no desire to go anywhere. You can't come in here and expect me to jump just because you say so."

"Actually, I can. We're going for a walk." His hand encircled her upper arm, and he pulled her to her feet.

"Hey! I—" Unable to pry his fingers from her arm, she was forced to take a few steps with him.

"Wait." He stopped and faced her. "You've forgotten something."

"Like what? You're the one dragging me. I don't even want to leave the house." She sounded like a bitch. Another lifestyle change to enjoy.

"Listen, sunshine, you're a fairy godmother now, and you'd better start thinking like one." He released her arm. "Where is your wand?"

She pointed to the armoire.

"Really? The cabinet still?" He retrieved the rosewood rod. "How do you expect to do magic if you keep it in there?"

"Look, buddy, I—"

"Never mind. Let's go."

"But I don't want to leave the house."

"Too bad." He shoved the wand at her.

She stuffed the wand into her back pocket and marveled as the wand slid all the way in without poking her or ripping the shorts. She looked up at him for an explanation.

"What did you expect? We don't advertise ourselves to Groundlings. You can't walk down the street carrying a wand. 'Cause that would look normal. Let's go." He grabbed her again.

She stumbled into submission beside him. When they reached the walk, he paused. He waved his wand at the lock. "So you don't have any other unwanted visitors."

"You lumped yourself into that category. You must be smart." Sarcasm—her new best friend.

He didn't respond. For about a block she said nothing, but when they reached the beach, she stopped. "If

I'd've known you wanted to surf, I would've brought a wet suit."

"I don't surf." Holding her shoulders, he aimed her gaze toward the sand. "What do you see?"

"The Pacific, sand, and people who probably need sunscreen." This time she was able to pry his fingers from her upper arm. "I know I have a lot to learn, and I *was* studying when you showed up. Are we done here?"

"We haven't started." He pointed back at the beach. "Look again, and give me details."

The puff of air that left her lips was louder than she intended, but she surveyed the beach again. Nothing extraordinary. The sand was crowded with people. Three teenaged boys clutching boogie-boards sprinted into the surf. Two men in their late twenties lay on frayed beach towels with a Styrofoam cooler between them. Probably contained beer. If the police saw it—

"Don't get distracted."

Tennyson's voice elicited a groan. She turned toward the small playground. A mother, her expression that mixture of vigilance and boredom only a mother could achieve, watched her child climb a giant concrete sea turtle. Children clambered on the slide and squealed with the reckless abandon of innocence.

Kristin blinked.

The children laughed, ran around, and threw sand at one another.

She scrunched her eyes shut, then opened them slowly. "Oh my God!"

"What do you see?"

Rubbing her eyes, she leaned forward. It wasn't possible. Above the heads of the children, tiny little golden crowns glowed and twinkled. They flickered on and off, appearing and disappearing in no apparent pattern or rhythm, but the crowns were there. She looked at the beachcombers on the sand. No crown, no crown, wait. That child building a castle by the edge of the water had a distinct shining tiara.

"Well?" Tennyson spread his hands open in a gesture of impatience.

She spun on her heel and faced him. "Can you see the crowns?"

"Do I look like a fairy godmother?" But his expression relaxed, and a ghost of a smile lit on his lips. "You see crowns."

"Yes." The word was almost a squeal. "Floating over the heads of the children." She peered back out over the playground.

His gaze followed hers, but he shook his head. "Nope. Nothing."

"Really? You can't see it?" Satisfaction shot through her. She could do something he couldn't.

"Really, I can *not* see the crowns." His arched brows signaled his impatience.

She pulled her bottom lip between her teeth to keep from laughing and continued her scrutiny of Mission Beach. Crowns blinked on and off over children's heads, and every time one appeared her smile renewed itself. "Why do the crowns disappear?"

"From what I've been told, wishes aren't constant. When a new thought occurs, the crowns vanish."

She inspected the sunbathers again. Slowly her joy dissipated, and questions started to flood her mind. She turned to Tennyson. "Only the children have crowns."

"That's because most of the adults don't believe anymore. It's a good thing actually. Keeps us safe."

"Safe? Safe from what? What do you mean?"

"What do you think would happen if Groundlings knew about us?"

She thought about that for a moment. "I guess people would be asking us to perform magic for them all the time."

"Right, but most of the world doesn't believe in magic. Adults especially, so we Arcani are relatively safe from discovery. When Groundlings witness something we've done, some act of magic, they explain it away or dismiss it as a hallucination."

"Um-hmm." It made sense. "What of those people who discover we *do* exist?"

"Their stories appear right next to the sightings of Bat Boy and Elvis."

She stared at Tennyson in surprise. His face was the portrait of earnestness until a large grin split his lips. "Just kidding. I stole that idea from *Men in Black*."

Against her will, she chuckled. The troll had a sense of humor. "So what does happen?"

He shrugged. "Most of the time we can arrange a memory-altering spell."

She winced. "That sounds painful."

"It's harmless. We had lots of practice in the Middle Ages. That was a tough time for us. Everybody believed in magic then, and we had a harder time keeping ourselves hidden. If we were discovered, we were plagued by people asking us to perform magic for them. Of course that was preferable to being killed by those who feared us."

"Did they really do that?"

"Yes. That's why we have rules now. We live in this world, just like Groundlings. We can survive better if they don't know about us. Anyway, altering memory became our best defense."

Repugnance shuddered through her at his tale. "Were you ever persecuted?"

"What?" He looked insulted. "How old do you think I am?"

"I don't know. How long do you people live?"

"*We* people live normal lives. Okay, maybe a little longer. We live around 130 years. I'm only thirty-five."

"Sorry." She shrugged. She'd better get used to putting her foot in it. There was still so much she didn't know.

"Sometimes, though, we do trust Groundlings. In fact, it's not unusual for Groundlings and Arcani to marry."

"Really?"

"Considering the ratio of Groundlings to Arcani, it would be hard to avoid it. We can fall in love with Groundlings and they with us."

"And that's allowed?"

"Yes. We aren't some totalitarian regime with strict rules of conduct."

"You could've fooled me," she muttered.

"That's the theory behind Rare Ones. A Groundling/Arcani union can produce Arcani or non-Arcani children. Our scientists believe that a Rare One occurs when two Groundlings mate who have Arcani in their ancestral lines. The right genes mix and, poof, a Rare One. They tend to have stronger powers because of the long dormancy of the trait."

"Wait. There are Arcani scientists?" Disbelief colored her tones.

"We're our own regular little world. Newspapers,

doctors, teachers, historians." He pointed at his own chest with that final word. "We try to blend in, but there is a thriving Arcani society."

"Why haven't I ever noticed?"

"Because Groundlings aren't very observant." He was mocking her now. "And we hide it."

"Like you have your own mall?" Her deadpan delivery didn't hide the sarcasm of her words.

His gaze narrowed. "Are you always a smart-ass?"

"No, I just like shopping."

The scowl returned to his face. He opened his mouth to retort, but she raised her hands. "I'm kidding."

What was it about him that brought out the worst in her? She'd have to work on that.

She gazed back over the children. One small boy sat by himself on a towel. His gaze focused on the horizon as he sifted sand between his fingers. She waited for a crown to appear over his head. Nothing happened. The boy looked at the large man sleeping next to him. A faint flicker materialized over his head, but it vanished so quickly she thought she imagined it. "Why don't all children have crowns?"

Tennyson sighed. "Some of them are exposed to things children shouldn't see. They lose their belief much earlier than they should."

She directed her attention to the boy who was once again staring out at the horizon. Her heart cramped and her breath stalled.

A squeeze of her shoulder brought her gaze back to Tennyson. He had a look of sympathy on his face. "You can't help everyone. You're not supposed to help everyone."

"I know." She drew in a deep breath.

"Good. Are you ready for the next step?"

"Why not?" She faced him.

He turned her toward the children. "Listen."

She waited, but he didn't speak again. "Excuse me?"

"Listen."

"To what?"

"To them."

"I'm too far away." Skepticism crept back into her voice.

"Are you going to argue every time I tell you to do something?"

She drew her brows together. "Probably. Look, a little sympathy wouldn't be out of line here. You're asking me to do things I don't know I can, hell, that I didn't even believe in yesterday. So forgive me if I'm a little dubious."

Tennyson inhaled deeply. "Sorry. I keep forgetting you're a Rare One. Now, *please* try to listen."

She set her lips together firmly, but turned toward the children in the playground. And tried. Little by little a hum grew in her ear. She clenched her teeth and focused on one little boy who was playing with plastic dinosaurs in the sand. The humming grew into buzzing. Then the buzzing cleared and a tiny voice popped into her head just as a golden crown appeared over his head.

"I wish I could see a real T. rex."

She clapped her hand over her mouth and looked at a girl at the top of the slide with her arms held out at her sides.

"I wish I could fly."

Another child jumped off a swing in midair. "I wish Daddy could see me now."

A fourth youngster eyed another child with a huge, dripping vanilla cone. "I wish I had one of those."

"I wish I were a real princess."

"I wish I had a puppy."

"I wish I had superpowers, so I—"

"I wish my brother would—"

"I wish he liked—"

"I wish Mommy—" "I wish I—" "I wish he—" "I wish—" "I wish—" "I wish—"

Tennyson was startled when Kristin slapped her hands over her ears. Pain twisted her features. Tears filled her eyes.

"Stop. Make it stop." She faced him, her bottom lip quivering.

With a quick glance to make sure no one was watching, he snatched his wand from his back pocket, stood in front of her, and brandished it between them. *"Quietus."* The shimmer of magic flowed over them like a curtain of dry water. He returned the wand to his pocket and placed his arms around her. "Shhh. It's okay now. You can uncover your ears."

As if she didn't quite trust his words, she slowly lowered her hands. At the silence that greeted her, she sniffed once and brushed away an escaped tear. "What did you do?"

"I put us in a kind of bubble. You can't hear anything out there now." He led her to a bench. "Here. Sit down."

Bright splotches of red mottled her complexion, and her eyes sparkled with unshed tears. Her breath snagged as she inhaled, and she twisted her wand between her fingers. "That was terrifying. I never want to do that again."

"Tell me what happened."

She gazed out over the sand. "I listened, and then I heard a wish, and then another, and another, and it became too loud and too fast, and"—she hiccupped—"it frightened me."

He laid his arm over her shoulders.

"I couldn't control it. It just grew louder and louder, buzzing like some horrible swarm of bees coming to attack me."

He smiled at that.

A rueful smile curved her lips. "It sounds silly, doesn't it?"

"Not really. I've heard the military is looking into weapons that use sound as an alternative to missiles. Sounds are powerful. Think of what a movie would be like without the background music."

She chuckled then, but her mirth was ephemeral. "I can't do that again."

"No, but you can control it. You can focus and hear just one wish at a time, and then only when *you* want to."

Her eyes welled anew. "How do you know I can? And how do I know which wishes to listen to? How do I pick and choose one wish over another? How can I disappoint all those children? And even if I choose one wish, how do I know I can grant it? I can't do magic yet. I can't even listen." She buried her face in her hands and released the pent-up sobs. "I-it's t-t-too m-m-uch."

He nearly panicked. Sobs? No one told him he'd have to deal with full-blown female hysterics. Twice. For the second day in a row. He grimaced, then put his other arm around her. He patted her back. "There. There." Even to his ears it sounded ineffectual.

She gazed at him. Her nose was runny, her eyes

were red, her cheeks were wet—she looked pathetic. But a fierceness burned in her deep green gaze. She had the power and the desire. Laying his hands on either side of her face, he brushed away her tears with his thumbs. "You'll learn."

"What if I don't?" Her gaze pleaded for reassurance.

He tilted her head so she could see directly into his eyes. "Why are you crying now?"

"Because I'm a failure."

"No. It's because you want the magic. You feel it so deep inside of you it hurts. You'll learn because it's who you are."

She swallowed hard. The tears ceased, but she still sniffled. "Do you really think so?"

"If I didn't, I wouldn't waste my time with you."

A tremulous smile played at her lips, parting them. Her breath eased out of her, and her essence wafted up to him. She was cotton candy and coffee. A fine wine and a great book. Vanilla and leather.

Before he knew what he was doing, his lips brushed against hers, and he almost groaned at their softness. They were ripe and rich, a full treat against his mouth. His fingers burrowed into her hair as he pressed harder against her. She tasted every bit as delicious as he had imagined, and he wasn't nearly contented. Too many nuances in her flavor eluded his senses, and the longer he sampled, the more there was to discover.

She lifted her mouth for an instant to draw in a deep, ragged breath.

Whoa. What was he thinking? He pushed her back from him. "I shouldn't have done that." He dropped his hands to his sides. To his annoyance, they trembled slightly.

She blinked once and drew in a sharp breath. He couldn't tell if her reaction was from her crying jag or from his kiss. She opened her mouth to speak, but then her mouth crimped shut, and her nostrils flared. She eyed him for a moment. "Then why did you?"

"I . . . I . . . I don't know." He stuffed his hands into his jeans pockets. "You were crying, I thought you needed comfort and . . ." He shrugged.

"And so you kissed me. Okay, good to know. Don't cry in front of Tennyson. I'll add it to my list of things to remember. The kiss was a mistake. At least you succeeded in taking my mind off the wish thing." She straightened her shoulders and waved her arm at the beach. "I'm ready to try again."

He shook his head. *He* wasn't ready to try again. "No, maybe tomorrow. You should work on simple spells this afternoon."

"Sure, whatever." She shrugged and gazed out over the ocean. "I can't hear the waves."

"Sorry. I forgot." He swiped his wand from his pocket and flicked it twice.

The masking spell disappeared, and the sounds of the beach crashed over him, almost an intrusion to his senses. The shouts of children playing, the roar of the waves, the cries of the gulls grated on his nerves. Clenching his teeth, he shoved his wand into his back pocket. "Are you okay?"

"Just peachy."

"Good." He paused, and an awkward silence threatened. He hurried to fill it. "You should practice some simple spells this afternoon."

"You already said that." She flicked her fingers casually in the air.

"Easy ones, like levitation." He clamped onto this safe subject with relief. "With a little practice—"

"Right. I'll do that at home." She started up the street toward the house.

"Hey," he said as he fell into step beside her.

She stopped short. "Look. Tennyson. I don't need a babysitter. I promise I'll practice. Easy spells. At home. By myself." Her gaze narrowed. "Unless you need to show me something else."

"No."

"Then I'll see you tomorrow." Without another glance at him, she pivoted and headed up the street.

Releasing a breath, he watched her stalk off. She had every right to be angry. He shouldn't have kissed her. He had crossed the boundaries. He had taken advantage of her moment of weakness. Hell, he still couldn't explain to himself why he had done it.

As she marched away, her posture was rigid, and she didn't look back. Yes, she had every right to be angry, but she had handled herself with dignity and class.

Although he was pretty sure he had heard her mutter the word "troll."

5

HOW TO BE A FAIRY GODMOTHER:

•

Never Use Your Magic in Anger.

"'YOU WERE CRYING,'" mimicked Kristin in a snide voice as she pulled five empty Diet Coke cans from the recycle bin. She walked to the bench she had placed in the middle of the garden. "'I thought you needed comfort.'" Her anger had not abated. The bottom of each can banged hard against the wood as she smashed the cans down along the top of the seat. "'I shouldn't have done that.' Darn right you shouldn't have." She stomped back to her starting place facing the bench about ten feet away from it.

Apparently the kiss had meant nothing to him. Just because she was an idiot and her world twisted when his lips touched hers didn't mean *he* reacted the same way. Her world had twisted enough in the past two days. She didn't need any other complications in her life. Especially from someone who felt nothing for her. She could forget about the kiss as easily as he would. He had told her to practice her spells. Simple ones. Fine. She'd master so much magic before he saw her again that he'd have to be impressed. Then he'd see. She wasn't some weak, fragile flower who needed "comfort."

She pointed her wand at a can. Levitation. Easy. A simple spell.

"Troll," she spat before she concentrated.

A startlingly loud bang rocketed the first Coke can into the air, where it disintegrated into a sparkly aluminum dust shower.

Kristin's eyes shot wide and she cringed. Whoops. Total destruction had not been her goal.

"Remind me not to get in front of that." Lucas stepped around the corner of the house with his hands held out in front of him.

Humiliation slunk through her. Count on her luck to bring a second witness to her magical failures. She needed another embarrassing moment today like a shark needed a machine gun. Pointing the wand toward the ground, she smiled at Lucas. "Sorry about that. I was practicing."

He eyed the still sifting powder as it settled to the ground. "I heard you in the backyard and invited myself to come see you. I take it you didn't mean to do that." His mouth pulled to the side in an expression of good-natured doubt.

"It was supposed to be levitation, not destruction." She looked at her wand. "I may have used the wrong word."

"Well, whatever it was must have held a lot of passion. And you never know. It could come in handy someday."

"Yeah, if I ever want to pulverize something." She shook her head in disgust.

Lucas smiled. "As long as it's not me."

"No worries." She relaxed at his easygoing banter.

"I didn't mean to interrupt your practice." Lucas swept his hand in a gesture that took in the remaining cans on the bench. "I came to invite you for a coffee. Is this a bad time?"

She pulled her bottom lip between her teeth. She should be practicing. She wanted to prove to the troll that she wasn't witless or helpless. Of course, her attempts at magic today had all been a disaster. Lucas watched her patiently. *He* wasn't putting undue pressure on her. *He* wasn't patronizing her. *He* was actually supportive.

Hell, yes, she could use a break.

"I'd love some coffee."

A broad smile curved his lips. "I saw a little shop just around the corner. We'll walk. I'll tell Dimitri to come back in an hour."

"Who is Dimitri?"

"My chauffeur."

"I'll get my purse and meet you in front." She started for the door.

"No, no. This is my invitation." He held out his arm in a gesture reminiscent of the nineteenth century. "I'll tell him on the way."

She wondered if he was trying to impress her. Okay, it was a simple coffee, but he was so . . . gallant.

The coffeehouse was a dingy storefront that overlooked Mission Boulevard and the Pacific beyond. The sea-foam green paint was flaking and in need of a redo, but the windows were clean and boasted gold and black letters that read: "Java Joe's." As Lucas pushed open the door, bells tinkled around them.

They sat on red vinyl seats around a chrome-edged table. A waitress wearing cargo pants and a camouflage T-shirt hurried to their table. She pulled a pencil from out of her curly hair. "What can I get you?"

"A double espresso for me, and . . . wait, let me guess." He looked at Kristin and tapped a finger on his upper lip. "A café au lait for you?"

"Yes." She was surprised.

"And bring us two of your cookies. One oatmeal walnut, and one chocolate chip . . . no, scratch that. No chocolate chip. Sugar."

"You got it." The waitress scratched on her pad. "H-two-O?"

"Yes, thank you." He dismissed her with a dazzling smile, then gave his attention to Kristin.

The waitress finished her notes and scurried away.

Kristin leaned over the table and dropped her voice. "How did you know what I wanted? Did you use magic?"

He laughed. "No, but yesterday I noticed there was no coffeemaker in the kitchen. If you liked coffee, that would have been the first thing you unpacked. So I took a chance and ordered you a milky coffee. And I saw the note your aunt left about the chocolate chipless cookies."

Kristin smiled. "You cheated."

"Guilty. And just a little observant."

"So you're from France?"

He sat back with a look of disappointment. "Is my accent that strong?"

"Not at all. I'm just observant."

Lucas chuckled at their shared joke.

Their order came. Lucas took a sip of his espresso and placed it on the table. "I'm only sorry I waited too long to look up your aunts, but my business kept me from pleasure calls. I am building my house, but I have grown so tired of hotel living that I wanted to take care of that first."

"Where have you been staying?"

"La Valencia in La Jolla. A lovely hotel, but still a hotel."

Her jaw dropped, but she quickly regained her composure. His Armani suit wasn't lying. The guy had money. "Forgive my indelicacy, but are all magicals rich?"

"No, like any group, we have all levels." He patted her hand indulgently. "You really are an innocent, aren't you?"

Heat flared in her cheeks. "I know. I'm sorry." She hid her face behind her hands.

"No, no, I find your candor charming."

When she peeked through her fingers, he was sitting back and watching her patiently. His teeth flashed with his grin.

She slid her fingers from her eyes. "So tell me about yourself." She sipped her café au lait.

Keeping his gaze on his cookie, he broke off a chunk. "What do you wish to know?"

She shrugged. "What do you do? What part of France are you from? Do you have any hobbies?"

He picked at the bit of cookie in his fingers. "I've been pretty isolated for the past years. My life is unremarkable really. I was in southwestern France, in the Pyrenees."

"That's right. Is that where you learned about that water you gave me yesterday?"

For a moment he looked puzzled, then he nodded. "Yes, yes, of course."

"So what do you do?"

He chuckled. "Kristin, I am a sorcerer."

"So I suppose you can just conjure up rubies and diamonds and gold when you need it."

He laughed. "Nothing so crude. I am . . . hmmm, how shall I put it . . . a diplomat of sorts. I work on power struggles in the Arcani world."

"Wow. That sounds important."

"Not as much as you might think."

"Are there many? Power struggles, I mean?"

"Few, but when they happen, they can be huge." His gaze drifted off beyond her shoulder as if he was remembering some past event.

"Someday you'll have to tell me about your adventures. If they're not classified or something." Kristin took a bite of the sugar cookie.

"I'm sure my adventures would just bore you. I simply do a job."

"So how do I earn money? As an Arcani, I mean? Do I keep my job as a CPA and do the whole fairy godmother thing in my spare time?"

He shook his head. "While I don't know the details, I'm sure the Council has set up a stipend. You'll have to ask your arbiter."

Every new piece of information brought new questions. "Council? What council?"

"The Noble Council of Wise Men and Women. They're the governing body of the Arcani. They set rules, pass judgment, try to ensure our safety."

The information made her frown. "There's a bureaucracy?"

He laughed again. "Certainly. You don't expect the Arcani world to work without orders and rules. The

Primary Council is in London, with smaller branches around the world."

She rubbed her face. "There's so much to learn."

"You're overwhelmed. That's to be expected at the beginning. A Rare One has much to learn, but he or she usually grows to be one of the most powerful Arcani in our society." He took her hand. "That's only one of the reasons you're so special."

She squinted at him in doubt. "Maybe. But I still feel stupid right now."

Lucas pulled his billfold from his coat pocket and peeled a few bills from the stack inside. He laid these on the table, stood, and held out his hand. "You are far from stupid, but you are still ignorant."

"Don't I know it." She placed her hand in his and allowed him to help her up from the table.

Lucas led Kristin from the café into the bright sunshine. "I would be happy to help you learn more if you allow. Will you have dinner with me tomorrow evening?"

"I'd love to." A sense of relief flowed through her. Here was someone willing to answer her questions without the attitude.

"But I must be honest with you." He frowned slightly.

"Is something wrong?"

"No, I just . . ." He chuckled as they turned onto her street. "You make me feel like an awkward schoolboy again. I am not asking you out merely to be your tutor. I enjoy your company and would like to get to know you better."

A rush of satisfaction swept through her. An attractive, distinguished man wanted to go out with her. She had to feel good about that. He probably wouldn't apologize for kissing her. He probably would want to kiss her. Unlike the troll.

She clamped down that thought in a heartbeat. She was not going to spoil the rest of this day with thoughts of Tennyson.

"I realize there is a difference in our ages—"

She held up her hand. "I'd love to go on a date with you."

"Excellent. I'll pick you up at seven."

They reached the front of the cottage. Glancing up at the house, he smiled. "It looks like you have visitors."

She looked at the front door but didn't see anything. Then she caught some tiny movements in the bushes. Sprites flitted among the bougainvilleas. If she didn't know they existed, she would have thought the sprites were merely the leaves flashing in the wind.

"I won't come in. I've taken too much of your time already, and it seems you are popular today. My driver is waiting."

The black BMW stood at the curb. She couldn't tell if Dimitri watched them from behind his shades, but he climbed from the car and opened the door as they approached.

Lucas bent over her hand and kissed it. "I'll see you tomorrow."

"Great. See you then."

He climbed into the back of the BMW. Dimitri closed the door and drove away.

She turned to her house. Okay, so her heart didn't race at Lucas's touch as it had with the troll, but *Lucas* was civilized. She had had enough jolts in the past two days that she didn't need any more heart racing.

She strode up the walkway to the front door. "Hello, Callie."

The tiny sprite flew to Kristin's shoulder. "Good. You're home. I brought some of my friends. We thought we'd give you a magic lesson."

"Thanks. I could use one." She glanced at the other sprites. There were five more of them. "Hi, everyone. I'm Kristin." She pushed open the door and let the six sprites enter first.

TENNYSON SAT AT the heavy oak table in the library and stretched his arms overhead. This had been a good idea. Delving into his research had driven Kristin and her green eyes from his mind.

Damn. She was back.

With a groan, he pushed back from the table and went into the stacks to find another text. His research on the *Lagabóc* was going well, except when he thought about *her.* He even believed he had found a new interpretation of the laws, one that hadn't been covered in the past. No one would doubt his position among the finest Arcani historians. As long as he stopped thinking about *her.*

He closed his eyes. *Concentrate.*

He inhaled. The dusty, slightly mildewed scent of the long rows of books entered his core. He loved this place. Sure, the library wasn't that old, although it was built to look that way, but its reputation was good. As was that of the Arcani university attached to it. Oops. Other way around. While this Academia Artis Magicae was only fifty years old, its wizards had carried out much of the revolutionary modern research into magic. Of course, his field was history, and the library housed fine archives. He could have popped over to other learning centers in the world, and often did, but that magic cost energy he couldn't spare today. No, this branch suited him. Especially since his mentor was in residence at the moment and Tennyson had to remain close to San Diego anyway. Because Kristin lived here.

Damn. There she was again.

In a dark humor, he pulled a book off the shelf and returned to the table. Why had he kissed her anyway? And now that he had, why couldn't he forget it? She was irritating, rude, difficult, and had curves that made a man's mouth hunger for a bite.

Argh.

He flipped the book open to a random page and started to read. Anything. So he wouldn't think of *her.*

Too late.

Resenting her continual intrusion, he almost growled. Then he froze. A deep rumbling far beneath his feet captured his attention. A moment later he heard it. Then he saw and felt it.

The library swayed. The floor undulated, bouncing the table. On the ends of their chains, the light fixtures swung. The clinking of bolts against nuts, the thumping of shelves against their housing, the low murmur of the earth as it rolled filled the air. Books began to fall off the shelves, and he heard the window creaking as if trying to hold back the glass from shattering. It wasn't strong enough. The crash of the pane shrieked through the air.

Earthquake.

He dove under the table and heard the raindrops of broken glass hit the wood. Knowing the heavy oak would protect him, he moved with the table as it skittered along the floor. As the shaking grew, the added cacophony of fire alarms and other sirens joined the roar of the earth. Another crash nearby told him a shelf had toppled; then the closest shelf teetered, hit the tabletop, and showered books around his shelter. The table stopped moving because it was pinned.

Then, just as it had started, the earthquake died away. The ground rolled one more time, then stilled. For an instant, the sweet, safe stillness reigned, only to be replaced by the heavy footsteps of people running for the emergency exits. Around him he heard the frightened cries of people who couldn't run.

Tennyson poked out his head. The library was in shambles. Books littered the floor, shelves had fallen over, and great cracks ran through the walls. Most of the windows had fractured.

Students climbed out from under the other library tables. Living in Southern California, they all knew what to do in a temblor, although their pallid faces told him they were a bit shaken up. No pun intended.

Okay, he had to be a bit shaken up if he was making poor jokes like that last one.

At times like these, he realized just how little real power he had, even as an Arcani. The same thoughts must have been going through the minds of the students.

He pulled out his wand. "Does anyone need help?" With a quick flick of the wrist he made a neat stack of the books nearest him.

Many of the students around him pulled out their wands to help. Within moments, they cleared a path to the main door. Only a few students with minor injuries had cropped up, and they were escorted to the school's infirmary. Tennyson and the head librarian made a sweep of the building before magically locking it against vandalism or theft.

Tennyson stared at the destruction he saw outside. Most of the buildings still stood, but with considerable damage. It would take weeks, if not months, to get them fixed. Would there be enough wizards to complete the job? They'd probably have to call in help from around the world. Maybe even some gnomes to rebuild. Restoring the campus would take much magical energy.

"Excuse me." A young girl looked up at him. "You're Tennyson Ritter, right?"

"Yes."

"I've been asked to find you. Professor Montrose has been injured."

A shiver of dread shook Tennyson. "Where is he?"

"In his office, but I'm afraid—" The girl broke off as tears filled her eyes.

Tennyson didn't wait. He sprinted across the grounds toward the administration building, dodging groups of dazed and confused coeds and staff who gathered together to give one another strength.

He reached the building and stopped short. Little more than a pile of rubble remained. Emergency workers were already on scene lifting the heavier chunks with their wands. To the side several cots held injured faculty and students. Another EMT waved his wand to put up a tent to protect those below from the sun.

At the corner of the building where Professor Montrose's office once stood, a large group huddled by the stones. Tennyson sprinted to them.

"Tennyson, are you there?"

"Yes, I'm here." He pushed through the shield of bodies and swallowed hard at the sight that greeted his eyes. Professor Montrose lay on a foam pad to protect him from the rubble beneath him. A collapsed wall covered the bottom half of his body.

"Don't look so serious, boy. I can't feel a thing." The old man attempted a smile, but the humor never reached his eyes.

Tennyson climbed over the ruins to get closer. A wave of panic gripped him. The last time he had spoken to Aldous was when the man had assigned him the position as arbiter to Kristin. And Tennyson had lost his temper.

"The rest of you, get away." The professor's voice sounded surprisingly strong.

When a huge man wearing protective clothing started to protest, Aldous lifted a finger. "I admire your dedication, but you know as well as I that my life is finished here. I need to speak with this young man here in private. Give me the little time I have left to do so."

The EMT frowned but moved away.

"Have they gone?" Aldous kept his gaze on Tennyson.

"Yes." He struggled to keep his voice and expression calm. His mentor's pale skin lost even more color.

"Good. I don't want people to panic."

"Panic? We've already had an earthquake."

"No, we haven't. This wasn't natural."

Tennyson stared at his mentor. "Are you saying—"

"Don't argue. I don't know how much time I have."

Guilt assailed Tennyson. "Aldous, about the girl. I was wrong."

"I know. I picked you for a reason."

"But I was angry—"

"Yes, yes, and now you're sorry. I know. Stop arguing." Aldous drew in a deep breath. "I'm proud of you. I love you as if you were my own son."

Tennyson's chest constricted. He pulled out his wand. He couldn't let Aldous lie there.

"It won't help. I'm dying and I need to tell you something. The earthquake was an attack. This was revenge." The old man's voice began to falter.

"How do you—"

"Right before it happened, this arrived. By magic." Aldous opened his fist and revealed a medallion emblazoned with a wand crushing a hammer and sickle. On the reverse were the words "We are the stronger." He drew in a labored breath. "It's her. Elenka. Or one of her supporters. Find her. Follow her."

"But I—"

Aldous pressed the medallion into Tennyson's palm, then dug his fingernails into Tennyson's skin. "You know more"—another breath—"than anyone right now. You"—Aldous closed his eyes—"are young, smart . . ."

"Aldous." Tennyson grabbed the old man's hand, trying to will life into him.

A feeble smile appeared on Aldous's lips. With clear blue eyes, he gazed into Tennyson's face. "You are my best legacy." Another breath; this time it rattled. "Time of Transition. Dangerous."

Tears welled up in Tennyson's eyes.

"Do this. You'll need . . . help . . . the Rare One . . ." Aldous's hand went limp in his.

Tennyson stared at the lifeless eyes and closed the lids with a pass of his hand. This man had practically raised him. Without thinking, he fisted his hand around the medallion but did not rise from his position beside his mentor. Tennyson needed time to compose himself. Hell, time wouldn't help.

A beefy hand on his shoulder startled him. "Are you okay?"

He glanced up at the EMT, blinked a few times, then nodded.

"There was nothing we could do."

"I know." He should have been here sooner. He could have done . . . something.

"He probably wasn't in any pain."

Tennyson only nodded.

"You'll have to step back now."

Swallowing the burning knot in his throat, he rose from the ground and climbed from the rubble. Like a statue, he watched the emergency crew lift the wall with their wands and drape a sheet over Aldous's body. Beside the ruins, a gurney appeared, onto which the body was levitated and gently placed.

A hardness in Tennyson's palm roused him from his stupor. He opened his fist and saw the hammer and sickle gleam in the sunlight.

As he stared at the emblem, a cold foreboding gripped him despite the summer heat.

6

HOW TO BE A FAIRY GODMOTHER:

•

Feathers Before Bricks.

KRISTIN STRETCHED HER arms overhead, then winced. Her muscles ached, but a deep satisfaction filled her. The sprites had pushed her hard. By the end of the session, she could levitate small objects, bring them to her, and send them back. But she couldn't lift her arms. Who knew magic required such a physical and mental effort? As she downed a bottle of mineral water, she debated whether she wanted dinner or just a hot bath and bed.

A loud knock interrupted her musings. Before she could even start for the door, she heard it open. The troll. It had to be.

He appeared in the kitchen a moment later. His hair was tousled, his jacket hung open, and dirt streaked his shirt. His fierce gaze pinned her to her spot. The fire in his copper eyes burned, but not with anger. Nor with desire.

She couldn't read his expression.

This would never do. She had to stop wondering what he thought. It didn't matter. And it led to actions that were out of character. Like kissing him. At the memory of their last meeting, embarrassment engulfed her. She summoned as much irritation as she could. "It is customary to wait until someone opens the door and invites you in."

He shrugged and didn't look overly concerned. "I knocked this time."

"What if I had been in the bath?" She shouldn't have said that. Visions of steamy water filled her fantasy, but this was no simple bath. In her mind, glistening limbs entwined with each other as vapor rose off the water's surface. A blush heated her face.

"You weren't." He looked around the kitchen.

"How are you going to torture me this time?" She crossed her arms over her chest and tried not to let her expression reveal any of her soreness or chagrin.

"No torture." He opened a cupboard and grimaced. "Don't you believe in food?"

She narrowed her gaze and scrutinized him. Something was different about him. His responses lacked the sarcasm she associated with him. Instead he seemed subdued, as if making only a halfhearted effort to achieve his earlier cynicism. No hint of impatience glinted in his eyes. "Does this fairy godmother thing come with empathy?"

"I don't believe so." He opened the refrigerator and shook his head. "You know most people consider dinner a daily requirement."

He was hiding something. "I haven't been shopping. I've been busy these past few days." She closed the refrigerator. "Are you here to take inventory of my food supplies?"

"No. Don't be stupid."

"Okay, that's just rude. You come into my house and start baiting me. I'm not required to feed you as part of my test, am I?"

"Don't be . . . Never mind." He turned away.

Something *was* wrong. His words didn't hold the same bite they had before. She placed her hand on his arm and waited for him to look at her. "What's happened?"

To her surprise, an expression of intense grief covered his features. "Did you feel the earthquake today?"

She thought back to the afternoon. Callie and her friends had her levitating, summoning, vanishing, and attempting to conjure at such a rapid pace, she hadn't been aware of anything outside the garden. But there was a moment when the sprites had held still, cocked their heads at something she couldn't hear, and she had felt a disturbance of some kind, something she couldn't recognize. That feeling had never quite dissipated. "No. There wasn't one on the news."

"There wouldn't be. The earthquake was highly focused. Under the Academy."

"Academy?"

"The Academia Artis Magicae."

"What's the academy . . . ?"

"Academia Artis Magicae. It's one of our universities. The Southern California Branch." He sat at the kitchen table. "Do you have anything stronger than water?"

"Diet Coke?"

A wan smile lit on his lips. "Stronger."

"I don't know what my aunts kept in the house."

"It doesn't matter." He pulled out a glass and waved his wand. The glass filled with a brown liquid and ice. "Scotch. Want one?"

"Sorry. I'm a margarita girl myself."

Another wave of his wand produced the yellow-green liquid in a taller glass. Crystals of salt clung to the rim.

She sat beside him. "Thanks. Now do you want to tell me what happened?"

"An earthquake hit the Academy today. A powerful earthquake."

A shudder ran through her as if she were doused with cold water. "Were you there?"

He nodded. "I was doing research in the library."

"Are you hurt?"

"No. I'm fine." He took a slug of the scotch. "But Professor Aldous Montrose died today. A building collapsed on him."

"Who is Professor Aldous Montrose?"

"My mentor." Tennyson finished off the scotch and refilled the glass with a tap of his wand. "My friend."

Shock didn't express what she felt at this moment. Her aggravation with him vanished. She placed a hand on his forearm. "I'm so sorry."

"The earthquake wasn't natural." His dark eyes stared into hers, and her feeling of disturbance grew. "It was focused on the Academy, on Professor Montrose."

"But why?"

Tennyson reached into his pocket and pulled out a coin. "Do you know what this is?"

She picked up the round disc. It wasn't a coin. On one side the words "We are the stronger" appeared, and on the other a hammer and sickle crumbled under the power of a wand. The medallion lay heavy in her hand. If she wasn't mistaken, it was gold and newly minted. "A hammer and sickle? Communism?"

"Do you know the Groundling history?"

"Sure. I don't understand the wand part, but this is the symbol for communism. But that's been over for two decades. For the most part. Why would anyone engrave an outdated symbol on it?"

With a deep sigh, he took another sip of his scotch and closed his eyes. "Then you know that after World War Two the Russians took over Eastern Europe."

"Of course." She sat back and waited for the history she didn't know.

"We, the Arcani, have always had our greatest footholds in Europe. When Russia fell to the communists in 1917, we relocated most of our people to other places. Some stayed behind to help the Groundlings in the Soviet Union, and for the most part, they blended in."

He took another swallow of his scotch. "World War Two was devastating on so many levels, even for us. We couldn't save nearly as many people as we wanted, and thousands of our own were killed. After the war, when the Russians rolled through Eastern Europe, we had to relocate from all those countries. We couldn't hide that many people in that sort of regime. That's when we became a real presence here in the United States. There were Arcani here before, but this was the most logical place to resettle the refugees. One of those refugees was a woman named Elenka Liska. She was a fairy godmother who lived in Prague. She lost everything twice—first to Hitler, then to the Soviets."

"Poor woman." The upheaval of Kristin's own life seemed trivial compared to this tale.

"I'm not saying your sympathy is misplaced, but

you may want to save it. Elenka refused to move here. She didn't want to start over. She believed she had the right and the power to do as she wished. She fought the Council on their plans for the Arcani. It was a time of confusion and turmoil. I'm afraid the Council wasn't as strong as it should have been. Unfortunately, people started to listen to her and believe her. That we are stronger than the Groundlings. That we should stand up to them. And against them."

"So some Arcani saw her as a hope for the future."

"Right. Elenka grew more powerful in the next few years. She gathered people to her side and eventually led a revolt of sorts against the established Arcani community. She wanted to . . ."

"Rule the world?"

He chuckled. "A little melodramatic perhaps, but close enough. You know we try to stay hidden from the Groundlings. She believed that showed weakness. She believed with magic we could be the ruling power on earth. She never understood the strength of Groundling will, nor that Groundlings outnumber us five, ten thousand to one. No magic can overcome those numbers."

"So she started a war?"

"A civil war of sorts. It's known as the Great Uprising. There's a lot more to it, but essentially she was defeated and exiled."

"How does this tie into the earthquake?"

He picked up the coin. "Professor Montrose was one of those who helped exile her. Just after he received this, the earthquake struck. Before he died, he told me it was her. This was her symbol, the symbol of the Great Uprising. Elenka is back."

"But that would make her . . . old."

"She'd be the same age as your aunts. It's not impossible. The Great Uprising happened only sixty years ago. Chaos in the Groundling world often spills over into the Arcani world and vice versa. Have you watched the news lately?" He swirled the scotch in his glass and stared at it a moment before speaking. "Your aunts helped put her away as well."

"What?"

"The fairy godmothers. Elenka was one of them until she started the uprising." He placed the glass heavily on the table. "Her anger left scars among the Arcani. Older Arcani remember which side they were on and may still harbor those ideals. The fantasy of Arcani rule lures younger ones. Even the Council became overly protective of themselves and distanced themselves from the very Arcani they are supposed to govern."

"But the aunts never seemed worried." Kristin furrowed her brow. Her drink remained untouched.

"They wouldn't be. To their knowledge, Elenka no longer posed any threat." He straightened up and leaned toward Kristin, his gaze penetrating into her. "The last thing Aldous said to me before he died was that danger exists now because it is the Time of Transition. This period leaves us vulnerable, and Elenka would know that. Aldous believes . . . believed there's a threat. To you. So I'm moving in."

"Excuse me?"

"I'm moving in."

"Where?"

"Here."

She snorted. "I don't think so."

"Look, you're a Rare One. You have no idea yet how important you are, nor do you have any idea how much power you possess. Until you do, you need someone to watch over you, protect you. That became my job when Aldous was murdered." He downed his drink and then made both glasses disappear.

She hadn't even taken a sip of the margarita, and after his story she could use a drink. "But you can't stay here. You have other things to do, and I have—"

"You need protection. If I don't watch out for you, who will?"

"I am capable of looking after myself." She knew the moment she said the words they were stupid, a mere reaction. She didn't know magic or the Arcani world. The chaos of the past two days had already left her emotions on a roller coaster—one minute laughing, the next crying. She had lost all control of herself and couldn't predict how she would act next.

But to depend on the troll? She was more afraid of her reactions around him than some unknown danger. "You don't know for certain that I'm in danger."

"No, but Aldous told me to watch you. That's good enough for me. How many bedrooms do you have?" Apparently he wasn't listening to her protests.

Even now when he ignored her, when he was disheveled from the earlier events, when sorrow occupied so much of his spirit, she found him fascinating. If he lived here . . . The earlier image of them in a bath together popped back into her head. She couldn't possibly bathe while he was here. "Can you read minds?"

"No."

Thank God. He was right. She didn't know enough about her powers or the Arcani world, and if she was in danger . . . "You can take the back bedroom."

His eyebrows shot up. "You agree?"

"Despite what you may think, I am not foolish, and I do believe you're here in my best interests." She set her mouth into firm lines. "But if you think this gives you leave to interfere in my life, you have another thing coming. I have a date tomorrow night. I expect you to stay in your room until after we leave and be there when we get home."

"Fine."

"Fine." She pushed away from the table. She stormed to the doorway, then stopped. Turning back to him, she said, "I am sorry about your loss."

As she flounced away, she swung her head. Her hair bounced, giving Tennyson a tantalizing glimpse of a spot at the base of her neck. He wanted to lick that spot.

Damn. He had just lost his mentor, and he was thinking about sex. All the stereotypes about men must be true. Men were dogs.

He buried his face in his hands. More scotch sounded good right now, but he had to keep his senses about him. He was here to protect her, and he couldn't do that if he was drunk. Rubbing his face, he tried to banish all thoughts of her.

A date?

Wait. Had she said something about a date? Tomorrow night?

"Shit."

There was no way he was going to let her go out without knowing where and with whom. Hell, he might as well follow her.

Not a bad idea. It would take some planning, but he would follow her.

He rose from the table and went to find his room. He found it—in a sea of chintz and roses. Pinks and yellows adorned every surface. Doilies covered every flat spot, and the bedspread was poufy and frilly.

"Argh." It was late, he was tired, and he didn't have the energy to deal with this ruffled nightmare. Redecorating could wait until tomorrow.

He waved his wand, and a pair of brown pajama bottoms, a concession to his housemate, appeared on the bed. A small satchel held his toothbrush, shaving kit, and shampoo—enough to get him through the night and morning. Five minutes later, he flopped onto the bed and shut his eyes.

He tried to keep his mind from the grief that still pounded in his thoughts. Aldous would have wanted him to carry out his duty, but duty didn't make accepting the murder easier. The horrific events of the day raced through his mind, over and over again, until they sapped his senses from him and he fell into a fitful sleep.

A scream woke him the next morning.

"Kristin!"

He jumped out of bed and raced to her room. Flinging the door open, he scanned the area looking for an intruder.

She screamed again. "Get out of my room. I'm not dressed."

No one appeared to be attacking her. He searched the room again. No, she was alone. She stood in the middle of the floor wearing nothing but a tank top that reached to the middle of her thighs.

"You screamed."

"Hell, yes, I screamed. I'm shrinking." She tugged at the hem of the tank.

"You're what?"

"Shrinking. As in growing smaller. Look at this." She stepped into a pair of tennis shoes that lay at odd angles against the wall. Her feet swam in them. "These fit yesterday." She kicked them off. They bounced off the wall and landed in new odd angles.

"And my shirt used to hit my hip bone. Now look."

Her shapely legs stuck out from beneath the bottom of the top. The material clung to her like a sexy mini-dress, showing off every curve and the outline of a lacy bra and panties.

Focus, Tennyson.

He stepped beside her. She only came up to his chest. "Yup, you're definitely shrinking."

Panic rode into her features. "What do you mean I'm shrinking? People don't shrink."

"But you're not people, remember?"

"But I can't shrink. I have a date tonight."

That stupid date again. He frowned. "Turn around." He grabbed her shoulders and twisted her so that her back faced him.

"What are you doing?"

"Checking for wings."

"Wings?" The word was a shout. "What do you mean, 'wings'?" Twisting from side to side, she tried to view her back.

Holding her still, he lifted the shirt to her shoulders. There. Right beside the shoulder blades. Wing buds. She would hurt before this day was through. Lowering the shirt, he turned her around. "How do you feel right now?"

"Achy. I did a lot of magic yesterday and my muscles are sore—" Her bones crunched, and she grimaced. "It hurts."

"You're going through your first transfiguration. Do you have any ibuprofen? You might want to take a couple."

She grabbed his arm in a wicked grip. "What is a transfiguration, and what the hell did you mean by 'wings'?"

"Time for another lesson. Magical transformation is a rite of passage. We all go through it, only usually we're a lot younger because it hurts less as a child. To change into another form requires the bending of bones, the stretching of skin, the growing of hairs or gills or whatever. Children are more resilient—so the first transformation usually occurs then. Unfortunately, you're an adult."

"Which means . . . ?"

He shrugged. "Unless you're a ballet dancer and incredibly flexible, it will hurt. That's why most Arcani don't bother with transfiguration. Every new one hurts."

"But I'm shrinking, not transforming." Her skin popped as the wing buds pierced her skin. She winced and rolled her shoulders.

"Yes, you are. As a fairy godmother, you can't always serve your charges at your full size. There is a reason you're called a *fairy* godmother."

He didn't have to wait long for understanding to dawn. "I'm getting small, like Callie?"

"Who's Callie?"

"A fairy. I met her two days ago."

Then you understand. All fairies can be as large as a human, but they also have the need to be small. Sprites tend to remain small." He hated to admit it, but she looked shorter. He took her hand. "This first time is nature taking control, helping your body accept the change. The next time won't be so bad, and it gets easier with each transfiguration. But it will still hurt."

She closed her eyes in dismay. "How small will I get?"

He shook his head. "I don't know the specific measurements, but you won't disappear."

"And the wings?"

"You have to fly, don't you?"

"Fly? I can't fly." She froze. "Oh God. I can't go on a date with wings."

No, you can't, sunshine. He knew the glee he experienced at that news wasn't right, but he couldn't prevent it. "So, ibuprofen?" He lifted his hands waiting for her to answer or point or something.

"In the bathroom, second shelf."

He went into the bathroom and retrieved two caplets and a glass of water. He hurried back to her. "Here. Take these before they become too big."

"Right." She snatched them out of his hand and swallowed quickly. "How long does this change thing last?"

"As long as you need it, but this first time? Around six to eight hours. And you won't feel like doing much afterward. Transfiguration is exhausting. Especially the first time." Just in case she still planned on keeping her date.

"Thanks for the news flash." She looked up at the ceiling. "It hasn't been that far away since I was ten."

"Yeah, but wait until you fly."

She eyed him. "Can you fly?"

"Only in a plane."

"What, no broom?"

"You've been reading too many fairy tales." He walked to the door. "I'll be here. I won't let anything happen to you."

"Thanks."

"One more thing." He crossed to her and peeled off her tank top.

"Hey!" She flung her arms around herself. "What are you doing?"

He gave her a wolfish leer. "Gotta make room for them wings." He walked back to the door and turned around again. "And I'd do something about that bra. It's beginning to hang on you."

He left the room with her howl of rage blasting out behind him.

7

HOW TO BE A FAIRY GODMOTHER:

•

Magic Comes with a Cost.

"THANKS FOR UNDERSTANDING. I just couldn't have gone out last night." Kristin climbed into the backseat and wrapped her shawl around her shoulders.

"Of course I understand." Lucas gave her a polite bow and climbed in beside her. Dimitri closed the door.

She leaned back in the leather seat. The car was as classy as its owner. While the floor of her Camry was decorated with empty soda cans, a few napkins, and wrappers from a local taco stand, his car didn't sport a speck on the carpeting. The wood of the dash gleamed as if it had just been polished. She was almost afraid to breathe.

Dimitri climbed into the driver's seat and started the engine. It purred, and she could barely hear it. Soft classical music floated from the speakers, surrounding her with sound.

"Was the transformation painful?" Lucas asked as they pulled away from the curb.

"Definitely. But I took ibuprofen before the major changes."

"So are you eager to try again?"

She considered for a moment. Once she had realized that her shrinking was a natural process, she had calmed down and waited to see what would happen. By the time the transformation was complete, she was no bigger than Callie and had the most beautiful gold and black wings. Kristin's attempts at flying had been clumsy, but exhilarating. "Oh yeah. Only I have to figure out what to do about clothes." She had been tiny and naked.

Laughter rumbled from his throat. "I keep forgetting how new all this must seem to you."

She sighed. "It's hard to believe only four days have passed since I found out about magic. I've never felt quite so stupid before."

"I expect you were a bright student . . . for a Groundling." He smiled at her as he maneuvered onto the northbound freeway.

"I was, which makes this transition thing really hard to take. I feel like I'm playing some game and no one has told me the rules."

"Give yourself time, Kristin. You will learn. As you said, you've only had four days. I have a suggestion. Let's not talk about magic tonight. How about we just enjoy ourselves?"

"Agreed." She settled in to enjoy a normal evening. Although how normal was it to be driven by a chauffeur? "Have you always had a chauffeur?"

Lucas chuckled. "I confess I find it easier to leave details like driving to Dimitri, but he also serves as my butler and all-around second-in-command. And he has bodyguard skills. I trust him explicitly."

Kristin looked at the back of the driver's head. Lucas must be more important than she thought.

As they headed north, the buildings and lights of San Diego proper vanished behind them.

"Where are we going?"

"Mille Fleurs."

Whoa. If Lucas wanted to impress her, he just had. The sky was darkening, and the stars began to peek out as they drove toward Rancho Santa Fe up the 5 Freeway. Small talk filled their conversation as they drove the twenty miles to the restaurant. Dimitri's driving was flawless. Spaces opened up for him, and he maneuvered through them effortlessly despite the traffic. It was almost supernatural.

Wait a minute. *Was* he using magic? She concentrated a moment. A slight humming tickled her senses like background music or a white noise machine. Its source was magic because it tingled through her. She hadn't even known she could sense that. Satisfaction flowed through her, along with a sense of power. For the first time, she believed she might be able to handle this new life. After she learned more.

As they pulled up in front of the restaurant, she was glad she had worn her Donna Karan. The little black dress was a classic, and hadn't been *too* expensive when she bought it off season on the sale rack at Neiman Marcus. Her mother had always told her to have a nice dress ready for special occasions.

The slight humming and tingling tickled at her senses again as Lucas helped her from the car. In fact, it intensified when he took her elbow to guide her into the restaurant.

Her face must have registered her consternation, for Lucas stopped. "Is something wrong?"

The feeling became more powerful. She examined him but detected no evidence of magical activity from him. For a moment the tingling increased, then dropped to nothing. "No, I just . . . Did you use magic just now?"

His eyebrows arched. "No." He stopped and focused. "I don't feel anything."

With her gaze, she searched the parking lot. "Neither do I now, but for a moment it felt like it was focused on me."

"There are other Arcani in the world. We may not be the only ones here."

"I suppose." The tingle had been there. Coming from that direction. She stared at the restaurant's facade, then gasped. Tennyson was here. Behind that corner. Spying on her. Anger bubbled in her. "Troll."

At once, wariness covered Lucas's features. "Where?"

"There." She grabbed his hand and pulled him along the sidewalk to one side of the entrance.

"Are you mad? Trolls are dangerous."

"Not this one." She pointed to Tennyson, who had pressed himself against the side of the building.

With a shrug, Tennyson came out from behind the bush that entirely failed to conceal him.

A deep frown creased Lucas's forehead. "Who are you?"

Kristin crossed her arms. "Tennyson Ritter, and he has a lot of explaining to do."

Tennyson brushed a few twigs off his trousers and stuck out his hand to Lucas. "Tennyson Ritter. I'm Kristin's arbiter and, at the moment, guardian."

"Why are you here?" she asked, narrowing her gaze at him.

The two men shook hands. "Lucas Reynard. I did not know Kristin required a guardian."

"I don't."

"It's a new development," said Tennyson, ignoring her protest.

"How did you find me?"

"I transported. Since you don't know how to shield yourself yet, I focused on you and here I am."

That must have been the magic she sensed. "Couldn't your crystal ball show you I was fine?"

"I don't use a crystal ball."

"Whatever."

"I can't protect you from sudden danger at a distance." A definite note of annoyance rang in Tennyson's voice.

"Kristin, if you are in danger, you should have told me." Concern filled Lucas's tone.

"I'm not in danger."

Tennyson looked about to protest, so she held up her hands. "Okay, I don't know if I'm in danger, but Tennyson seems to think that I might be. Something about the Time of Transition." She scowled at Tennyson and placed her hands on her hips. "But I'm on a date. With. A. Sorcerer. What could happen to me here?"

Lucas nodded. "I would, of course, protect her even without knowing your concerns. Unless you think *I* am a threat to her." He smiled.

A look she couldn't identify flitted across Tennyson's features, but it disappeared in an instant. She looked at the two men. Tennyson was taller than Lucas. His posture showed strength and vitality, whereas Lucas exuded power in a debonair package. They stood on either side of her, and for an instant she felt like the bone two dogs were fighting over.

Tennyson returned the smile. "I'm sure she's safe with you, but I'll feel better if I'm near."

Lucas nodded. "We were about to have dinner. Won't you join us?"

"No, he won't," she said.

"Thank you," he said over her. "I'd love to. Just act like I'm not here."

"Like that's possible." She fumed. Of all the embarrassing things to have happen, this was the worst. She almost wished she could shrink now instead. What was she? A sixteen-year-old who needed an escort? Trolls should stay where they belonged—under rocks.

"I'll even watch from the bar." Tennyson's tone sounded exactly as if he were a magnanimous robber baron gifting the poor with some trifle. "So you won't have to curb your conversation."

"No, you won't," she said.

"An excellent idea," said Lucas on top of her words.

She waved her hands. "Hello. Am I invisible? You two seem to think that what I want doesn't matter."

"Not if you're being stubborn," said Tennyson.

"Kristin, you're not being reasonable. Mr. Ritter is only trying to protect you," said Lucas.

Argh. The last time she had put up with such macho bull was in college when her statistics test scores beat all the men in her class. Her fingers brushed against the clasp of the small beaded purse she carried. Hmmm. If Tennyson could transport here, then maybe she could transport away.

"Why don't we have a nice dinner, then the three of us can go somewhere and discuss the situation?" Lucas clasped her elbow again.

"I don't think so." Kristin flipped open her purse and pulled out her wand. "I want to go home."

Dizziness seized her, and her vision went black. She couldn't breathe, but before she had time to panic, a solid floor materialized beneath her feet, and she gulped in a deep breath. Her vision was still black. Then she realized her eyes were closed.

When she opened her eyes, she wasn't sure where she was. This wasn't a room she recognized. A huge bed occupied one wall, and a series of bookcases lined another. The large windows looked out over the ocean and an expansive backyard led to the edge of a cliff. Great. She must be in La Jolla somewhere. On top of a ruined evening, she was going to be arrested for breaking and entering.

She ran out of the sumptuous bedroom and down the stairs to the front door. *Please don't have a dog, please don't have a dog.* Luckily the house seemed empty. *Or an alarm. Please don't have an alarm.*

She saw no entry pad on the wall by the door, but that didn't mean there wasn't an alarm. Well, there was nothing for it. She grabbed the knob and flung the door open. No mechanical screeching filled the night sky. Relief weakened her knees for a moment, until she heard the dog next door start barking. His muzzle pushed through between slats in the fence. Time to leave.

Her high heels were going to be a problem, so she took them off. In her stockings, she ran up the walk and into the street. A moment later, she retraced her steps and pressed herself into the bushes that lined the drive. The neighbors' door opened and a man stepped outside.

"Zeus, you stupid mutt, shut up."

The dog barked more wildly.

"Dumb dog." The voice was beside the fence now. "Get inside before someone calls the police."

The barks drew away from the fence. She imagined the owner was dragging the dog into the house. When she heard the door close, she climbed from the foliage.

Terrific. Her little black dress was filthy, her stockings had huge holes in them, and she still had to find her way to the cottage. Maybe if she tried to shrink herself, she could fly home.

No way. She would not abandon her little black dress and killer shoes to the street.

She pulled off the ripped pantyhose, stuffed them into her purse, and took off in the direction of what she hoped was a street she could recognize so she could call a cab.

TENNYSON BLINKED TWICE before it registered that she had disappeared.

"Did you know she could do that?" asked Lucas.

"No. And I don't think she can." Tennyson pulled his hand down his face. "She has got to be the most stubborn, willful, stupid—"

"She isn't stupid. We handled that poorly."

"Maybe." The guy was right. He had handled that badly, but something about her made him crazy and caused him to forget everything he knew about proper behavior. And that little black dress that clung to her curves had not helped his thinking any. Nor did the fact that she seemed to enjoy being with Old Man River here.

The selfsame old guy pulled out his cell phone and punched in some numbers. "Change of plans, Dimitri. Come pick me up."

The guy had a driver? Who the hell was he?

Lucas returned his attention to Tennyson. "You transported here?"

"Yes."

"Do you want to drive back with me? It will give her some time to calm down," Lucas said.

"That would probably be smart, but right now, I'm not ready to be smart. Thanks anyway." Tennyson pulled out his wand and transported to the cottage.

He could feel the drain when he arrived. Transporting twice in such a short period cost energy. He needed food.

He stumbled to the kitchen and then remembered she hadn't gone shopping yet. Damn. He pulled out his wand again but knew he wouldn't have the strength to summon much. But he could teach her to.

"Kristin!"

No answer. In fact, the house was remarkably quiet. He would have thought she'd be throwing things or yelling or something.

"Kristin?" He started through the rest of the house. No sign of her. Each room was empty. Where was she? Icy tendrils of panic grabbed his mind. Even if he could succeed in locating her, he doubted he could transport himself without serious risk. He ran back to his room and pulled out a map of San Diego County. He didn't like scrying—it was much too inaccurate—but he was out of options. He didn't have the energy to do anything else. Holding his wand loosely between two fingers, he dangled it over the map. "Kristin."

The usual surge of power didn't come. Instead, the wand gave a weak jerk and landed on La Jolla.

That couldn't be right. He was drained. He needed food. He went back to the kitchen and found a container with cookies. Tearing off the lid, he grabbed one and shoved it in his mouth. It was good, but strange. It tasted like a chocolate chip cookie without chocolate chips. Who the hell ate chocolate chip cookies without chocolate chips?

He gobbled down two more, grabbed a fourth, and went back to the map. He wasn't at full magical strength, but he had to find her.

As he lifted the wand again, he heard a car drive up and stop in front of the cottage. He rushed to the window. Kristin climbed from a taxi. He ran to the door and threw it open.

"Thanks, Benito. I'm so glad it was you who stopped. My aunts will love the story of how you rescued me. Now wait here. I have money inside." She started up the walk. Clutched in her hands were her shoes and a take-out bag from a local taco stand.

"Where the hell have you been?"

She plastered a smile on her face. "Oh, good, you're here. Do you have some cash? I need twenty-five for the fare."

"You haven't answered my question."

"No, I haven't, but it isn't fair to make Benito wait." She held out her hand.

"Who's Benito?"

"The driver."

With a growl, Tennyson dug in his pocket and found two twenties. "I don't have anything smaller."

"That's okay." She snatched the bills from his palm and went back to the taxi. "Here, Benito. Keep the change. You are a spectacular driver."

"Thank you, Miss Kristin. Call me again if you need me. Have a good night." The cabby turned on his available sign and headed down the street.

Tennyson watched in disbelief as Kristin waved to the driver and came back up the walk. That little black dress clung to her in all the right spots. No wonder Benito had been so friendly. And on a first name basis with her.

"Where have you been?" Tennyson asked as she came in to the house.

"Away from the testosterone display. Now if you'll excuse me, I'm going to eat my dinner." She walked into the kitchen and pulled down a plate. She placed her shoes on the table and pulled a massive burrito from the bag.

He stared at her. "You can't just sit there and eat."

"Why not? I'm starving. I didn't know magic could make you so hungry." She took a huge bite of the burrito. The aroma of spiced meat and guacamole filled the kitchen. She pulled out another item wrapped in paper. Peeling it back, she revealed three rolled tacos drenched in more guacamole. She lifted one and waited for the melted cheese to separate.

His stomach growled. Four cookies did not a meal make, but he'd be damned before he asked for some of her food. "What you did tonight was unconscionable. You can't just disappear like that."

"Clearly I can." She crunched down on the rolled taco. "Mmmm, this is heavenly."

"You could've put yourself in danger." He ran his hand through his hair.

"I didn't." A bite of the burrito followed that pronouncement.

He paced the linoleum. "Your powers aren't fully developed yet."

"I am aware of that." She ate without looking at him.

"Your actions were childish."

"Probably. But it felt good." She chewed, holding her finger in the air until she swallowed. "Have you ever noticed that when you make a strong move that someone else doesn't like, they tend to call it childish?"

"It was irresponsible and dangerous. You don't know what might have happened."

"Nothing did."

The phone rang.

"Get that, will you? My mouth is full." She bit down on the burrito like a snarling lion.

With an impatient groan, he picked up the receiver. "What?"

"Mr. Ritter, I presume?"

He recognized Lucas's voice, and a fresh surge of discontent ran through him. "Yes."

"Is she there? Safe?"

Even Reynard's calm tone irritated him. But then the man had had decades of practice in holding his temper. "Yes."

"May I speak with her?"

"Sure." He handed the phone to her just as she took another bite.

She rolled her eyes. Chewing furiously, she swallowed the mouthful, then put the receiver to her ear. "Hello?"

He watched as slowly a smile replaced the aggravation that highlighted her face when she was speaking with him. What was that smarmy jerk telling her anyway?

"Apology accepted," Kristin said.

Reynard apologized to her? For what? She should be apologizing to them. She's the one who left them standing outside Mille Fleurs not knowing where she had gone.

"No, I'm not living with him. He's occupying the back bedroom, that's all."

Nosy bastard. The guy was old enough to be her father. He shouldn't be interested in her sleeping arrangements.

"I'd like that. Tomorrow night? I'll make sure my guard dog understands." She glared at him.

Guard dog? A low rumble started in his throat.

"Terrific. See you then. Good night." She handed him the receiver and picked up the burrito again. "Hang it up for me, would you?" An insincere smile punctuated her request.

He slammed the receiver into its cradle. She widened her eyes and gave him an innocent look. "Is something wrong?"

"You're going out with him?"

"I like him. He talks to me, not *at* me, and he asks me things instead of telling me."

Tennyson placed both hands on the table and leaned over her. "You are still an innocent. The Arcani world isn't some rainbow candyland with prancing unicorns here for your entertainment. You have no idea of the threat out there, and you refuse to act sensibly."

She dropped the burrito on the table, jumped up, and mirrored his position. "Sensible? What the hell is sensible about this situation? I have been through more than can be expected from one person in the past few days, but instead of helping me learn, you want me to obey your commands. Well, I don't work that way. You say I need protection. Fine. But don't exclude me from your plans. I have the right to decide what I am willing to risk. Teach me what I need to know, but don't expect me to accept your *help* without explanation."

Above her the light fixture glowed brighter. Tennyson glanced at it, then back at her. "Would you have let me follow you?"

"No." The light fixture flickered.

"Then why should I have asked?"

"You are insufferable." She pushed away from the table.

Her eyes flashed with an emerald fire. The auburn curls bounced around her face, adding to the image of flames. The light fixture glowed red now and would probably explode in another minute. There was no doubt she was a powerful creature. He could feel anger radiating off her in waves. God help anyone who crossed her when she had her full strength. She was magnificent and the most frustrating woman he had ever met.

Before he knew what he was doing, he buried his fingers into the riot of hair on the side of her head and pulled her to him. He needed to hold her, to punish her, to own her. His mouth slanted across hers. His tongue slid into her mouth, taking, drinking, reaching for her. She tasted of spices and warmth, fire and guacamole.

For an instant she froze; then her tongue responded, chasing his, teasing all his senses. A soft moan rose from her throat and filled his ears with music. Her hands came up to his neck and jaw, taking from him as much as he took from her.

His hands moved to the scoop back of the dress where they met warm skin. His fingers danced over her spine. A simple sweep would brush the dress from her shoulders. Anticipation thrummed in him. This woman sang to his blood.

He swung her into his arms and carried her to her bedroom. He placed her on the bed and knelt beside her. Cradling her head, he kissed her again, and put every nuance of his hunger into it. She turned to fit herself more intimately against him. Her lips, soft, full, yet firm, urged him on. She placed a hand on his chest and splayed her fingers. Her touch burned through his polo.

He broke away. Every breath seemed a roar. His heart thundered in his ears. Closing his eyes, he leaned his forehead against hers. "Tell me now, if you want to stop. Tell me now, because in a moment I won't be able to."

8

HOW TO BE A FAIRY GODMOTHER:

•

Not All Wishes Should Be Granted.

KRISTIN'S BREATH CAUGHT in her throat. "Don't stop." She dropped her head back.

His lips traced the exposed curve of her neck. With a gentle swish, he swept the material from her shoulders. Her nipples puckered when the cool night air hit them, then tightened further as his mouth took first one, then the other into the moist warmth. His hands cupped their weight as his thumb lazily brushed their sides.

Blood rushed through her, effervescent and playful, as sensation after sensation rolled over her. What was she doing? She tried to hang on to her anger, but rational thought was no longer possible. The maelstrom of the past day had left her emotions raw and her sensibilities in confusion, and the magic of his mouth on her body wasn't helping her thought process. She braced herself on her arms. Nothing had ever felt so powerful before. But it wasn't enough. She wanted to feel him, to touch him.

She leaned forward and pulled his polo up. He snatched the material from her hands, yanked the shirt from himself, and flung it into a corner. She splayed her palms on his chest, then slowly slid them down the ridges of his abs. At his waistband she hesitated, then leaned forward and licked his nipples.

"God, woman." He pressed her back onto the mattress and pulled her dress down the length of her legs until only the small, black, lacy excuse for panties covered her. With a hungry glint in his eyes, he moved back over her, running the tip of his tongue up from the waistband to her neck.

With a wicked grin, she popped the buttons on his jeans. He pushed them from his hips along with his boxers. His erection brushed against her thigh, eliciting a tremor of pure anticipation in her, and for an instant she wondered if magic might change the whole experience.

He braced himself above her and bent his head to her lips. She welcomed him, his heat covering her like a blanket. As the kiss deepened, he pressed forward, rubbing against the material of her panties; then he shifted above her and nestled his hardness between her legs. A delicious tension started in her core.

He slid down a little and once again feasted at her breasts. Her hand burrowed into his hair, holding him there. She gasped as his hand delved beneath the lacy triangle, stroking and coaxing her insides to melt. She felt her dampness, the slickness of herself flowing into the material. Her hips twitched as he slid a finger inside her, and she sucked in her breath as she clenched around him. When he left her, she gave a little whimper, but he toyed with the bud hidden in the thatch of curls. Her breathing grew more ragged.

"You like that." He licked the little hollow at the base of her neck. "What else?"

"More. I want more." Her fingers clenched the side of his head, and she brought his mouth to hers.

His laugh echoed in her mouth. Grabbing the fragile material of her panties, he pulled down on the diaphanous fabric until it ripped. She didn't care. Her blood raced at the heightened excitement.

Kneeling on the bed between her legs, he opened his palm and focused on his hand. His wand appeared. "*Requiro.*" A silver packet appeared on the bed. He reached for the condom and without a break in movement said, "Sanctum." The wand disappeared.

He sheathed himself, then settled himself between her legs. His penis traced the entrance to her innermost self. He moved up and down against her, making himself slick with her juices. The lightness of his touch teased her, sent shots of energy jolting through her. Reaching between them, she enfolded his erection, raised her hips, and guided him inside.

Unintelligible sounds mingled in their throats, their breath. Her skin, hot and moist, quivered as their bellies touched, and his quivered in return.

Their hips met, and she arched against him so she could feel every inch of him stretching her. He pulled out and drove himself into her again. She gave in to the enchantment roaring in her blood. She met his thrust, tilted her hips, and took him in again and again and again.

The spell crescendoed, lifting her higher, higher still, until, on a gasp, the world shattered into a thousand shimmering stars. "Oh, Tennyson."

Above her, he pushed into her one last time and a

great shudder overtook his body. He drew in an uneven breath, and lowered himself to her side.

For several minutes she didn't move. The enchantment of what had just happened enveloped her in a comfortable fog. She snuggled into his warmth and lay in the circle of his arms. Dear God, her body still hummed.

He pressed his lips to her forehead. His every breath seemed to her ears an effort to regain his equilibrium. A sense of satisfaction filled her. He was as affected by the experience as she. Words had no place in this afterglow.

Contentedness seeped into every pore. She felt languid and relaxed and . . .

"Mmmm." The sound of his enjoyment brought a smile to her face. "I can't begin to describe that."

She rolled her cheek against his chest. "Mmm-hmmm."

"You're beautiful."

"So are you." She lifted her gaze to his. Within the deep burnished copper of his eyes a fire shone.

"We probably broke a million rules. We'll never be able to explain this." He stroked her hair and let the strands trickle through his fingers.

"Rules? What rules?" She furrowed her brow.

"The ones about an arbiter and his charge."

Oh God, she was in bed with the troll. Reality snaked back into her senses. She was a fairy godmother and he was a wizard. She bolted upright, grabbed the comforter, and draped it around her. "Oh God, oh God, oh God!"

One eyebrow cocked, he gave her a puzzled look. "That part usually comes before now."

She stared in horror at the rumpled bed. "Did you do this? Was this magic?"

He chuckled. "I suppose you could call it magic, but, no, it wasn't *magic*."

Disbelief welled in her. "What have I done?"

"We had sex. Are you telling me you've forgotten?"

"No, you idiot. I just . . . Oh God, oh God, oh God." She buried her face in her hands.

"Hey. What's wrong?" He swung his legs off the bed and picked up his clothes. In a matter of seconds he was wearing his jeans again.

"I've never done this kind of thing before." She jumped from the bed, dragging the bedcover with her. She paced the floor. "I don't do this kind of thing."

"You could've fooled me." He was frowning now.

She stopped and faced him. "I don't jump into bed with men I barely know. Hell, I barely jump into bed with men I do know."

"I'll admit it's a little dicey, since I am your arbiter, but we don't have to tell anyone."

"I can't have a relationship with you."

"Nobody's asked you—"

"I have a date tomorrow night."

He was scowling now. "You can't seriously be thinking of keeping it."

She shook her head. "I don't need this complication now. I don't even like you."

"Well, you certainly liked parts of me a little while ago." He grabbed his shirt from the floor. "Look, sunshine, I don't know how your mind works, but what happened here was as much your fault as mine."

"Oh God, oh God, oh God." She sank onto the bed.

"Right. I'm outta here. We'll just pretend this whole thing didn't happen. That's probably best for you and me." He pulled the shirt on with jerky movements. "I'll be in the back room if you need . . . hell, if someone attacks."

"You're staying here?"

"As pleasant and not awkward as this interlude has been, I have a duty. I promised Aldous." Tennyson strode to the door, then faced her again. "That's the only reason I haven't left already." He left the room. A few moments later she heard the bedroom door slam at the back of the house.

She buried her head in her hands. Oh yes, she was a genius at this sort of thing. She tried not to think about how she had just broken every rule she had ever had for herself. Tears welled in her eyes. Too much had happened in the last few days. Too many new things, too much to learn. Too much to take in. No wonder she had behaved out of character.

How was she going to face Lucas tomorrow? She'd have to tell him she couldn't handle dating anyone now. *Especially* now.

After she had just had the best, mind-blowing sex of her life.

With the troll.

KRISTIN SAT AT the kitchen table and stared at the morning newspaper. She'd been staring at it for ten minutes and still hadn't read a word. Her orange juice sat untouched and her toast had turned to stone. Anger, exhaustion, confusion, and fatigue roiled within her. And she was tired too. And mad. And she couldn't think. She hadn't slept all night.

Callie fluttered into the kitchen. "Good morn—Ewww, you look terrible."

"Thank you, Captain Obvious." Kristin dug her fingers into her hair and rubbed her scalp.

"Did you get any sleep at all?" asked the sprite as she flitted from one side of Kristin's head to the other.

"Not really."

Callie landed on the table and peered up into Kristin's face. "I was going to suggest we try some more spells, but I don't think you're up for it."

"What I'd really like is to get out of the house." She glanced toward the back bedroom. *What I'd really like is not to face* him *today.*

A moment later her inner voice added, *Coward.*

"Do you have someone stashed back there?" Callie took to the air again and zoomed to the doorway.

"In a way. Tennyson Ritter is here."

The fairy's mouth dropped open, and she zipped back. "*The* Tennyson Ritter? He's a dish."

"You can have him." Despite Kristin's foul mood, tears welled in her eyes. Why did she feel like she had screwed up?

"Oh, honey, you look like you need a friend." Callie landed on Kristin's shoulder. "You really want to leave the house?"

She sniffed. "Uh-huh."

The fairy nodded. She pulled out her wand and waved it over herself. In a few moments, Callie stood beside her, without wings and human sized. She wore a beautiful diaphanous rose and green dress that flowed around her like the wind through leaves. Her strawberry blonde hair looked sun-kissed and gently tousled by a warm breeze. Her cheeks had lovely pink blooms and her eyes were the blue of an aquamarine. She looked ethereal and lovely. Callie shuddered and shook herself as if removing the last vestiges of a bad dream.

For a moment, Kristin said nothing. "You're big."

"Of course." The fairy's voice had a richer timbre in this form. "But I prefer to be small. I can do my work better."

"What work?"

"Sprites tend plants and flowers. And small animals. Bees and spiders are my favorites." Delight sparkled in Callie's eyes.

"You tend . . . No, wait. I can't deal with anything new right now." Kristin studied Callie. She was beautiful. And that dress looked fairy-like, yet fit in with the human world. It must have been hard to find such a fitting style. Wait a minute. "When I shrank, I was naked. How did you keep your clothes?"

"Honey, I've done this a lot longer than you have." Callie padded through the kitchen as if testing the space. "You'll learn in time. It's easy really. Except for shoes. I hate shoes. Nasty confining instruments of torture." She wiggled her toes against the linoleum.

A crooked smile lit on Kristin's lips. "I'd think you'd say that about bras."

Callie waved her hand. "Oh, please, I never bother with those horrible things. Come on. You said you needed to get out of the house." Callie grabbed Kristin's arm and pulled.

The misery of the morning returned with vengeance. Tears threatened anew. "You're coming with me?"

"Hey, I don't put on shoes for just anybody." With a quick snap of the wand, a pair of flip-flops showed up on Callie's feet.

"I should leave a note—"

With another flick, a white sheet with writing scrawled on its face lay on the table. "Done. Now come on. Let's get you some fresh air."

The two women strolled down the street and turned onto a more commercial road. Here tables were set outside for enjoying food, boutiques exhibited their wares—three T-shirts for twenty dollars—on racks blocking the sidewalk, and New-Age stores claimed crystal healing powers and psychic readings. Chimes tinkled in the breeze.

"Don't you just love how humans think they know magic?" Callie giggled as they passed a palmistry shop. "They're so cute. Even *we* can't read the future."

Kristin smiled as expected but didn't say anything. Her thoughts were still on the man she had left at home.

"Okay, spill it. What's troubling you?" Callie said.

With a deep sigh, Kristin said, "I slept with Tennyson last night."

Callie's eyes grew wider. "Oh my God. That has to be against so many rules."

"That's what he said." Kristin stopped in front of a juice bar and sat on a bar stool at an elevated high table. "But it's just so unlike me. I don't jump into bed with men this fast."

"Really? Why not?"

"Because sex has always felt like sharing a part of my soul. It's too intimate for me to take lightly."

"There's nothing wrong with that. Was it good?"

Her face flamed.

Callie laughed. "I'll take that as a yes."

"I know, but I've only known him for five days." She buried her head in her hands. "And he hasn't been the nicest individual I've ever met."

"So maybe it was your body talking for a change instead of your head."

Her body had never talked before, and if it was about to start, she needed to set some rules for it.

A waitress approached them. "What can I get you?"

"Two pineapple mango smoothies," said Callie. "With a vitamin supplement. She needs it."

The waitress left, and Callie took Kristin's hand and squeezed it. "You don't know who Tennyson Ritter is, do you?"

"No." Oh God, she was going to feel worse, wasn't she? She had no idea who he was.

"He's a brilliant wizard. His talents were recruited by all the top Arcani firms, but he turned his back on all of them for academic study. A lot of Arcani thought he was crazy. They changed their minds when he found the *Lagabóc*."

"The what?"

"*The Book of Rules*. An ancient text filled with the most powerful magic the world has known. It was lost in the Dark Ages, and we believed it was legend until Tennyson found it."

"So this book is important?"

Callie gave her a look of exasperation. "You know the Dark Ages weren't just called that because Groundlings had little learning. The Arcani world didn't have set boundaries. Some Arcani considered Groundlings little more than vermin, even debating whether those creatures had souls. When Merlin rose to power with Arthur—"

"Wait. Merlin? *The* Merlin? As in Arthur? Knights of the Round Table?"

"You've heard of them then. Good." Callie smiled at her like a teacher smiled at a prized pupil.

The waitress appeared with their drinks. "Thanks," Kristin said. She dug into her pocket for a few bills and paid the girl.

Callie took a long pull on her straw. "I love these

things. Next time you have got to try the piña colada one."

Kristin gave the sprite an impatient glance and cleared her throat. "The story?"

"I'm getting to it." Callie gave a little pout. "Merlin tried to form a society where Groundlings and Arcani could coexist for each other's benefit, but some Arcani rose against him. They believed Groundlings inferior and worth less than animals. They had no desire to coexist with such base creatures."

A protest rose to Kristin's tongue, but Callie held up her hand. "Their words, not mine. The Groundlings fought this idealized society as well. They wanted to enslave the Arcani and force them to use their powers to benefit only the Groundlings. Society broke down, one side fighting the other with more fighting within the groups. Eventually Merlin emerged victorious on the Arcani side, but Arthur couldn't control the Groundlings. Too many Groundlings wanted what the Arcani could provide for them, and too many Arcani had urged the rebellion. Merlin realized that Groundlings and Arcani couldn't live together, so he separated the worlds. His rules and teachings appear in the book, but there's also a section on the spells he used to defeat the most powerful Arcani of the day." Callie shuddered. "Those spells are really dangerous. I don't even like to think about them."

"So these rules . . ."

"Govern our society. We have a high Council, courts, all that stuff. He came up with your job, you know."

"Who?"

"Merlin. He liked Groundlings despite his failure, and he wanted to help them. So he made the position of fairy godmother. You're a sort of liaison between our world and the Groundlings."

"And Tennyson found this book?"

"Yes. We had rules before, but people believed they were just the natural course in the development of a civilized society and the *Lagabóc* was just a legend."

"And the spells?"

Callie shuddered again. "They were real too. Of course, you'd have to be a really powerful Arcani to cast them."

Like a Rare One? But the question remained unasked. Kristin was beginning to understand Tennyson's concern for her safety. And his impatience at being made her arbiter.

Still, he could have shared some of this information.

A young mother walked toward them pushing a stroller. The infant was strapped in and looked unhappy. His cheeks were red and he squirmed ceaselessly. A tiny crown appeared over his head. Kristin hesitated. The last time she had tried to listen to a child's wish, the noise had overwhelmed her, but maybe if she concentrated . . . Kristin focused on the child and drew in a deep breath. A moment later she looked at the mom and frowned.

"What's wrong?" asked Callie.

"It's a beautiful day. Warm, sunny."

"And this is a problem?"

"I hate it when parents wear shorts and a tank top, then dress their kids as if they were going on an arctic expedition. That child is miserable." She pointed to the baby who was fussing in the stroller.

"How do you know?"

"I can hear his wish." Without thinking she summoned

her wand and hid it under the table. She cupped her free hand slightly, tapped it with her wand, then blew into it in the direction of the child. When the breeze hit him, the infant hiccupped, and then he smiled as the air moved over him. It carried his hat away, opened his little jacket, and popped the booties off his feet. He gurgled as his toes wriggled in the air.

Of course the breeze also took the baseball cap from the head of a boy skateboarding by them, scattered the papers from an open briefcase of an already harried-looking businessman, and lifted the skirt of an old woman walking her bichon frise. Oops.

"How did you do that?" Callie asked.

"I don't know. I just did it." Her actions had felt right, and her instincts had taken over. Her guilt melted away as she watched the child grin toothlessly at her.

Callie looked smug. "My lessons must be paying off."

The mother rolled past them. She glanced at her son, then frowned. "Oh, Brian, what have you done with your booties?"

"See? I told you shoes were an instrument of torture," Callie whispered to Kristin.

Biting her lip to keep from laughing, she watched as the woman tucked a thin blanket around her son. As soon as the mother's back turned toward Kristin, she swirled the wand and saw the end of the blanket trail out of the stroller and fall to the sidewalk.

"You were born for this job," Callie said with a grin.

"It did feel good." Kristin placed her wand in her pocket and slurped up the last of her smoothie.

"So you're feeling better?" Callie touched Kristin's arm.

Her uneasiness returned. The smoothie had smoothed

over nothing about the situation with Tennyson. "I still have to face Tennyson."

"And what a great face he has. Whatever else you may think, he is hot, and great sex is still great sex." Callie slid from the chair. "Now let's take care of me. The sooner we get back, the sooner I can have my wings. I feel naked without them."

9

HOW TO BE A FAIRY GODMOTHER:

•

Never Fly in a Thunderstorm.

TENNYSON SHOT OUT of the chair as Kristin walked through the door. He wanted to throttle her. Or kiss her. No, wait. He couldn't kiss her. She didn't like him, remember? Anger swirled through him. Okay, he'd settle for throttling her. "Where have you been?"

She wasn't alone. Some woman was with her. They exchanged a look. Kristin said, "Callie, this is Tennyson. Tennyson, Callie."

Her sprite friend. He nodded his head without really looking at the woman. Kristin couldn't distract him with an introduction. "Why didn't you tell me you were going out?"

"We left a note."

He waved a white sheet in front of her. "You mean this? This just says you're going out. How was I supposed to know where you were?"

"And this is where I leave," Callie said. She waved

her wand, and in a matter of seconds, she sprouted wings and was tiny again. "Much better. See you later, Kristin."

"Bye, Callie, and thanks." Kristin's voice was full of warmth, a warmth he had never heard her use with him. Great. Now he was jealous of a sprite.

Jealous? He wasn't jealous. He was angry.

Callie fluttered around Kristin's cheek and gave her a fairy peck. "Any time, kiddo." Callie flew out the still open door, which then gently closed behind her.

"How does she change so fast?"

"She's a sprite, and don't change the subject." He crossed to Kristin and gripped her arm. "What were you thinking?"

Her gaze met his. "I wasn't. Thinking, that is."

"You are driving me insane." He saw his hold on her arm, and chagrin swamped him. He released her and drew his hand down his face. "My life was so . . . calm before you. Now look at me."

"*Your* life was calm? Five days ago I didn't even know magic existed." She stopped, drew in a deep breath, and rubbed her arm. "I told myself I wouldn't lose my temper. I mean to say I understand now."

"Understand what? That you're in danger?"

"Why you're worried about me. Callie explained about Merlin and the *Lagabóc*. And then I helped a kid get his wish. . . ." A hint of a smile lit on her lips. "It was amazing."

"You were able to do that already?" Tennyson eyed her with surprise and a little doubt.

"It was an easy wish. But it felt great." As she exhaled, her posture relaxed, and she looked pleased with herself. "Anyway, I understand my role. I'm a liaison, a conduit between the Arcani world and the Groundling world. Merlin liked Groundlings and didn't want to leave them completely without magic, so he created my job."

She had summed it up accurately and concisely. Tennyson's estimation of her grew in that moment. He had known she was intelligent. Now he had to tell her the rest. "The godmothers also provide a barrier between the worlds."

"What do you mean?"

"The idea of magic, the idea of something special or unexplained, seems to excite Groundlings. They go searching for it in so many ways. If they knew we were real, they wouldn't stop hunting us. Merlin understood this, so he created the godmothers. They provide the magic Groundlings crave. To distract them. At the same time, their magic protects us. When a godmother grants a wish, Groundlings forget about the search."

"But wish granting isn't big magic. How does having a wish granted satisfy a Groundling?"

"It doesn't in the long run, but godmothers keep the Groundling world under surveillance. They are the first to sense the undercurrents of unrest or trouble. Hitler was strongly into the occult. He was searching for more power. The godmothers knew this and kept him distracted by creating little magical events that drew his attention away from the real search."

She frowned. "Could they have stopped him?"

He shook his head. "Sometimes even magic isn't enough to stop evil." He hadn't lived during that era, but just thinking about it sent a profound sadness through him. He shook himself. "Because the godmothers must mingle so deeply in the Groundling world, they require a special ability to love both worlds. According to the *Lagabóc*, godmothers don't have power in their early years, so they can sympathize with how Groundlings live. So in a sense, godmothers have the power to keep Groundlings from discovering the Arcani but also help Groundlings satisfy their need for magic. The strength of the godmothers keeps the worlds separate."

She sighed. "Okay. I think I get that."

"But it works both ways. Since godmothers are part of the Groundling world too, they are also required to protect Groundlings from Arcani who would do them harm."

"So now I'm a cop?"

"No. You just try to stay aware of anything off in both worlds."

"Which is why they assign an arbiter to a new godmother. To see if we can hack it." She watched him with intensity. "Right?"

He smiled. "Pretty much."

"Gee, that's not asking much." She squinted at him. "If this job is so important, why can't you help me with the Transition?"

"Because you have to discover for yourself if you want this life."

Kristin drew in a deep breath. "That's a lot of responsibility."

"Precisely. And during the Time of Transition, the Arcani world is at its weakest. The old godmothers start to lose some of their powers, and the new ones aren't used to theirs yet. New Council members are chosen and others must step down." He raked his hand through his hair and started to pace. "Someone could take advantage of that weakness. And now Aldous

Montrose is dead. Someone killed him. An Arcani." Tennyson paused. "I believe someone is trying to gain power."

She plopped into a chair. "You sure know how to make this job sound attractive."

"I may be wrong—"

"No, it's better that I know." She leaned forward. "When I helped that child today, it felt so . . . so . . . I don't know how to describe it, but I liked it. I can do this. I want to do this."

"Good. Then we have to make plans. If I'm going to keep you safe, you have to—"

"Wait." She held up a hand. "I said I want to do this, but you can't order me around. I'm not stupid, and I don't want to take risks with my life or"—she chuckled nervously—"upset the balance of power, but you have to trust me."

He frowned. "You're not ready yet. Your magic is—"

"Still new. I know that. But I have things to do. You want me to trust you. I'm asking the same in return."

He thought for a moment. "Fair enough."

"Good. I'm going out tonight. With Lucas."

A hot jolt of fury pierced him. He should have listened to his initial impulse to throttle her. "You can't seriously be going on a date after last night."

Color flooded her cheeks, but her gaze didn't waver. "Yes, I am. And you are *not* coming with me or following me. Is that understood?"

Her answer left him speechless. How could she see another man after last night? She had told him she didn't like him—hell, he didn't much like her at the moment—but she had also said she wasn't the type to sleep around. "Oh yes, I understand."

She eyed him, then sighed. "No, somehow I don't think you do."

SEVEN O'CLOCK FOUND Kristin in the lobby of La Valencia Hotel. The stucco glowed pink in the evening sun, and the furnishings were fancy yet comfortable. Large floral arrangements graced the lobby. She couldn't begin to guess how much just one of those bouquets cost. Money spoke here, and she wasn't sure she knew the language.

The desk clerk had seemed reluctant to send a message to Lucas's suite. Kristin's blue jeans and T-shirt probably caused his hesitation. He had inspected her attire with some disdain, as if he couldn't believe someone dressed as she was could have business with the impeccable Mr. Reynard.

The elevator expelled its passengers, and Lucas stepped out. He scanned the lobby, then smiled as he saw her. He strode to her reaching his arms forward, clasped her hands, and pulled her in to kiss her cheek. "Kristin, such a surprise. I thought I was coming to pick you up."

"You were, but I needed to talk to you." She stepped back from him, needing to create a little space between them. Dimitri hovered in the background, not close enough to eavesdrop but enough for her to feel his presence.

"This sounds serious. Let me buy you a drink. We can sit in the lounge." He indicated an area off the lobby.

"Let's stroll instead."

"This *is* serious." He took her arm in his and led her through the lobby. Dimitri followed at a discreet distance. "What can I do for you?"

The cooling air refreshed her as they stepped outside. She drew in a deep breath. The fragrance of the hotel grounds' flowers mixed with the tang of the sea. The distant sound of waves crashing against the rocks hummed in the air. "As you know, it's been an interesting week for me."

He chuckled softly. "I can imagine."

"I've learned so much this week. Mostly that I have so much more to learn."

"Ah, but you're bright, intelligent, graceful—"

She laughed. "I wish I could be as sure about that as you are."

"Nonsense. Why else would I be drawn to you?"

"You're too kind."

He opened his mouth to protest, but she held up a hand. "That's what I wanted to talk about. Your friendship has helped me a lot this week. You've been honest with me, so I want to be honest with you. This Time of Transition thing is hard. I don't quite know what I'm doing yet, but I know I want to succeed."

"And you shall."

She smiled. "Yes, I will. But it will take work, and right now I can't worry about dating when I have so many other things to worry about."

"I see." Lucas's face lost all expression as if a mask had dropped over it.

"I'm truly flattered by your interest in me, and perhaps in a few months, when I'm not so overwhelmed—"

With an enormous boom, a crushing wave crashed into the rocks below the hotel. Its spray exploded high into the air. Seagulls and other shorebirds shot up into the sky scolding the disturbance raucously.

Lucas turned to her, an odd smile on his face.

She looked for signs of anger—lips set, eyes narrowed—but saw none. He looked . . . hmmm, not hurt, but frustrated? "Lucas, I'm not—"

"No, no, no. I understand completely." His smile was genuine again.

She exhaled. "I'm so relieved. I didn't want to disappoint you."

"No, it is I who should apologize. I shouldn't have troubled you in this time of change. I hope you will still consider me a friend, here to help you in any way I can."

"Watch what you're offering, because I may have to take you up on that."

He frowned. "What do you mean?"

"According to Tennyson, this Time of Transition may not be so smooth. He believes someone is trying to seize power."

Lucas's eyes widened. "Impossible."

She shook her head. "Yesterday an earthquake struck at the magical academy."

"The Academia Artis Magicae?"

"Yeah, that one. Tennyson's mentor was killed."

"Such a tragedy, but earthquakes happen." Lucas gave a very continental shrug.

"Not like this one. Before he died, Tennyson's mentor told him that it was an attack."

Lucas fell silent for a moment. "Has Tennyson shared his concerns with anyone?"

"I don't know. I don't think so. He's been too busy ruining my life." She let out a snort of disgust. "All right, guarding me. He thinks I'm in danger, so he won't let me out of his sight. Believe me, he is not my idea of the perfect roommate."

"But he's not here right now?" Lucas swept his hand around the hotel grounds.

"Only because I threatened him with bodily harm if he came. I wanted to speak with you alone. But I did promise him that after tonight I will behave and he can follow me around like a good watchdog."

"As it should be. If he hadn't offered to protect you, I would." His lips formed a stern line.

"Oh, please. Not you too?"

"You are a fairy godmother." He counted off his first point with one finger, then lifted another. "And you're a Rare One. You cannot yet realize how special you are."

"Maybe not, but it's hard to believe that *I* am so important." She shrugged. "I'm just Kristin Montgomery, former CPA."

"Greatness is seldom planned. More often it is thrust upon one." Then he patted her hand. "I accept your decision with one small request."

"What's that?"

"That I may continue to call on you, as a friend, to check on your welfare. I do wish to help you."

"I'd like that." She held out her hand. "Thanks for understanding."

He took it in an exaggerated manner and shook it. "Of course. That's what friends do."

WHEN KRISTIN RETURNED to the cottage, she almost smiled until she remembered the troll inside. Her conversation with Lucas had been, well, if not pleasant, at least friendly. He was so refined, so civilized. She didn't feel as if she was pushing against a stone wall when she spoke with him. Logic and manners worked with Lucas. Unlike with Tennyson.

She opened the door to find the troll in a chair staring at her.

He raised a single eyebrow. "You're home early. Date not go well?"

"It was fine if you must know." She walked toward the kitchen and heard him plod after her. Dropping her purse on the counter, she glanced at the fruit bowl. Empty. Her stomach growled. She needed energy.

"When's your next date with this guy?" he said in a disagreeable tone.

She almost snarled back. "You promised—"

He held up his hands. "I'm not being nosy. You made the boundaries very clear. I was just thinking I could put some sort of protection spell on you when I can't be there."

She sighed. "Don't worry about it. I told him I couldn't see him until the whole Time of Transition mess is over."

Was that a grin she saw fleeting over Tennyson's face? Couldn't be. His expression was businesslike. "Good. I'm glad to see you've started showing some sense."

Irritation flared in her. "I told you I'm not stupid. I just didn't need you hanging around while I told Lucas."

"Yeah, I would've hated to see the smarmy fellow cry."

Were all men this obnoxious? And she had slept with him. Her heart started to pound at the memory of their searing sex. Image after image assailed her, and her body trembled at the sensation running through it. Heat spread through her, and she turned away to hide her face. It must be the lack of food. She opened the refrigerator. It was empty too. The cupboards provided nothing either. She grabbed her purse again. "Come on."

"You're going out again?"

"Not me. We. We're going shopping. There's no food in the house." She didn't wait to see if he followed her as she walked back to her car and sat behind the steering wheel.

He stood by the passenger side. "You're driving?"

"I know it's hard to accept, but I've been doing it for years."

He climbed in, his face set in a distinct frown.

She set the car into motion and pulled away from the house. "So why didn't you offer to zap us some food?"

"Magic takes energy. You've felt it yourself."

"I thought that was because I'm not used to it."

"Partially, but magic cannot be used without a cost. It takes a physical toll on an Arcani. People have died from overuse of magic. Usually that happens only in battle or times of high stress, but normally we don't like to waste energy on 'zapping' if it's more convenient to go to the store."

"Makes sense."

A few minutes later she pulled into a Vons parking lot.

"What do we need?" he asked as he grabbed a cart.

"The usual. Fruit, lettuce, tomatoes, bread, milk, Diet Coke."

"What about meat?" he asked.

She shot him an exasperated look. "I'm a vegetarian."

A look of horror exploded on his face. "If you expect me to go without real food—"

Her laugh burst out of her. "Just kidding. You saw

me eat a burrito last night. I just wanted to get a rise out of you. I love hamburger as much as the next guy."

He glowered at her, clearly not amused.

She smiled and started to stock the cart with food for the week. A distant rumble of thunder reached her ears, and she saw a couple of customers dash into the store and shake water drops from their clothes. A summer thunderstorm was rare for San Diego. How refreshing.

An hour later, the grocery cart full, they stood in the cashier's line. Kristin opened her purse and, frowning, pulled out her wallet.

"Something wrong?" Tennyson asked.

"What am I going to do about money?" She removed her debit card and ran it through the machine. "I mean, I'm a CPA, but I get the feeling I'll need to quit that job. So how do I get money?"

"I don't know the details, but you'll receive a generous stipend from the Council." He paused. "You haven't quit yet?"

"No, I was on vacation this week." She tucked the receipt into her purse. "I haven't had time to quit."

"Well, you won't have to worry about money."

"What about taxes?" she muttered under her breath.

They loaded the groceries into the car. The rain still sprinkled, and the air smelled wonderful. No stars shone because of the clouds covering the sky.

A few minutes later as she drove onto her street, she found a crowd blocked the traffic.

"What's going on?" Tennyson asked. He lowered the window and peered out.

She parked the car and climbed from the seat. He joined her.

Smoke billowed into the sky despite the rain. Her mood started to plummet. They moved forward through the crowd until she gasped. "It's the cottage!"

Tennyson used his bulk to push through the crowd. Unable to feel more than shock, she followed in his wake.

A fireman stopped them at the perimeter. "You can't go any farther."

"That's my house," Kristin said. Tears filled her eyes.

"Is there anyone in there?"

"No." She pressed the back of her hand against her mouth, her legs buckling. Tennyson grabbed her, but she barely noticed.

"Okay. You'll have to wait here for the captain. I'm sorry about your loss."

She watched as flames licked the wooden sides of the small bungalow. The facade appeared wavy through the heat. "What happened?"

"Lightning." The fireman scanned the crowd to make sure no one tried to get through the hastily erected tape barricade. "It hit the back of the house. These old structures don't have much protection against energy like that."

Everything she owned was in there. Logically thinking, she shouldn't care. Things could be replaced. But all of the aunts' stuff was there too. And she had never had the chance to look for the rules on the aunts' computer either.

She stared at the destruction in horrified silence. The flames did seem to be growing smaller, but half the house had burned. A whimper escaped her throat.

Tennyson's arm tightened around her.

She turned to find Tennyson watching her. He stroked her shoulder. "Are you okay?"

"I guess." She leaned into him, trying to draw comfort and a little warmth from his presence. "Did you lose much in there?"

A mirthless chuckle escaped him. "I can't believe you're worried about my things."

"Not really." She gave him a hollow laugh in return. "The food is going to spoil in the car."

"No, it won't. Wait here a moment." He pushed his way back through the crowd.

"Where are you—" But he had already disappeared.

She watched as the firemen doused the last of the flames. The rain was no more than a memory now, and she sat on the curb, suddenly too tired to remain standing.

The crowd slowly dispersed as they realized that the pyrotechnic display had ended. A dark-haired man turned away quickly as her gaze fell on him. She sat up. Dimitri? When she stood up she no longer saw him. Shaking her head, she sank back to the curb.

Tennyson returned and sat beside her.

"Where did you go?"

"To the car. You don't have to worry about things spoiling now."

"What do you mean?"

"Camry on ice." He eased the handle of his wand from his pocket and pointed to it.

"Weren't you afraid people would see?"

He shook his head. "They were all watching the fire."

"Thanks."

He placed his arm around her and drew her to him. "Just one more thing in a week filled with excitement. You didn't need this."

Tears threatened again. "What will I tell the aunts?"

He kissed the top of her head. "Don't worry about that now. We have time to figure things out."

The fire captain approached them. "You the owner?"

She stood. "Sort of. I'm house-sitting for my aunts."

"The fire's contained now. The back bedroom is completely gutted, and the front has a lot of smoke and water damage. You can go in tomorrow to see if anything's salvageable."

"Thank you."

The captain looked back at the house. "Damnedest thing, lightning. Never can predict it."

"What do you mean?" asked Tennyson in a wary voice.

"Normally, it would've struck the telephone pole, or one of the eucalyptus trees. They're much taller than the house. But you never can tell with lightning. Hell, when was the last time we had a thunderstorm in San Diego?"

Tennyson stiffened. She glanced up at him and saw his brow furrow. He asked, "You're sure the fire was caused by lightning?"

"Absolutely. The burn marks indicate a burst of heat in the back." The chief looked at him. "Why? Do you know something?"

"No. I guess you just can't tell about lightning." He glanced at Kristin. And a nervous flutter erupted in her gut. Foreboding trickled through her.

"Ain't that the truth," said the fireman.

Tennyson's arms tightened around her.

10

HOW TO BE A FAIRY GODMOTHER:

Magic Isn't Always the Answer.

THE FIRE CAPTAIN'S words chilled Tennyson. The ugly thought that had snaked into his consciousness wouldn't leave.

The lightning had been another attack. If he had had any doubt about Aldous's warning, he had none now.

As the fireman had said, thunderstorms, especially summer storms, were rare in San Diego. That and the way the lightning had struck the house rather than a tree or telephone pole.

Elenka wanted to kill Kristin and upset the balance between the worlds.

"Kristin?" a deep voice called out.

She turned out of his arms to look for the voice.

Tennyson looked up to see Lucas hurrying toward them.

Lucas pulled Kristin into a hug. "Are you all right?"

Good thing the man released her a moment later.

Tennyson's brows drew together. Lucas still held her hands.

"Yes, I'm fine, but I'm afraid my aunts' house isn't. What are you doing here?" she said.

Tennyson wanted to know the same thing himself.

"I saw the house on the news. I came to see if you needed anything." Lucas surveyed the damage and clicked his tongue in a Gallic manner. "Such a tragedy."

She managed a smile, although the corners of her lips trembled. "Not really. No one was hurt."

"No one?"

Lucas searched the area, and his gaze landed on Tennyson as if he had just spotted him. Right. Tennyson almost snorted. Lucas was a good actor, but the caring pretense wasn't real.

"Ritter. How fortunate you are safe as well."

He wanted to wipe the insincerity off Lucas's face. "Yeah, I'm good." He looked down at his smoke-scented jeans and T-shirt. The slick bastard wore a silk shirt and trousers, just rumpled enough to look as if he had thrown something on and transported in the next instant to see about Kristin's welfare.

Great. The guy even dressed up for disheveled.

And since when had he begun to notice what other men wore?

Kristin searched the street. "Where's Dimitri?"

"I sneaked out without telling him. He will not be pleased." Lucas lifted a finger to his lips.

Kristin raised an eyebrow and scanned the crowd but then gave her attention to Lucas.

Lucas said, "Where are you staying tonight?"

"Don't know yet," Tennyson said.

"Then you must come back to the hotel with me."

Kristin's face lit up. Tennyson rushed to respond before she could do something stupid like accept. "Thanks, but no. We'll figure something out."

"No, no. I insist." Lucas faced Kristin. "I'll get you a nice suite. Mr. Ritter can stay with me."

"No, sorry, we can't," Tennyson said before she could speak. He placed his hand on her shoulder in a proprietary manner.

The daggers she shot from her eyes were almost tangible. She was angry. No harm then in plunging forward. "You understand Kristin's safety is paramount. After tonight, this incident, I can't let anyone know where she is. Not even you."

Lucas's brow furrowed briefly, which gave Tennyson a perverse pleasure. "Of course I understand. Thus the reason for my offer."

Kristin's gaze narrowed, and she shook off Tennyson's hand from her shoulder. She faced him with her hands on her hips. "Wait a minute. Are you saying the lightning, the cottage burning, was done on purpose?"

"It's a definite possibility," Tennyson said.

Her forehead crinkled, and a slight frown curved her lips down. She looked back at the house. Black scars of soot defaced the once pretty bungalow. As she stared at the ruins, a tremor shook her.

Lucas moved beside her and placed his arm around her shoulders. "I shudder to think you might have been injured."

"But I wasn't." She still stared at the house.

"Please, let me get you a room at La Valencia."

She shook her head and stepped away from him. "No, I can't afford it."

With a gentle smile, Lucas turned her to face him. "You misunderstood. I shall pay for it."

Touching his arm, she said, "Thank you, but I can't let you do that. I need to take care of myself."

"But you have Ritter—"

"He doesn't count."

Tennyson scowled. Wonderful. She sure knew how to make him feel important. He faced Lucas. "Reynard, thanks for the offer, but I have another place in mind."

"Where?" Lucas asked.

"Sorry, old chap, but I'm not telling." So what if it sounded childish? And he liked the "old" dig.

Kristin let out an irritated puff of air. "I am not some toy you two children can fight over. Lucas, I appreciate your offer, but I cannot accept such generosity." She faced Tennyson. "As much as I hate to admit it, I think you may be right, and since you are my inquisitor—"

"Arbiter."

"Whatever—I'll let you decide." She raised a finger. "For tonight."

Lucas said, "If you're sure . . ."

"I am." Strength burned in her eyes, but beneath the display Tennyson saw the fear and determination not to be weak. God, he admired her.

Lucas took her hand and kissed the back of it. "Then I shall bid you good night. I am relieved you are safe. Please let me know where you are as soon as you can."

"I will," Kristin said.

Lucas's dark gaze landed on Tennyson. Tennyson didn't like him, and clearly the feeling was mutual. But Lucas obviously cared for Kristin. So Tennyson moved beside her.

Lucas's eyes narrowed. "Good night, Kristin. Stay safe." With a curt nod, the sorcerer left.

AN HOUR LATER, they pulled up in front of the multiple garage doors of a large house facing the beach at Windansea. The three-story structure was dark. Kristin yawned and glanced at the clock on the dashboard. Just after midnight. No wonder she was tired. "Where are we?"

"At a friend's house."

"You have friends?" Not so tired as to forget her sarcasm.

Tennyson frowned. "One."

He opened her door and helped her from the car. How had he managed to take over the driving? She *must* be tired.

"Is he expecting us?"

"No." Tennyson led her to the stairs that led to the front door.

She stopped "We can't just barge in on him."

"Yes, we can."

"It's after midnight."

"Doesn't matter. Zack will help us."

"Zack?"

"My one friend." Tennyson rang the doorbell; then he knocked as well.

She cringed. This was so far out of her comfort zone, she couldn't make out where the boundary had been. She didn't know Zack, but who could like being woken in the middle of the night and asked to put up a stranger?

Tennyson rang again, and a light flicked on in the house. A minute later the brightness shone through the window beside them. The door opened and a man with tousled blond hair grinned out at them. No, "tousled" was too nice a word. His hair bushed out in every direction. His face was tanned and white teeth gleamed from the sun-darkened skin.

"Dude, it's great to see you." The man grabbed Tennyson's hand and pumped it up and down. "What are you doing here?"

"We need a place to stay." Tennyson pointed at her.

The man peered at her, and his grin grew wider. "Nice. I can always make room for a hot babe."

She didn't know whether to feel awkward or honored.

He thrust his hand out to her. "I'm Zack."

She took his hand gingerly. "Hi. I'm Kristin."

"You are totally welcome, Kristin. Come in. Where's your stuff?"

"No stuff," Tennyson said. "We had a fire."

"That's tragic." Zack's face morphed into an expression of sadness. "I saw a house burning on the news. Was that you?"

She nodded.

"So sorry, dudette. Did you save anything?"

"No, but we do have groceries," she said.

"I like guests who bring food." Zack bounded out of the doorway and ran to the car.

Tennyson leaned to her. "See? I told you it was okay." He retreated to the car and opened the bag-filled trunk. The two men grabbed the sacks and came back to the house.

"No clothes, huh?" Zack said as he passed her. "I've got extra sweats and stuff in the back room. Help yourself."

"Thanks, Zack," Tennyson said.

They followed Zack into the kitchen, where he flicked on the lights and dropped the bags on a black granite counter.

She took in the room. "Wow." A gourmet cooktop glistened next to a block of knives she'd have real trouble identifying uses for. A stainless steel sink broke up the stone counter farther down, and even though all sorts of gadgets and appliances littered the space, there was plenty of room to work. A floor-to-ceiling refrigerator blended in with the oak cabinetry, and every surface shone.

"It's what Mrs. Pendelton wanted," Zack said.

"Who's Mrs. Pendelton?" she asked.

"My cook, nanny, housekeeper, and domestic goddess. She knows how to use all this stuff. I usually buy hot dogs from the vendors at the beach." Zack held up a bag. "Any ice cream in here?"

"No," she said.

"Bummer." Zack opened the fridge and shoved the bag onto a shelf without unpacking it. "Mrs. Pendelton will sort it out tomorrow."

Kristin glanced at Tennyson, who merely shrugged.

"Sorry about the late hour," she said.

"No problem." Zack put away the other bags in a similar manner. "Normally I'd be up, but the surfing will be classic tomorrow because of the storm."

"We know," Tennyson said.

"Right, the fire. I forgot." Zack led them from the kitchen. "I'm getting up at five. Do you surf? I've got extra wet suits if you want to come."

"I can't surf," she said. His exuberance coaxed a smile from her despite the events of the evening.

"Tragic. But you probably didn't want to surf after

the fire anyway." He cocked his head. "Although surfing is nature's way of making things cool again."

"Next time," Tennyson said. "Right now we really need to shower and sleep."

Zack snapped his fingers. "You got it." He led them through a darkened hallway and upstairs. A thick carpet covered the hall floor here, but Zack tiptoed past the second door. "Shhh, the spud's asleep."

She glanced at Tennyson.

"His son," he whispered back.

Zack opened a door farther down. "You can camp here."

Blue walls with hints of green gave off a peaceful glow as the light hit them. A queen-size bed with a deep blue cover filled much of the room. Two chairs with a low table between them provided a cozy conversation area in one corner. The large sliding glass doors led out onto a balcony. A copper seaweed sculpture rose from the floor along one side, and fish prints decorated the walls.

"Wow," she said again as she surveyed the room. "This is beautiful."

Zack ruffled his hair. "The decorator called it the 'Ocean's Deep' room. Doesn't actually have an ocean view, but you should be comfortable here." Zack pointed to a door on the other side of the room. "Bathroom's through there. You'll find towels and soap inside. Make yourselves at home." Then he stopped and smacked himself on his head. "I almost forgot." He zipped from the room.

"What's he doing?" she asked.

"Don't know. I've never been good at predicting Zack's moves."

Great. She had put her life in the hands of a Spicoli. "So who is he?"

Before Tennyson could answer, Zack let himself back into the room after a quick rap on the door. A pile of clothes filled his arms.

"Here. Try these" He tossed them on the bed. "I had to guess at the sizes."

She held up a huge black T-shirt with a lime green logo that read, "Z-foam."

"I thought you could sleep in that," Zack said. "Unless you guys like to feel the breeze."

"Thanks again, Zack," Tennyson said.

"You know you don't have to thank me. We'll talk in the morning. Good night." Zack paused in the doorway. "Sure you don't want to go surfing tomorrow?"

"Good night, Zack." With a chuckle, Tennyson pushed him out of the room.

She sorted through the pile of clothes and pulled out a pair of sweats and a French T-shirt. They were both emblazoned with the Z-foam logo. "What is 'Z-foam'?"

"A new sort of neoprene that makes a better insulating wet suit. Zack invented it."

Her mouth dropped open.

One corner of Tennyson's lips drew up in a smirk. "Zack has a degree in chemistry and owns the Z-foam company. He's a multimillionaire. All the best surfers use Z-foam, and most scuba divers do too."

Chagrin swamped her at her own prejudice as she remembered how she had misjudged Zack.

Tennyson put his arm around her. "Don't feel bad. Zack fools most people."

"Yes, but I'm supposed to be a fairy godmother. I'm

supposed to help people. You'd think I'd be more in tune with people's inner selves."

"Hey, you're new at this, and besides, Zack hides it."

"You saw through it, didn't you?" Alongside her chagrin was a smidgen of irritation with him. He was enjoying her embarrassment.

"Well, I don't invest in companies run by fools." He pulled off his smoky T-shirt and threw it into a corner. His abs stretched, and she found herself staring at the play of muscles in his chest and abdomen.

She cleared her throat. "You invested in Z-foam?"

"Yes. It made a lot of sense, and Zack had a good product. I was his first major investor. He considers me a friend and a business partner." He pulled out a long pair of sweats and a T-shirt from the pile.

"Then he isn't Arcani?"

"Nope. As Groundling as they come. He was in a car wreck five years ago. His wife died, and he was hospitalized for a while. I ran the business while he recuperated."

"Oh God, I'm so sorry."

"It wasn't easy, but Zack is a good sort." Tennyson shrugged. "He had his son and the business to pull him through the tragedy."

"Does he know about you? You know?" She wiggled her fingers as if casting a spell. At least the way they did it in the movies or on television.

"No, and he shouldn't find out. He thinks I'm just some guy who helped him start his business."

"Wait a minute. If Z-foam is successful, then aren't you rich too?"

"I guess. So, you want the shower first?"

She stared at him. She didn't know anything about

him. Not that money changed anything, but she thought he was a historian, some important muckety-muck in the Arcani world. He clearly hadn't shared much about his life with her. He was simply . . . infuriating. In a fit of pique, she grabbed the clothes she had selected and hurried into the bathroom.

Ten minutes later she was clean but still tired. Wearing the large black T-shirt, she brushed her teeth with a toothbrush she had found and returned to the bedroom. Still shirtless, Tennyson was asleep on the bed.

One bed. The only bed.

There was no other place to sleep. No cushions to place on the floor. No couch. The chairs in the conversation corner were straight backed, not conducive to pushing together to form a bed.

Luckily he had not fallen asleep in the middle. She peeled back the cover on the free side and gingerly crawled between the sheets. She stretched out on the cool cotton and almost cried at how good it felt.

Tennyson sprang up. "What?"

"You fell asleep. I'm about to do the same."

He stood, blinked a few times, then rubbed his face. "You're done in the bathroom?"

"Yes."

"Good." He walked toward the room.

"Where are you going to sleep?" she asked in an innocent tone.

He froze. As he turned to face her, his gaze narrowed. "I'm sleeping on the bed. If you don't like it, you can sleep on the floor. It isn't as if we haven't shared a bed before."

She wished she could control her blush. "Fine. It doesn't matter to me." She flipped onto her side so she couldn't see him. Only when the door to the bathroom closed could she draw her next breath.

Share a bed?

Oh God.

11

HOW TO BE A FAIRY GODMOTHER:

Don't Use Magic to Manipulate Emotions;
It Doesn't Work Anyway.

HER EYES FLUTTERED open. She was warm and clean and comfortable. A sense of security enveloped her. Her skin tingled and erupted in goose bumps. Her senses took in a unique aroma that hit her at a visceral level, a scent that left her languid and loose. The soft sound of breathing blew in her ear. With a contented sigh, she snuggled closer to the broad expanse of chest behind her.

Chest?

With a sharp cry, she flung the covers back and sat up. The T-shirt she had worn to bed was hiked up to her waist. With another sharp cry, she yanked the covers up to her neck.

Tennyson grimaced. "Do you always wake up so loudly?"

"Only when I'm sharing a bed against my will." She

jumped out of the bed and ran to the bathroom, grabbing the sweatpants and a clean shirt along the way.

She washed and changed clothes quickly. Looking down, she frowned. The sweats bagged, and the shirt clung a little too tightly for her comfort. Shopping was definitely on the agenda for today.

But the clothes did little to erase the feel of Tennyson's bare chest against her. His heat still seared her skin, and she couldn't stop thinking about the sleepy-eyed look he wore when he woke. His face was creased and frowning, the sweats he wore were rumpled, and his eyes were mere slits, but she had never seen anyone so enticing. Okay, he looked better when awake, but something about the vulnerability in his expression had her wanting to take advantage of it.

Ugh. She would not think about the troll.

She marched back into the room, her eyes blazing. He was pulling on a T-shirt as she entered. Great. Just what she needed. Another image of his bare chest to torment her through the day.

"Sleep well?" he asked.

Yes. Deeply, soundly, safely. "As well as can be expected." She wasn't about to let him know how wonderful she felt lying next to him.

"Good. Let's grab some breakfast." He opened the door for her and they descended to the kitchen.

A small boy sat on a stool at the granite island while a neat, prim middle-aged woman fussed at the cooktop. The boy looked up. His face split into a grin, and Kristin saw the resemblance between him and his father.

"Uncle Tennis." The boy launched himself at Tennyson, who caught the child in midair.

"Tennis?" Kristin raised her brows.

"Don't start," he answered with a scowl, then turned his full attention to the boy. Tennyson hugged him, placed him on his feet, and ruffled the boy's hair. "How's it going, Jake?"

Jake frowned. "You haven't been here in forever."

"I know and I'm sorry, Jake, but I've been really busy." He hoisted Jake back onto the stool and took a place on the next seat. "But I'm here now. Good morning, Mrs. Pendelton."

The woman at the stove turned and smiled at Tennyson. "Hello, Mr. Ritter. It's lovely to see you again. Would you like one of my special omelets?" Her crisp British accent gave her words a definite authority.

"You know I would," Tennyson said. "Make two, one for me, one for her. Let me introduce Kristin Montgomery. Kristin, this is Mrs. Constance Pendelton."

Mrs. Pendelton nodded at her. "Mr. Glass told me you'd be staying. I'm happy to meet you. Do you like green chile?"

"Trust me, you want Mrs. Pendelton's green chile," Tennyson said. "She studied cooking in Santa Fe, and you've never tasted anything like it."

"Sounds intriguing." Kristin took the third stool. "Can I help with something?"

"That's kind of you to offer, but no." Mrs. Pendelton poured out two cups of coffee and placed them with an expert hand in front of Kristin and Tennyson. "Cream, sugar?"

"No," Tennyson said.

"Yes," Kristin said, and glowered at him briefly. "Lots."

Mrs. Pendelton laughed and retrieved a small creamer

from the fridge. "That's right. Don't let them think they can order you around."

Jake had been eyeing Kristin with a look of curiosity.

"I'm Kristin," she said, sticking her hand out to the young fellow.

He shook it solemnly. "I'm Jake. Are you Uncle Tennis's wife?"

"No."

"Are you his girlfriend?"

"Jake," said Tennyson in a warning tone.

"What?" The boy shrugged. "I'm just asking."

"Actually, Tennyson's just helping me with something right now," Kristin said.

"Cool. Then maybe you could marry my dad."

"Jake," Tennyson said in surprise.

Spreading his hand wide in a gesture of blamelessness, Jake said, "Well, she's pretty."

With a smile, Kristin looked at the boy. A moment later she saw a shimmering crown appear over his head. Concentrating on him, she heard the wistful voice in her head.

"I wish I had a mommy."

Poor kid. Was she allowed to mess with love? In her own mind she believed love was something sacred, and the thought of casting a spell to manipulate it seemed dishonest. But she was a fairy godmother. Where were those rules the aunts had promised to leave her? She reached for Jake's hand and squeezed it. "Thank you. I think you're sweet myself."

Jake twisted his mouth to the side. "I don't want to be sweet. I'm a man."

"Right. I should've noticed. You're definitely not sweet," she said, hiding her smile behind a serious mien.

Mrs. Pendelton placed a glass of fresh-squeezed orange juice in front of her. "Mr. Glass told me that your house burned down. Please accept my condolences."

"Thank you. I'm just grateful he was able to put us up."

"As if we wouldn't welcome a friend of Mr. Ritter."

"Your house burned down?" Jake's eyes widened. "Were you there too, Uncle Tennis?"

"Yes, but don't worry. I wasn't hurt."

"Did all your stuff burn up?"

"Some of it. Not much. Most of my stuff is at my house, not Kristin's."

His house? He had a house? He never told her he had a house.

Before she could ponder her thoughts longer, Jake bombarded her with another question: "Did you lose all your stuff?"

"Pretty much. But it's just stuff." She smiled to reassure him. And possibly herself as well.

"Wow." Jake fell silent for a moment, then he pursed his lips and nodded. "Yeah, I wouldn't care about my stuff either as long as Dad and Mrs. Pendelton were okay. But I'd hate to lose my Xbox right now. I've reached a new world in Spyro. Wanna see, Uncle Tennis?"

"I'd love to." Tennyson lifted his hand for a high five.

Jake jumped off the stool, but Mrs. Pendelton lifted a finger. "After Mr. Ritter eats, young man."

In a picture of childhood dejection, Jake let out a long sigh and dropped his shoulders dramatically. "Okay." He climbed back up on the stool.

Tennyson leaned to Jake. "Don't worry. I'll eat fast."

Kristin's brow furrowed. Tennyson kept surprising

her. Yes, he had been impatient and mean when he first met her, but now . . . His reaction to his mentor's death, his fierce protection of her, his clear affection for Jake . . . it was getting harder to remember Tennyson was a troll. Especially when she remembered her body's reaction to him. Like now. A delightful shiver danced up her spine, raising goose bumps on her arms. She rubbed them vigorously.

Stomping on the stairs announced the arrival of Zack. He appeared in the kitchen, wet, clean, and grinning.

"Dad," yelled Jake. He jumped off the stool again. "How was surfing?"

Zack scooped his son into his arms, then placed him on the floor. "It was amazing, dude. The waves were incredible."

"Can I come next time?"

"Not yet, little man. You still have much to learn."

Jake's face creased into abject dejection. "Aww, you always say that."

"That's because I know the waves. But I can take you for a lesson today."

Jake's smile returned. "Cool. What time?"

"Surf will be good at one. Right after lunch."

"Yes." Jake pumped his arm back and forth. "That gives me time to show Uncle Tennis where I am in Spyro. I'll go set it up." Jake scampered from the room.

Zack turned to his guests. "Good morning. How'd you sleep?"

"Fine, considering. We've only been up a short time," Tennyson said.

"You missed an awesome set. We don't get waves like those in San Diego often."

"Did you hang up your suit, Mr. Glass?" asked Mrs. Pendelton.

"Yes, ma'am. I even folded the towels." He grabbed the mug the cook passed to him. "I used to track sand and sea into the house, but Mrs. Pendelton threatened to quit if I didn't clean up after myself. So I had a shower installed in the garage. Actually, it works great. I can rinse off my suit there and store it with my board." He reached for the paper that was neatly folded on the counter. "You made the news."

She glanced at the headline. "Unusual Storm Burns House." Her house was the main photo on the page. The picture showed the firemen battling the flames at the cottage. The enormity of her loss was just beginning to strike her. She closed her eyes and dropped her head back.

"Are you okay?" asked Zack, his forehead wrinkled with concern.

"I know it sounds stupid, but my black dress and killer shoes were in there." Tears welled in her eyes.

Tennyson's arm slipped around her. "It doesn't sound stupid."

A crooked smile appeared on Zack's face. "No, it sounds like the shock is wearing off. Like your mind is focusing on a small thing, so that it doesn't hit you with everything at once."

She shot Zack a glance. Okay, he really was pretty smart. She wiped her eyes. "Yeah, but I'm crying over a dress."

"One thing at time." Zack folded the paper and placed it to the side. "Besides, I like you in this shirt. I guessed really well on the size."

"It's a little tight—"

"Yeah. Nice and," said Zack with a grin.

She laughed, and to her surprise she saw a hint of color creep into Tennyson's cheeks.

Mrs. Pendelton placed two omelets in front of them. "Your clothing line is nice, Mr. Glass, but a lady needs more than sweats and a tight T-shirt. Eat now; then you have to go shopping."

"Hey, I have other sizes," Zack said.

"Yes, but you don't make bras." Mrs. Pendelton shook her finger at him.

"Hmmm, maybe I should. Surfing bras. Let me think about this." Zack gulped his coffee. "You know, I'd think better if I had an omelet too. Don't forget the green chile."

Mrs. Pendelton harrumphed, but turned back to the stove with a smile on her face.

The exchange brightened Kristin's mood. She was safe, as was Tennyson, and things could be replaced. Even if her black dress and killer shoes had been all that.

An hour later, after Tennyson had checked out Spyro, she and Tennyson were in Target buying essentials. Their cart was already halfway full, and they hadn't bought nearly all the things they needed. As she walked through the store, she noticed children with their parents. The tiny sparkling crowns twinkled over the children's heads. Just for fun she practiced listening in to their wishes.

"I wish we'd go home."

"I wish I had that doll."

"I wish Mom would buy me that new video game."

Kristin realized that her skill had improved. The cacophony of sounds didn't overwhelm her this time, and she was able to focus on one wish at a time.

A moment later, she blinked. An adult had a tiny crown over her head. The woman had two young children with her and dark circles under her eyes. She was picking things off the shelf, turning them over in her hand, and placing them back.

Kristin concentrated. Instead of the usual childish tone, she heard: "I wish I had more money," in an adult voice.

Sympathy filled her. But how did she know the woman deserved her wish to be granted? With a child, one could assume an innocent desire for something and grant the wish based on practicality. But how did one know if an adult deserved his or her wish? Kristin needed a test.

"Tennyson, give me five dollars." She held out her hand.

An eyebrow arched. "What do you need five dollars for now?"

"Just give it to me."

He pulled out his billfold and handed her the requested money.

She crumpled the bill up in her hand until it was little more than a ball. Then she sneaked up behind the woman. "Excuse me, but did you drop this?"

The woman hesitated, then smiled. "Yes. Yes, I did. Thank you." She took the crumpled five and stuffed it into her pocket.

Kristin smiled back with no warmth. "You're welcome." As the woman turned away and went back to her shopping, Kristin focused on the twinkling crown. The crown turned black, then faded.

"What was that about?" Tennyson asked. He had caught up to her and now stood beside her.

"She lied." Kristin's frown held all the emotion her smile had lacked. "She had a wish, but she wasn't worthy of it."

He searched her gaze. "Maybe now isn't the best time to explore your powers. You've had an emotional night, and you're bound to hit disappointments as you discover—"

"No. Now is the perfect time. The faster I learn the job, the sooner I can deal with the danger facing me." She grabbed the handle of the shopping cart and pushed it in the direction of underwear and socks.

IN A RESTAURANT that served massive hamburgers and great ice cream, Tennyson relaxed . . . a little. They had replaced a number of Kristin's things and hadn't fought once, but his constant vigilance had drained him. He was hungry, and his burger looked delicious.

"So how do you tell if someone is Arcani or not?" Kristin asked, and then took a bite of the hamburger that required two hands to hold.

"You can't really." Without thinking, Tennyson reached across the table and with his napkin wiped a dot of mayonnaise from her cheek. "Sure, there are some places where you're almost guaranteed that everybody is Arcani—"

"Like the Academy?"

"Like the Academia Artis Magicae," he corrected. "Or like your aunts' house."

"But that's just an ordinary house on an ordinary street. Anybody could live there."

"True. We have to live somewhere, so most of the time we live in regular Groundling neighborhoods. When I was a kid, I played with the neighborhood children, but they all thought I went to some private school, since I didn't go to school with them."

"What school did you go to?"

"An Arcani one." He dipped a fry into some ketchup. "Sometimes we congregate in certain neighborhoods, but sometimes there's only one of us in an entire city. You can't legislate personal taste. Anyway, you can't say for sure who is and who isn't just by looking."

"So any of these people might be Arcani?" She waved her hand at the customers in the restaurant.

"They might. The only way to tell if you don't know the person is if you see them do magic, although sometimes you can tell by the magical footprint."

"Footprint?"

He nodded. "Magic leaves a sign, a sort of mark that you can feel sometimes. You can't really see it."

Her face lit up. "You mean the tingle."

"What tingle?"

"That's how I think of it. I can feel a sort of tingle, a sort of low vibration or hum, when magic is being used." She pointed at him. "That's how I found you outside the restaurant that evening."

He stared at her. "But I used a special cloaking magic. You shouldn't have noticed anything."

"Well, I did." She shrugged and took a sip of her soda.

She fascinated him. She really didn't know how powerful she was. In the past few days, she had faced so much, yet each setback left her more determined to succeed. Each day brought new discoveries, and she handled them all with aplomb. Her abilities surprised even him at times. When she came into her full powers she'd be formidable. No wonder the enemy wanted to kill her.

Elenka wanted to kill her.

He put down his food and observed her. In this ordinary setting, it was easy to forget the danger. Was it bravery or ignorance that she displayed? She was eating a hamburger as if nothing unusual was happening. Okay, nothing unusual was happening now, but it could, yet she ate calmly. She showed no outward signs of nerves. Was she afraid? Last night she had been. But she had trusted him to help her.

A sense of responsibility weighed on him, but he didn't feel it as a burden. Instead, determination to protect her from all danger intensified in him.

Her gaze narrowed. "What? Do I have something in my teeth?"

"No." He picked up his burger again and watched her surreptitiously. Her auburn hair bounced around her shoulder as she brushed it back to take another bite. He laughed to himself. She enjoyed food. Every bite was a sensual experience. That was a good term for it. After all, the last time he had watched her eat with such exuberance was right before they'd made love.

Heat arced through him like an electrical shock. For a moment he couldn't draw a breath. Every nerve buzzed with the memory of their lovemaking. Ugh. This reaction was the reason he tried not to think of it. Last night had been especially difficult. She was in the bed next to him, asleep, but his body had known. He hadn't slept until well into the morning. The icy shower at two A.M. hadn't helped at all.

"Are you okay? You look like you're in pain." She reached out and placed her hand on his arm.

He jerked it back. Touching him—anywhere—was the worst thing she could do right now. Not when his control threatened to slip away entirely. "I'm fine." He forced himself to breathe deeply and evenly. "I just bit my tongue." A little lie couldn't hurt.

He was in deep trouble.

Her attention fixed on a table near them. He followed her gaze to a girl who was staring off at the ceiling. Her parents were speaking on cell phones, not to each other. She looked bored, poor kid.

Kristin smiled. She took out her wand and flicked it under the table. He raised an eyebrow at the covert move. The napkins on a nearby table fluttered out of the holder to the floor.

"Ignore the mess. Just wait," she said.

A minute later, a waitress approached the girl's table. She held a large, gooey sundae. "Excuse me."

The father looked up.

"The kitchen made this by mistake and instead of throwing it out, we'd like to give it to your daughter. Would that be okay?" the waitress asked.

The pleading look in the child's face was almost comical.

"Sure," the father said, and went right back to his phone conversation.

The girl's expression lit up, and the waitress placed the ice cream and a long spoon in front of the child. "Here you go, hon. Enjoy."

The child dug into the sundae and came up with a whipped cream and chocolate smile.

"Well worth the risk," said Kristin with a hint of smugness in her tone.

"How did you . . . ?"

She shrugged. "I just did. I can't really describe it. Something just felt right, so I did it."

Amazing. "What was her wish?" he asked.

"Not to be bored." Kristin slipped her wand back into her pocket and surveyed the restaurant again. A moment later, her smile vanished and her gaze riveted to the television above the bar.

"What is it?"

"Look."

He turned and focused on the television. Although the volume was down, he could read the caption at the bottom of the screen.

"Freak wave capsizes cruise ship in the Pacific."

He faced her. "You don't think—"

"My aunts."

12

HOW TO BE A FAIRY GODMOTHER:

•

Use Magic Judiciously. Magic Has Its Limits. We Are Not All-Powerful Beings.

IF KRISTIN HADN'T been so concerned about her aunts, Zack's office would have surprised her. The room was the epitome of modernity and didn't seem suited to its laid-back owner. A chrome and glass desk dominated the room and two state-of-the-art computers sat on the smooth surface. Along one wall, a leather couch provided seating, and the window looked out over the ocean. She didn't see the view. Leaning over one keyboard, she punched yet another word into the search engine.

"Anything yet?" Tennyson read over her shoulder as she gazed at the information on Zack's computer screen.

"Nothing. The travel itinerary burned up in the house, so I don't know if this was the ship or not." Frustration spiked in her. She pushed away from the computer and rolled her neck. "But it is the only one that left in that time frame, so I think we can pretty much assume they were on it."

He placed his hand on her shoulder. "Try not to worry."

"Argh. Easy for you to say." She jumped up from the chair and started to pace.

"No, really. Think about it." Tennyson stopped her and forced her to look at him. "Your aunts are powerful magicals. They were probably able to save themselves and many others as well."

She drew in a deep breath. "Do you really think so?"

"I do. Even though it is the Time of Transition—"

"Wait a minute. I thought that only affected me."

He hesitated. "No, their powers are fluctuating now. Some are diminishing and some have already disappeared."

"Great." She flopped onto the couch and buried her head in her hands.

"Kristin, they aren't powerless. Look how much you've accomplished after a few days. They had far more power than that. They haven't gone from being godmothers to being completely helpless. They still can do magic."

He wasn't making her feel any better. She felt guilty and incompetent. She rubbed her face. "It's just . . . In the space of two days, I've been burnt out of my house, and now my aunts are on a capsized ship in the middle of the Pacific. It's like I'm the unluckiest person in the world." She froze. That wasn't right. This was the third big occurrence this week. The earthquake at the academy was the first. The earthquake that had sent Tennyson to protect her. She thought back over all the magical history she had learned in the past week. "Didn't you say that my aunts helped put that Elenka away?"

The same thought must have occurred to Tennyson because his brow was furrowed and his lips were set in a grim line. He nodded. "Freak waves do happen. They can occur naturally, but that would be too big a coincidence."

The knot in the pit of her stomach grew even more tangled. "Is there any way to reach them? Any way to see if they are all right?"

He hesitated. "I could try to image them. I'd need a large mirror."

She perked up, more hopeful than she'd been in hours. "Would you? Do you think you can?"

"I *know* I could, but they are far away. Somewhere in the South Pacific right now. I'd have to cast the spell over a vast area and then I could hone in until I found them." He raked his fingers through his hair. "It would cost me a lot of energy." A note of reluctance hung in his tone.

"Energy you want to save in case we need it here." She was torn. She wanted to assure herself that the aunts were safe, but if he cast the spell and then needed to protect her, he could push himself over the limit and injure himself. She didn't want him to risk himself. If he hadn't been at the grocery store with her last night, she would have already lost him. The lightning bolt had hit the back bedroom of the cottage. His bedroom.

"You're important to the Arcani world, Kristin. If something happens to you . . ."

"I know, I know." She didn't fool herself into thinking she could protect herself. "I'm not ready to be on my own yet. I still need you."

His crooked smile told her to review what she'd said. She blushed. "I mean, I haven't passed the test yet. You haven't decided if I'm suitable. For the job," she hastened to add.

His grin widened. "You're suitable. That doesn't mean you still don't have a lot to learn."

"I know that." Her inadequacy taunted her. She wanted to know if the aunts were safe but understood the limitations on his magic.

Then a notion struck her. "How long does it take you to recuperate, to regain full strength?"

"A good meal and a good night's sleep. Why?"

"If this Elenka has used her powers to cause a thunderstorm last night and a freak wave today, won't she be feeling it?"

"Probably. She won't be able to push herself for much longer without permanent damage."

"And she's old. So it's pretty safe to say she won't be attempting anything today. Besides, she doesn't know where we are." She waited for him to get there.

With a soft chuckle, he said, "Manipulative, aren't you? Go find me a mirror. I'll start preparing myself. Meet you in the bedroom."

Grinning with satisfaction, she dashed from the room. A large mirror. Did Zack have such a thing in his house? The ones in the bathrooms were attached. Bright paintings and framed posters hung on the walls in the hallway. She didn't feel comfortable exploring in the bedrooms, so she headed for the stairs. There. At the bend in the staircase a large mirror hung on the wall. It was around two feet by one foot and had a leather frame. Unusual, but it suited the owner.

Carefully she lifted it from the wall. Thank goodness it wasn't as heavy as it looked. She carried it back to the room she and Tennyson shared. He had pushed the bed to one side and cleared the center of the room. In a triangle, he had placed a rock with some kind of rune on it, an undyed beeswax candle, and a sprig of white sage.

She raised her eyebrows. "Did you bring that stuff with you?"

"No. I summoned it from home."

That's right. He had a home somewhere. All his stuff hadn't gone up in flames. She stifled the jolt of envy that flashed through her. "Where should I put the mirror?"

"In the center of the triangle."

She placed the mirror, face up, on the floor. "Like this?"

"Perfect." He retreated to the bathroom and came back with a paper cup filled with water.

"Snazzy. You don't need a special goblet?"

"Nope, just the water and it doesn't matter how you carry it." He poured nearly half of it onto the mirror's surface so that it formed a flat pool.

"This looks complicated." She watched the water and for some reason thought of her middle school lessons on surface tension. The water's reflection in the mirror and the play of light on the various surfaces almost made her dizzy. She wasn't sure where reflection began and the reality ceased between the two elements.

"It isn't really, but it is advanced. You'll learn it with time." He held out his palm. "Here, take my hand. I'll need your energy and your image of your aunts to help."

She slipped her hand into his. The warm, dry strength in his palm sent a note of courage through her.

"Now concentrate on your aunts. What they look like, how they speak."

"Will we be able to hear them?"

"Not with this spell, but anything that brings the search closer to them will help." With his free hand, he drew out his wand. *"Speculum spectá."*

The surface of the water clouded over, mixing gray and white whorls into a foggy view. The surface undulated a little but didn't bubble or burst. Then the swirls in the water grew lighter and lighter still, then cleared, showing an immense expanse of blue. Light sparkled and glinted in flashes.

"The Pacific," said Tennyson.

The image on the mirror grew more distinct. She could see waves and tiny whitecaps as the image flew across their viewing port. It looked as if she were in a low-flying airplane staring down at the ocean.

"Concentrate. Since we don't know their exact location, we have to be thinking of them." He too stared at the image on the water.

She was growing dizzy from the constantly changing yet strangely constant picture. A minute passed, then two, and then the scene seemed to slow down, gradually at first, then distinctly slower. The waves took on details, and she could distinguish green in the blue of the ocean. Then she gasped. "Look."

A lifeboat appeared in the image, then another. Soon the whole view was filled with tiny boats floating next to a huge cruise liner that listed on its side. Rescue boats were already in the area pulling the survivors from the sea.

The image focused on a lifeboat. Around fifty people sat in it. The picture tightened onto a group of three elderly women who sat in the back of the boat.

"My aunts," cried Kristin.

"DID WE GET them all?" asked Rose. She wiped the sweat off her brow and drew in a deep breath.

"I believe so," Lily said. Surveying the capsized ship, she gave a stealthy wave of her wand. Her hand trembled slightly. "I'm not reading any more lives on board."

Hyacinth placed her hand on Lily's wrist. "Enough. You can't do any more." Hyacinth was paler than usual. "We did good, ladies. Now I could use a vacation. I'm tired."

"That's because you're old," said Rose with a teasing smile.

"Speak for yourself," Hyacinth said with a frown. "I'm in fine shape. I feel like I'm eighty."

"Are you ladies okay there?" asked a uniformed crew member. "The ships will pick us up shortly, but if you are feeling ill or need anything now—"

"No, no, dear boy, we're fine. Just a little high-spirited at the moment," Lily said.

"If you're sure . . . ," the crew member said.

"We are," Rose said with a wide smile. "Don't worry about us. We haven't had such excitement in decades."

A few passengers snickered at her words, then fell silent.

Even Hyacinth smiled. "Don't be afraid to laugh. As long as everyone is safe, we have every reason to celebrate. Life is good, and we've just had it affirmed."

"Hear, hear," said one of the civilians.

The tension in the survivors seemed to ease with those words, and a few leaned in close to one another and started conversations as they waited for their turn to be rescued.

"I will admit that I'm tired myself," Lily said, rolling her shoulders. "I haven't done that much magic in weeks."

Rose nodded. "And it is the Time of Transition."

"How do you think Kristin is faring?" Lily asked.

"I'm sure she's doing fine. She's a brilliant child," Hyacinth said.

"Not so much a child. I wonder who her arbiter is." Rose tilted her head, and a faraway look splashed over her face.

"Just because you married yours doesn't mean the same thing will happen to her." Hyacinth clicked her tongue. "And that was highly irregular if you remember."

"I do, but breaking the rules was half the fun," Rose said.

"Poor Kristin. I don't see her breaking any of the rules," said Lily.

"Maybe not, but she is brilliant. And a Rare One." Rose sighed. "I do so like that child."

"Suppose her arbiter is an ass?" asked Hyacinth.

"We'll just have to trust that the Council sent the right person to judge her," Lily said.

"In any case, we can do nothing about it now." Rose waved her arm at the many lifeboats and people surrounding them. "We can't pop home. Not only would we have a hundred witnesses to our disappearance, we performed so much magic last night that we'd run the risk of never making it home."

"I hate to add one more worry, but if we're going to get worked up about things, let's do it right." Hyacinth paused. "When the wave struck, did you feel anything?"

"Yes," Lily said, her voice dropping in dismay. "I had hoped I was wrong, so I didn't say anything."

"The footprint? Oh dear, I felt it too." Rose reached into her pocket and pulled out her closed fist. "And the purser delivered this just before the wave struck." She opened her palm to reveal a medallion with a hammer and sickle emblazoned on one side.

"I received one too." Lily pulled hers from her pocket and presented it to the others.

"I left mine on the boat. And I don't want it back." Hyacinth scowled. "Do you think it means what I think it means?"

"I hope not." Lily frowned.

"Right. So now what?" Hyacinth asked.

"We recover." Lily lifted one finger. Her face took on a look of efficiency. She began to tick off the points on the rest of her fingers. "We rebuild our strength, rest, and—"

"—get rescued," added Rose.

"Exactly." Lily nodded. "Then when it is safe to do so, we go home."

"And until then? What about Kristin?" Hyacinth stared into her companions' eyes.

"We hope she has a competent arbiter."

"YOU FOUND THEM." Kristin tugged on his hand and pointed to the image.

A surge of pride ran through Tennyson at the success of his spell. The three women were in a lifeboat. Safe and sound.

"I wish we could hear them. They look like they are

bickering." Kristin smiled. "You know they bicker all the time. They're best friends, but they bicker."

He drew in a deep breath. "I have to break the connection. I don't want to leave myself much more drained than I am now."

"I understand." She nodded at him and released his hand.

He waved his wand and the image disappeared. The water became a clear puddle on the mirror's surface almost at once.

"Thank you." She threw her arms around him and kissed him.

Although he knew the kiss was an expression of her relief and exuberance, the heat of her touch shot straight to his groin. He pulled her closer and melded his lips to hers. A slim ribbon of reason filtered into his mind: *She doesn't want this, she doesn't want this*. But to his surprise, she pressed herself against him. He could feel the soft flesh of her breasts molding against his chest, searing him even through the fabric of their clothes. She tilted her head under his to mesh their lips more firmly together. Her hand tunneled into the hair at the base of his neck and she grabbed on as if she was fighting to steady herself.

He rounded his hands over her rear and drew her in against him. Her hip applied a delicious pressure to his already thickening penis, and she wriggled in closer, tighter—

His foot hit the edge of the mirror, tipping it, sending the water over their feet.

The sudden dampness had the effect of a cold shower. They sprang apart. Kristin's mouth was parted, still moist and pink from the kiss.

His heart pounded, and he summoned all his remaining strength to not step back into her.

"I . . . I . . ." She sputtered for a moment, then fell silent.

So, she wasn't as indifferent as she contended. Satisfaction swelled throughout him. He'd claim this small victory over her emotions and work from there. He grabbed a towel. "You're welcome."

She looked at him without comprehension.

He stifled a laugh. "Your aunts. I told you they'd be all right. They're outstanding women."

She drew in a deep breath, as if relieved he wasn't speaking of the kiss. "Do you know them?"

"Not well, but I have met them." He blotted the water with the towel.

"And they probably know of you," she said.

He paused, then finished cleaning up. "Probably."

She scrutinized him, and he felt her gaze almost as if she had touched him. "It must be hard to be famous."

"You'll know soon enough. When you go through the official ceremony declaring you a godmother, all Arcani will know who you are."

"There's a ceremony?" She paled. "Oh God."

"What's wrong?"

"I don't do well in front of people. I freeze up."

He squeezed her hand. "Don't worry. As your arbiter, I'll be right beside you."

"Believe it or not, that helps."

He picked up the mirror from the floor and handed it to her. "I'll take care of the towel while you return the mirror to its rightful place."

She opened the door and stopped short. Zack stood

right in front of the door with his arm raised as if to knock. He glanced at her, then at the mirror in her arms, then at Tennyson holding the towel. A slow smile stretched across his mouth.

"Dude." Zack gave him the thumbs up. "But I've got a bigger mirror that will work even better. Let me know when you want it, okay?" Zack gave him a wink.

Tennyson watched her eyes widen. Color slipped in under her tan. "But I . . . we . . ."

"No need to explain, pretty one. I understand completely. Mrs. Pendelton baked some cookies, but if you're busy . . ." Zack nodded knowingly.

"We'll be right there," Kristin said, nearly tripping over her words.

Tennyson chuckled. It was amusing to see her so rattled.

"We're in the backyard." Zack disappeared.

She turned back to him. "This is your fault."

He arched his eyebrows. "My fault. How do you figure?"

"I don't know, but somehow it's your fault." She carried the mirror out of his sight. "It always is."

His shoulders shook in silent laughter. Zack had really gotten to her. Hmmm, a mirror. He'd have to remember that if he ever had the chance to—

Instantly heat flared through him, tightening his chest and surging into his loins. Sparks danced on his nerves, igniting them. He tingled all over. Damn. He gulped and tried to divert his thoughts. He could be in major trouble if just thinking about her caused such a reaction.

She returned, poking her head into the room. "They're waiting for us."

"Coming."

But a soft tapping at the window caught his attention. He looked at the sliding glass door and saw something glitter in the sunlight.

"Callie." Kristin ran across the room to the balcony door. Sliding it open, she let the sprite into the room.

"I've been so worried about you," the sprite said as she fluttered around Kristin's head. "When I saw the cottage in ruins, I didn't know what to think. I've been searching for you all day."

"I'm sorry, Callie. Tennyson thought it best that we went into hiding."

"Hiding? Why?"

"Tennyson seems to think the fire was deliberate, and I'm afraid I agree." Kristin twisted her mouth to the side expressing her uneasiness.

"Oh my goodness." The sprite landed on the edge of the dresser. "Then you aren't being very clever about it."

Tennyson frowned. "What do you mean?"

"If I could find you, anyone can."

"How did you find us?"

"I followed the footprint. You did magic. I know every Arcani house in this area, and this isn't one of them. So when I found a footprint, I came to investigate, and there you were."

"I didn't think about the tingle," Kristin said.

"Tingle?" asked Callie.

"It's what she calls the footprint." This talk of tingling led his thoughts and body down an entirely different path. He drew a deep breath and exhaled, willing his body to obey. Tennyson faced Kristin. "I did, and I masked it as best I could, but a full blown shield would announce our presence as surely as the footprint."

"And you did pretty good, but I was looking for a footprint, so I found it," said Callie.

"Then we aren't safe here?" Kristin asked. Her brow furrowed and she looked worried.

"I think we are. With the exception of Callie, no one is looking for us. Today." He placed his hands on her shoulders. "You made the argument yourself. After all the magic she expended on the storm and the wave, she has to be taking a down day or risking herself. As long as we don't use any more magic—"

"I know, but . . . Wait." Kristin went onto the balcony. She waved at Jake and Zack in the garden. She watched for a moment, then out of the side of her mouth, she spoke back into the room: "Can you feel the tingle now?"

Tingle again! She was going to be the death of him. *Remember your job, Tennyson.* He concentrated and sensed the faint imprint of a magical footprint from her. "Are you doing magic?"

"Not really, but there's a crown over Jake's head."

Tennyson fell silent.

She looked him straight in the eye. "And yesterday I heard another of Jake's wishes."

Tennyson fell silent. The last thing he wanted was to place Zack and Jake in danger. "The footprint isn't strong, and if you didn't know what you were looking for, you'd never find it. With one child, the footprint will be weak indeed. But I can't risk Zack and Jake."

"I know." She came back into the room and closed the sliding glass door.

"Damn."

"Exactly." She perched on the edge of the bed.

"I'll put the strongest protections on the house, but after the viewing, it will leave me weak."

She shook her head. "We can't stay here."

13

HOW TO BE A FAIRY GODMOTHER:

•

The Barriers Between the Arcani and Groundling Worlds Are Meant to Protect Both Sides. But Sometimes You Need to Knock a Hole Through the Walls.

A SOMBER MOOD SETTLED on Kristin. Her aunts were safe, but now Zack and Jake weren't. Because of her. Guilt pressed hard on her conscience.

"Are you ready to go down?" asked Tennyson.

"Yes," she said with a sigh.

"No, you're not." Callie fluttered to her. "Now that I've found you, I'm keeping my eyes on you."

"You can't come down," Tennyson said.

"No one will know I am here." Callie landed on Kristin's shoulder, then hid in the hair by her neck.

"Fine. Just make sure no one sees you." Tennyson opened the door for Kristin. "They're waiting, and we have to tell them we can't stay."

Callie's feet tickled her neck.

"Settle down, or I'll shake my head," she whispered.

The sprite peeked through Kristin's hair. "Do you see a good place for me to hide yet?"

"Not yet, but there're lots of trees and plants in the backyard. We'll find something. Now shush." She followed the stone path to the outdoor table and chairs.

Jake was running through the yard, stopping on his next pass to grab a cookie.

"I don't know where he puts it," Zack said, snagging a cookie for himself. "The kid eats more than I do, and he's still skinny."

"Da-a-ad." Jake frowned at his father.

"It's true, little dude. You eat like a machine," Zack said. "It's awesome to behold."

"*Who* is that?" whispered Callie at her ear.

Kristin didn't answer. There was no way she could speak to the fairy without being noticed by Zack.

"Lemonade, Miss Montgomery?" Mrs. Pendelton asked.

"Thank you."

Mrs. Pendelton filled a glass with ice and poured.

Kristin took a sip and her eyebrows rose in surprise. "This is fresh."

"Yeah, Mrs. Pendelton refuses to use anything processed. She's into health. I couldn't get fat if I tried." Zack grabbed another cookie, then leaned toward Kristin. "Course, she doesn't know about the chili cheese fries I eat when I go out."

"I heard that, Mr. Glass," Mrs. Pendelton said without looking up from pouring a glass for Tennyson. She carried the pitcher back into the house.

"Is he single?" asked Callie.

The fairy's breath tickled Kristin's ear. She tossed her head to discourage the sprite from talking. She couldn't have a conversation with Callie now.

Callie pinched her neck.

Kristin jumped. "Ouch."

"What happened?" asked Zack.

"Nothing. Just a little pain in the neck." Kristin walked to a foliage-filled basket hanging from the lowest branch of a tree. "Here," she hissed. "Get off."

Callie fluttered quickly to the leaves and hid.

Jake squinted at Kristin and cocked his head. His gaze focused on the planter.

Could Jake see Callie? Kristin looked up at the fairy, who was still peering out from behind a leaf. She looked back at Jake. He was watching the planter intently.

She turned her back to the others. "Callie, hide. I think Jake can see you."

The sprite ducked behind the leaf and disappeared from view. But a moment later, Kristin heard a tiny, despair-filled voice. "He's a Groundling. Why did he have to be a Groundling?"

What did Callie mean by that? Kristin couldn't ask about the comment now, but she couldn't understand why the sprite sounded upset.

Tennyson sat on a chair beside Zack. "We need to talk."

"You sound serious." Zack squinted at Tennyson. "Should we go inside?"

"No, that's okay," Tennyson said.

Kristin pulled out a chair to join the conversation. Wait. Where was Jake? Searching the backyard, she frowned. Then she saw the boy. He had climbed into the tree and was crawling along the branch. He reached for the hanging basket.

"No!" she cried, dashing for the tree.

The gazes of both men flew to her, then to the tree.

Jake never lost his focus. He snapped forward with both hands. A loud crack burst from the tree; and the branch, the basket, and the boy plunged toward the ground.

Zack jumped to his feet. "Jake!"

Tennyson whipped out his wand. Kristin had hers out an instant later. They both pointed at Jake.

The boy floated gently to the ground, oblivious to the injury that might have befallen him. "I caught her, Dad! I caught her."

Kristin glanced at Zack. His mouth hung open and all color blanched from him. He had seen them then. Well, of course he had seen them. They were standing right in front of him. She glanced at Tennyson, who didn't look much better.

"Look, Dad." Jake bounded up from the ground, unaware of the drama unfolding among the adults. He ran to the table holding out his cupped hands. "Look." He spread his fingers.

For an instant, Callie sat in the boy's palm, knees drawn up to her chest, curled into a ball, but the moment she realized her prison had opened, she shot through Jake's fingers, sprang into the air, and darted away. Only a slight effervescent sparkle followed her path, which faded in the next second.

"Awww, she flew away." Jake screwed up his mouth.

"Did I just see what I think I saw?" asked Zack as if a wad of cotton was stuffed in his throat. He stared after the glittery trail.

"Dad, can I search for some more fairies, huh? Can I?" Jake bounced on his feet in front of his father.

"What? Uh, sure, go ahead." Zack still hadn't regained his color.

Jake scampered into the garden and started his search.

Zack looked at Tennyson.

Tennyson opened and shut his mouth a few times, but he formulated no words. At last he said, "I am a wizard."

Zack plopped into a chair but said nothing.

"I am a wizard and Kristin is a fairy godmother." Tennyson's voice was calm and soothing.

"I know it sounds crazy," she said, trying to ease Zack's clear discomfort. "I didn't know a thing about it until last week myself. I pretty much reacted as you have."

"We try not to let ourselves be known to you, um, non-magical folk. There aren't many of us, and we live amongst you. Can you imagine how the world would react if it knew about us?" Tennyson gave Zack a smile.

"Probably a lot like Zack is now," said Kristin under her breath.

"Sometimes, however, we must reveal ourselves. I couldn't let Jake get hurt." Tennyson stared at his friend.

Zack didn't move. He didn't blink. Kristin looked for the pulse in his neck. It beat steady and regular.

After quickly checking to see that Jake was still occupied, Tennyson pointed his wand at a cookie. "Watch."

The cookie rose gently into the air and landed directly into his fingertips. "That's not impressive, I know, but I didn't want to freak you out. Too much."

Zack's face still maintained that open-mouthed, shocked look.

"You don't have to be afraid. I'd never hurt you."

Still no reaction.

"I suppose you have a lot of questions. I know I still do," said Kristin. She held her breath. She was unable to read Zack's expression.

In the next instant, Zack jumped to his feet. "This is abso-freakin'-lutely awesome. I can't believe this. My best friend is a wizard. Magic is real." He pumped his arm into the air as he danced around. "Totally freakin' cool. I am the luckiest dude in the world."

Jake looked up at his father's outburst. "Did you find a fairy, Dad?"

"No, little man, but keep looking." Zack lowered his voice. "That was a fairy Jake caught, wasn't it?"

"Her name is Callie, and when she comes back—"

"—if she comes back—," said Tennyson.

Kristin nodded. "—I'll introduce her."

"Wicked." Zack's grin lit up his face, and the resemblance between father and son was clearly visible. "I've got a million questions. Let's go inside where the spud can't hear us." Zack called out to Jake, "Found any yet?"

"No."

"Keep looking. But don't leave the backyard."

"YOU USE THE phone?" Zack's lip curled, and his eyes scrunched up. "That's so lame."

They were in the office. She and Tennyson sat on the couch while Zack sat behind his desk. Kristin had been right. This man with the sun-kissed hair, T-shirt, and flip-flops contrasted sharply with the ultramodern room.

Tennyson laughed. "Landlines and cell phones. We even use the Internet. Hey, they're good technologies, and they don't cost us energy. Otherwise we'd be wasting our time conjuring up communication spells half the day. What did you expect?" He lifted his arm to rest on the back of the leather couch. His fingertips were a hair's breadth away from her neck, but he didn't touch her.

"Owls. Like in the book. You know. Harry Potter?"

"That's fiction. Besides J. K. Rowling knows better than to reveal all our secrets."

Zack's eyes rounded. "She's one of you?"

Tennyson shrugged. "We all have to earn a living somehow. We *do* live in your world."

"Well, she succeeded, didn't she?" Zack paused, then he lifted a finger. "Is that why you invested in Z-foam?"

"I need money too."

Zack frowned slightly. "You didn't use magic?"

"It was a solid product, Zack. You made an amazing discovery. No magic, bud. It was all you." With a smile, Tennyson added, "I guess you could call that your own magic."

"Cool." Zack leaned back in his chair. "So you guys can't just conjure up cash, huh?"

"I keep telling you that magic costs energy. We can't just use magic recklessly." Tennyson thought for a moment. "You went surfing this morning."

"Yeah, but—"

"Why did you come home when you did?"

"Hey, I was tired. The surf was epic. I caught eight, ten waves. That's a lot of work, dude."

"So why didn't you keep going?" Tennyson asked.

Zack furrowed his brow. "I told you I was tired and these were monster waves. One little mistake and . . ." Enlightenment dawned on his face. "Ohhhh. I get it."

So did she, in a way she had not understood before. Magic was not easy, and she was far from an expert. One little mistake in magic and you could end up anywhere. Like in an unfamiliar house in La Jolla at night in your killer shoes and black dress. Not that the shoes and dress mattered anymore. She sighed.

"You sound sad, pretty woman." Zack gave her his attention.

"Because you've turned out to be quite a delightful person, and I wish we could stay until I got to know you better."

Zack bowed his head in a gesture of humility, but she didn't miss the frown on Tennyson's face. What was wrong with him?

"So why do you want to leave?" asked Zack.

"It's not a question of want," Tennyson said, and he explained his theory about the Time of Transition and the attacks on them.

Zack's face grew somber as Tennyson's story spilled out. When Tennyson finished, Zack sat back in his chair. "Where would you go if you left here?"

"I don't know. I brought Kristin here because nobody in the Arcani world knows you," Tennyson said.

Except you, dude," Zack said.

Tennyson smiled. "Except me. I couldn't take her to my place. Too many people know where I live."

That explained why he hadn't taken her to his house. But she didn't find it fair. Tennyson knew everything about her life, but she didn't even know where he lived. She wondered if his home reflected the man—stuffy on the outside, with a wealth of depth beneath the arrogant exterior.

"We don't want to put you or Jake in danger," Tennyson added.

Zack fell silent. His forehead wrinkled as if he were debating with himself. Then he faced Tennyson. "When I needed help, you stepped in without hesitation, without questions. I'm here for you now."

Raking his fingers through his hair, Tennyson stood. "You don't know how serious—"

"You said yourself no one knows you're here. So we'll be careful. You stay here, incognito, and, as much as I hate to say it, no magic."

"But I'll still see Jake's wishes," she said hesitantly.

"Tennyson said he could put protections on the house. Besides, you said that the fairy found you only because you did some big magic." Zack paused. "I wish I could have seen it."

Pacing, Tennyson frowned. "But the protections will tell Arcani that someone is here."

"But you'll be protected. Isn't that what the magic is for?" Zack argued.

"As long as we stay in the house—"

Zack held up his hand. "Will that fairy tell anyone?"

"Of course not. She's a friend," Kristin said.

"Then it's settled."

Tennyson paced a few more steps, but the agitation had left his movements. He walked over to Zack and extended his hand. "Thanks. You're a good friend."

Zack gripped Tennyson's hand around his thumb, withdrew his hand, then bumped knuckles. "Hey, I can finally do something for you. Let me enjoy it."

KRISTIN RETREATED TO the bedroom. The boys were playing video games—she believed Jake was beating them both—and all she wanted was some quiet time, maybe with a good book. She also had to figure out how to quit her job. She could take some notes, come up with some kind of plausible excuse.

Bags from their morning shopping expedition littered the room, which wasn't the most conducive for relaxing or thinking. At least the damp spot in the carpeting was dry. Zack and Tennyson had carried everything upstairs after "The Talk." She smiled to herself. They hadn't understood her need to change out of the Z-foam sweats and T-shirt for dinner.

Pushing open the door, she stopped. Something wasn't right. She thought she heard crying. But no one was upstairs. The guys were in the TV room, and Mrs. Pendelton was cooking.

There it was again, a tiny sob.

She peered into the room and spotted Callie sitting on the dresser.

Callie stood and wiped her tiny hands across her face. "Oh, good. You're back."

"Are you crying?" Kristin bent to take a closer look at the fairy.

"Of course I'm crying. It's been a hideous day." Callie sniffed.

"I'm sorry Jake trapped you. That must have been frightening," Kristin said.

"What?" Callie looked taken aback, then shook her head. "Oh, the child. That wasn't a big deal. It was my own fault." A fresh round of tears burst forth from her eyes.

Kristin was surprised. "Is being caught bad? Will you be punished?"

"No, you don't understand."

Kristin bit back the impatient retort that rose to her lips. She didn't need to upset Callie further. "Then why . . . ?"

"It's *him*. Zack. The boy caught me because I wasn't paying attention. I was staring at Zack." Her wails grew louder.

"But—"

"He's a *Groundling*. I can't fall for a Groundling."

Fall? For Zack? "You haven't even met him."

"And I don't wah-ah-ah-ant to." Callie sobbed, her wings heaving with every breath.

Flummoxed, Kristin sat on the edge of the bed. "Are you saying you're attracted to Zack?"

"It's . . . more . . . than . . . that," said Callie between gulps of air. "He made my heart zing. My heart has never zinged before."

Kristin hid her smile. "Well, Zack is a nice guy, and he's intelligent as well."

"You're not helping." Callie forced her tears into submission and paced the dresser top.

"Tennyson told me early on that it wasn't forbidden for Groundlings and Arcani to get together," Kristin said in a cheerful voice.

"I know that." Irritation sharpened Callie's tone.

"Then what's the problem?"

"Don't you see?" Callie faced her and placed her hands on her hips. "If I dated Zack, I'd have to be big."

14

HOW TO BE A FAIRY GODMOTHER:

•

Take Your Time.

CALLIE'S COMPLAINTS AMUSED Kristin more than roused her sympathy. Love was something, oh God, special, if not sacred. She believed in love so fully that it formed the foundation of her outlook on life. She had seen her parents share their love with each other; and she knew that love was not just sex and chemistry, but heartache and hardship and hard work too. It was having a secret strength that you could call on when you needed it, that could get you through anything because you knew you were not alone. You weren't one person; you were part of an entirely new whole.

She tried not to laugh at Callie's dilemma. "Nobody said you had to marry him. Geesh, he may not even want to date you."

Callie struck a pose with attitude. "Oh, he will want to date me."

Kristin held up her hands. "My mistake."

As if she had deflated, Callie sank to the dresser top and sat cross-legged. Elbows on her knees, she propped her chin on her palms. "You don't understand. I'm a sprite."

Kristin struggled to make sense of those words. "Uh, I know you're a sprite."

"But you don't know that we recognize our heart mates the moment we see them." Callie sighed.

Now Kristin understood the reason for Callie's distress but still didn't understand the sorrow. "Callie, love is a gift, the greatest gift life has to offer."

"I know, and I've had friends who married big people, and they were happy."

"Then what's the problem?"

"I just never wanted to be one of them. I like being little." Callie scrunched her face into an expression of resentment.

Kristin had to bite back a smile. She already knew Callie had a strong sense of self worth, but Kristin also knew the sprite wasn't truly selfish. "Well, when you're ready, I'll introduce you."

"Yeah, *if* I change my mind."

"We're staying here for the time being. Tennyson seems to think it's still the safest place for us to hide." Kristin updated the fairy with the plans and watched in dry amusement as Callie's expression turned grave.

After giving a solemn vow of silence, Callie zoomed into the air and brushed a fairy kiss onto Kristin's cheek. "I'll see what I can find out from my sources. We sprites get around." She gave a wry smile, then zipped through the open sliding glass door.

Callie's visit set Kristin musing. She was discovering a new community, a new set of rules, many of them unexpected. She hadn't really considered the drawbacks of a sprite like Callie falling for a Groundling. Why would she have? She'd never believed in the existence of such beings. How many more creatures didn't she know about? How many more unusual circumstances were sure to arise?

Tennyson's image sprang into her mind. He certainly was an unexpected consequence of the past week. Her impression of him had changed. Impatient? Yes. Domineering? Yes. Control freak? Definitely. But he was also dedicated and loyal and kind. And sexy as hell.

No, she couldn't think along those lines. Could she?

Too late. The memory of his long, sinewy limbs wrapping around her burned into her consciousness. Her skin remembered the heat of his chest and abdomen, and his penetrating coppery gaze flared into her mind. A tight ball of embers unfurled in the pit of her stomach and sent heat surging through her every fiber. Her body throbbed in a thrillingly aching way, and she quivered with need.

An urgent knock at the door broke her reverie. "Kristin?" Tennyson called through the wood. The door cracked open.

"Yes?" Her cheeks flamed as the object of her musings walked in.

"Is anything wrong?" he asked. The fiery gaze so recently called up in her memory now peered into her eyes. It was more intense in person.

Why *was* he staring at her? "No. Everything's fine."

He examined her for a moment, then crossed to the bed and sat on the edge. "You were taking so long."

Oh God, he was on the bed. Trying to act as casual as possible, she shrugged. "Callie was here, and we talked."

He pointed at Kristin. "I thought you were changing."

"I was." She dove into the bags to find some clothes. And to hide her face. She tossed one thing after another from the sacks.

"Are you sure you're okay?" Doubt filled his voice.

"Of course." Her voice squeaked. "Why wouldn't I be okay?"

"I don't know, but you made a mess."

She glanced down at the floor. Clothes littered the carpeting. The bags were strewn about, half-empty. "Found it." She grabbed something, anything, and walked into the bathroom.

"Dinner will be ready soon. Want me to wait?"

No. "Sure."

As she pulled off the T-shirt, she couldn't help but remember Tennyson sat just a few feet away. A closed door stood between them, but her skin prickled, and she ignored the insane thought that she wished it were his hands stroking her, not the material of the shirt as she lifted it from her body.

With a quick push, the Z-foam sweatpants joined the T-shirt on the floor. Catching a glimpse of herself in the mirror, she turned and examined her reflection. The simple white underwear was serviceable, not sexy, yet her nipples pushed through the fabric. Great. If just thinking about him did this to her, what would his touch do?

And that thought brought a thrumming to her inner core.

Stop it. You need to get dressed. She lifted the clothes she had grabbed from the bags and groaned. Sweats and a T-shirt. Why did she have to be a victim of life's cruel irony? She couldn't possibly get away with changing into inferior quality casual clothes, not after the search Tennyson had witnessed.

"Uh . . . Tennyson?"

"Yes?"

"Could you leave?" Well, *that* sounded brilliant.

"Why?"

Good question. "I'll be down soon." Not an answer, but it would have to suffice.

"All right."

She waited a minute and then poked her head out. He was gone. She rushed to the bags and pawed through them. Again. This time she focused and found a kicky skirt and blouse. She pulled them on, slipped her feet into a new pair of flip-flops, and went downstairs.

The skirt was a mistake. The air that hit her thighs sent her nerve endings into a frenzy. It didn't help that Tennyson's steamy gaze shot to her the moment she walked into the dining area. Maybe the "steamy" was in her imagination, but that's how she perceived it.

Mrs. Pendelton laid dinner out, and everyone tucked in. Kristin knew she ate, but for the life of her she couldn't remember what she ate. She was sure it was delicious, and her plate was nearly empty at the end of the meal, but she had spent the time sneaking glances at Tennyson, and wondering if he was looking at her.

God, what was she? In middle school?

She couldn't stomach dessert. She pushed back from the table. "Please excuse me. I think I'll go lie down for a while."

Tennyson stood to follow her, but she hurried from

the room. God, she was so stupid. She fled up the stairs and ran into the room she shared with him. How was she going to get through another night with him? After today? After everything she had been thinking?

She liked him.

It was more than that, but she couldn't even contemplate the other "L"-word after only a week. That just wasn't possible.

Neither was magic.

She flung herself on the bed, rolled to her back, and stared at the ceiling.

The door opened. Tennyson walked into the room and sat beside her on the bed. She kept her focus on the ceiling.

He laid his palm on her forehead. "Are you ill?"

She shook off his hand. "No."

He peered at her and tilted his head. "Cramps?"

"Don't be an ass."

"Well, what am I supposed to think?" He shot to his feet and paced the room. "You ran away from the table with no explanation. They're all concerned about you."

"I'm sorry about that. I just couldn't stay any longer." She couldn't face him, afraid he'd see her desire for him in her eyes. "I just needed some time alone."

"Look, I'm sorry you're stuck with me. As soon as we figure out how to stop Elenka, you'll be rid of me."

She bolted upright. "Is that what you think? You think I want to be rid of you?" She swung her legs off the bed.

He lifted his hands in front of him. "You've made it clear that you don't like me much. I'm sorry for that because I find you admirable."

"Admirable? *Admirable?*" She strode and stood no

less than an inch in front of him. "That's all? Admirable?"

"I have to admit that you do things to me that you shouldn't, but I know the rules and boundaries. I won't step over them again." His face took on an impenetrable mask. Even his eyes lost their fire.

"You arrogant, righteous, uptight . . . Ohhh." She grabbed his shirtfront. "You stupid man."

She pulled his lips down to hers and kissed him fiercely. His eyes widened and his eyebrows arched high, and she reveled in his look of surprise. Then she closed her eyes so she could taste him more fully.

His arms curled around her and drew her into him. She nestled into his embrace and pressed herself against him. His solid strength exuded heat, and she shivered in its glow. His one hand moved to cradle her head, and the other splayed against her back, holding her so securely she believed she could never fall again.

She angled her lips to fit better against his and slipped her tongue in to chase his. He tasted of forest winds and brown sugar and his own unique spiciness. She could subsist on this forever.

Her blood coursed through her, like wind in a storm. She felt wild and free and powerful. She tilted her hip against his loins and rubbed against him. A delicious throbbing ached for attention, so she twisted into him, wanting more. He matched her movements, and his hardness stroked her to higher sensation.

His hand delved beneath her blouse, and with a feather touch, he brushed her nipple through the thin cotton of her bra. Her aureole puckered into a pebbly circle, and she craved more attention for the hard center. As if he read her thoughts, his thumb and forefinger rolled the hardened point gently between them. She let out a soft moan as the jolt shot straight to her core.

With his other hand, he lifted her skirt and placed his palm against the roundness of her buttocks. His touch claimed her.

He pulled back and whispered against her cheek, "Does this mean you like me now?"

She worked her fingers into the top of his waistband. "Uh-huh." She wasn't capable of intelligible speech.

"Good, because I like you too." Capturing her lips again, he ground his erection against her hip.

She wanted him. Now. Drawing her hands to the front of his sweats, she untied the string.

With a growl of anticipation, he swept her into his arms and carried her to the bed. Laying her gently on the cover, he bent over her and nipped at her breasts through her blouse. She squirmed with pleasure.

The tension simmered within her, growing stronger and more insistent. She pulled his T-shirt over his head, revealing the hard planes of his chest. In return he grabbed her blouse and yanked. The buttons popped off and landed with soft plops onto the carpeting.

Another shirt destroyed and she didn't care. As he wrestled with her bra, she pushed the sweats off his hips.

He raised the hem of her skirt and pulled down her panties. His fingers delved into the newly exposed flesh. She moaned against his cheek. His expert touch sent jolts of desire through her.

Rolling to her side, he grabbed his wand from the floor where it had fallen and flicked it. A shower of little foil-wrapped packets fell on the bed beside her. He grabbed one and ripped it open with his teeth, all the while maintaining his intimate contact with her.

She could barely lie still any longer. Her back arched as he tweaked the sensitive nub at the apex of her legs. She tugged at his boxers and freed his erection. When his free hand placed the rubber ring at the tip of his penis, she brushed away his hand and rolled the condom over him herself.

As soon as she had finished, he rose above her and settled between her legs. She held his hot length and guided him into her. He thrust forward, filling her.

She lifted her legs and hooked them around his waist, drawing him farther into her. He rocked his hips, in and out, in and out, until his gliding overtook her senses. She dropped her head back and opened her mouth. He covered her lips and pulled on her tongue as she fractured into a million diamond facets, sparkling and full of light.

Above her, he broke his lips from hers. His breath grew ragged. He pushed deep into her and ground himself against her. A guttural purr rose from his core as he shuddered above her and exhaled in a long, forceful push of air. He stilled, then melded himself to her curves. His arms encircled her and he drew in a deep breath.

She closed her eyes and let a smile creep onto her face. No regrets this time. He touched her, deeply, in a spot she wasn't sure she could identify as a physical part of her body.

He withdrew from her and rolled to her side. His hand entwined with hers. "I'm glad you like me."

She laughed. "Me too."

"You aren't going to yell at me this time?"

A pang of guilt shot through her. "No."

"It's still against the rules. I am still your arbiter."

"And I'm still a novice fairy godmother. And a woman." The need to analyze what had just happened rose in her, but she tamped it down. "And we aren't out of danger yet."

"Yes, but this magic didn't have a footprint." He kissed her forehead. "Although maybe they could hear your screams."

"I screamed?" Heat bloomed in her cheeks.

He kissed her forehead again. "Yes, but I caught it all in my mouth."

"Quit trying to scare me." She hit him playfully.

"Watch it. I haven't passed you yet. Officially." He grinned at her. "If you're not nice to me . . ."

"That sounds distinctly like sexual harassment." She traced a circle in his chest hairs.

"Hey, if I thought I could coerce you or threaten you, I'd have tried it when I first met you." He kissed her nose. "You're too strong for that."

"Strong? After all the grief you gave me?"

"Grief? I was stuck with a newbie who didn't want anything to do with me."

She let out a good-natured groan. "Well, you weren't very nice at first."

"I know, and I'm sorry. I thought you'd be a burden and a hindrance to my work. I didn't know how much I'd come to like you."

She was beginning to hate that word "like."

"Of course, you're still hindering my research, but I don't think I mind so much anymore." Then his face grew serious. "But we do have important work here. We still need to find Elenka and stop her."

A knock at the door startled them. Kristin jumped up from the bed and looked down. Her blouse, panties, and bra were gone, but she still wore her skirt. For some reason, that sent an aftershock of sensation through her.

She grabbed clothes from the floor and ran to the bathroom. Great. She had grabbed the Z-foam T-shirt again. At least she didn't have to worry about buttons. As she tried to restore some semblance of propriety, she heard Tennyson call out.

"Who's there?"

"It's me. Zack. You guys all right?"

"Yeah. Come on in." She heard the laughter in Tennyson's voice as he answered.

She peeked through the slim opening in the door. Tennyson wore only his sweats and no shirt. Wonderful. Zack would think they were animals at this rate.

Zack came in, took a look at the rumpled bed, and the now-familiar grin appeared on his face. "Dude."

"Zack, did you want something?" Tennyson grabbed his T-shirt and pulled it back on.

"Yeah. There are three ladies at the front door claiming to be Kristin's aunts. Should I let them in?"

15

HOW TO BE A FAIRY GODMOTHER:

•

Have Faith in the Magic.

"WELL, THAT WAS rude." Hyacinth stared at the closed wooden door in front of her.

"Do you think we came to the wrong place?" asked Rose. "It is the Time of Transition. Maybe our magic hasn't worked."

"Don't be silly. We haven't made a mistake. She's inside." Lily frowned at the door. "Though I can't imagine why she's here, in a house covered with protections, and not at home."

"We could blast the door," said Hyacinth.

"We cannot," said Lily.

"It wouldn't be polite," said Rose.

"But we're not godmothers anymore. We don't have to be nice." Hyacinth rubbed her hands together.

"We are still godmothers, just in Transition. Besides, we can't risk it." Rose wagged her finger. "We just transported from a Pacific island. More magic might push us over our limits."

"I wasn't serious," said Hyacinth.

"I know, dear. We're all tired, and we're concerned about Kristin." Lily patted Hyacinth's shoulder.

"Not to mention we just survived a shipwreck. Not bad for a bunch of old broads." Rose grinned.

"Stop calling me old," said Hyacinth, but she had no real rancor in her voice.

A light inside the hallway came on and shone through the opaque glass in the door. A moment later the door was flung open, and Kristin ran out. Tennyson hung back in the doorway and watched as the four women cried, laughed, hugged, and talked at once:

"We were so worried about you."

"What are you doing here?"

"Were you frightened?"

"How did you get here?"

"Have you been eating?"

"You're not hurt?"

"I'm so sorry we didn't tell you more."

Tennyson cleared his throat. "Ladies, I think this conversation would be more productive inside."

Zack stood at his shoulder, looking from one woman to another. "And if they took turns talking."

"Hey, I never said we could perform miracles," Tennyson said.

The aunts stopped suddenly as if just realizing they had observers. Lily stepped forward. "Tennyson Ritter, I believe." She held out her hand.

He shook it. "A pleasure to see you again."

Hyacinth narrowed her gaze at him. "You're Kristin's arbiter?"

"I am."

"Perfect," said Rose with a bright grin on her face.

Tennyson indicated his friend. "And this is Zack Glass. It's his house."

"A pleasure to meet you," said Lily, extending her greeting to Zack.

"Welcome to my house, O bodacious examples of mature feminine pulchritude," said Zack, opening his arms to include all the aunts.

Stunned silence dropped over them as Lily's mouth dropped open, Rose blinked up at Zack, and Kristin stifled a laugh.

Hyacinth narrowed her gaze for a moment, then nodded. "It's about time someone recognized our value." She took Lily's arm. "Come on, old girl. I like this place." She led Lily into the house.

Without hesitating, Rose took Zack's arm and bestowed a beatific smile upon him. "Aren't you a charming young man?"

"I try my best," said Zack as he took her inside.

Tennyson waited by the door for Kristin. She released the chuckle pent up inside her. "I've never seen them at a loss for words before."

"Zack can do that to people." Tennyson touched her cheek. "We were interrupted. We should talk about . . . Are you . . ." He didn't know how to continue.

"We probably do need to talk sometime, but apparently now isn't it." She tiptoed and pressed a kiss to his cheek. "I think the real world, or the unreal world, has just intruded upon us." She slipped her hand in his and pulled him into the house. "Come on. We have a lot to discuss with the aunts."

The unusual congress was meeting in Zack's living room. Zack played host.

"Ladies, can I get you something to drink?" asked Zack. "Wine? Beer? Margarita?"

"You'd make us margaritas?" asked Lily.

"Not to generalize, but I've found drinks with umbrellas go over well with the ladies, so I always keep a supply at hand." Zack eyed Hyacinth. "Let's see, tough exterior, stylishly efficient do. I'm guessing you're a piña colada lady."

"You're good," said Hyacinth. "But you can forget the umbrella. Don't need the thing poking me in the eye."

"You got it. One umbrella-less piña colada. Anyone else?" Zack took additional orders for two margaritas, one scotch, and a bottle of club soda. Rose's stomach was a little upset from all the travel.

Tennyson watched in amusement as Zack charmed the three old ladies. They giggled at Zack's jokes and flirted with him as he brought them their drinks. Tennyson found it hard to believe that these women were counted among the most powerful Arcani in the world. At least they had been. All fairy godmothers were.

His gaze fell on Kristin. She was laughing with the others. It was hard to see her as one of the guardians of his world, but she was, and already she showed talent few had—truly a Rare One. If he was right, if Elenka was making another attempt at power, Kristin was probably destined to play a key role in the upcoming battle. But he couldn't interrupt the mood right now. He knew they had a vital topic to discuss, but he also knew they all needed this time to celebrate the happy outcome of events. The aunts, as he had come to think of them himself, were home safely.

But for how long?

He placed his scotch nearly untouched on a side table. A cold shiver snaked down his spine. Despite the ebullience in the room, a sense of foreboding rose in him. The contrast between his thoughts and the celebration left him sober.

As he struggled with putting words to his feelings, Jake burst into the room. Mrs. Pendelton followed behind with a chiding scowl and glanced at the ladies apologetically.

Jake launched himself into Zack's arms. "Dad, I'm ready for bed."

"Brush your teeth?"

"Yup." Jake nodded.

"And your hair?"

"Why bother? I'm just going to sleep."

"That's my boy." Zack tousled Jake's unruly mop. "Say good night to our guests."

Jake looked around and gave the newcomers a shy smile.

"A child," said Rose, beaming at Jake. "I knew I felt welcome here."

"And he's so handsome too," said Lily.

"Handsome, shmandsome. Anyone can see the kid's strong," Hyacinth said.

"I am," Jake said. "I caught a fairy today."

The three women fell silent.

Kristin quickly turned to the aunts. "I'll tell you about it in a moment."

Zack saw the expressions on the three women's faces and turned to Tennyson. "Hey, are they—"

"And I'll tell *you* about it after you've put Jake to bed." Tennyson recognized the surprise of the three women.

Zack nodded. "Come on, little spud. Tomorrow's a workday for me. Time for bed."

"Good night, Kristin," said Jake. "Good night, Uncle Tennis."

"And the ladies?" prompted Zack.

Jake drew himself up and struck a serious pose. "And good night to you, beautiful creatures."

The three women giggled. "Such a charmer," said Rose.

"Takes after his father." Zack winked at the aunts.

As Zack took his son from the room, Mrs. Pendelton nodded. "If you don't need anything else, then I'll go to bed too."

"We're fine. Thanks for everything. Good night, Mrs. Pendelton," said Tennyson.

"Breakfast's at seven when Zack goes to work. See you then." Mrs. Pendelton left the room.

The three women turned to Tennyson expectantly.

"He's a friend, a Groundling, and he found out about our world today." Tennyson avoided the censure he knew was in their gazes.

"Oh dear. It seems we do have a lot to talk about," said Lily, and she straightened up. "Why don't you start by telling us why you are here and not at home?"

Kristin's eyes filled with tears. "The cottage burned down." Her voice quavered. He moved beside her to offer support.

"What?" said Hyacinth. "How—"

"What happened, dear?" asked Lily kindly.

"Lightning struck the house," said Tennyson.

"Lightning? Here?" Rose's eyes widened.

Lily's expression grew stern. "Lightning destroyed the house?"

"Exactly." Tennyson saw the implication wasn't lost on the women.

"Have you called the gnomes to work on it?" asked Lily.

"Gnomes?" asked Kristin.

"They're the best builders." Tennyson knew she had questions, but they had more important things to discuss than the work of gnomes. He turned his attention to the aunts. "I can't call the gnomes because they're all busy rebuilding the university."

"The university?" said Hyacinth in a shocked tone.

"An earthquake struck." He paused. "Aldous is dead."

The three women gasped. "Oh, poor Aldous," Rose said and pulled a handkerchief from her bag.

Lily bent her head.

Hyacinth scowled. "We leave for a few days and the world goes to hell."

He reached into his own pocket and retrieved the medallion emblazoned with the hammer and sickle. "This was sent to him just before he died."

Lily opened her pocketbook and retrieved a similar coin. She passed it to Tennyson. He examined the two medallions. They were identical. When he looked up, Rose handed him another. He looked at Hyacinth.

She shrugged. "Mine went down with the ship."

"You all received a medallion?" Kristin asked.

"We did." Lily folded her hands in her lap and struck a listening pose. "Perhaps you'd better tell us what you know. Start at the beginning."

"Wait." Kristin hurried out of the room and returned a few minutes later with a tablet of paper. Tennyson raised his eyebrows.

"Notes," she said, and poised her pen over the yellow sheet.

He smiled inwardly, then related the events of the past week. The discussion began in earnest. Kristin added an occasional comment, but he did most of the talking for them. However, organized notes soon filled her paper.

"And so we assumed the wave was a magical event," finished Tennyson.

"It was," said Rose. "We all felt the footprint."

"Aldous believed Elenka was behind the earthquake. It makes sense. The medallion was her token to her followers." Tennyson glanced down at the three coins in his palm.

Lily had a deep frown on her face. "I don't see how it could be Elenka. We isolated her nearly sixty years ago."

"But it's not impossible," Tennyson said.

"No, it's not impossible," Hyacinth said in a somber voice.

"Would someone tell me what you mean by 'isolated her'?" Kristin tapped the pen against the paper in a rapid tattoo. "What did you do to Elenka?"

Rose looked at Hyacinth, who looked at Lily in turn. Lily spoke. "Aldous Montrose and the three of us caught her. Her rebellion fell apart without her leadership. The Council wanted to execute her." She shuddered.

Hyacinth said, "We convinced them that she only needed to be isolated from the magical world so she could no longer pose a threat."

"She was one of us, after all," said Rose with a bob of her head. "We were based in Europe then."

"So we arranged for a prison of sorts to be built in a crevasse in the Pyrenees. We sealed off the mountain from the Andorrans, and any wayward Spaniards or Frenchmen." Hyacinth's gaze grew unfocused, as if she were picturing the memory.

"We recruited three wizards and one sorcerer to stand guard over the area," added Lily.

"And to serve as company for her." Rose frowned. "We weren't cruel. She had every amenity."

"Except freedom," Hyacinth said. "Aldous placed a powerful and intricate spell to contain her magic within the crevasse so she could never escape. We placed many enchantments over the area so no one, neither Groundling nor Arcani, would ever stumble upon her."

"And to discourage her followers from seeking her, the Council expunged the details from the record and forbade us to ever speak of Elenka and moved us to America." Lily sighed. "Aldous and the three of us kept the secret all these years with the blessing of the Council."

Kristin's pen scribbled on the page. She paused. "So as far as you know, Elenka is still in the mountain."

"She'd be our age," Lily said. "And I've never heard anything from the Council about her."

"But would they tell you if she escaped?" Kristin said.

"We can't really say," Rose said slowly. "But she'd hardly be a threat now. She'll be losing her godmother gifts just as we are."

Kristin fell silent.

Tennyson believed they were overlooking something, but he didn't know what. "We have to find out somehow."

"I think the best thing would be for one of us to check on Elenka," Hyacinth said.

"I'll ask the Council," said Rose. "I'll go tomorrow."

"And if we're granted permission, I'll visit Elenka," said Lily.

Hyacinth crossed her arms over her chest. “Which leaves me to do what?”

“Teach Kristin magic, of course,” Lily said. “Make sure she’s safe. She has a lot to learn in a short time.”

A contented expression settled on Hyacinth’s features. “I can do that. Good idea.”

“I thought I had to make the Transition on my own,” Kristin said.

“You do,” said Tennyson. “But the situation has changed, and as your arbiter, I think we can bend the rules this time.”

Zack returned to the room. “Did I miss anything?”

“Yeah, but I’ll fill you in in a minute,” Tennyson said.

“Do you think it’s a good idea to involve him?” asked Hyacinth.

Tennyson nodded with resignation. “He’s already involved. He’s giving us shelter. The least we can do is keep him informed of the possible dangers.”

“You’re right, of course. Mr. Glass needs to make his own decisions.” Lily smiled at Zack.

Zack’s face grew its customary grin. “Count me in. And call me Zack. ‘Mr. Glass’ sounds so uncool.”

“Now we all need some rest.” Lily stood.

“But where shall we go?” asked Rose. “Our house no longer exists, and I couldn’t transport any great distance again this evening.”

“Whoa, your house got destroyed too?” Zack’s eyes widened.

Kristin shook her head. “My house was their house. I was just house-sitting until they came back from their cruise.”

“Bummer. I’m so sorry.” Then Zack snapped his fingers. “Ladies, I’d be honored if you would consent to stay here. I have more bedrooms than I know what to do with."

"Zack, you may be bringing more attention to your house than is safe," said Tennyson. He tamped down a rill of unease. He didn't like exposing Zack and Jake to more danger.

"Just for tonight then. Let me help that much." Zack waited expectantly for their answer.

"It would be nice to find a bed about now," said Rose.

"And we shall leave in the morning," said Lily. "That can't cause too much risk."

"All right, but no magic," said Tennyson, feeling a little overwhelmed. "The house is under protection, but if there's a sudden increase in the footprint, Elenka might know something's going on."

"Oh dear," said Rose. "We lost our clothes on the ship. We were going to conjure some up—"

"No need. I have a supply of T-shirts and sweats. Perks of my business," said Zack.

FORTY-FIVE MINUTES LATER Tennyson found himself staring at the door to the bedroom. The aunts were tucked away in rooms nearby; Jake was long since asleep. Mrs. Pendelton was in her suite, and Tennyson had just finished talking to Zack about the aunts and their pooled knowledge. The only unfinished business was Kristin.

Tennyson listened at the door for a moment. Nothing. Was she already asleep? He cracked it open.

She sat in bed, tablet on bent knees, end of a pen in her mouth, brows furrowed as she stared at the page. Then she scribbled on the paper and drew arrows connecting one line of notes to another.

"Working?" he asked.

She jumped, startled. "You could've knocked. No, wait. I forgot who I was talking to."

He smiled. "Hey, it's my room too."

"I know." She focused on the page again.

"Find something new?"

"No, but some things don't make sense. Aldous was killed, the cottage burned down, and the aunts were attacked, all in the space of a week."

"Right."

"So why didn't Elenka attack me before I learned about my powers? Before the aunts handed over the job? Before you?"

"No one knew who you were until you chose your wand and your name appeared on a marble scroll in the Council hall. When the new godmothers are born, the magic reveals their names to the outgoing ones, but the godmothers keep those identities secret until the new ones receive their powers. Elenka had to wait for the Time of Transition to begin." Tennyson pulled off his shirt and couldn't help but notice how Kristin's gaze followed his movements. He stretched for good measure. "Besides, she doesn't just want to stop the Council and future godmothers; she wants revenge. On the ones who locked her up."

"And for all she knows, she's succeeded."

"She did. With Aldous."

Kristin reached out and squeezed Tennyson's hand. "The attacks have been too general, too prone to failure. Why not be overt? It doesn't make sense."

"Well, if she's trying to hide her actions, trying to make the deaths seem natural . . ." He stopped. Kristin was right. Why would Elenka need to try? Especially after sending out the coins as a calling card? One other thing troubled him. "She has to have someone who's helping her. She'd have to have followers, like-thinking Arcani."

Kristin paused. "You're right. Why haven't we spotted them?"

"For one thing, you're too new. You don't know a thing about the Arcani world." Her brows drew together in irritation and her mouth opened ready to protest. He spoke before she could form the words. "But you're learning. Fast."

The irritation vanished from her face, and she nodded with reluctance. "You're right. Have you noticed anyone?"

"Only your boyfriend, Lucas."

She shot Tennyson a look of exasperation but then froze. "Lucas has a servant. Dimitri. He gives me the creeps. I've seen him a couple of times. He's always watching me."

"You mean the chauffeur? It's possible. And the name is Slavic. Elenka was from Prague." Tennyson flipped the tablet back to its front page and set it aside. "We're still missing some piece of information, something we're not seeing. We need to know what the Council knows. For now we're safe."

"Rose talks to the Council tomorrow. Will they help?"

"It depends on whether they believe her." He shook his head. "This Council has been prone to ignoring news they don't like."

"Then I guess we have to wait to see what they tell her." Kristin scooted down in the bed. "Which reminds me. Someday you'll have to explain the whole

Transition thing. Just how am I expected to know all this stuff?"

"Sure. Every seventy years—"

She held up a hand. "Not now. I don't think I could handle more tonight. I just want to go to sleep."

"Ah . . . Kristin . . ." He waited until she gazed up at him. "Where am I sleeping?"

Her brows drew together, and she blushed. "Look, I'm not like this. I don't believe in cohabitation, and I don't sleep around, but I think, for now, I'll feel safer with you beside me."

He forced down the grin that threatened to erupt on his face. Until that moment, he didn't realize how knotted his stomach was.

"Just don't get used to it." She fluffed her pillow.

"I thought you liked me."

"Yeah, but you don't have to keep throwing that in my face."

16

HOW TO BE A FAIRY GODMOTHER:

•

Sometimes a Subtle Touch Is Best.

KRISTIN SLIPPED OUT of the house in the lavender-gray predawn. She hadn't slept well. Oh, worry hadn't kept her awake. Tennyson had. Sharing the bed with him hadn't been uncomfortable. In fact, she had felt safe, especially when his arm had draped over her as he turned. No, what had kept her awake was how right it had felt.

Fog lay heavily on the coast. The "June Gloom" concealed the other side of the street. As she stepped to the asphalt, the tingle of magic lifted from her as if she had slipped off a heavy raincoat. Vulnerability hit her and she felt exposed. She had left the protection of the house. She drew in a deep breath.

"Callie," she whispered. She had no clue what she was doing. How did one contact a sprite who wouldn't carry a phone?

Kristin concentrated. "Callie?" she said louder. "Can you hear me?"

"Over here." The sprite flew out of a bush and hovered in front of Kristin.

The initial elation at having contacted Callie with magic faded as Kristin realized the fairy had been close by. "Have you been here all night?"

"Yes." Callie's voice was flat. Even flying, even sparkling in the softness of first light, the fairy looked dejected. "Were you looking for me?"

Obviously, but Kristin didn't think sarcasm would go over well right now. "Is something wrong?"

"No. I was just peeking at Zack." Callie sighed.

"How long have you been here?"

"I never left."

Kristin grimaced in sympathy. "You've got it bad."

"Tell me something I don't know," said Callie with a little pepper in her voice. "What did you want me for?"

Kristin glanced back at the house. "I needed to get out. I was feeling restless, so I thought I'd take a jog on the beach."

"So?"

"So, I'm not stupid. If I leave the house, I leave its protection." Kristin peered at the sprite. "I was hoping you might want to fly with me. Do you have enough magic to help me if there's trouble?"

"I'll let that question slide only because I know you know so little about everything." Callie's fists landed on her hips.

"Do you want to get a little exercise?" Kristin raised her brows.

"You bet. I was tired of that bush anyway." Callie blew it a kiss. "No offense, green one."

Kristin had stretched inside the house, so she started off at a jog. Callie flew beside her. On the other side of the street, Kristin followed the steps leading down to the beach and then headed for the harder sand where the ocean met the shore.

"So you've fallen hard," said Kristin when she reached her desired track.

Callie blew out a puff of air. "It stinks. This time I've really done it. A Groundling. Ugh."

"You don't have to do anything about it. You'll get over him."

"No, I won't. I'm a sprite. When we fall, we fall for good."

"That does stink." But Kristin secretly felt a little jealous. Her own life was in such chaos, she'd love to be sure of something.

Immediately an image of Tennyson leapt into her mind. Oh sure, she'd had sex with him, and she even admitted she liked him, but she was no sprite. She wasn't falling for him. Not after one week.

She wasn't.

For the next minute, she concentrated on her stride, feeling the sand beneath her step, inhaling through her nose, and exhaling out her mouth. The spray from the waves left a salty tang on her tongue.

Callie zipped in front of her. "Will you introduce me?"

"To Zack? Sure."

"Thanks." Callie fell in beside her again. A moment later Callie's voice sounded in her ear. "Do you think he'll like me?"

"Yeah, I do." Kristin moved farther inland as a wave came up higher on the beach.

"Kristin," a voice called.

She stopped suddenly, causing Callie to shoot forward and then dart back to her with a frown. "If I'm supposed to protect you, you can't do things like that," said the sprite. "Warn me if you're changing direction."

"I heard my name." Kristin tried to peer through the thick whiteness.

At this hour few others were on the beach. The day had grown older, but the morning fog obscured the sky. She could see only a few feet down the beach in either direction.

"Kristin," came the voice again. A dark figure appeared in the mist and jogged toward her. A moment later she recognized Lucas. Wearing a slick black training suit, he stopped in front of her. The suit accentuated that he was in excellent shape for a man his age. His hair, damp from the fog, curled around his face in disarray that Hollywood stars would pay mucho money to achieve. The gray at his temples only added to the air of distinction.

Yet she took in his appearance more clinically than emotionally.

"Good morning, Lucas." She smiled at him.

"It is now that I've seen you." He took her hand and kissed it.

If she hadn't known he was from Europe, she might have laughed at the affectation. "How did you see me in this soup?"

"You forget I'm a sorcerer. This is my element." He waved his hand indicating the beach.

"Ah-hummm." Callie cleared her throat.

"Oh, this is Callie." Kristin pointed to the fairy floating by her ear.

"Calliope." The sprite darted forward and examined Lucas with squinted eyes.

He laughed. "I'm pleased to see you have a fierce guardian. I was about to chastise you for being out without protection." He bowed to Callie. "I am Lucas Reynard."

"Pleased to meet you," Callie said in a tone that sounded like forced politeness.

Lucas focused again on Kristin. His face grew serious. "Seriously, Kristin. Are you fine?"

She nodded. "I'm good. We're . . ." For some reason, she didn't want to tell him about her aunts.

"Is Ritter taking care of you?"

A blush crept into her cheeks. She thought she saw Lucas's gaze narrow briefly, but she might have imagined it. "We're being careful."

"I hope so. I don't want to see anything terrible happen to you." He placed her hand in his palm and cupped his other hand over it.

Callie flew over the connection and shot a look to her. Kristin ignored the accusation in the fairy's eyes. Instead she peered through the fog but saw nothing. "What about you? Is Dimitri here?"

"He wouldn't let me jog without him. He takes his job seriously."

Kristin repressed a shudder. If her suspicions about Dimitri were true, no wonder she had run into Lucas.

"You're staying around here then?" It wasn't really a question. Lucas's gaze searched through the fog as if it could penetrate the thickness.

"She can't tell you," Callie said, hands on her hips.

"I wasn't going to tell him anything, Callie," Kristin said with a hint of exasperation.

"I wouldn't want her to," said Lucas. "Her safety is more important to me than my ego. Although I can't say I don't wish she would have chosen me to protect her. It's enough to know you are safe. I've missed you."

Like she missed a normal life. She couldn't prevent the sigh that rose in her. "Things have gotten a little crazy. I still find it hard to believe someone wants to hurt me."

"We won't let that happen." Lucas squeezed her hand.

Kristin saw Callie's eyebrows shoot high, and, in truth, she wasn't comfortable with Lucas. Especially now after the thing with Tennyson. Lucas cared for her, but she didn't want his touch, not even on her hand. She couldn't explain all this to Callie right here.

"Ah-hummm." Callie cleared her throat again, more loudly this time.

Kristin pulled her hand out of Lucas's. She shook her head. "I should get going. I want to get a little more running in before I return to the house."

Callie lifted a warning finger.

"I didn't say anything," Kristin said in exasperation.

"And I won't ask," Lucas said with a laugh. "May I run with you for a bit? I'm not done with my workout just yet either."

"No, you may not," said Callie. The fairy turned to Kristin. "And you need to head back. We've come too far already."

"Then I shall accompany you a little way. Since I am headed in that direction."

She didn't really have a choice. She had to return that way, unless she transported, and she really didn't trust her ability to do that. The last thing she needed was to end up somewhere far from the protection of Zack's house. But if Dimitri was watching . . . "Let's go."

Callie waved her arms in protest.

"But you'll have to leave me before we reach the end of the beach."

"Very sensible," Lucas said.

Callie glowered at her but acquiesced.

The fog gave an eerie glow to the beach, and when they came upon the few souls and surfers who braved the weather, they made wide arcs around them. With Lucas's keen vision, this never proved difficult.

"My house is nearly finished," Lucas said as they jogged along.

"That's terrific news. When do you move in?" Kristin asked between breaths.

"Next week. I would like to show it to you."

"I don't know. Right now—"

"I mean after all the danger has passed."

Kristin glanced at him. The jogging hardly seemed to affect him. She was beginning to fight for every breath. "That sounds good."

Callie zipped in front of her. "You're beginning to sound like an asthmatic seal."

"Thanks, Callie." Kristin glared at her.

Lucas looked as if he could run another five miles without effort. Kristin had definitely reached her three-mile limit. Grateful that Lucas no longer attempted to talk, she focused on her stride. Boy, one week of not running was killer on the stamina. All the magic workouts in the world couldn't keep her in shape like a few miles on the sand. Different muscles entirely. So did this new lifestyle mean that she'd have to exercise as well as practice? Great. Twice the workouts.

With those pleasant thoughts on her mind, she puffed her way back toward Zack's house. Lucas kept pace easily at her side. He wasn't even breathing through his mouth.

A few minutes later Callie zipped in front of them. "Okay, that's far enough."

Yes, Kristin's mind rejoiced. She drew in an uneven breath and bent at the waist, clutching her sides.

Lucas smiled. "Now I *can* leave you with an easy mind. You've proven yourself an excellent guard, Calliope."

"Thank you, but flattery won't get you past me either."

He laughed. "Delightful." He took Kristin's hand in his and pressed another kiss on it. "I am so relieved to have seen you. Please let me know if you need anything."

"Okay," Kristin said, struggling to stand upright.

"I shall call your cell."

"Do that," she panted.

"Good-bye, then. Calliope, it was a pleasure to meet you." Lucas jogged off in the opposite direction and disappeared into the fog.

Callie looked at Kristin. "You sure you can make it back?"

"Ha-ha. Come on." Kristin jogged forward, albeit at a slower pace.

Callie flew beside her. "So that's Lucas."

"Uh-huh." Now was not the time for a conversation.

"Does Tennyson like him?"

"Nope."

"Can't blame him. For an old guy, Lucas is hot."

"I got the feeling you didn't like him."

"I don't, but that doesn't mean I can't appreciate his form. And he likes you."

Kristin stopped and drew her hands down her face. "I don't need a replay. I know all this."

"He's smooth. Suave."

"Who?"

"Lucas."

"I suppose." Kristin started running again, hoping her action would hide how poorly she lied.

Callie was laughing when she flew in front of Kristin. "You suppose. He *is* smooth. And you know it."

"Okay, so I know it." Why had she ever thought Callie was amusing?

"And you enjoy it."

She stopped. "I'm flattered that a suave European gentleman finds me attractive. Who wouldn't be? It doesn't mean I'm going to date him."

"Right. Because you have Tennyson."

"Tennyson? I most certainly do not have Tennyson."

"So you do feel something for Mr. Suave."

"No, I . . ." She didn't. She felt nothing for Lucas. Whereas Tennyson made her heart race and her blood sing.

Oh God, where did that thought come from?

Callie's mouth dropped open. "What aren't you telling me?"

"Lucas has a creepy butler. Come on; I need a shower."

Kristin ran the last few yards and reached the steps that led to the street. The fog was still thick. It wouldn't burn off until midmorning.

Callie flew beside her, then stopped. Whirling around in the air, Callie peered into the fog.

"What do you see?" asked Kristin.

Callie didn't answer for a moment. "I thought I

sensed . . . I must have imagined it. There's no one there."

They climbed up to the street. A moment later Tennyson burst out of the house.

"What the hell were you thinking?" He grabbed Kristin by the shoulders. "Do you know what kind of risk you're taking?"

Her teeth nearly clattered as he shook her. Tennyson had no trace of the debonair about him. Lucas had been concerned, but *he* hadn't resorted to rattling her eyes out. Those wayward thoughts on the beach must have been the lack of oxygen. Tennyson could still be a troll.

"Quit shaking me." Kristin stepped out of his grasp. "You really are the most annoying man."

"Annoying? Me?" Tennyson stared at her. "I'm not the one who took off in the middle of the night, alone—"

"I wasn't alone."

Tennyson stilled. "What?"

"Callie came with me."

Callie darted forward and waved.

"Oh." The lines eased from his face only to reappear a moment later. "Why didn't you tell me? I was worried."

"I had to get out, and you were still sleeping." Kristin wiped her forehead. "Can I go inside now? I need a shower."

"I'm coming back later," Callie said. "This afternoon. Remember?" She jerked her head in the direction of the house.

"Make it after five," Kristin said. "Some of us do have work."

"What work do you have to do?" asked Tennyson.

"I have to quit my job for one." Kristin stepped to the front door. "See you later, Callie. Thanks for the help."

"My pleasure." The pixie flew away.

"You could apologize." Tennyson held the door open.

"To whom?" Kristin walked past him into the foyer.

"Me." He frowned at her.

"You're just upset because I wasn't being as stupid as you first thought, and you have no reason to yell at me." She started up the stairs.

"Oh, please. You left without telling anyone where you were going. You didn't even leave a note." He dogged her every step.

She whirled on the landing and found herself eye to eye with him. "I didn't think I needed to ask permission when I wanted to take a jog."

A furrow formed between his brows. "You don't. But there are a lot of people in this house who care about you." His voice was soft, but not tender. In fact, it held more steel than if he had yelled.

She opened her mouth but held back the angry words. He was right. She had acted without thinking of anyone's feelings but her own. Her irritation dissipated. "You're right. I should've left a note."

The furrow between his brows deepened. "You are the most exasperating woman. How can you switch gears like that? I'm not done being mad."

She smiled. "That's why you love me."

Wrong thing to say. Her eyes grew wide in horror. All the feelings she had struggled with on the beach came flooding back, and her cheeks blazed. Why had she said that? Oh God, and now he was looking at her with the oddest expression. And his lips were right there, right at her level. She could just lean forward and—

"Just kidding," she said hurriedly. "I'm gonna take that shower now." She spun and ran up the stairs to the bedroom they still shared.

She sprinted to the bathroom, locked the door, and turned on the faucet. What had possessed her to say such a thing? She didn't believe in subconscious Freudian slips.

Then again, a week ago she hadn't believed in magic.

When had she lost control of her life?

She peeled off her clothes, stepped under the water, and nearly screamed. The water wasn't warm yet.

The cold stream quickly turned warm and she thrust her face under the drops. The words hadn't meant anything. They were just an expression. She was making too big a deal out of her slip. Tennyson had probably already forgotten it. Just because she had wanted to kiss him . . .

And so much more.

Suddenly her nerves flared to life. Her skin tingled under the shower. She tilted her head back and let the water cascade through her hair.

She was in so much trouble.

WHEN KRISTIN APPEARED in the kitchen an hour later, she was calm, clean, and clearly in the wrong dimension. The room bustled with noise and activity. Mrs. Pendelton and Rose pored over a spiral notebook with handwritten recipes, their voices raised in debate about the merits of walnuts over pecans and whether cranberries or blueberries made the better muffin. Jake stood on his chair taking bites of both kinds of muffin and passing judgment with great oratorical style. Lily had cornered Tennyson, and if Kristin had to guess from his furtive glances at her, they were talking about her. Hyacinth had the newspaper open and her face buried in the front pages with the other sections on her lap, and Zack wore a suit.

"A suit?" The words were out of Kristin's mouth before she could stop them.

"Yeah. I have a meeting with a real square client, but don't worry." Zack lifted up a drawstring sack emblazoned with the Z-foam logo. "I've my shorts and flip-flops right here."

"Good. I'd hate to think you're becoming part of the establishment." She grabbed a cup of coffee and before she realized what she was doing she took a sip. Her face crinkled. "Why do I keep trying this stuff?" She dumped more than a dollop of cream into the liquid, then added four teaspoons of sugar.

Zack drew his lips back. "Ewww. How can you drink it like that?"

Tennyson spoke from the corner. "She also likes chocolate chip cookies without the chips."

"How did you know?" asked Kristin.

"Now, that's just gross." Zack exaggerated a shudder. "I take back everything good I ever said about you."

"How did you know about the chocolate chip cookies?" asked Kristin again, glaring at Tennyson.

"I found some at the cottage," he said.

"And I told him," said Rose with a smile. "That's the kind of thing a man should know about a woman."

Kristin's jaw dropped. Mortification burned through

her. Please. The last thing Kristin needed now was a matchmaking aunt. "I don't . . . I'm not . . ."

Tennyson grinned.

"Well, I'm off," said Zack. "Mrs. Pendelton, don't get any ideas about making cookies without chocolate chips." Zack turned to Jake. "Come here, spud."

Jake jumped off the chair and into his father's arms.

"I almost flew that time," Jake said.

"I think you're getting better," said Zack with a nod. "See you all later." He brushed a kiss on the top of Jake's head, placed the boy onto the floor, and left the kitchen.

"I should be off too," said Rose. "Who knows when the Council will see me?" She reached for her wand.

"Not here," said Lily. She ticked her head toward Mrs. Pendelton.

Luckily, Mrs. Pendelton had her head bent over a recipe that Rose had written out for her. In a lowered voice, Rose said, "I almost forgot."

"I'll go with you. I want to see if any rumors are flying around." Lily linked arms with Rose and they left the kitchen together.

"Jake, it is time for you to dress," said Mrs. Pendelton. "Maybe later we can convince Mr. Ritter to take you to the park."

"Can you?" Jake's eyes pleaded with Tennyson.

He ruffled the boy's hair. "Only if you change out of your pajamas."

"Yippee." Jake galloped out of the kitchen.

"But later," Tennyson called after him. He turned to Kristin. "We have to get some practice in."

For having a child? Oh God, she was doing it again. He meant magical practice. That's what they had planned for today. "I'm ready." If she could concentrate.

Suddenly a tremendous roar rumbled through the house. Mrs. Pendelton grabbed the edge of the counter. "*Dear heavens.* An earthquake."

17

HOW TO BE A FAIRY GODMOTHER:

•

Always Consider the Consequences of Your Actions.

But it wasn't an earthquake. The floor remained still, but the roar grew.

Tennyson's eyes widened and he glanced at Kristin. In tacit agreement, they ran to the front door. By the time he stepped onto the stoop, car alarms were sounding. About one hundred yards away, cars tilted toward an indentation that had formed in the street. The road cracked and sank a few more feet, revealing the dirt beneath the asphalt. A hole opened up and started to swallow the street. A car toppled into the crevice.

"Oh my God." Kristin peered over his shoulder. "She's found us." Kristin shivered, and his body absorbed the tremor.

"The house is protected." But his words rang hollow. Cold seeped into his gut despite Kristin's presence beside him. Danger had found them, and now it threatened more than just the two of them.

Kristin started forward, but his arm shot across her middle, holding her back. "Stay here where it's safe."

He watched as neighbors clustered on the edges of their lawns and gaped at the growing chasm. The sinkhole's maw spread, eating another car and taking a bite of the sidewalk. One woman scurried into her house and returned a moment later with a purse and baby slung over one arm. The other arm hooked around a protesting toddler. The woman's action spurred the others into motion. Their faces masks of horror and disbelief, people up and down the street gathered children and pets and fled their houses.

The monster in the road yawned again and consumed another car. Pipes and culverts reached to the sky as if pleading for help.

"What should we do?" Kristin's eyes glittered with fear.

"I don't know what we can do." His insides coiled in frustration, and he clenched his fists. "The house should be safe with the protections."

"Oh no." Kristin pointed to the edge of the sinkhole. "Look."

A puppy scurried along the brink. None of the fleeing residents noticed the dog, and none, in their hurry, seemed to care. The little creature barked futilely and then whimpered at the encroaching monster.

The road gave an ominous crack.

Kristin jumped over the front steps and sprinted for the spot.

"No, Kristin. Wait!" He puffed out his exasperation.

"We can use magic," he said under his breath. *If I have the chance to concentrate.* He jumped after her.

The hole stretched closer now. As if taunting him, it swallowed a fire hydrant. Water shot into the air, sending a barrier between him and her.

Tennyson ran into the artificial rain. Water dripped into his eyes from his hair. He swiped at them, giving his sight a momentary clarity. "Kristin, stop!"

The first, distant siren wails hit his ears. Help was coming, but would it come in time to save her? Through the undulating curtain of water, he spied her beside the sinkhole. The puppy teetered on the cracking asphalt, yapping incessantly.

"Kristin!" He couldn't run through the shower. A huge chasm opened in front of him.

She scooped up the puppy and sprang back just as the ground crumpled away.

"Run, Kristin!"

The road ruptured beneath his feet. He leapt to the side, but the street continued to crackle. A fissure opened and furrowed toward him. He dodged it, but it drove him away from her. Damn it. He had lost her in the chaos. Where was she? Had she fallen?

The fissure devoured the purchase under his right foot. He jumped back and ran up the street. The crack followed him and forced him back into the cascading water. He pulled out his wand, but the water blinded him. He couldn't see her. Frustration and fear reached panic levels in him. His job was to protect her and he couldn't do that if he couldn't see her. His wand slipped in his palm. Clasping it tighter, he wiped the drops from his brow, but it didn't help. He couldn't clear his vision. The water forced him to retreat farther.

Looking like a lightning bolt, a jagged slash in the earth snaked toward him. His heel caught on something. Another crack had formed behind him. The asphalt pushed upward, leaving the surface of the street looking like a volcanic field. More and more fractures opened around him. The street crackled.

He closed his eyes and concentrated.

"Tennyson!"

For an instant he opened his eyes. Kristin ran toward him. His concentration faltered.

"Get out of here!" he shouted. The ground crumbled beneath him, and then she vanished from his view.

Watching in horror, Kristin screamed as Tennyson disappeared. The puppy squirmed in her left arm, but she ignored its scratching claws and sharp little teeth. The street still buckled and cracked. She couldn't get closer to the hole that had swallowed Tennyson.

She searched the opening, trying to find him. Tears filled her eyes. Where was he? Was he hurt? She had to get to him.

On the opposite side of the sinkhole, the first fire trucks had arrived. The fire department was directing people away from the scene and preventing the curious from coming closer.

"Lady, move away from the hole," a voice boomed over a loudspeaker.

"Tennyson . . . my . . ." God, she didn't even have a word to call him. "My friend has fallen in there." She pointed to the crevice.

"Back up, miss. We'll get him."

"No, you'll be too late." How could she save him? Helplessness raged through her.

A moment of clarity descended over her. She wasn't

helpless. She was an idiot! She reached into her pocket for her wand.

A hand grabbed her wrist, preventing movement. "No magic."

She whirled around. Tennyson stood right behind her. He released her arm. "Too big a chance of exposure."

"Tennyson!" She threw her free arm around his neck and pulled him to her. The puppy wriggled between them. "How did you . . . I thought . . ." Her voice hitched on a sob. "I thought . . ."

The puppy sank its sharp little fangs into her finger. "Ouch."

"Here, give me that thing." Tennyson took the puppy from her, then squinted his eyes at it. The puppy squirmed harder. "Kristin, get back."

"What?" Kristin looked at him in confusion.

The puppy was struggling in Tennyson's arms. Its coat was changing from a soft black fur into a muddy gray hide. Tennyson dropped the thing. Kristin bit back a scream as wings erupted from its back and its tail became elongated, with a sharp point at the end. Its fur had entirely disappeared now. It was covered in a dull gray leather-like skin. Its eyes were huge, black, and bulging. Tiny horns had sprouted from its forehead. The creature was two feet tall and stood on its back legs. It grinned hideously up at her for an instant, then disappeared in a puff of black smoke.

"What was that?" asked Kristin in horror.

"An imp."

"That thing bit me."

"Don't worry; it's not poisonous." Tennyson grabbed her arm. "It just likes to create trouble. Let's move back." He led her away from the hole.

"An imp?" The tears she had been fighting flowed freely now. Her emotions overwhelmed her. That thing had disgusted and frightened her. Her heart still raced and adrenaline buzzed through her.

But there was more. When she believed Tennyson had fallen, she had felt devastation and intense loss, emotions she shouldn't be feeling after knowing him for one week. Girls like her didn't fall in love in a week. They weighed options, measured someone for suitability, used their hearts *and* their heads. Love was not an option. She didn't need another complication in her life right now. She wouldn't and couldn't be in love with Tennyson. She was just happy that he was safe.

Good she focused on that. The important thing was that Tennyson was safe. He was safe and standing beside her. "How did you get out of the sinkhole? I saw you disappear."

"Exactly. I disappeared. As the street crumbled, I transported away. The timing made you think I fell."

Despite the relief, the joy, and the fear, she felt stupid. Of course he used magic. She had forgotten. "Well, don't ever do that to me again."

"Me? I didn't do anything. You're the one that darted into danger. I aged a century because of you." He raked his hand through his still wet hair.

"But I had to save the puppy . . . that thing." Anger at herself for being so gullible mixed with the other emotions.

"And we could've used magic to do that," he said with a scowl. "It was a lure. To get you to come out. Whoever did this would've known you wouldn't think to use magic."

Now she really felt stupid. Avoiding his scrutiny, she

looked out over the destruction. The hole had stopped growing. It was massive. She reached out with her senses. The footprint diminished even as she searched for it. But something was wrong with the whole scene. Something about the spread of the hole as it had cracked open.

Tennyson frowned. He pointed at the hole. "This was weak, ineffective."

"Weak? Look at the damage." She waved her hand over the damage. "It'll cost the city thousands to repair the street. Not to mention the money people will need to replace their cars and property."

He shook his head. "But as an attack, it wasn't well thought out."

"It almost got you."

"I know, but that doesn't matter. I am irrelevant."

"No, you're not."

"That's not what I mean. Right now, you're important. Not only are you the next godmother, you're a Rare One. But you were never in danger. Not really." He wrinkled his forehead as if confused. "It's almost as if Elenka wanted to frighten you, not hurt you."

She did a good job. I thought I'd lost you. Suddenly Kristin's thoughts gelled, and she knew what had troubled her about the scene. "This wasn't an attack on me. It was something else."

"You mean besides a magical sinkhole meant to swallow us?"

"Very amusing." She wanted to shake him. "It wasn't here for me."

"Right. Someone else decided to open a sinkhole on this street by coincidence." His features eased into a look of compassion. "It's hard to accept someone wants to hurt you. I understand that, but I don't believe in coincidences. At least not of this size."

"No. That's not what I mean."

Tennyson looked at her. "Then what are you talking about?"

She puffed her breath out in exasperation. "The sinkhole was an attack, but I wasn't its intended victim. You were."

His jaw dropped and his eyebrows arched in disbelief. "That's ridiculous."

"No, I saw it. The street cracked toward you, around you. It looked like the filaments of a spiderweb trapping its victim." She stared at him intently, willing him to believe.

He looked back at the hole. "But why would someone want to kill me? It makes no sense."

"Yes, it does." She drew in a deep breath. "Think about it. When the cottage burned down? The lightning struck the back of the house. *Your* bedroom."

He stilled. "Why would *I* be the target?"

"I don't know."

A firefighter strode toward them. "Hey. Move back. You can't stay here."

"We're going." Tennyson took her by the elbow and led her back to Zack's house, leaning toward her as they walked. "The other attacks make sense. Elenka hated Aldous and your aunts for what they did to her. But I haven't done anything. I wasn't even alive when she was banished."

"But you found the *Lagabóc*. You're important to the magical world."

"Not that important. I'm not the only scholar with access to the *Lagabóc*."

She tsked her disbelief. "What are you working on now?"

"Nothing. I had to put everything aside when I became your arbiter."

"Oh." She felt a little deflated. Maybe she was wrong. . . .

"Unless they wanted to get to you through me." His voice was hesitant, but his scowl was fierce. "If you didn't have an arbiter, you'd be pretty vulnerable."

Finally. He was beginning to believe her. "They want you out of the way."

"It's possible. . . ." Tennyson reached for the front door, only to have it snatched open before he could touch the knob.

Mrs. Pendelton's worried face greeted them. "Mr. Tennyson, are you safe?"

"We're fine."

Jake jumped off the sofa. "Mrs. Pendelton wouldn't let me watch." He frowned.

Aunt Hyacinth's face was grim. She stepped away from the window and gave Kristin a fervent embrace.

For the first time since Kristin met her, Mrs. Pendelton looked rattled. She clasped a hand to her chest. "I was so frightened. The street cracked, and that awful hole opened up."

"We were careful. I wouldn't let Kristin take chances with her life," Tennyson said.

"You'd better not," Hyacinth said, still glowering.

Kristin knew her aunt well enough to understand that Hyacinth wasn't truly angry. Her fright caused her to bristle so.

"I thought I saw you fall, Mr. Ritter." Mrs. Pendelton shuddered. "But I must have been mistaken."

Luckily the house was far enough away from the sinkhole that Mrs. Pendelton couldn't have had a good vantage point. Kristin shook her head. "It was chaos out there."

A knock at the front door stopped the conversation. Mrs. Pendelton answered it. A policeman stood on the stoop. "Good morning. I'm afraid I have to ask you to evacuate. Until the city can assess the danger, we're asking everyone to leave."

"Yes, of course," Mrs. Pendelton said. The unflappable woman had returned. "How much time do we have?"

"Ten minutes. We aren't sure the gas lines are safe."

"I understand," Mrs. Pendelton said. "I shall call Mr. Glass."

"I'll call Zack," said Tennyson. "You pack for Jake and yourself."

"Thank you," Mrs. Pendelton said. "Jake, come along. I need your help."

They disappeared up the stairs. Tennyson turned to Kristin. "Can you handle the packing?"

"Yeah. We don't have much, remember?"

Hyacinth took out her wand. "Go pack. I'll find Rose and Lily. Call me when you know where you're going." She stepped outside the door and vanished.

"Where did she go?" asked Kristin.

"She transported," Tennyson said. "Probably to the Council chambers to find the others. You could take a cue from your aunt. It can't hurt to practice." He turned from Kristin and grabbed the phone.

"Easy for you to say," Kristin muttered beneath her breath as she climbed to their room.

She entered the room and stared at the mess awaiting her. When had she become so slovenly? She grabbed a draw-string duffel bag that Zack had given them and started to stuff everything on the floor into the bag. A moment later she stopped. She'd never get it all packed in time. Maybe . . .

She took out her wand, and its handle warmed her hand. "Come on; we can do this."

As if in response, the wand twitched in her palm. She took it as a sign of encouragement. She drew in a deep breath, closed her eyes, and concentrated. *"Vení."*

The wand grew hot in her hand. Power rose within her and channeled down her arm into the wand. A coil of air swirled through the room and up her body. She opened her eyes to peek. A few articles of clothing rose gently and floated to her.

"Yes." She pumped her arm. In the next moment, however, clothing flew at her from all directions. Shirts, sweats, shorts, and pants struck her in the face and torso as she twisted from side to side to avoid the deluge of clothes. The clothing flight subsided a moment later with a final slap from a sock. In her mind she could hear Tennyson telling her to focus. No celebrating until the task was done. At least it hadn't hurt.

She opened the duffel and shoved everything inside. In little time the sack was filled. She drew the string and tossed it to the side. Only the toiletries and a few other miscellaneous things remained. Those she threw into a backpack. Done.

"You ready?" Tennyson appeared in the doorway.

"Yup." She grabbed the stuff sack, hoisted it over her shoulder, and slung the backpack over her arm. "No, wait. Callie's coming back here later. How do I—?"

"I'll take care of it." He took out his wand and

tapped a piece of paper. The sheet glowed for a moment, then returned to normal.

"What was that?"

"A note. Callie will find it when she comes back. Or rather it will find her." Tennyson took the duffel from Kristin and walked toward the front door. "She really should get a cell."

"But Callie doesn't like—"

"Yeah, yeah. Sprites can be stubborn."

SEVERAL HOURS LATER, after Kristin had stopped at her office and handed in her resignation, much to the astonishment and over the protest of her boss, their private war council sat in a corner of La Valencia Hotel's comfortable lounge. Kristin sat on a yellow armchair and eyed her allies. They were only three at the moment. Fortunately, the lounge was sparsely occupied. As she shielded him from view, Tennyson cast a muffle spell to hide their conversation from any curious Groundlings, as well as a repellent to keep them away. Except Zack.

Zack pressed his palm against the picture window as he watched Jake playing on the lawn. Mrs. Pendelton stood at the edge of the grass, watching Jake. A scowl marred his usually jovial expression.

Tennyson had a like frown on his face. He stood behind her chair and stared at Zack.

Kristin took inventory of her own expression and discovered she had the third frown in the room.

Zack turned to Tennyson. "I didn't think I could be chased from my home."

Tennyson's scowl deepened. "I know. I can't tell you how sorry I am."

Zack raised his eyebrows. "You think I'm angry with you?"

"Well, yes. I put you and Jake in danger."

"To hell with that. I'm pissed that there's someone out there trying to hurt you. Yeah, I'm pissed that the slime pulled this stunt near my kid, but, dude, you could've died."

A shudder ran through Kristin. She had not forgotten her earlier fear. Tennyson placed his hand on her shoulder.

"You don't blame us?" asked Tennyson.

"No. I just wish I had the magic to put a whammy on this guy. So how do we get him?"

"Her. She's a woman, actually," Tennyson said. "We have a theory, and we're waiting for the aunts to confirm our suspicions. Then we'll come up with a plan."

As if on cue, Lily, Rose, and Hyacinth entered the lounge. The three women scanned the room and spotted them. But their expressions held little optimism.

"We heard what happened." Rose hurried to Kristin and hugged her.

"Important thing is that you're all safe," said Lily.

Tennyson gave his attention to the ladies. "What did you learn?"

Lily faced him with a grim expression. "Elenka is dead."

Tennyson's eyes widened. "But how . . . what . . . ?"

"She died ten years ago, fifty years after we placed her in the cavern. The Council didn't publicize the death because they were afraid her name might stir up the malcontents." Lily paused. "She hasn't been the cause of the attacks."

"Then who?" Tennyson raked his hand through his hair.

"She had a child." Lily's words brought a silence into the air.

"How is that possible?" asked Tennyson.

All gazes turned to him.

Zack said, "Well, you see, when a man and a woman—"

Tennyson drew his hand down his face. "Very funny. I meant how is it possible that Elenka had a child while imprisoned?"

Lily sighed. "Elenka was always charismatic. She was able to seduce one of her guards. It seems her plan was to get the man to fall for her and then help her escape. It worked to a degree. The sorcerer fell for her, but the other guards learned of their liaison and reported the traitor. But Elenka was already pregnant. She had a child. A boy."

Kristin was stunned. "What happened to the baby?"

"From what the Council told us, Elenka raised him until he was around seven or eight, then the Council sent him to school. In Switzerland. They were afraid of her influence on him." Lily clicked her tongue. "The poor thing."

"Looks to me like they were too late," Hyacinth said.

"I'm afraid she's right, Lily," Rose said, nodding. "The boy would've already been influenced by her."

"But the Council claims that they were supervised . . . ," Lily said.

"You can't supervise one hundred percent of the time. And they probably underestimated the bond between mother and child." Rose's sweet tone gave her stone-cold pronouncement a bitter irony.

"Where is this son now?" Tennyson asked.

"Nobody knows." Lily clasped her hands. "I hate to think Elenka's poison has passed into the next generation."

With a glower on his face, Tennyson started pacing. Kristin could almost hear him thinking, rearranging his thinking to accommodate the new information.

"It still fits." Kristin stood and drew everyone's attention to herself. "If her son is carrying on her legacy, he'd want revenge. Aldous's death, the attack on the aunts, the attacks on Tennyson."

"What attacks on Tennyson?" Hyacinth asked.

"There were no attacks on me," Kristin said. "He's not after me. Not yet anyway."

Tennyson stood beside her. "Kristin thinks that I'm the target."

She faced him. "You're my arbiter. You're here to guide me into the next stage of my life. He needs to get rid of you to get to me."

"What do you mean?" Hyacinth asked.

"I'm a Rare One. Apparently that means I have great powers."

Aunt Rose nodded. "And you do, dear."

"I don't know anything about the Arcani world. At least I didn't until a few days ago. I wouldn't know about Elenka, the Great Uprising, or any Arcani history. I wouldn't have a clue who the bad guys were or even if someone was lying to me about everything."

Tennyson looked offended.

Kristin touched his cheek. "Let's face it. I've had to take a lot on trust these days, and I can only hope I've chosen the right side to believe."

"Very sensible," Lily said.

Tennyson opened his mouth, but Kristin shook her head. "For what it's worth, I believe I've chosen the right side."

Tennyson still didn't look very happy with her.

Kristin continued. "So, if you wanted to take over the world, wouldn't you try to recruit someone like me to help you?"

"That is so devious," Zack said. "But brilliant."

18

HOW TO BE A FAIRY GODMOTHER:

•

Don't Be Distracted by Flash.

IN KRISTIN'S HEAD thoughts whirled. She was trying to make sense and organize everything she'd learned. The number of new people in her life was few: Dimitri, Lucas, Zack, and Callie. And Tennyson. In the name of fairness, she had to include him. "The sorcerer who was the father, who was he?"

"Ivan Dimitrov. His family was displaced during the Russian Revolution," Rose said. "But they had resettled in France and were by all accounts happy there."

Kristin lifted her gaze to Tennyson and exchanged a knowing look. He was thinking of Dimitri. As was she.

"So who is this son?" Zack asked.

Lily's brows knitted together. "The boy was named after his father."

Not such a far stretch from Ivan Dimitrov to Dimitri.

"The Council has lost track of him," Lily said. "He was a good student and graduated from a top academy at the Council's expense, but they don't know where he is now."

"Kristin and I have an idea, but we need to know more about a magical named Dimitri, who works for a sorcerer named Lucas Reynard," Tennyson said.

"I'll see what we can find out," said Hyacinth. "We'll set our feelers out for him."

"Yes," Rose chimed in. "Oh, this is so exciting."

"Rose, please," Lily said with a frown. "This man is dangerous."

"Yes, yes, of course. I didn't mean it as it sounded." Rose looked properly chastised. "I just meant it's good to be doing something."

"Something constructive," added Zack.

Rose smiled at him gratefully.

"Then let's get started." Hyacinth stood.

"Good idea," Lily said. "We're off."

"You're not staying here?" asked Kristin.

"No, love," Rose said. "A big group is harder to hide."

"But we'll be in touch." Hyacinth shook her cell phone. "You gotta love these things."

The three women left the lounge and stepped into the stairwell. A moment later, Kristin felt the tingle of magic from there.

"They've disappeared, haven't they? That is too cool," Zack said with a sigh. "What's next?"

"Time to get us settled in." Tennyson looked around and quickly removed the spells on the lounge.

"Great. We'll have dinner, and—"

"Zack, we're not staying here either," Tennyson said.

Zack looked surprised. Kristin *felt* surprised. She had no idea they weren't staying at the hotel.

Zack frowned. "But you can't exclude me, dude. That's

bogus. You let me in on this big secret, then cut me out? That's just not right."

Tennyson held up his hand. "Kristin and I need to go to a safe place."

"Where?" Zack asked.

Tennyson hesitated. "I'd rather not say."

Hurt sprang into Zack's eyes.

Tennyson clapped Zack on the back. "It's not that I don't trust you, but whoever is after us found us at your place. This time I'm not telling anyone."

Not even me. Kristin was annoyed. She was about to confront him when Callie appeared in the lounge.

Ethereal and willowy, Callie wore a gauzy green dress belted with a loose chain. Two thin braids formed a sort of crown around the rest of her hair, which flowed down her back. And shoes. Okay, the shoes could barely be called shoes, but they were on her feet—strips of leather with laces that crisscrossed up her legs.

Zack's jaw dropped.

Smiling at Zack's reaction, Kristin crossed to the sprite. As Kristin hugged Callie, she whispered, "You got the note."

"Yes. What's going on?"

"I'll tell you later. But now it's time to meet Zack. You look great."

"Do you really think so?" Callie whispered back. She glanced at Zack, who was still staring at her. "Really?"

Kristin had never heard uncertainty in Callie's voice before. "Are you kidding? He can't take his eyes off you." Kristin took her by the hand and led her to the others. "Callie, I'd like to introduce you to Zack Glass."

"How do you do?" Callie's voice glided through the room like audible brandy—smooth, rich, and warm.

Zack didn't exactly blush, but his face glowed. His gaze had cemented itself on Callie, his expression lightened, and an appreciative tilt curved his lips. He took her hand and shook it. " 'Pleased to meet you' doesn't come close to expressing what I'm feeling now."

Callie giggled. Giggled? Kristin shook her head. This Callie was unsure of herself, shy, almost demure, not the outspoken, brash, mischievous sprite Kristin had become friends with.

Zack leaned toward Tennyson. "Is she a . . . you know?" He winked outrageously at Tennyson and cocked his head toward Callie. "One of you?"

"Zack, anyone can hear us now," Tennyson whispered.

"I am a sprite, a fairy," said Callie in the same low tone as Tennyson.

"Wicked." Zack bobbed his head.

"No, I'm not. I help animals and plants." Callie looked confused.

"No, no. I meant that's wicked cool," Zack hurried to reassure her. "It's an expression and a good thing."

Callie smiled. "Oh, I see. You like magic?" Callie asked. Hope glittered in her voice.

"Yeah," Zack said.

"You don't mind that I'm a sprite?"

"Why would I?" Zack shrugged. "I think it's monster cool."

Jake ran into the lounge. "I'm hungry, Dad."

"And you're interrupting, little dude."

"Sorry, big dude." Jake stepped back and looked up at Tennyson. "My bad, Uncle Tennis."

"And the ladies," prompted Zack.

"Please forgive my rude and unacceptable disruption," said Jake and gave a little bow.

Kristin laughed at the boy's clearly memorized speech. He had his father's charm, that's for sure. She crouched down and said, "Jake, I'd like you to meet a friend of mine. This is Callie."

As Jake looked up at Callie, his eyes widened. "Whoa. You look just like the fairy I caught the other day. Only big."

Zack looked at Callie, then at Jake, then at Callie again. Callie drew her mouth into a halfhearted smile, shrugged, and nodded.

"Sweet," said Zack.

Callie's smile slid into a pleasure-filled grin.

"I have got to learn more about you. Will you have dinner with us?" Zack asked.

"I'd love to," Callie said.

"Filthy," Zack said with a wide grin.

Callie's brow furrowed.

Jake tugged on her hand. "Surf speak. It means outstanding or great."

"Oh. I guess I'll be learning a new language." Callie winked at Jake, who giggled.

Zack turned to Jake. "Where's Mrs. Pendelton?"

Jake pointed toward the front of the hotel. "She's waiting for us outside."

"Always one step ahead of me," Zack said. "Shall we?"

But Callie didn't answer. She was staring at the entrance to the lounge.

Kristin followed Callie's gaze. Lucas stood in the archway. His clothing was as impeccable as always, but he seemed paler than usual. Shadows under his eyes made him look tired. His shoulders drooped slightly.

"Kristin?" he said with a look of surprise. "What a wonderful treat. Did you come looking for me?" He came forward and took her hands.

Dimitri stood in the arch, wearing the ever-present non-revealing sunglasses. She stared at him and realized Tennyson was doing the same. But had he realized the same thing she had?

The son of Elenka would never hide himself in a menial or subservient role.

In that instant, Kristin had a flash of insight. It wasn't magical—Tennyson had told her magic did not extend to mind-reading abilities—but she *knew*.

Lucas Reynard.

His soft French accent. His age. His demeanor. His desire to ingratiate himself to her.

For someone who claimed he had feelings for her, his reaction to the danger she faced was wrong. He was too calm. Tennyson always lost his temper or yelled at her. Lucas seemed to know she was safe.

She had seen Lucas just before the lightning strike and right after. And she had seen him this morning, just before the sinkhole opened up.

He was Elenka's son.

Kristin felt stupid. Why hadn't she seen it before? Okay, she couldn't explain the name discrepancy, but she knew she was right. He always showed up at odd moments, times that couldn't quite be explained by coincidence.

She clamped her teeth together and steeled her expression.

"Kristin, is something wrong? You seem disturbed." Lucas scrutinized her face. "Has something happened?"

Oh, he was good. But she couldn't reveal her theory here. Who knew how Lucas would react? She had to play along until she could tell Tennyson.

And what would Tennyson think of her latest wild idea?

"There was a sinkhole, Reynard," Tennyson said, his gaze on Dimitri. "Another attack. We had to evacuate."

Lucas drew his brows together. "Kristin, why did you not call me?" Lucas eyed Tennyson with concern. "I trust no one was hurt."

Concern, ha! Disappointment more like. Kristin shook herself mentally. She couldn't keep reading things into Lucas's demeanor. She'd give her suspicions away.

"We're all fine," Tennyson said as he moved beside Kristin.

"And your friends?" Lucas indicated Zack, Callie, and Jake.

"We're all safe," Kristin said, believing she could trust her voice. "But we couldn't stay at the house."

Lucas nodded. "Thus your presence at the hotel." He stepped to Zack and held out his hand. "Lucas Reynard."

"Zack Glass. And this little spud is my son, Jake."

"Hi," said Jake. "Dad, can I go outside?"

"Go. Find Mrs. Pendelton. I'll be there soon," Zack said. Jake dashed from the room.

"Ah, the exuberance of youth." Lucas chuckled.

Kristin bristled at the performance. In every way Lucas was acting like a well-bred gentleman. Why hadn't she seen through his pretense sooner?

"And the delightful Miss Calliope." Lucas lifted Callie's hand to his lips. "You look charming full-size."

"I looked charming before, Mr. Reynard." Callie's brows had slight furrows. She let her hand drop to her side and with a subtle motion wiped the back of her hand on her skirt.

"Please call me Lucas. In fact, all this formality is troublesome." With a serious expression, he focused on Zack. "You were helping Kristin. I wish to thank you, Mr. Glass. I shall invite you to my house next week. I move in on the weekend and I'd love to celebrate the housewarming with you. All of you." He swept his arms wide.

"How kind of you." Kristin smiled because she knew they would never make it to the housewarming. Not after she spoke with Tennyson.

"Excellent. Then I shall be in touch." Lucas returned to Kristin. "Are you staying here?"

Tennyson took another step closer to her. "No, but you can leave a message at the desk. I'll get it."

"At the desk?" Lucas looked surprised. "Why can't I just send a—"

"You won't find us. No one will."

"Still in hiding?" Lucas nodded. "Good. I'm happy to see you aren't taking risks with Kristin's life. She's too important to us now."

"Now?" she asked.

"At the Time of Transition. I heard about the accident at sea. Any word on your aunts?" Lucas asked.

"No." Kristin was aware of Tennyson's questioning look, but she ignored him. "I've been worried."

"I can imagine." Lucas clicked his tongue. "You have so much to shoulder right now. Perhaps it is lucky you are a Rare One. Your powers can help you in these difficult times."

If I only knew exactly what I can do, she thought in frustration. What use was it to be a Rare One with great powers if she didn't know just what her powers consisted of?

"Of course your last attempt to hide didn't succeed. Perhaps I can help you this time," said Lucas.

"Don't worry, Reynard. I know my job." Tennyson stepped even closer to her.

Lucas laughed. "It was just an offer, my friend. I wouldn't dream of overstepping your bounds." He bowed to the occupants of the room. "Until next week then. I shall be in touch."

"Can't wait," said Tennyson in a particularly unenthusiastic tone.

Lucas bent over Kristin's hand and lowered his voice. "And as always it was a particular pleasure seeing you again." He pressed a kiss on her hand.

She struggled to prevent a shudder and forced a smile to her lips. "I look forward to our next meeting." *When I can expose you.*

"Au revoir, *mes amis*." With a wave, Lucas left the room. Dimitri followed him.

"That is one smooth dude," said Zack. "And I think he has a thing for Kristin."

Darkening storm clouds filled Tennyson's gaze. "I . . . don't like that guy."

"Really? We couldn't tell from your expression," Kristin said, but a rill of excitement danced up her spine. Maybe his feelings ran deeper for her than she thought.

"You seem to eat it up, that whole Mr. Continental bit." Tennyson crossed his arms over his chest.

He was acting like a troll again, but this time she enjoyed it. Not that she'd let him off the hook. "Manners are never misplaced."

"Manners?" Tennyson's eyebrows arched high. "If you call acting like some fop from the nineteenth century—"

"I think we'll go to dinner now," said Zack, watching their exchange with a grin. "Will we see you later?"

Tennyson shook his head. "No. Kristin and I have to get settled, and you have a date, remember?"

"Most definitely." Zack glanced at Callie and a light glowed in his eyes. "See you dudes later." He took Callie's hand and led her from the room. Callie turned at the doorway and winked at Kristin.

Tennyson drew in a deep breath as if he were trying to control his temper, then he turned to face her. "Do you mind telling me why you lied?"

"Not at all. In fact, I had planned on telling you."

"Before or after Reynard charmed you?"

She exhaled exasperatedly. "He didn't charm me."

"Right." Tennyson's voice took on a falsetto. "I'm looking forward to our next meeting, Lucas, when you can kiss my hand again."

She stared at him open-mouthed.

"The guy doesn't know how to kiss a woman. That wasn't a kiss. This is a kiss."

Before she could breathe, Tennyson pulled her into his arms and planted his lips on hers. For an instant she straightened, and his embrace tightened around her, molding her to him. Her surprise dissipated and she gave herself over to the exhilarating sensations. The sweet, heady manna of his touch brought her renewed energy and a desire for more of his nourishment. She angled herself to feel more, touch more, taste more.

His tongue searched her mouth until it met hers, and

she nearly buckled to the ground. A deep, primal moan of satisfaction started low in her gut as heat built up at her core and spread through her. Liquid pleasure pooled between her legs as his hand buried into her hair.

"Ah-hem."

A nearby clearing of a throat—loudly—broke through the haze of her entrancement. She stepped back. A dignified concierge regarded them calmly with an unperturbed expression.

"Pardon me, madam, sir. Perhaps you would be more comfortable in private?"

Flame rushed into Kristin's cheeks as she realized that the concierge wasn't the only witness to her and Tennyson's kiss. Several other onlookers with amused expressions watched them, as well as one older woman with a pinched look on her face. Clearly *she* didn't approve of such behavior in public.

"Thanks, uh . . . Tomás," Tennyson said, reading the man's badge. Mortification was an unknown emotion for Tennyson if his smile was any indication of his feelings. "We're leaving."

"Thank you, sir."

Tennyson took her hand and led her from the lounge. Her face still blazed, but she felt like giggling. The whole episode seemed surreal. Tennyson had acted jealous. Jealous of Lucas.

She sobered. For a moment she had forgotten her suspicion about Lucas. Cold rushed through her, destroying all the delicious verve she had felt moments ago. "Tennyson. It's not Dimitri."

He shook his head. "Not here. We need more privacy." He led her through the lobby and pulled her into the stairwell. "Hang on to me."

"What?"

"Don't let go." He grabbed her around the waist.

Instinctively she threw her arms around his neck just as the world tilted and her breath squeezed out of her. Darkness enveloped her. She scrunched her eyes shut, but before nerves could overtake her, she touched solid ground again. She blinked.

She stood on a cliff overlooking the Pacific Ocean. The breeze played with her hair, and she smelled pines. Tennyson released her waist, and she turned around. Scrub and chaparral covered the area, but many twisted Torrey pines grew around them. Canyons unfurled from the edge of the cliff, exposing its red clay to the sky. The ground was dusty, littered with the detritus of many seasons.

Tennyson opened his arms wide. "You can't get more private than this."

19

HOW TO BE A FAIRY GODMOTHER:

•

Discomfort Is Sometimes Necessary to Achieve One's Goals.

TENNYSON WATCHED AS first confusion, then amusement played in Kristin's expression.

"Well, I'll grant you the privacy thing." She picked up a pebble and started rolling it between her fingers and tossing it from hand to hand.

He climbed up and sat on the top of a picnic table. "So now tell me. What did you mean by 'it's not Dimitri'?"

"He's a servant. He's not important enough." She paused. "But Lucas is."

Tennyson's breath rushed out of him as if he'd been punched in the solar plexus. "Lucas?"

"It fits. His age, his accent, his interest in me." She started pacing. "It's hard to explain, but I know I'm right."

"I didn't say I didn't believe you." Tennyson followed her with his gaze. "In fact, I want it to be him. I don't like the guy."

A ghost of a smile bent her lips.

"Is that why you didn't tell him the aunts are safe?"

"If he's the one, if he tried to kill them . . ." She pinched the bridge of her nose. "I don't usually go by instinct. Hell, I don't act like this. I need proof, facts, figures. Things need to add up. And I believe they do."

"Add it up for me."

"He's French." She held up one finger.

"Yes."

A second finger joined the first. "He's the right age, I think. I don't really know how old he is."

Tennyson chuckled. "He is."

Third finger. "I spoke to him just before every attack."

"What of the earthquake at the academy and the shipwreck?"

"He's a sorcerer. He told me himself that his magic works with the earth." She raised a fourth finger.

Of all the things she could have said, this one struck Tennyson most deeply. Lucas was a sorcerer. He drew his power from nature and the earth. She had convinced Tennyson even if the proof was flimsy.

"He's trying to worm his way into my life, and supposedly I have these great powers. He's here, where my aunts live, and they put Elenka away."

"So did Aldous." Tennyson wanted her to fight for her argument. He might believe her, but they had no proof, no real evidence. "What of his name? Elenka's child was named Ivan Dimitrov, not Lucas Reynard."

"What if he took on a new name? What if he decided Ivan was too well known? What if he didn't like the name?" She paced the site. Agitation rolled off her and a glow of light encircled her head. She could be dangerous if her magic took control. The stone she had picked up now did loops and spirals as she tossed it from hand to hand, but she seemed not to notice. "I can't explain the name yet, but if he wants to take power, he'd want some stealth, at least at the beginning. Changing his name would make him more difficult to trace.

"And a couple of times when I was with him, weird things happened. When he was disappointed. I didn't think about them at the time, but now . . ." Her aura glowed brighter.

Tennyson put up his hands. "Maybe you should sit—"

She went on as if she hadn't heard him. "I know, I know. It sounds ludicrous, but it makes sense. At least to me."

As she tossed the stone one last time, the pebble flew into the air, looped twice, then burst into a mini-firework of brilliant green color. Her eyebrows shot up. "Did I do that?"

He nodded. "Must've had copper in it."

She stopped. "You think I'm crazy."

He climbed from the tabletop and grasped her shoulders. "If you are, then I am too, because I believe you. Not just because I want Lucas to be the bad guy, but because I think you're right."

Her eyes widened.

"But I think we've had enough excitement for today. We're safe here. And we need to set up camp."

He swished his wand and a cooler appeared by the table. Next to a blackened fire pit, a stack of wood piled up, and a crate of supplies materialized at the end of the table. A small dome tent righted itself, swaying slightly in the soft wind.

She stared at the tent, then at Tennyson. "You have got to be kidding me." Horror and disbelief exploded on Kristin's face.

He was tempted to laugh. "What? It's safe, remote, and no one will think to look for us here."

"No kidding. I don't camp." Kristin fisted her hands and placed them on her hips.

"You'll love it." Tennyson moved to a pile of wood and tossed some logs into the fire pit. With a flick of his wand, flames licked the wood. "It'll take a while to burn down, but it's worth it. Food tastes great cooked in the open air." He pulled out a folding grill and placed it over the flames.

She looked out over the cliffs again, examined the trees and plants, and frowned. "Wait a minute. This is Torrey Pines State Park, isn't it?" Kristin's gaze narrowed at him.

"Yes."

"There's no camping here. You can't ask me to break the law." Her voice held a note of triumph.

"No camping for Groundlings, you mean." Tennyson walked to the cooler and retrieved several bags of vegetables and a cutting board. He placed them on the picnic table. "We've got our own rules here."

"Since when?"

"Since we protect this spot." He grabbed a grilling basket from the milk crate of supplies.

"Protect?"

"Why do you think this last stand of Torrey pines exists on the mainland? We saved this bunch two hundred years ago." He grabbed a knife from the crate too. "So we have a few campsites hidden in the reserve. Magic protects the sites from detection, and magic protects the woods from our campfires or any other harm."

"Terrific," she said in a tone that indicated it was anything but. She kicked a rock.

"It's not so bad," he said, placing a zucchini on the cutting board. "We're having steak and roasted vegetables tonight."

"Argh!" she cried. "I don't care about dinner. I can't do this. Where's the bathroom? Where's my bed? Where do you expect me to shower?"

"No worries. I think you'll look cute all rumpled from camping." He swung the knife so it sliced through the squash, lopping off the round end.

She just glared at him.

"I'm kidding. The bathroom and showers are just up that path." He pointed at a dirt trail with the tip of the knife. "And your bed is in there." He pointed at the tent, then returned to the chopping. He hoped he had repressed his grin, but really she would look cute climbing out of a sleeping bag in the morning. Even cuter if she was climbing out of his.

That thought sent an electric jolt right through him.

She eyed the tent warily. "Please tell me it's a magical tent. You know, bigger on the inside than the outside."

"I keep telling you Harry Potter is mostly fiction." He shook his head. "Don't worry. We'll be cozy and comfortable."

"Only if there's a pillow-top mattress in there," she muttered under her breath.

An image of her stretched out on said mattress, on top of silk sheets, her hair fanned out around her, a look in her eyes that had nothing to do with hunger for food, filled his head. He swallowed hard. *Don't think about it,* he warned himself. *Banish the thought. Concentrate on something else. Like dinner.* He waved at the cutting board and the fire. "We have some great food coming, and we need a break. How about we just enjoy this evening and start worrying again in the morning?"

A reluctant smile curved her lips. "Sounds great." Then she whacked him in the shoulder. "But it's still camping."

THE FIRST HINT of dawn brightened the inside of the tent. Tennyson squeezed his eyes shut tighter. He wasn't ready to face the day. Despite the pad beneath him, a rock had stubbornly poked him in the side all night long no matter where he turned. Of course he wasn't ready to concede the comfort question to Kristin yet. After their dinner, which had been delicious, a dessert of s'mores, and a round of storytelling, they had climbed into the tent and settled in for the night. Although the thought of holding her all night had stayed with him, he believed he might be pushing his luck trying to be amorous in a tent. But he hadn't heard a peep out of Kristin all night. She must have found a nice sandy spot to sleep on.

The dawn refused to go away. The light inside the tent grew brighter and he knew he was fighting a losing battle to stay asleep, or rather return to sleep. He suppressed a groan as he rolled onto his back and stretched. That pesky rock dug into his hip. Unzipping the sleeping bag, he threw back the cover, grateful that they weren't in the mountains so he didn't have to fear the cold. Boxers had served as pajamas enough.

"Good—" He froze. She wasn't there. Her sleeping bag, rumpled and mussed, was empty of a body.

Kristin.

He rolled to his knees and darted for the door. He unzipped it only as much as he needed to crawl out, then dove through the opening.

Sitting on the picnic table, Kristin eyed him with some amusement. "Do you always leave a tent like that?"

"Always. It's much more efficient." He stood, dusted himself off, and scowled at her. "How long have you been up?"

"I don't know. An hour, I guess." She twirled her wand in her fingers.

"Why didn't you wake me?"

"I wasn't going anywhere." She pointed the wand at the cooler and squinted slightly. The lid rose and a small plastic bottle of orange juice floated to her.

Tennyson raised an eyebrow. "That was pretty smooth. You didn't even have to use words."

"It's not enough." She unscrewed the lid on the OJ and took a swig.

"A week ago you couldn't even do this."

"A week ago I wasn't facing some bad guy." She slammed the plastic container on the table beside her, ignoring the juice that sloshed over the side. Her gaze pierced him. "We can't keep hiding. If we're facing a threat, we need to act, not run away."

He shook his head. "You're not ready yet."

"Then you need to teach me to use my magic."

He shook his head. "I can't do that. My job is—"

"To hell with your job. You're supposed to judge if I can handle being a fairy godmother. Well, I can. But now I need to know how to protect my aunts, my friends, and—" She broke off and glanced at him. Color glowed on her cheeks.

"Yourself?" He climbed onto the table beside her and took her hand. "Our tradition is clear on the matter of godmothers. They need to ease into their powers so the Magic doesn't overwhelm them. Even Merlin wrote as much in the *Lagabóc*."

"But I'm a Rare One. Most other godmothers had the advantage of an Arcani upbringing. They at least understand how magic is supposed to work. I don't know anything."

"Which is why you especially need the time."

She snatched her hand from his. "I don't have the time."

She was right about that. He couldn't imagine the turmoil within her. That strong desire to protect her rose in him again. "I don't know that I can teach you."

"Of course you can. You just don't know if you want to. You aren't sure you want to break the rules."

He raised his brows. "And you do?"

"Yes. For once in my life. I want to break the rules." Tears filled her eyes. She cradled his cheek. "I have to. The rules are putting people I love in danger."

For a moment he saw something in her eyes that filled him with hope. Did she count him among those she loved?

But a moment later she drew back. "If you won't help me, I'll find someone who will."

Tennyson studied her. She wasn't smiling. In fact, her green eyes blazed with fierce determination mirrored in the heightened color of her cheeks. A soft breeze lifted her auburn hair from her face. She looked like a warrior princess girding for battle, strategizing her victory.

"Boudicca," he whispered in admiration.

"What?" She sent him a quizzical look.

"Nothing." He nodded and took her hand again. "When I said I can't teach you, I didn't mean I wouldn't. I meant I don't need to. The Magic. It's already inside of you. You just have to discover it. But for what it's worth, I'm in."

She threw her arms around him. "Thanks."

"Thanks nothing. Just remember how you're feeling now when we're called up in front of the Council." He nudged her shoulder. "Okay, show me what you can do."

She hesitated, then tilted her head. Biting back a smile, she said, "Maybe you should, uh, change your attire first."

He looked down. Perhaps boxers weren't the best things to wear for performing magic. "I'll be right back."

A few minutes later, they stood side by side overlooking a sharp canyon that cut into the cliff. The other side of the canyon wasn't more than thirty feet away, but the floor of the gorge lay seventy feet below them.

"How would you get to the other side?" he asked.

Her forehead wrinkled. "I could turn myself into a sprite and fly."

"You could. But what if you didn't have the time? Transformations happen faster as you have more experience with them, but remember how long it took you last time? And they hurt. There's a faster way. Think."

She pursed her mouth as if she were biting back a retort. Only her eyes betrayed her impatience.

"If I tell you, you won't learn as fast."

"I know. Doesn't mean I have to like it," she said. She stared at the other side. Suddenly her expression cleared. "The way we popped here. From the hotel."

He smiled. "Go on."

"But I tried it once and ended up lost." She pointed to the opposite cliff and looked at the bottom of the sharp canyon. "Are you out of your mind?"

"It helps if you have more at stake."

"What if I miss?"

"Don't." He turned her head, so she gazed at the flat spot a mere thirty feet in front of her. He didn't feel as flippant as he sounded. His heart pounded as she focused on where she wanted to be. If she missed, came up short, he'd have to be ready with his wand to keep her from plummeting to the bottom of the gorge. A trickle of sweat rolled down his neck. He gripped the handle.

For a moment nothing happened. Then she shimmered at his side and vanished. A moment later she re-formed on the cliff opposite him.

"I did it!" she shouted, waving her hands and jumping up and down.

He let out his breath as relief gushed through him. And a little pride at her accomplishment. His hold relaxed on his wand. "You did. Now come back."

She tugged on her lower lip with her teeth but focused. She shimmered out of view again and reappeared about five feet from him. She panted as if she had just finished a sprint. "Whoo-hoo!"

"Good work. With practice, you can go wherever you want, even if you've never been there before. You can focus on someone's face and go to them."

She stilled. "Then why can't Lucas find us here? Why can't he focus on me and get here?"

Tennyson shook his head. "Because I placed a shield on you after your date. No one can follow you without your permission. You haven't given Lucas your permission, have you?" He smiled.

"I didn't even know I had a shield." She huffed out a breath of air.

"Don't worry about Lucas here. I also cast a blocking spell. No one can find us here, not even those who have my access spell. This area is protected. That's why camping is called getting away from it all."

"A spa would be getting away from it all." But her retort was tempered with the look of exultation still on her face. In the next moment, she grew sober. "Then how did Lucas find me on the beach?"

Good question. Tennyson drew his brows together. "I am such an idiot." He laid his left hand on her chest and his right on her head.

"Hey." She tried to pull back, but he pressed down on her head.

"Stand still. I have to read you." He sent his energy into her searching for a mark, a sign that Lucas had attached a find spell to her. Nothing. If it was here it would have to be small and attached to something elemental, since Lucas was a sorcerer. Wait, there. In her femur. Never underestimate the importance of calcium. He closed his eyes and said, "*Remové*." He felt the spell detach from her and dissipate.

She shuddered. "What was that about?"

"Lucas placed a locator spell on you. He could find you any time he wanted. Unless you were in a protected location. So when you left Zack's house and went jogging on the beach, he found you." Remembering her inadvertent disclosure of their hiding place still sent a chill through Tennyson. He should have told her more. Maybe she was right about her education.

"What's to prevent him from doing it again?"

"He only got away with it because you didn't have the knowledge. Parents can place locator spells on children, but by the time they're teenagers, they can remove them."

She frowned. "If I was protected by the spells over Zack's house, then how did my aunts find me?"

"Godmother magic. According to the *Lagabóc*, godmothers have a bond with one another. Since they help each other so often, they can tap into special magic."

"So no one can find me if I don't want them to. For the most part."

"There's still scrying, but that's hardly reliable, and there's always this." He pulled out his cell phone.

She chuckled. "Ah, the bane of man's existence. I suppose shielding should be the next spell I learn."

"Small steps, grasshopper." He watched as her face took on the expected expression of irritation edged with impatience. "You can't do it all in one day."

"I know, but it's frustrating." She straightened up and clapped her hands together. "Let's do this again."

He glanced to the other side of the gorge. "Okay, one last time. I don't want you to use up all your energy."

"No problem. I'm in great shape."

No kidding. Her jogging pants molded against her ass in beautifully rounded curves. He swallowed hard and closed his eyes for an instant to banish the image. Composed again, he nodded. "Go ahead."

She focused on the spot and this time disappeared with less shimmering. She waved from the opposite side. "Ha. I'm good."

"Now come back."

She reappeared a moment later. Her shoulders heaved with every breath.

"You okay?"

"Yeah. Just winded." She clasped her side.

"Now you know why we don't do this several times in a row. And it's harder the farther you go."

"Got it." She nodded.

"But you still might be attacked when you're winded. You need a good spell that delivers a hard blow. One that's easier on the energy."

She nodded. "Don't worry about that one."

"Are you kidding? That's the one you'll probably need most."

"I've got it."

He stared at her. "How could you have one? You've never needed to use one yet."

She shot him an impatient glance. "Nevertheless, that one I know."

His impatience matched hers. "You aren't taking this seriously. If you're attacked—"

Kristin straightened and pointed her wand at a rock. "Troll," she said.

The rock flew into the air and a moment later disintegrated into a fine powder. Tennyson stared at the spot. No trace of the stone remained except a fine dusting of dirt on the ground.

"How did you . . . ? Never mind." He examined her. A smug smile lit on her lips. "Wait a minute. You use the word 'troll' for that spell?"

"Uh-huh."

"You used to call me troll."

"Coincidence." She walked toward the campsite. "I need some water. How about you?"

20

HOW TO BE A FAIRY GODMOTHER:

Don't Forget to Take Care of Yourself.

THREE DAYS OF camping had left Kristin physically and mentally beat. Camping itself was bad enough, but she could no longer deny her deepening feelings for Tennyson. In the close shared quarters, she had spent the night hours observing him. His even breathing in sleep fascinated her. His tranquil expression drew her gaze. Hell, counting his heartbeat proved more enticing than sleep. She felt like an idiot. A sapheaded, giddy-schoolgirl, rose-colored-glasses idiot.

They had spent the daylight hours practicing magic. They laughed together at her mistakes and celebrated her successes. But it wasn't all fun. In the past three days, Tennyson had drilled her in rudimentary magic until she didn't want to see her wand anymore.

Her wand poked her from her pocket.

"I didn't mean it," she said in a weary voice. Her wand wasn't alive exactly, but it seemed to read her thoughts. When her magic wasn't working, it lay cold and stiff in her hands, but when things were going right, it seemed supple and warm and a graceful extension of her body. And at times, like now, it reminded her of the burden she had inherited.

No, not a burden. She loved magic, and she loved being a part of this new world. But now the threat of danger scared her.

Sinking onto the bench of the picnic table, she dropped her head into her hands. She was tired. Tired of practicing, tired of eating outdoors despite Tennyson's claims of better flavor, tired of lukewarm showers, and, most of all, tired of the tent. She hated that thing. Not enough room to really stretch out, or get dressed in or relax in. She glared at the small nylon dome that stood to the side of the campsite. A moment later a glow flared from within the tent.

She drew in a deep breath. "Control." She exhaled. "Control."

The glow vanished. Another crisis averted.

With a towel slung around his neck, Tennyson appeared on the path. His long legs extended from his shorts, and his T-shirt melded to his body, rippling with his muscles. His hair was damp, but already an unruly wave was asserting its dominance. Her fingers itched to run through his dark locks.

He rubbed his head with the towel, leaving his hair tousled. "I thought you were practicing."

"I was." She reached behind her and pulled out a stone shaped exactly like a bird. "I finished."

He whistled softly. "Brilliant. A bird. They're hard. They move too quickly to pin down easily. You've got more ability than I gave you credit for. Next time I'll give you something really tough. Like a mosquito." He touched the rock with his wand, and the stone transformed into a sparrow that flitted away. "Good work."

"Yeah, but I almost burned down the tent." She sighed.

He glanced at the dome, then nodded. "The key word is 'almost.' Only you are in command of your power." He tucked his knuckle under her chin and tilted her face until she looked directly at him. "You look sad."

"What use is turning a mosquito into stone? I'm useless." Her frustration made the words crackle.

"You're exhausted. You've done more work in three days than most wizards do in three months." He climbed behind her and sat on the tabletop. His fingers splayed out over her shoulders and started to knead.

"Ummmm." All she could do was moan with relief. She wanted to melt into him, let his fingers and thumbs dissolve her until nothing remained but a puddle.

"I think you need a break. No more work today, okay?"

"Okay." She answered so quickly, he chuckled.

"What would you like to do?"

"Nothing. No, wait. More of what you're doing now." Her head dropped forward as his touch outlined her spine with a deep, firm stroke.

He laughed again. "The shower was rejuvenating. Why don't you try one?"

"Is the water hot?"

"Not exactly."

"I'll pass."

"You really hate camping."

"I've never camped before, and while I can understand how some people might enjoy the outdoors, it's not for me." She sighed again as his fingers hit a mass of nerves. "Maybe if I had gone as a young child . . ."

"Right, because you're so ancient now." He kissed the top of her head and jumped down from the table. "Do you think you're up to doing a little research on our friend?"

"As long as I don't have to use magic." She rolled her shoulders and stood up. The brief massage had helped. "Let me put on something besides these sweats, and I'll be ready to go."

Ten minutes later, her hair pulled back in a ponytail, she zipped up the entrance to the tent and stood in Capris and a soft cami. An unbuttoned blouse billowed in the ocean breeze.

"Well, you can try, but you still don't look like a CPA." Tennyson took her hand. His hair had dried, and its unruly waves still tempted her.

"That's okay. You don't look like a historian." She smiled into his copper gaze. "Where to first?"

"I thought we'd check in with your aunts to see what they've discovered. I've already called them."

"Sounds good."

"Okay, hang on." He tightened his grip on her hand. "This time we travel on me."

The now-familiar shimmer that accompanied transport enveloped her, but she felt none of the energy drain. Her breath squeezed out of her, a brief weightlessness, and in the next instant solid ground supported her again. She looked around. They were in some sort of closet.

"Lovely place. Let's book our next vacation here too." She drew her mouth to the side.

"Oh, ye of little faith." He opened the door, and they stepped out.

Colorful buildings, like something out of a storybook, surrounded her. A huge merry-go-round, a storybook castle, and flying elephants filled her vision. Beyond the castle, the Matterhorn.

"Disneyland?" Disbelief filled her. "You zapped us into *Disneyland*? I love Disneyland, but you can't just magic us into the park—"

"Magical entrance. Just wait a moment." He was breathing deeply but still didn't appear as winded as she did traveling over much shorter distances. And alone.

Sure enough, a park attendant dressed in a dirndl and sporting a happy smile and a nametag that displayed the name Brandi walked to them. "Welcome to the Magic Kingdom. To whom shall I charge this visit?"

"Tennyson Ritter." He cocked an eyebrow at Kristin as if to say, "I told you so."

Brandi took out a clipboard. "Two?"

Kristin stared. Where had Brandi been holding that clipboard?

"Yes, thank you."

"No. Thank *you*, Mr. Ritter." She gave them two tickets. "Enjoy your stay with us." Brandi waved and turned from them.

Tennyson pushed the tickets into his pocket. "See. We don't break the rules."

"Wait a minute. Are you saying she was Arcani?" Kristin watched as Brandi walked into the closet.

"Of course. I told you we have jobs everywhere. We couldn't just let Arcani go wherever they pleased without paying. That wouldn't be fair."

That explained the clipboard.

"Your aunts should be around here somewhere." Tennyson scanned the crowd. "And there they are."

The three women were exiting Peter Pan's Flight.

Lily saw them first. "Kristin. Tennyson. What a wonderful surprise. I'm so happy you could join us." She kissed Kristin on the cheek.

"Disneyland?" said Kristin, still dumbfounded.

"We love this place," said Rose. "Look around."

Kristin did and noticed all the children, some crying, some dragging their feet, but most smiling and laughing with excitement sparkling in their eyes. Their parents too held their hands and pushed strollers, and carried balloons and ice cream and toys. She concentrated harder. Hundreds of tiny golden crowns appeared over the heads of the children and a fair number of the adults as well, but when she tried to focus on the wishes, she wasn't able to hear them.

"See, they think they have something to wish for, but those wishes vanish with every new view." Lily smiled. "Here we don't have to fulfill wishes, because the park does it for us. We just enjoy watching the happy children—"

"—and adults," broke in Rose.

"And adults," said Lily with a nod, "who are getting their fantasies fulfilled."

"So it's kind of like a break for you," said Kristin.

"Not to mention how much fun this place is. I love the rides, and now that you guys are here, I have someone to ride Space Mountain with." Hyacinth clapped her hands together. "Let's go."

For the next two hours, they strolled through the park, rode some of the attractions, and just pretended they were normal people. Tennyson held Kristin's hand as they walked; his thumb occasionally brushed over the top of her knuckles. With each stroke, Kristin felt more secure and relaxed. Beside this man she found safety and strength. Even if he had made her go camping.

When they reached the roller coaster, the group stopped. A serious pall settled over them.

Rose sighed. "I suppose we can't just play all day."

"Come on. Get in line with us," said Hyacinth to her two companions. "There's an exit inside so you won't have to ride, but we can talk while we wait."

As the group joined the line, the conversation turned serious. Lily cast a muffle spell over the group. "I'm afraid to say we don't have much information," said Lily.

"We wanted to know if you've discovered anything new about the boy," said Tennyson.

"We tried, but all we found was coincidental." Rose clicked her tongue. "Elenka was very secretive, even after her capture. She kept her pregnancy a secret until after the child was born."

"How is that possible?" asked Kristin.

"Almost anything is possible if you plan it well enough," said Hyacinth. "And Elenka had great organizational skills."

"But the Council did discover his birth. Little Ivan went to school when he was old enough, but as soon as he came of age, he disappeared from the Council's radar."

"What of the father?" asked Tennyson. "What happened to him?"

"The Council reprimanded him, and he lost his position. They couldn't trust him any longer. But Elenka taught him well. He became her liaison to her son. He managed to visit Ivan at school and was able to show his son how to visit his mother." Lily shook her head.

"He died evading the Guards on one of his attempts to visit Ivan. Ivan was only twelve at the time."

"Who are the Guards?" asked Kristin, frustrated by her continuing lack of knowledge.

"They're an elite group who serve as our law enforcement," said Tennyson. "We don't use them often. They're kind of a secretive group." He turned back to Lily. "They had the Guards on Ivan?"

Lily nodded. "The Council knew that Elenka had somehow been keeping in touch with him. They wanted to know how and put a stop to it before she had too much influence over the boy."

The story of Lucas's childhood stirred sympathy in Kristin, but she tamped it down. Lucas was responsible for his own choices.

Rose crinkled her brow. "About that wizard you asked us to find out about, Lucas Reynard? The Council has no records of anyone with that name. They tried to track him down, but they can't find a house, an address, any record of him. And then they accused us of wasting their time."

"Oh, he exists all right," Tennyson muttered.

"Who is he?" asked Lily.

"He's Elenka's son," Kristin said.

"But what of this Dimitri you told us about?" Hyacinth asked.

"Wrong guy. He just works for the bastard," Tennyson said.

"We think he's been using a different name," Kristin said before the aunts could chide Tennyson for his language. "But we still have no proof that Lucas and Ivan are the same person."

"We did find one interesting fact," Lily said. "Apparently Elenka's father was named Lucas." When the others looked at her, she shrugged. "I remember things like that. It's not proof, but . . ." She shrugged.

"Oh my gosh." Rose jerked upright. "Elenka *Liska*." She stared at the others as if willing them the information in her head.

"You'll have to be more specific than that," Hyacinth said.

Rose pointed at them in short staccato movements. " 'Liska' means 'fox' in Czech."

"And 'reynard' means 'fox' in French." Tennyson's voice held an icy note.

"Proof enough for me," said Kristin.

They fell silent as the line moved forward. The exit out of the ride was now at their left. "Somehow I've lost my taste for fun," Rose said.

Fun? Kristin mulled over the information the aunts had shared. They still had no conclusive evidence that Lucas was Ivan, but her instincts told her she was right. If he was gathering Arcani to him . . .

She faced Tennyson. "We need to find out if the Council has heard of any rumblings, any signs of discontent—"

"I thought we were taking a break," Tennyson said, slipping his arm around her.

"I know, but I can't have fun if Lucas is plotting something."

"Neither can I. Let's go—"

"You'll bloody well leave after I've had my ride," Hyacinth said. "I don't get to ride this thing often because those two are chicken."

"I heard that," Rose said with a smile.

"I'm going with Rose," Lily said. "We'll see you

outside and talk about it then." The two women slipped through the turnstile and left the building that housed the indoor roller coaster.

Hyacinth harrumphed. "At least you didn't desert me."

Kristin smiled. "I wouldn't disappoint you for the world." And then she hoped that her words weren't prophetic.

AN HOUR LATER Tennyson and she stood in the lobby of La Valencia Hotel. Tennyson approached the front desk. "Any messages for Tennyson Ritter?"

The clerk tapped on his keyboard and nodded. "You have several. Just a moment." The clerk disappeared for a moment and returned with a collection of envelopes. "Here you are, sir. Is there anything else I can do for you?"

"Yes, can you have room service deliver two lobster dinners to room seven-oh-one? And some mineral water too?"

"Of course, sir. What would you like with your lobster?"

He turned to Kristin. "Baked potato?"

She nodded, sending him a look of confusion. Zack still occupied a suite here because the city had not yet reopened his street, but how was Tennyson ordering room service?

"Yes, sir," the clerk said, tapping on his keyboard.

"With all the fixings," Tennyson said.

"It will be there in half an hour."

"Thank you." Tennyson slipped the clerk a tip, took Kristin's arm, and led her to the elevators.

"Where are we going?" she asked.

"To the room."

"We have a room here?"

"Yes. How else did you expect me to get messages here?" He pressed the button. The doors opened, and he let her enter the elevator first.

Kristin could feel her blood pressure rise. "You mean all this time we were camping, you had a room here?"

"Yup."

The doors closed. Her mouth hung open in disbelief. She had hated the tent. He knew she had. "You forced me to live in that cramped, dirty—"

He placed a finger on her mouth. "I couldn't keep you safe here. The room was a decoy."

"But I—"

"I'm sorry. We needed space to practice and safety. We had neither here." Then he grinned at her. "But since we know who the bad guy is now, I can set up an alarm to warn us if he's coming. We can stay here now."

The elevator dinged as they reached their floor. He let her out first again.

Sliding the key into the slot for the electronic lock, he said, "Why don't you take a bath? A long, hot, luxurious bath?"

"A bath?" The thought of soaking in a tub of hot water took the argument right out of her. He was right, after all. He had kept her safe. And a bath . . . "Show me the way."

Tennyson chuckled. "Right through there. And I have a gift for you." He pulled out a bag decorated with Disney characters.

She crinkled her brow and opened it. Disney Princess Bubble Bath. She laughed. "I'm going to use this, you know."

"That's why I got it."

"Thanks." She closed the door to the bathroom and turned on the faucet.

"I'll let you know when dinner is here," he said through the door.

"Okay." She poured the pink liquid, and the water erupted with fruity-smelling foam. She needed this.

She peeled off her clothes and let them puddle on the ground. She didn't know what she'd change into after, but she couldn't be bothered to pick these up right now. She slid into the hot water and sighed. The bubbles reached her neck as she sank into the bath.

"There's a message here for you," said Tennyson through the door.

"Bring it in."

He walked into the steamy room and stopped short, staring at her. "Damn. I am never buying you bubble bath again."

"Why not?"

"I can't see a thing." A wolf-like grin slipped across his face.

"That's too bad, because I like bubble baths." She lifted a leg and let the bubbles trickle down her calf.

"Now you're just being cruel," he said. "I could just take out my wand and—"

"Don't you dare. I said I like bubble baths." She sat up a little, but not enough to show anything important, and wiped her hands on the towel hanging beside the tub. "Where's that message?"

"Here." He handed her an envelope.

Her name was written in neat, almost calligraphic letters. Curious, she tore open the seal and scanned the signature. "It's from Lucas."

Tennyson scowled. "What does he want?"

She read it quickly. "Dinner with me tomorrow night. At his house."

"Where is his house?"

She reread the note. "It doesn't give the address. He says he'll pick me up at seven o'clock."

"You can't go."

"Why not?"

Tennyson's gaze narrowed. "You can't go out to dinner with him."

"I wouldn't be going out with him; I would just be having dinner. At his house. I can figure out where he lives, and maybe learn even more."

Tennyson shook his head. "It's too dangerous."

"He doesn't know we suspect him."

"I don't know where he lives." Tennyson paced the small room. "I can't rescue you if you need help. He probably has the house cloaked. Even the Council hadn't heard of him or known of any house being built. If something happened to you . . ." His voice broke as if he were choking on something.

She reached out her hand to him. "Nothing will happen to me."

He cleared his throat. "You don't know that."

She sighed. "Are we in agreement that Lucas poses a danger to the Arcani world?"

"Yes."

"Then I have to go. Right now I'm the only one who can get to him."

A knock at the room door interrupted their argument.

"Go get our dinner. I'll be right out." She shooed him from the bathroom.

As soon as he left, she stepped from the tub. The truth was she didn't feel quite as brave as her words. She didn't have the power to face a threat like Lucas alone. Not yet anyway. Three days of practice did not equal a lifetime of magic. But she had a day to plan.

And she was good at planning.

21

HOW TO BE A FAIRY GODMOTHER:

•

Sometimes Truth Can Be a Hindrance.

KRISTIN ADMIRED THE green marble floor that shone under the high chandelier in the entrance.

"What do you think?" asked Lucas. He placed a hand at the small of her back as he guided her through the foyer.

The walls glowed with a reddish hue sponged over a burnt orange base. A sweeping staircase flowed upward to a second story, and a massive domed skylight adorned the ceiling.

"Impressive." Kristin set her lips in a moue of admiration, but inwardly she was frustrated. When Lucas had picked her up, she tried to memorize the street names or at least the directions to the house, but all details slipped away from her and she could remember nothing. Only when she sought a footprint did she realize that magic shielded the house. Lucas didn't trust her. Smart of him. "The color is so vibrant, so unusual."

"Ox blood gives the red its life."

"Actual blood?"

"Yes. The process is more expensive, but well worth the expense." He brushed his hand over the wall. "Quite beautiful."

"Um-hum." The color was beautiful, but she wasn't sure she'd want blood on her walls.

"Not as lovely as you, of course." He lifted her hand and kissed the back of it. "You look delightful."

"Thank you. I went shopping this morning." She smoothed the front of her new black dress.

"I'm honored you would shop for me." Lucas led her into a vast living room where glass made up the west-facing wall.

She reached out with her magic, and a strong tingle of power pushed back at her. She concentrated on her location. Nothing. She couldn't remember whether they drove north, but she assumed they had. Between San Diego and the border, she didn't believe there were any open spots with such a magnificent view of the ocean. And no hills like the one this house perched on.

The sun was setting, and the orange spectrum added even more warmth to the walls. Any minute she expected the walls to start undulating. Like the belly of some beast.

"Champagne?"

His question startled her from her fancies. "Yes, thank you." She walked to the window. The uninterrupted view was dotted with lights of houses below them and between them and the sea. If she could just remember this scene, maybe they could find Lucas again later. "Are we celebrating something?"

"Of course. My house. I am no longer a nomad." He

pressed a flute into her hand and filled it with the golden bubbles of Dom Perignon.

"But this isn't your housewarming," she said, putting a hint of panic into her voice. "I didn't get you anything. You didn't tell me this was your housewarming party. You invited the group of us—"

Lucas chuckled in an amused fashion. "No, no. Your presence is gift enough for me. I wanted you to be the first one here."

"I'm flattered, but I don't know why I deserve this honor."

"You think too little of yourself. I want you to like my home, to feel comfortable in it."

She faced him and placed her hand on his arm. "Lucas, you're reading too much into my visit tonight. I told you I'm not ready for a relationship. My life—"

"Hush." He lifted his hand. "I know that. I just wanted to remind you of what I want when you're ready."

He had charm, she had to give him that. His manner oozed sophistication and maturity. His suavity, his wealth, could easily sweep a weaker woman from her senses. Not her, of course. She let a moment of smugness fill her and allowed herself a genuine smile.

"That's better," he said. "Come. Let me give you a tour of the rest of the house." He took her drink and placed it beside his on the bar counter at the side of the room.

She had never seen such grandeur in a house. The kitchen was vast and cried out for servants to bustle in its depths. The first floor also housed a study attached to a library, a theater, and a gym. Upstairs were four bedrooms, a sitting room, and the most sumptuous bathroom she had ever seen—a sunken tub big enough for two, a two-person whirlpool steam shower, a sauna, and a massage room off the master suite. Of course maybe she was just partial to bathrooms after the camping ordeal of the past week.

At the end of the upstairs corridor, another flight of steps led down. "Where do these go?"

"To the kitchen," Lucas said with a flip of his hand. "This is the servants' staircase. There's no need to see them traipsing through the house."

That made sense in Lucas's world. Although she hadn't noticed any servants on the tour, she realized a house this size must have several. Lucas didn't seem the type to scrub his own floors.

Beside the staircase, painted into an arch was an elaborate trompe l'oeil. "And that painting?" She pointed to the realistic portrayal of steps ascending to a third story. It was expertly done, drawing the vision up the imaginary flight of stairs. The depiction of shadows and light gave it a 3-D effect, and the perspective was deceptively true. Even a basket of brightly colored, painted pillows rested on the third step as if left there to be taken up later.

Lucas smiled. "A touch of whimsy. No house should be without it."

"I think it's charming."

The tour finished in the living room. Lucas retrieved her glass from the bar and returned it to her. "What do you think?"

"It's fabulous. I don't believe I've ever seen anything so beautiful."

"But is it livable as well?"

"Definitely. You'd have to be dead not to appreciate all the amenities."

"Thank you." He bowed his head. "I strove to make it lovely, yet homey. I do plan to settle here. Find a wife. Have children." His gaze landed on her.

She sought escape in her glass. The sip of champagne didn't ease the discomfort she felt. She wasn't meant to be a double agent. Her acting wasn't that good. But she supposed it would have to be to fool Lucas. She strolled the length of the room. "You haven't told me much about your past."

As he settled onto a ruddy brown leather couch, he followed her with his gaze. "There isn't much to say."

"I don't believe that. Where did you learn so much? You seem to know a lot about my role as a godmother."

For a moment he was silent. "My mother was one of the chosen ones, a godmother as you call her."

She let her eyebrows arch as if the information surprised her. "Really. What was her name?"

"It doesn't matter now."

"You sound unhappy."

Watching her intently, he twirled his glass slowly between his fingers. "She gave her life for what she believed in."

Crossing back to him, Kristin placed her hand on his arm. "She sounds noble. Was this in France?"

"It was. I grew up in the mountains. She showed me how to use my sorcerer's powers to touch the earth and her elements before the Council restricted her and sent me away to school." His gaze hardened.

"My parents didn't even know magic existed."

A movement in her peripheral vision caught her attention. In black jeans and turtleneck, Dimitri stood at the entrance to the dining room. "Sir?"

Lucas turned his head. "Yes?"

"Dinner is ready." A slight guttural tone made Kristin think of the steppes of Russia.

"Excellent." Lucas held out his arm to her. "Shall we? Bring your drink. We'll enjoy the rest of the champagne as we eat."

She took his arm. "Dimitri serves you here as well?" she whispered.

"He is a man of many talents, my most loyal assistant. The first of many. He serves me at all times."

There were others? Interesting. "You've known him for a while then."

"Dimitri joined my employ before I moved to the United States." He helped her into her chair. "There are many like him in our world, Arcani looking for a leader, a new order."

"Really? What's wrong with the old order?"

Lucas chuckled. "I always forget how new you are to our ways. You don't know the history or the workings of the Arcani." He settled himself at the table. "Do you realize we are a hidden society? Secretive, as if we had something to hide, something to be ashamed of?"

"I hadn't thought of it that way."

"As you learn, you will see how many of us long for true freedom."

"And they look to you as their leader?"

He bowed his head. "I have that great honor, yes. But I do not claim the ultimate power. There are others who are . . . or will be . . . far more powerful than I." He lifted his glass in her direction.

"I don't know what to say." She pulled her bottom lip between her teeth.

"So humble. Ah, our dinner arrives."

Kristin observed Dimitri as he came forward with

individual bowls of salad. He served her first, then Lucas.

"Thank you, Dimitri," Lucas said.

The man gave a polite bow and disappeared from the room. His behavior was creepy. The man didn't smile or acknowledge her. And the formal behavior appeared almost militaristic to her. Of course it had since she first saw him.

"He isn't very friendly, is he?" Kristin said.

"He isn't paid to be. Besides, he knows you are a Rare One, one deserving of great respect. I wouldn't tolerate any rudeness toward you."

"I hardly think a smile is rude."

"Ah, you are still so innocent. You aren't aware of your status, your importance."

Now she felt uncomfortable. "Come on. I'm just like anyone else."

"But you shouldn't be. You have great power, great gifts. You should be a leader, someone people fear and revere." Lucas pointed at her. "The Council hasn't told you that, have they?"

"No." She pushed the lettuce around with her fork. The thought of so much influence disconcerted her.

"Of course they haven't. They are afraid to give you too much information." Lucas stabbed his salad with his fork. "But you deserve adulation. You are a Rare One. You should be queen."

Oh no. She wouldn't want the life of a queen at all. She took a bite of her salad, hoping that Lucas took her silence as evidence of her mulling over the possibility. She was playing a risky game here.

"You are surprised." Lucas smiled at her. "Did that Tennyson fellow never tell you of your potential?"

"No. He's actually told me very little."

"Then he's a poor arbiter. He should have been guiding you to your greatness, not holding you back." Lucas nodded knowingly. "He has been holding you back, hasn't he?"

A cold shiver snaked up her spine. Tennyson had been helping her, breaking the rules, teaching her the extent of her powers. He hadn't wanted her to come but knew she had to. They had discussed an extensive list of possible outcomes to this evening just to prepare her, prepared responses to possible topics of conversations, worked on ways she could use her magic if she needed to. But Lucas couldn't know that. She closed her eyes. The charade was difficult, but she could handle it. Too much depended on her.

"I see you're distressed. Forgive me, *chérie*. The last thing I want to do is upset you. But I want you to understand that you are special. That you should not be undervalued." He clapped his hands, and Dimitri appeared a moment later. "Take these dishes away and bring the main course."

"Of course, sir." The butler cleared the table.

Kristin took a fortifying sip of the champagne. "This is all so much to take in."

"You need someone you can trust, someone who isn't afraid of your powers. Someone to guide you to the supremacy within you."

"You." She focused her gaze on him.

"That is entirely your decision, but I would be more than willing to serve you, stand by your side as consort." He lifted his glass. "You already know how I feel about you."

"I know."

"Together we could lift the Arcani to their rightful place above the Groundling. We shouldn't have to hide from those weak beings as the Council thinks we should." He spat out the word "Council" as if it were a curse.

Here was the crux. She understood her part in his plans and now needed to find out more. "But what can we two do against the Council? My power can't be that great."

He let out a low chuckle. "There are many who believe as we do."

Dimitri returned with their dinners. Filet mignon, asparagus spears, and new potatoes in a light brown sauce lay on the plates. The food looked delicious, but she had lost her appetite.

"We are not alone," Lucas continued. "Dimitri here is but one of many followers I have gathered. Is that not so, Dimitri?"

"Yes, sir." Dimitri turned to her and bowed. "It would be an honor to serve you as well, Great One."

Great One? That's when she peered behind the austere veneer and saw the thug beneath the polished exterior of the servant. She swallowed the bile that rose in her throat. Dimitri retreated from the room.

"They know of your destiny," Lucas said. "You are young yet, but with the proper support, you can be the mother of a long line of royalty."

She pushed her plate from her.

"You aren't hungry?"

"I don't think I can eat. How many women are offered the world, literally?" She gave a nervous laugh.

"You are overwhelmed. I can understand that. I have given you much to think about."

"I don't know what to say." Her voice was quieter than she expected.

"Say you will take on the mantle that has been offered to you. Say you will join me in the fight for our rightful place, our place in the sun, our place at the control of the world. Say you will accept your destiny."

"I'll need to think about it." She needed to get out of here. Now.

"I understand. I'll have a room made up for you."

Shock jolted through her. "Here?"

"Certainly, *ma chérie*. We can't risk your arbiter learning anything about this. He's part of the group that wants to own you, oppress you, keep you in your place." He clapped his hands. Dimitri responded within a few seconds. "Have the east room made up for Miss Montgomery. And see to it she has someone to help her with anything she may need."

She bit back her panic. Although she and Tennyson had discussed what might happen if her ruse was discovered, this little twist in events wasn't anticipated; her charade was still intact and she wasn't a prisoner, but the principle of captivity remained the same.

Play along, her inner voice said. *Anything to buy you time until you can escape*. "Lucas, I hardly know you. I know it's old-fashioned, but I can't just—"

"Another part of your charm, *chérie*. Separate rooms. We will maintain decorum until we wed," Lucas said. "Although I can't say I'm not eager."

Willing herself to remain calm, she inhaled deeply. "You expect me to stay here?"

His eyes narrowed slightly. He placed his glass on the table and pressed his fingertips together. "Are you unhappy here?"

She grasped at the first ridiculous thought that entered her head. "You haven't even given me a ring."

For a moment he stared at her, and then Lucas threw his head back and laughed. He rose from his seat and walked around the table to her. "Ah, *ma chérie*, you shall have all the jewels of the earth." He kissed the top of her head.

She smiled up at him. "Not that I want you to think I'm greedy or anything."

"Never." He held out his hand. "Come. I find I am too excited to eat."

Placing her hand in his, she followed him into the living room. Darkness had settled over the land, and dots from house lights seemed an inverse of the starry sky. How could such beauty exist in the presence of such wickedness?

"The lights remind me of diamonds," Lucas said. He came up behind her and placed his hands on her shoulders. "The queen of gems for my queen. I shall collect them for your ring."

"Diamonds? Are you sure they suit me?"

"Definitely. Pure, brilliant, and most highly valued." He turned her around. "I shall design a magnificent ring for you." He cupped her chin with his hand and kissed her.

Oh God, oh God, oh God. She didn't want this, she didn't want this, she didn't want this. His kiss left her feeling dirty, and when he reached into her mouth with his tongue, she steeled herself against the utter revulsion that swamped her. No warmth accompanied his touch, and her every instinct told her to push away. But she endured it. He mustn't suspect her, not yet.

He pressed his hips against her, grinding against her

lightly, so she could feel his arousal. He let out a guttural sigh, and then he backed away a few inches. "Ah, my sweet queen. Soon we shall enjoy all the pleasures we must deny ourselves now." His hand dropped from her chin to her collarbone. He slid his hand down to her waist, pausing at the side of her breast. "But for now we should say 'good night' before we go too far to stop."

Not trusting herself to speak, she could only nod.

Lucas stepped away from her. "Dimitri."

The butler appeared in the doorway.

"Were you able to find a suitable chaperone?"

A chaperone? She felt as if she were trapped in a time warp to the past.

"Yes, sir."

"Then show the lady to her room. Make sure she has everything she needs." Lucas turned back to her. "Good night, my queen."

"Good night, Lucas." With a swell of relief, she followed Dimitri up the stairs to the room on the second story.

Airy and bright, the room held a queen-size bed covered in fat pillows and a golden comforter. Surreal. It was the only word for the situation. The contrast between her emotions and the sumptuous lodgings was overpowering. A chaise stretched in front of a large television, and a desk was pushed against a broad window. The view was dark from this vantage. No dots of lights indicated any sign of civilization in this direction. She was trapped in a gilded cage, except . . . perhaps—

The door pushed open and she jumped. A stout, middle-aged woman entered with her arms full of towels. Her graying hair pulled back in a severe bun, she gave a curt nod of her head. "Miss Montgomery, I am Ilse." The long-drawn-out "e" sound of her name indicated another person of foreign birth. "I hope you find everything satisfactory."

"It's lovely."

A grim smile appeared on the woman's face. "I am here to serve you. Would you like a bath?"

Yes, but not here. "No, thank you."

"I took the liberty of acquiring some suitable clothes for you." Transferring the towels to one arm, Ilse pulled open the door of an armoire. A variety of undergarments, shirts, and loungewear greeted Kristin's sight. "You'll find nightgowns in here. Unless you prefer pajamas?"

"No, I like nightgowns." Kristin picked up a slinky, satiny gown. As the material slid through her fingers, it shimmered in the light.

"The closet holds day clothes. The bathroom is through here." Ilse opened the door to a private bath. "You'll find everything you need in there. Please let me know if you have any preferences in shampoo or soap."

"I'm sure it's fine."

Ilse put the towels onto the bars hanging on the bathroom walls, then returned to the bed and pulled back the sheets. "Tomorrow you shall tell me what else you desire. Please forgive me if I've overlooked something."

Kristin shook her head. "Everything looks great."

Ilse gave that curt nod again. "Would you like help undressing?"

"Goodness, no." Kristin's eyes widened.

"A glass of milk or a snack perhaps?"

"No, thank you, Ilse."

"Very well then, I shall be just outside if you need me." Ilse walked to the door, then turned back. "And if I may be so bold, it is a pleasure to serve someone of your stature, Miss Montgomery." Ilse backed out of the room and closed the door.

As she puffed out a long breath, Kristin sank down on the bed. All the attention was almost enough to turn her head. Good thing she didn't believe the hype. All right, she was a Rare One, and supposedly that brought great powers with it, but she made mistakes almost as often as she succeeded.

"Wand," she said aloud as she opened her palm. Her wand appeared in her hand. She still hadn't mastered the knack of calling her wand without the word. She surveyed the room. How was she going to get out of here?

She pressed outward with her magic and discovered the strong answering tingle of power. The house radiated with it.

Pointing the wand at a book, she said, "*Vení*." The book floated easily across the room and landed in her hand. So her magic worked here. But how well?

Lucas couldn't expect her skills to be strong yet. Tennyson had said she was progressing faster than usual, but she was still new to her powers. If the shield around the house worked like the one at the campsite, then she should be able to transport out of here. Trouble was she had never attempted such a large jump before. Nevertheless, it was her only idea. She couldn't stay here. She had to try before Lucas realized she could do more than he believed. He couldn't suspect anything yet, could he? Was the magic on the house capable of holding her here?

"Oh, focus," she told herself. She visualized the room at La Valencia. "I want to go home."

A moment later, the air around her squeezed. Her skin tingled and her breath froze in her chest. Then her vision grew black. She disappeared.

22

HOW TO BE A FAIRY GODMOTHER:

•

Never Forget to Celebrate.

TENNYSON PACED IN the room. It was after midnight. Where was she? She should have been home hours ago. Okay, not hours ago, but she should have been home. How long did a dinner take? He shouldn't have let her go. They knew Lucas couldn't be trusted. Hell, Tennyson hadn't liked the guy even before they decided he was the villain.

Tennyson pulled out a map of San Diego County. Maybe he should scry for her. Scrying was an inexact science at best. It could point out a general area, and a good shield could block even that, but he couldn't do nothing any longer. She had been shielded from him earlier when he tried to find her. What if she was in trouble?

Before he could summon his wand, the doorknob rattled and the door opened. Kristin stumbled into the room. Her dress had fallen off one shoulder, revealing a lacy black strap. With a little cry, she ran to him and threw her arms around his neck.

He engulfed her in his arms as she buried her face into his neck. "What happened? Are you hurt?"

"No," she said, muffled against his neck.

Reluctantly he unhooked his arms from around her. He cupped her face between his hands and looked at her. Tears fell from her eyes, and her face was flushed. "You don't look good."

"Too much magic," she said, and licked her dry lips. "Water."

He sat her on the bed, grabbed a glass, and filled it. "Here."

Swiping the tears from her face, she drank in huge gulps, then held out the glass. "Better. More."

As he hurried to fulfill her request, questions filled his head. What had happened? Why was she so exhausted? What had happened? Oh right, he'd already asked himself that one. He gave her the second glass of water. She downed it almost as fast as the first.

"You need to eat something."

"I don't suppose you could zap me up some homemade chocolate chip cookies without the chips." She waved her hand. "Never mind. We don't have time anyway. We've got to leave."

"What?"

"We can't stay here. If we're lucky, he won't notice I've gone until the morning, but we can't count on it." She stood up from the bed, then nearly lost her balance.

"You're not in any shape to go anywhere. You don't have the strength of a puppy right now."

"That doesn't matter. He knows we're here, so we have to go." She tugged on Tennyson's hand and leaned toward the door. "Nothing's wrong with me a little time won't cure."

"And food." He waved his wand and a plate of sandwiches appeared.

Her expression lit up, and she moaned with hunger. She snatched one and bit into it. Through her chewing she said, "Good. They're mobile. Grab two and let's go."

Shaking his head, he grabbed a couple. "What about our stuff?"

"Leave it. We'll get it some other time." She shoved another bite into her mouth. "Please come on."

"Where to?" He flourished his wand.

"Can we go back to the campsite?"

Now he was worried. She wanted to go camping? "I gave up our site today. Someone else has it."

She dropped into a chair. Her sandwich fell unheeded to the floor. Renewed tears gathered in her eyes. "Then where can we hide?"

He knelt in front of her. "You're really frightened."

Her eyes wide, she made a slight choking sound, then nodded.

Every nerve in his body cried out to ease her fears. He placed his sandwiches onto the bed. "Okay. We'll leave. There are lots of places we can go where he'll never find us." Tennyson took her by the hands and pulled her to her feet. "Are you strong enough?"

"I have to be."

"Then come on." He grabbed one of the sandwiches from the bed, passed it to her, then led her out the door.

"Where are we going?"

"I don't know yet," he said, frantically searching his memory for a safe place. "But we're leaving here."

Even that vague answer brought some relief to her

features. They took the stairs all the way to the garage and jumped into her Camry. He didn't even ask if she wanted to drive. Clearly she wasn't able to. He pulled out of the hotel's garage and followed the ritzy streets lined with name stores out of La Jolla and into San Diego. Now, where to go?

The roads were essentially empty. He drove with no real destination in mind, but if Lucas was scrying for them, moving would throw him off.

Tennyson passed a hotel that was missing letters so it was just an "ote," but its facade spoke of fleas and cockroaches. Not a place to take her after the camping experience. A B and B would be perfect—small, private, and unknown—but what B and B would accept guests after midnight?

Then he knew. He cut across two lanes and made the next on-ramp to the freeway. He glanced at her. Her eyes were closed and her legs were curled up beside her.

"Kristin?" he said loudly.

"Huh?" Her eyes fluttered open, and she stretched out her legs. "Where are we going?"

"My office. The academy is already covered with magic, and unplottable, so Lucas can't find us there."

"But the earthquake . . ." She sat up straighter.

"My building is fine. We might find books on the floor, but my office is safe. There's a couch in there you can sleep on."

"What I really want is a shower. I feel so dirty." She shuddered.

"You want to tell me now what happened?" he asked gently.

She drew in a hitched breath. "His house is cloaked

and there's some kind of confounding spell on visitors. I couldn't—can't—remember how I got there or where it is."

Tennyson nodded. "I have the same protection on my place. It makes sense that Lucas would protect his lair."

"That's what made it so difficult to transport. The first jump landed me in this house in La Jolla." She shook her head and added, "Again," under her breath.

"You transported?" His gaze shot to her. She was strong, but long distance travel would still be hard for her.

"Twice. Once I figured out that I wasn't back at the hotel, I had to transport again." She leaned her head back. "That's why I'm so tired."

"Why do you think Lucas will be looking for you now?"

Her mouth twisted into a moue of disgust. "Wouldn't you hunt down your fiancée?"

"What?" As he whipped his head toward her, the car crossed lanes.

Kristin grabbed the dashboard. "Hey! I didn't escape Lucas only to be killed by you."

Good thing the freeway was practically empty. He righted the car. "Sorry." Red-hot anger sat in a lump in his stomach. "What do you mean his fiancée? You agreed to marry him?"

"In a way." She rubbed her hands over her face. "I didn't know what else to do."

"Really. When's the wedding?" Anger filled his voice. The next exit would take them to the academy. He swung off the freeway and started to make his way into the chaparral-covered hills east of San Diego. He usually enjoyed the drive. Now he could barely concentrate on the road.

Her face scrunched up in a look of complete disbelief, she stared at him. "I'm not going to marry him. Why are you being so obtuse?"

Because he didn't want to think of her and Lucas together. All right, he was being stupid, but he wouldn't tell her that. He inhaled slowly. "Why don't you start at the beginning?"

As she related how Lucas had picked her up, Tennyson pulled off onto the hidden road known only to Arcani. They drove through the shimmering curtain of magic that shielded the academy from Groundling eyes. She told of the immense house Lucas had built and the apparent army of servants or minions that awaited his commands.

"Did you see them?" Tennyson asked quickly.

"No, but Dimitri was there, loyal as ever. And a maid. And Lucas spoke of many disgruntled Arcani who looked to him for leadership." She paused. "And me."

"You?"

She nodded. "He wants me to be his queen."

"Queen?" Tennyson pulled into a parking spot a little more abruptly than necessary. His temper bubbled on a slow boil in his gut. Lucas wanted her for his queen. "That's got to be hard to turn down."

"Not really." She climbed out of the car. "I don't want to be a queen, let alone his."

"Lucky for us then." Sarcasm gave Tennyson's words a sharp edge. He knew he was being an ass, but he couldn't stop himself. He grabbed her upper arm and led her from the car. "All I ever promised you is lots of work."

"Because being queen would be so easy."

"So you considered it."

She pulled her arm from his grip and whirled to face him. Fists on hips, she glared at him. "What is wrong with you?"

"I don't know. Maybe all this talk of royalty has me wondering about you." Even though he knew the words were idiotic, he said them anyway.

"You're insane, you know that?" She stormed away from him, only to stop about twenty feet away. "I don't know where I'm going. Of course, if you're not willing to help me any longer, I'll just get back in the car and find my own hiding spot."

Without a word, he strode past her and headed across the campus without waiting to see if she followed. What had happened to him? What had happened to his logical thought process, his objectivity, his ability to interpret information? Gone, it was all gone. Nothing was left except irrationality.

As they crossed the academy, evidence of the destruction was still apparent. They both maintained their silence when they saw the crumpled building where Aldous had died, when they passed scaffolded structures. Tennyson unlocked the door to a smaller structure that appeared to have been a family dwelling once but now housed history offices. He led her down a hallway and unlocked a second door to an office lined with bookshelves. Most of the books were on the floor, as he had predicted. A large desk occupied the center of the room, and a plump leather couch stood against one wall.

He kicked aside some of the volumes and lifted others to clear a path.

"So this is where you work," she said in a flat tone.

"Not for the past two weeks. I've been busy on another assignment." He gave her a pointed look.

She touched his arm. "Tennyson, I didn't know what else to do. Lucas had it all planned out. He wasn't going to let me go. He assigned a room to me and found me a chaperone without difficulty. A chaperone, can you believe it?" She shook her head. "I don't think he expected me to be able to transport yet."

Vowing to remain calm, Tennyson drew in a deep breath. "Tell me what happened. How did you get engaged?" Just saying the word stirred the embers in his stomach.

"I had to allay his suspicions somehow. And I'm not engaged." Her body quaked, and a look of contempt and revulsion crossed her features.

"What aren't you telling me?" A sharp pain plunged itself in Tennyson's chest. "Did you sleep with him?"

"No!" Her voice crackled with despair. "But he kissed me and . . ." She stopped.

"You kissed him?" Fury flamed now inside.

"No. *He* kissed me, and . . . he showed me . . . how much he wanted me."

An image of Lucas holding her, pressing her against him, grinding himself into her, burned into Tennyson's imagination. He could feel rationality slipping away again. "So, a position of royalty and an offer of sex. Quite an evening."

Her cheeks glowed. "My God. I didn't want to kiss him. I didn't want any part of him. I just thought I should play along."

"It's a good thing he only kissed you then. So glad you could take one for the team."

With a loud cry, she hit Tennyson's chest. "You're hateful. You're beastly, and awful, and horrible." Tears spilled from her eyes. "Right now I despise you." She pounded his chest again.

He caught her wrists in his hands. She didn't cower or back down but stared up at him in anger and defiance despite the rivulets coursing down her cheeks. He wanted to yell at her. He wanted to shake her, drag her to the couch, and put his mark on her. Own her. So that no one else could ever touch her again.

"You're mine. I know that isn't right, or proper, or politically correct, but you're mine. I can't let anyone else have you."

Her eyes widened, but not in fear. Her gaze held only questions. On a note that sounded almost like she was in pain, she swallowed a sob.

Tears welled up in his eyes. "God, Kristin, I can't think about someone else touching you."

She let out a little gasp. "Make me forget. Make me forget Lucas ever touched me."

Tennyson kissed her then, a kiss that assailed her lips because he couldn't be gentle right now. She returned the attack with equal vigor. He released her wrists and molded one palm against her back, the other against her rear. Her hands buried into his hair and gripped tightly. It was as if they couldn't be close enough to each other, as if even the smallest space between them would cause pain.

Her legs wrapped around him as he lifted her. Without breaking the contact of their lips, he carried her to the couch. Kneeling, he placed her on the cushion. Thank God she was wearing a dress. He lifted the hem and slid his hands up her body beneath the material. Her head dropped back.

He slid the dress from her, leaving her clad only in a lacy black bra and panties. And high-heeled shoes. He stood over her. "You are every man's dream." He peeled off his shirt and watched her suck in her breath. She moistened her lips with her tongue. "But my reality."

She reached out for his waistband. "Too far." She pulled.

He forced her back onto the cushions and ran the tip of his tongue over her neck, stopping to taste the small indentation at the base of her throat. A low purr resonated in her chest and reverberated through him.

His hand dipped into the elastic at her waist as his mouth toyed with the tip of her breast through the sheer lace he found there. A soft whimper came from her lips, and she raised her hips to meet his fingers.

"More," she whispered. She unbuttoned his trousers.

Pushing off her, he stood and removed his clothes, feeling her gaze on every part of his body and knowing she approved. He slid her panties down her legs, slowly, excruciatingly slowly, until she squirmed under his scrutiny. Her cheeks were flushed, and her chest rose and fell in jerks with her breathing.

The bra he left on her.

Snatching up his wand, he flicked it and grabbed one of the foil envelopes that appeared beside him. As he sheathed himself, he watched her breasts rise and fall with her breath, tantalized by the black lace covering the creamy skin.

With a slanted smile, he lowered himself over her. The couch would be a snug fit, but one he was eager to try. He rolled over the arm of the sofa, kissing her as he moved up her body, first the thigh, then the belly, then through the lace again, then her neck, her chin.

She arched her back beneath him. The lacy bra tickled his chest. His abdomen burned against hers in a glorious fire, skin to skin. Every nerve tingled with her, her every texture crackled through him until he thought he might fracture.

"I don't care what anyone else thinks. You are mine." He buried himself inside her.

A vocal sigh tore from her lips as her body closed around him. He pulled out slowly, then reclaimed her, again and again and again, until she shattered, uttering a cry so musical he wanted to record it and replay it again and again and again. But for now he was satisfied as he spent himself within her, deep within her, fixing his claim on her.

For long moments, neither spoke nor moved. Their limbs entwined, their breathing intermingled, he pushed to his elbows and brushed her hair back from her forehead. "I love you. I know I shouldn't. I'm your arbiter. We haven't known each other long enough, and I've never believed in love at first sight, but I love you. I can't tell you the number of rules this destroys, but I love you."

"You love me?" She gazed up at him in surprise and affection and adoration.

"I do." His finger traced lazy circles on her stomach.

A slow, delight-filled grin spread over her mouth. "Okay, I guess I love you too."

"You guess?" he said with an answering grin, and he leaned over and kissed her.

His hand stroked over her belly as he pulled on her mouth. He reached between them and teased her still sensitive bud until she writhed beneath him, and then he stopped. "You guess?"

She gasped, her body arching to resume the intimate contact with him. Half-laughing, half-panting, she said, "No guessing. You're mine."

"That's better." And he proceeded to finish what he had started.

23

HOW TO BE A FAIRY GODMOTHER:

•

Hardships Don't Always Befall Those Who Deserve Them; Trials Come to All People, Groundling and Arcani.

When Kristin woke up the next morning, she found it difficult to breathe. Maybe because a body lay tangled with her, on top of her, and around her. A quickening deep in her core sent waves of joy through her. Tennyson loved her. She was right where she wanted to be. Except she couldn't breathe well.

Light poured through the window. With a gasp she realized no drapes or blinds covered the glass. Anyone could see in, and neither of them had clothes on. Not to mention their position was one she preferred not to share with the public.

She shook his shoulder. "Tennyson, wake up."

Yawning, he wriggled a little, then tightened his arms around her. "Uh-uh. I don't want to."

That brought a smile to her lips, but she persisted. "You have to. It's morning, and you don't have curtains on your window."

"I don't think the door's locked either." He snuggled into her.

That brought a yelp from her. "Tennyson, we've got to get dressed." She rolled over him, ignoring the pain in her neck, and started searching for her clothes.

"Why bother? If you appear in that little black dress at this hour, you aren't keeping any secrets anyway." He leaned on his elbow and grinned at her.

His pose there on the couch was oh, so tempting to stare at, but she disciplined herself. "We don't have time to play. Lucas probably already knows I'm gone."

The grin disappeared. "Now you've spoiled a perfect morning." Tennyson swung his legs to the floor.

How could he look so good in the morning? And with no clothes on? "Get dressed." She threw his jeans at him, still searching for her little black dress. How hard could a little dress be to find? It was little, black, and, well, a dress.

From the corner of her vision she saw Tennyson grinning again. She faced him with a question in her gaze.

"I think I like you in what you're wearing now."

She glanced down at herself. A black bra and nothing else. She reddened. "Very funny." This she could take care of. "Wand."

Her wand appeared in her hand. Focusing on her favorite pair of denim Capris and the soft white T-shirt she loved, she waved the wand. *"Requiro."*

A moment later her requested clothing appeared on the floor in front of her, followed by her shoes, her panties from the night before, and the little black dress, which slid out from under the couch. "That's where it was." She secured her wand.

Pulling on his jeans, Tennyson nodded. "Good job. We didn't get the entire ladies' department of Target."

"Ha-ha." She hastily tugged her Capris on.

He arched an eyebrow. "No underwear?"

"I forgot to summon any." She pointed to the scrap of black lace on the floor. "And I'm not putting those back on. And I am not having this conversation with you."

"Okay, but if I'm distracted today, you'll know why." He wrapped his arms around her and kissed her. "Have I told you what a beautiful morning this is?"

"No. Now let me finish dressing." She pushed him away.

He turned to the window. She wasn't too worried about his shirtless appearance. It was early morning yet. Few people would be wandering the campus at this hour. That is, if Arcani students were the same as Groundling ones. She pulled her shirt over her head, then joined him at the window. "What are you looking at?"

Cocking his head toward the scaffolding, he said, "It's just starting. Lucas has played his hand with you and lost, so he can't remain hidden any longer. He has to know we'll go to the Council." He wrapped his arms around her.

For a moment she enjoyed the safety she felt in the circle of his embrace. Then she stepped out. "I almost don't want to go out there."

"I know what you mean." He walked away from the window and pulled on his shirt. "This room seems like a secret grotto, a hidden enclave that reality doesn't touch."

Books still littered the floor, the desk still occupied most of the room, and the couch was lumpy this morning in spots it wasn't yesterday. His office was bare of ornamentation—one plant withered in the corner—but she knew what he meant. Out there, outside, trouble was brewing, and as tempting as it was, they couldn't ignore it, and neither would ever suggest it.

"Are we wrong to feel happiness at a time like this?" she asked as tears welled up in her eyes.

Grabbing her hand, he shook his head. "No. This is the perfect time. It shows hope. It means we believe there is a future." He kissed the top of her head. "Celebrating love is always right."

Boy, she didn't want to leave this room. "So what do we do first? Go to the Council?"

"I can, but you haven't been officially presented yet."

"What?" Her disbelief arched her eyebrows.

"Before you can appear before the Council, you have to go through an official ceremony. You haven't been presented yet."

"That's just stupid. What if there's an emergency, like, I don't know, *now*?" She planted her fists on her hips.

He held up his hands. "Hey, don't get angry with me. I'm just passing on the news. The Council is protected by magic that no one who hasn't been presented can penetrate."

"How archaic, elitist, shortsighted—"

"It saved the Arcani world when Elenka was the only one who could appear before the Council," he said softly.

Kristin drew in a deep breath. "Tell me."

"Elenka was a godmother, and so of course could appear before the Council. But her followers couldn't. So as she led the Great Uprising, the Council remained safe. She had hoped to draw them out to battle, but they wouldn't meet her."

"So they hid."

Tennyson nodded. "Many of us do feel that the Council could've done more, but because they remained safe, our world was preserved."

"And you were presented to the Council . . . ?" Her voice ended as a question.

"Because I found the *Lagabóc*." He shrugged. "Aldous was grooming me for a position on the Council anyway."

Tennyson's importance among the Arcani had never struck her as deeply as it did at this moment. No wonder he had resented his assignment as her arbiter. She barely understood the Arcani world, and he was an integral part of it.

Before she could voice her self-doubt, he continued. "Aldous was on the Council until his death. His position is open now." Sadness tinged Tennyson's voice.

"Will they ask you to fill it?"

He shook his head. "Not yet. Aldous's seat won't be filled until the end of the Time of Transition. Even then my name may not appear among the chosen."

"No wonder Lucas thinks this is the best time to make his move. How many times have you told me the Time of Transition is the period of greatest instability in the Arcani world?"

His smile was one of approval. "Glad to hear you were listening. The year of Transition is always the most chaotic. Not only does the Council change members, new godmothers are chosen. Usually nothing happens. Even Elenka waited ten years after the last Transition to stir up trouble."

"Because she had to wait until she came into her full powers," Kristin said. "I couldn't lead right now. Not with my powers still so unsure. But Lucas is in his prime. He isn't affected by the Time of Transition. This is his best time to act."

"That's what it looks like." Tennyson hesitated. "You know Merlin created the job of the godmothers to protect both the Groundling and Arcani world from each other."

"Right."

"So Merlin understood that the boundaries would be tested from both sides. He explains it in the *Lagabóc*, but I haven't translated it fully. I'm still studying it."

She squinted at him. "Where are you going with all this?"

"Stopping Lucas falls into your job description."

She jumped to her feet. "Me? Me!" Her voice rose to a shriek. "I don't know anything! I'm a liability! Lucas nearly captured me!"

A strong wind erupted from the floor. Warm and cooling at the same time. It swirled around her, lifting her hair in a tangled mane above her head. A bright, golden glow enveloped her as the wind picked her up a few inches from the floor. Her eyes grew wide. Surprise mixed with fear, and the wind's force flowed through her.

"Kristin!"

His voice broke through the eddy of emotions. The wind ceased abruptly, and she dropped the few inches back to the floor.

He wound his arms around her and pulled her close. "I didn't mean to scare you."

"I'm not scared," she lied.

He pointed at the papers that littered the floor. Some of them were still settling. "That little storm wasn't because you were happy."

"I'm still doing that?" She stared at him.

A soft chuckle came from his throat. "You don't have complete control of your powers yet."

"But I . . . Crap." She exhaled a puff of air.

"You are a Rare One. You have powers you don't even know yet." He stroked her hair.

A total sense of incompetence swamped her. Why was *she* so important? How did *she* get this job? "How was Merlin able to set all this up?"

"He was very powerful. The most powerful wizard the world has ever seen. And when he finished, he disappeared."

"He must have made a mistake somewhere," she muttered.

Tennyson chuckled. "I don't think so."

"You have to say so because you love me." She gave him a watery smile.

He tightened his hold on her. "I'll go see the Council, and tell them what we know, but I don't want to leave you alone with Lucas out there. We'll check in with Zack and then find your aunts."

And get some more clothes. Her bare toes scrunched up against the floor, but she was not going to put those black spikes on with this outfit.

She nuzzled her cheek against his chest. "Tell me everything will turn out great."

"We'll do our best."

She didn't want to leave the security of his arms, but she stepped from the circle of his embrace. "Come on. Let's get some food. I'm starving."

They returned to the car. After a brief stop at a drive-through to cure Kristin's growling stomach, they drove toward La Jolla. The morning was still young.

She broke off some of whatever breakfast sandwich she was eating and fed him. As he took the food from her fingers, his tongue touched her. With a hard swallow, she clamped down the rush of desire that flashed through her. She had more important things to think about now than sex.

Alternating bites between herself and him, she emptied the bag. She wanted more food. She wasn't usually so ravenous in the morning, but she hadn't really eaten dinner yesterday, and last night's activities left her hungry. And a renewed blush heated her cheeks. So much for not thinking about sex.

They parked the car on the street. If Lucas was searching for her at the hotel, not finding her car in the garage might buy them a few seconds. She still didn't have shoes, but that wasn't quite as noticeable in this beach community. La Jolla might be rich, but no one walked on the beach with their shoes. She could always claim an early morning stroll. And then absentmindedness concerning the location of her flip-flops.

"I can't feel a footprint, but we should be ready just in case." He placed his hand over the end of his wand.

She nodded and summoned her wand. It lay steady in her palm. She stuffed it into her pocket until her fingers needed only to conceal the handle. "Let's go."

Nothing stopped them, no one attacked them, as they made their way to their room, but when they opened the door, they found everything in shambles. Clothes were strewn over the entire area, the pillows were scattered across the room, cushions were overturned, and the mattress was off the bedsprings. One chair lay in pieces on the floor, and cracks in the center of the vanity mirror radiated outward like a spider's web.

"I guess Lucas knows I'm gone," she said.

"Did he think we'd be hiding between the sheets?" Tennyson asked with heavy sarcasm.

"This wasn't a search for us. This is anger." She lifted one of her shirts. It was ripped in two.

They waded through the mess looking for anything they could keep. Not everything was destroyed. Kristin was able to find a pair of tennis shoes and a pair of underwear. "I'm going to put these on."

"Ruin my fun," said Tennyson, trying to coax a smile from her.

In truth, she wasn't disturbed at the loss of her things. Again. For the second time in two weeks. She had nothing of real value here. But the violence of the destruction, knowing that fury and rage were the only reason for it, filled her with anxiety. She didn't have enough control of her powers to fight Lucas yet.

The bathroom was surprisingly pristine. Lucas probably couldn't be bothered to vandalize this room. She re-dressed quickly, washed her face, pulled a brush through her hair, and returned to the main room. She stopped short. The room was back in order. The chair stood whole, the bed was made, and the mirror reflected without any distortion.

"I fixed everything, but I didn't waste energy on our clothes," he said. "I just stuffed those into the duffel. We'll throw them out on our way."

For a moment she had forgotten he could use magic. Some fairy godmother she was. The tricks she had learned in the past week wouldn't save her from someone with real power. "Sounds good."

"I also checked us out." He pointed at the TV screen. "Self-checkout."

"Good idea." She'd never had the chance to enjoy the hotel. For most of their "stay," they had been camping. And last night . . . right, she wasn't going to think about sex. The attempt at levity popped into her head automatically but didn't alleviate her mood at all.

"Let's see if Zack is awake." Tennyson grabbed the duffel and took her by the hand. "Then I'll take you to your aunts and go to the Council."

No sound came from Zack's suite. Tennyson rapped loudly on the door. A moment later, the door was flung open.

"Tennyson." Zack paced away from the door without saying anything else. He crossed to the sofa, where he bent over Callie.

Tennyson shot a glance at Kristin, then entered. She followed behind. Then she heard . . . crying?

Callie sat on the sofa with a white washcloth pressed to her head. Zack sat with his arm around her.

"Have you heard anything?" Zack asked.

"What should I have heard?"

"I left you a message on your cell." Zack placed his arm around Callie.

As Callie settled into his embrace, her face became visible. Kristin gasped. A huge bruise encircled Callie's left eye, and when she lifted the washcloth, blood trickled from a cut on her head.

Kristin rushed to the sprite. "What happened?"

Zack said, "I went to get Jake breakfast. Callie stayed here with him. While I was gone—" His voice broke, and he jumped to his feet. He stormed to the window and stared off at nothing. A tic in his jaw muscles showed how tightly his teeth were clenched. Agitation rolled off him.

Callie turned tear-filled eyes to Kristin. "They took Jake. I never thought he could be in danger. I never considered it. What kind of monster attacks a child? They caught me by surprise. Before I could stop them, before I even realized what was happening, they took Jake." Sobs overtook her and quaked her shoulders.

"Who?" asked Tennyson, his voice glacial.

"Lucas and his men."

24

HOW TO BE A FAIRY GODMOTHER:

•

Don't Be Afraid to Ask for Help.

COLD FEAR SEIZED Kristin's heart. Lucas had Jake. Now she understood the anguish in Zack's expression. Callie's tears weren't for herself, they were for the child. Tennyson too had lost color in his face.

Kristin knelt at Callie's knees and said, "This is my fault. I should've stayed with Lucas."

"No," came the protest from Tennyson's lips.

"If I had, he wouldn't have taken Jake." Anger sharpened Kristin's words.

Callie blotted the cut on her forehead. "It was my fault. I should've fought harder."

Zack returned to Callie and tightened his arm around her. "Right, because you haven't suffered enough. There were four of them, you said."

"It doesn't matter," Callie said. "I should've watched Jake better."

"You couldn't have known," Zack said.

"No, but *I* did. I knew Lucas was the bad guy. I just didn't think . . ." Tennyson's voice broke. "I didn't believe he would target an innocent. It goes against everything we believe in." Tennyson walked stiffly away from the group. He isolated himself by the window. "I should never have involved you."

"You're wrong, man. I needed to get involved," Zack said. "You're family too, dude, and if it hadn't been me, it would've been someone else."

Kristin stood. "It won't serve us any good to blame ourselves. We have to focus on getting Jake back."

Callie pointed to a glass sphere about the size of an orange on the floor. "He left a bubble."

Kristin's gaze shot to Tennyson.

" 'Bubble' is the slang word for a dictosphere, a holographic message holder," he said. "Who is it for?"

"Kristin," Callie said.

Tennyson picked up the globe and gave it to her. "Only you can open it."

"How do I—"

"Break it." Tennyson walked away from the group again.

She stared at the glass ball in her hand. It appeared empty. Nothing of substance was inside. Holding the bubble gingerly, she walked to a dining table that stood in the suite. Lucas left this for her? She thought of Jake, probably terrified, in the hands of that man. Rage and fear consumed her. Break it? In a sudden motion, she smashed the sphere against the tabletop.

The musical crash of shattering glass filled the room. From the shards arose a thick white fog that circled and swirled over the tabletop. Each wisp snaked toward a central point, then entwined with another, rising into the air forming a dense white column. The white fog faded leaving Lucas's image in a smoky gray haze.

He appeared as he might in real life, only smaller and indistinct. He had that same air of civility (ha!) and yet something was off. Something that diminished his look of control, as if the hold on his temper was ready to slip, as if chaos roiled just under the polished surface.

A low laugh emanated from the figure. "Congratulations, Kristin. Few have ever succeeded in deceiving me. I was correct in thinking you were magnificent. It's only too bad I cannot count you among my friends now. The world was ours."

Tennyson snorted. "Pompous ass."

The likeness continued. "Unfortunately, I still have need of you. Or rather I must prevent you from helping the other side. And so I propose a trade. You for the boy What say you, Kristin? Is your life worth his?" Again he laughed low, and a shudder ran down her spine. "Not hardly, but I'm willing to wager you think so. It's weakness, Kristin, weakness. His kind are insects. So far below you and me. But with your mixed-up sensibilities, you'll think the trade worth the price. I shall be in touch."

The smoke grew white again, unfurling into individual tendrils, and then dissipated, leaving a faint smell of ozone in the air.

"He can't be serious." Tennyson raked his hand through his hair.

"He is." Her voice was quiet.

Zack stared at the spot where the image had appeared. "He's going to kill Jake." Zack's voice was void of life.

Kristin grabbed his hands. "No, he won't. He knows he has to keep Jake safe if he wants me to cooperate. And I will."

From the corner of her vision, she saw Tennyson start at her words, but she focused on Zack. "Lucas is right. I don't consider myself above Groundlings. My parents were Groundlings. Lucas knows I respect and love them. Jake won't be harmed."

Zack released a quivering breath as if he refrained from crying. "What do we do now?"

She glanced at Tennyson.

"He'll know you've heard the bubble. The sender receives notice when the bubble is broken." Tennyson stared out the window. "He'll contact us again soon."

Callie lifted her gaze to Kristin's. "Maybe you could figure out where he's keeping Jake."

"Probably at his house," said Tennyson. "My bet is that Lucas considers it his fortress, his home base."

Callie stared at Kristin. "But you were there. Last night. You can show us where he lives."

Kristin shook her head. "I can't. He's protected his house with powerful magic. Every time I tried to remember the location, I couldn't. I don't know where it is."

Callie's voice dropped to almost a whisper. "You're a Rare One. You have great power."

But I don't know how to use it! Frustration exploded within her. She couldn't look at Callie's expectant face or Zack's hopeful one. She would only fail them. "Damn it." She glared up at the ceiling so she didn't have to see their expressions. "Which room is Jake's?"

"The one on the left," Zack said.

"Tennyson, come with me," Kristin said, then faced

the pair. "If another bubble arrives, just keep it until I'm ready."

She strode into Jake's room, and her heart broke again. His toys were scattered over the dresser and floor, and a comic book lay open on the rumpled bed. For a few seconds, she couldn't move. Jake's absence struck her like a blow. Was this the reason she had been picked to be a fairy godmother? Because she possessed a special affinity for children?

Tennyson moved in behind her. Before he even touched her, his warmth spilled over her back. She turned, and the torment in his eyes nearly destroyed her. Her arms longed to hold him, to comfort him. Her lips ached to soothe that distressed brow, her heart beat to renew his vitality, but she couldn't. Not yet.

"Tell me what spell to use. Teach me how to find my way back to Lucas's house. How do I relive yesterday?"

Tennyson let out a curt, hollow laugh. "You can't. If we could turn back time, we wouldn't need historians. My job would be unnecessary."

"Then I'll just have to remember." She sat on the edge of the bed and grabbed Jake's stuffed pelican. That brought a smile to her face. Leave it to Zack not to get his son a regular teddy bear. She held the toy and closed her eyes.

Last night . . . last night . . . the car arrived for me at seven. Lucas opened the door for me and we drove out of La Jolla and took . . . Torrey Pines Road. A thrill of triumph flashed through her. She could see the inside of the car, feel the leather seat beneath her, hear herself laughing at Lucas's wit, remember thinking the game had started . . .

Tennyson watched a smile slide across Kristin's face. He didn't dare ask her what she was thinking. Something magical was happening—he could feel the footprint—but it wasn't magic that he recognized. Slowly, as he watched her, a rich purple aura grew from and enveloped her, becoming more and more distinct with each passing moment. He had never seen such magic. What was she doing?

Concern prickled at his senses. What if she was putting herself in danger? If her grip on that pelican tightened any more, its head would pop off. Dread iced through him. He reached out to shake her, to break her from the spell. His hand hit a wall. But there was no wall. He pushed harder. Something blocked him. Panicking now, he pressed forward with both hands. A barrier prevented him from touching her.

"Kristin!" he shouted. He pounded at the barrier, disturbed by the lack of sound created by his hands. She sat there, unmoving, without any response to his shout or actions. "Kristin!"

He searched the room for a weapon, anything he could use as a sledgehammer, and spotted a heavy-based lamp on the bedside table. He raised it over his head.

The purple disappeared. Her eyes opened, and she gasped. "What are you doing?"

Heart beating in his chest, he dropped the lamp and grabbed her. Nothing stopped him this time. He yanked her into his arms and squeezed. "Saving you."

"From what?"

"I don't know. I've never seen anything like what you just did." His heart rate still hadn't slowed. "What did you do?"

"I remembered the way to Lucas's house. I know where it is." Excitement colored her voice, and her eyes sparkled into his. "We can rescue Jake."

He pulled back a little. "Are you sure? You told me Lucas had placed protections, confounding spells, on the location. Those spells can't be broken. Ever."

"I didn't break them. I just went through them." She frowned slightly. "Why are you looking at me like that? You're scaring me."

Could she really have done it? He ran his hand through his hair. "I've just never heard of anyone having the ability to get through cloaks. Not with magic."

"Then it's a good thing I don't know the rules. You forget my parents were Groundlings."

An interesting point. Was it possible? But they didn't have time to launch an investigation right now. "You know where Lucas's house is?"

She nodded.

"Then let's get Jake." Tennyson took her by the hand and led her from the room.

Zack and Callie looked up as they came in. Zack jumped to his feet. "What's happened?"

"Kristin knows where Jake is." Tennyson smiled at her.

"Then let's go get him." Zack started for the door.

"Wait, Zack. It's not so simple," Tennyson said. "We won't be able to march up to Lucas's house and demand Jake's return. We need a plan."

Impatience and frustration erupted in Zack's expression. He scrunched his eyes shut, rubbed his forehead, then drew in a deep breath. "You're right, of course." He paced the room.

"I can get into the house," Kristin said.

Tennyson looked at her. He didn't know what she had planned, but he knew he wouldn't like it.

"The bigger problem will be keeping Lucas from knowing we've arrived. I'm sure he has something set up to warn him of visitors." Kristin grabbed a pad of paper from the desktop. She started making columns.

An hour later they had their plan. Tennyson, Kristin, and Zack stood. Tennyson bit back his reservations. The plan was good, but he had been right. He didn't like it. Kristin had tossed back his arguments without a care for her own safety.

Zack crossed to Callie and cupped her face. "I'm glad you're staying here, babe. I can't worry about you too." He kissed her.

"Bring back our boy," Callie said when she had her breath back.

Zack nodded, then turned to the door. "Let's go."

They decided to take Zack's Beetle because Lucas probably wouldn't recognize it as belonging to them. Tennyson climbed into the driver's seat, put the key in the ignition, and then sat there. He couldn't drive.

"Why aren't we moving?" asked Zack.

"I don't know the way."

"Torrey Pines Road, north," Kristin said from the backseat.

Zack looked at him blankly.

He should have known that street. He knew his house was near it, but he couldn't remember how to get there. *Idiot.* He shook himself. "The spell."

Now Kristin gave him a blank look.

Tennyson climbed from the driver's seat. "I know the road. I know where it is, but not if I'm heading toward Lucas's house. It's the cloaking spell. Do you know how to get there?"

"Yes," she said.

He tilted the chair forward so she could climb out and folded himself into the narrow backseat. "You'll have to drive."

"Whoa. That is some weird feeling," Zack said. "It's like the ultimate brain fog. It's like I know, but I don't know."

She took her place behind the wheel and within minutes they were driving north from San Diego.

It was almost surreal, knowing exactly where he was in one moment and in the next being unable to state where he had just been. Lucas's spell was more powerful than Tennyson's own simple protection spell on his house. Both prevented transport to the property for anyone outside a trusted circle, and both would prevent Groundlings from stumbling onto their properties or even viewing them; both would require special invitations for guests. He could read the familiar magic, but Lucas's spell went way beyond that. Lucas had set up his residence like a fortress.

And Kristin had gotten through it all.

Tennyson glanced at the back of her head. If he didn't know her, if he hadn't seen her kindness, if he didn't love her so much, she would be scary.

Thirty minutes later, Kristin signaled and parked the car on the shoulder.

"Wait a minute. There isn't a road here," Zack said.

"You can't see it?"

"No."

"Lucas has protected it from Groundling eyes," Tennyson said. The road stretched into the hills, and an obscuring curtain pulsed ahead of them. As soon as they touched that screen, Lucas would know they had arrived.

"Can you see it?" Zack asked as he pressed his nose to the glass.

"I can, but I still can't tell where we are." Tennyson took out his wand. "Here. This will help."

He touched Zack's head with the wand. *"Potes videre."*

Zack's eyes widened as the road revealed itself to him. "If I wasn't so scared for Jake, this would be so cool."

"Don't worry. We're almost there." Kristin climbed from the car. "God, I hope he doesn't know we're here yet."

Tennyson unfurled himself from the backseat. "The curtain will warn him. Once we pass through, he'll know."

"Can you drive from here?" she asked.

"I should be able to." Tennyson eyed the road. He didn't know where he was or where he was headed, but all he had to do was follow the road.

"Okay, here goes." She pulled out her wand and focused. "Ibuprofen, please."

He poured out three pills, then closed his fist over them. "Kristin, I don't—"

Tiptoeing, she kissed his objection silent. "We talked about this. This is a good idea."

He knew she was determined. He handed her the pills and a bottle of water. She swallowed them quickly and then waved her wand over herself. He nearly winced when he heard the first cracking of her bones. This time would be easier, but it would still hurt.

Zack stared at her. "Hey, she *is* getting smaller."

"And she's about to lose her clothes, so if you don't mind . . ." Tennyson gripped Zack's shoulders and turned him away from her.

"Aw, can't a guy have even a little fun?" But Zack's attempt at humor was halfhearted, and he didn't peek.

Kristin stood behind the car and pushed her T-shirt from her shoulders. She stepped out of her pants next. "Now I know why Tinkerbell wears strapless only. You need room for the wings. It was nice of Callie to lend me a dress." She held up a tiny scrap of material. "I only hope it'll fit me."

As Tennyson watched, she shrank several more inches. Her bra flapped against her chest, and her panties clung by the merest wisp to her hip bones. "Turn around please," she said.

"But I've seen—"

"Nevertheless, turn around."

"Okay, okay." He pivoted just as the bra and panties fell to the ground. He was sorry he couldn't see more. To relieve himself of the temptation of peeking he moved next to Zack.

"Is she done?" Zack asked.

"Not yet. This is only the second time she's changed, so it takes longer than, say, Callie."

Zack grinned slightly. "Yeah, it's pretty cool how Callie can change." Then his expression grew serious. "We haven't had a chance to tell Jake yet. About her, I mean."

Tennyson patted Zack's shoulder. "Don't worry; you will."

They stood silently for a few minutes.

"Done." A tiny sprite flitted in front of them.

"Don't tire yourself out," Tennyson said. He opened his palm and she landed in the center. "You have a lot more flying to do."

"Are we ready?" Her voice was tiny, matching her body.

"Yes." He climbed in behind the wheel, and Zack took the passenger seat. Tennyson placed her on the dashboard. "Hang on."

He started the car and rolled onto the road. For a moment panic threatened to grip him as he realized he didn't know where he drove, but then he heard her voice.

"Just follow the road."

He concentrated on the pavement. As long as he stared at the road, he was fine. Whenever he looked at his surroundings, disorientation threatened. So he stopped looking at the landscape.

He drove slowly because every time he sped up, he felt lost.

"We're almost there."

When she spoke, his confidence returned. "Are you ready, Zack?"

Zack nodded and picked up a satchel.

Another bend in the road and Tennyson saw the house. Kristin disappeared below the level of the dashboard. Without any surprise, he saw three men with their wands aimed at the car as he pulled up. Lucas stood at the end of the walk, his face projecting a storm of fury. Tennyson pulled into an open space and parked. He exited the car, but left the door open.

"How the hell did you get here?" said Lucas. His fists clenched and unclenched.

"We drove." Tennyson smiled into the man's obvious anger.

"Where the hell is my son?" Zack asked as he circled the car to stand beside Tennyson.

Lucas eyed the two men. "Very foolish of you to come here. I was willing to leave the boy unharmed, but you haven't acted in good faith."

Tennyson pulled out his wand and pointed it at Lucas. As expected, the three magicals aimed their wands at him.

Lucas just laughed. "Go ahead. Try to use it. My men will rip you apart before you can invoke any spell. Your magic isn't fast enough."

"Good thing we aren't using magic then." Zack slammed the satchel to the ground. The crash of shattering glass filled the air; then a thick white and gray smoke obscured their view of the house and of Lucas.

"What the—," Lucas shouted. "Get them."

Zack grabbed Tennyson's arm, and Tennyson concentrated. The air tightened around them, his vision went black, and then they stood in the living room of Zack's suite.

Callie jumped up the minute she saw them. "Well?"

"Chemistry rocks," Zack said with a grin. "You should've seen the confusion on that bastard's face when I made fog. Most satisfactory."

Callie turned to Tennyson. "And Kristin?"

"We can only hope." The words offered shallow comfort, and he stared out at endless ocean trying to keep his apprehension contained.

25

HOW TO BE A FAIRY GODMOTHER:

•

Simple Magic Is Often the Best Magic.

KRISTIN FOUND AN open window on the second story. Why wouldn't she have? Lucas had no idea anyone would find his house. He believed he was safe here. She unsheathed the tiny but keen dagger at her waist and sliced through the screen. Two more perpendicular swipes and the hole was big enough for her to push through.

The smoke had worked perfectly. She had flown from the car behind the billowing chemical cloud and up to the second story. The cries and shouts of disbelief from Lucas and his men told her that Tennyson and Zack had escaped. And now she crawled inside Lucas's house to search for Jake.

Her memory had served her well. The second floor was exactly as she remembered, including the room she had occupied for such a short time. She flew from door to door and explored the rooms. Being small had its advantages. She was able to squeeze under closed doors and hide in places no one thought to look. Not that she'd had to hide often. Although more servants roamed the house than the last time she was here, they were occupied downstairs.

But her examination of the second floor proved fruitless. Jake was in none of the rooms. She checked to make sure the hall was clear, then flew down the main staircase to the lower floor.

"Check the back of the house," Lucas's voice boomed out. He was coming into the foyer. "Those two were here as a distraction, and I want to know what they were hiding."

She ducked into a large pot that decorated the entry hall. Three men bowed to Lucas, then ran outside again. Lucas's face transformed into a mask of fury. She ducked lower into the urn. His expression held no vestiges of the cosmopolitan man he had pretended to be.

"Dimitri!" Lucas shouted.

The expressionless butler, still clad in black, appeared from the kitchen area. "Sir?"

"Where's the boy?"

"He's still in his room. I checked on him first when I heard the commotion."

"Good work." Lucas moved into the living room. Dimitri trailed behind him.

Pulling her bottom lip between her teeth, Kristin left her hiding place and flew along the ceiling to follow. Both men faced away from the doorway. She darted to a bookshelf and hid behind a bronze statuette.

Lucas poured himself a brandy and stared out the window. "How did they find us? This location is hidden from everyone. I didn't even let Kristin know . . ." His head lifted. He placed his glass on the bar and turned to Dimitri. "Check the house. Every inch. She's here. Somewhere. I feel her."

"At once." Dimitri left the room, shouting orders for more men to follow him.

"Kristin." Her name was a curse on Lucas's lips.

Her heart hammered in her chest. She had to find Jake and get out of there. Fast.

Lucas picked up his glass again. In a sudden movement, he hurled it against the stone hearth. He didn't even watch it shatter, as he left the room.

Kristin drew in a deep breath. Fear ran like acid in her veins. She could scarcely hear the activity in the house over the beating of her heart. *Think*, she chided herself. *Focus*.

Dimitri had come from the back of the house. He said Jake was still in his room. So that's where she had to start.

Flying unobserved was more difficult now. The house bustled with men and women searching for her, but she made it to the kitchen and its myriad hiding places without being seen. Of course, Jake wasn't being kept in the kitchen. Beyond the kitchen lay the servants' quarters. She'd have to check in there.

The hallway in the servants' wing was almost void of decoration. Without decorations, she'd have to move quickly and hope she wasn't seen. She entered the hallway and was halfway down when she heard someone behind her. Speeding up, she flew into the light fixture. She bit back a scream as she burned her sole on the lightbulb. The glass panes were hot too, but she had no choice except to cling to them. Even so, if the person below her looked up, she'd be seen. Luck was with her.

The man continued down the hall without looking around. When he entered a room at the end, she darted to the first door and squeezed beneath it.

Hiding in the rooms would be easier because the occupants had more belongings. For servants some of them were downright messy, but she was grateful for their clutter. However, her search of these rooms passed without incident. All that she had lost was time. Where was Jake?

She flew up the servants' stairs back to the second floor.

"But, sir." She heard a voice from the room she had originally entered through. "It's just a small hole in the screen."

Lucas's voice rang with displeasure. "This is a new house. No holes should exist. Especially one cut so precisely."

"Someone would have to be pretty small to fit through there," said the first voice with a laugh.

Lucas laughed too, but his laugh held no mirth. "Clever, clever girl."

He burst into the hallway just as she hid in a flower-filled vase. At least the water soothed her sizzled feet.

"She's small. She's the size of a sprite."

Kristin's sprits sank. He knew. He knew she was here and that she had altered her size. Still she had the advantage.

"Search again," Lucas said. "And this time I really do mean every inch. You're looking for a fairy."

Men scattered throughout the hallway and into the various rooms. Damn it. The new hunt left her less time to rescue Jake. Where was he? She had searched the entire house but hadn't seen him.

Lucas stepped to the end of the hallway and stopped at the top of the servants' stairs. There. She hadn't seen it before. In the wall, hidden by the trompe l'oeil, was the slim cutout of a door. Lucas removed a key from his pocket and inserted it into a keyhole. The door sprang open and she could see a wide arch that opened onto an expansive room that stretched into a part of the house she had not toured.

Lucas loved his secrets, didn't he?

He entered the room and crossed to a small door in the wall to the left. A second key opened that lock. He peered inside. "Are you awake, boy?"

"Go away."

Her heart clenched to hear the fear and sadness in Jake's voice. *Hang in there, Jake. I'm here.*

"Watch your tongue, boy."

While Lucas's back was to the secret entrance, she took the chance to zip through the opening, right past Lucas into the wide room. It looked like a magical museum. A medieval tapestry hung in a glass case on the wall. A scarlet crystal sphere rested on a wooden stand in a niche. If she didn't know better, she'd think the globe was a solid ruby. Wait. Knowing Lucas, she surmised it probably was. A large, carved staff leaned in one corner, and some strange symbols decorated another spot on the wall. Ancient books lined a shelf against one wall, and a table stood against another. A mortar and pestle adorned the table, and various plants, stones, and powders filled glass vials and bottles on shelves above the tabletop. An intricate skylight domed overhead. Its panes looked almost like the petals of a huge flower. Magic permeated the room, and even with her limited knowledge, she recognized each item held some sort of supernatural association. She would have loved to explore everything and discover more of Lucas's secrets.

Leaning into the room, Lucas said, "You might want to be more polite next time. If you want to eat."

"I hate you, and I won't ever be polite to you."

"The feeling is mutual, I assure you." Lucas pulled back suddenly, as if he was satisfied with the reaction of the child. She darted behind the ruby globe and stood on the rim of the wooden stand. She pressed against the cool sphere, then pulled back slightly. A low glow burned in the center of the ball, but she forgot about it a moment later when she heard Lucas turn the key in the lock. A few footsteps, a loud click, and darkening in the room told her that Lucas had gone.

She peeked out from behind the sphere. No lamp burned, but the skylight provided plenty of light. She flew to the door that Lucas had opened and slid beneath it.

She blinked a few times to help her eyes adjust to the dimness. A thick shade hung over the one window. Even in bright light, the room would appear drab—no furniture except a simple bed. And then she saw him. Curled on his side on the bed was Jake. His back was to her. He was crying.

She flitted to him and hovered a little ways above his head. Approaching him would be harder than she thought. She was about to reveal the whole Arcani world to him "Jake?"

He stopped crying.

"Jake," she said louder. "It's me, Kristin."

Jake swiped the tears from his face and sat up. She maintained her distance above his head. "I can hear you, but I can't see you."

"That's because I need to tell you something first. Remember that fairy you caught last week?"

"Yeah." He wiped away an errant tear.

"That was Callie."

"No way." His voice grew louder. "She was the fairy? But she was little."

"Shhh," Kristin said quickly. "We have to be quiet so Lucas doesn't hear us."

"Okay." Jake looked under the bed. "So where are you?"

"Callie isn't the only one who can be small. Look up."

He did, and his mouth opened in wonder despite the tracks of his tears.

"Now don't try to catch me, okay?" She flew closer to him.

"Uh-uh." His eyes grew wider. "Wow. Did you come to rescue me?"

His eagerness brought a smile to her face. "I did."

"Yippee!" Then he clapped his hand over his mouth. "I forgot," he whispered.

"That's okay. I don't think anybody heard." She landed on the bed next to him and exhaled loudly. Finding him had taken longer than she had hoped, and staying this size drained her energy. *Stay focused. You can do this.*

"Is my dad coming?" Jake bounced on the bed. "Where is he?"

"He was here, but I'm the only one who could get inside. Don't worry; you'll see him soon."

"Okay." His little shoulders drooped as his enthusiasm deflated. He rubbed his stomach as it rumbled.

"Are you hungry?"

"A little." He tried to act brave.

"Let's get you some breakfast, then we'll make our plans." She focused and waved her wand.

A moment later a white sack appeared. She'd done it. Somewhere a McDonald's employee was wondering what had happened to the order he just filled. As thrilled as she was to see Jake rip into the bag and pull out the sandwich, dizziness overtook her and she sat on the bed. She didn't know how much longer she could hold the transfiguration.

The problem was if she tried to conserve her energy by changing back to her full size, she'd have no clothes. Okay, that wasn't a real problem, but she didn't need to make Jake more uncomfortable than he already was. Not to mention how much harder escaping the attention of the bad guys would become if she were full-size. But if she weighed how much less energy she'd expend against staying small, the option seemed clear.

"Jake, I'm going to need a favor from you."

His mouth full, Jake nodded. "Ho-kay."

"I need the sheet from the bed. Can you get it for me?"

He nodded again, stuffed the rest of the sandwich into his mouth, and jumped off the bed. She flew up as he tugged the blanket from the bed, then pulled the sheet off. "Now what?"

"Can you hold it up above your head and keep it there until I take it from you?"

"Sure." He braced his legs apart and held the sheet up over his head on outstretched arms. "Like this?"

"Perfect. Now, no peeking. I'm going to get big again." She landed on the floor and waved her wand over herself. A moment later the first popping of her bones announced her transformation. As fast as she could, she peeled off the tiny dress already beginning to constrict her. She hoped she had taken enough ibuprofen.

"My arms are getting tired," said Jake.

"Just a little bit more," she said. "Hang in there."

A minute later she grabbed the sheet and wrapped it loosely around her.

"Wow, you're bigger." Jake watched her.

"And I'm not done yet." She attempted a smile through the pain. She adjusted the sheet around herself as she grew taller.

Three minutes later the transformation had finished. The sheet hung like a loose toga around her. She tugged on a corner and found another corner to tie it to. Not the most comfortable, but it would suffice. Her breath was labored and her legs wobbled beneath her, but the constant drain on her power vanished. "Did they give you any water or anything to drink?"

"Yeah, but I threw it." He scrunched up his face and scanned the room. Then he ran to the corner. "Found it. It's a little squished, but it's still got water in it."

"Perfect." She took it from him and drained half of it in one breath.

"Boy, you were thirsty," Jake said, his eyes wide.

"Magic will do that." She sat on the edge of the bed. "Jake, I need to sit just for a little while. Just to catch my breath."

His face crumpled. "Aren't we going home now?"

"As soon as I catch my breath. I promise." She closed her eyes and finished the rest of the water. The cool liquid helped, but she knew she wasn't at full strength.

She forced herself to breathe slowly, to calm and soothe herself as best she could.

A minute elapsed, then another before she opened her eyes. Jake was sitting on the floor, his knees drawn up to his chest, his head hanging down, a picture of abject misery.

"Am I such a terrible rescuer then?"

Jake's head lifted. His struggle between politeness and honesty played out in his expression. "No, you're fine," he said finally.

"Then let's get you home." She stood and her legs didn't collapse. That was a good sign. She hadn't completely recovered yet, but she felt somewhat stronger. She placed her hand on his shoulder, focused on Zack's room at the hotel, and waited for the familiar tingling to begin.

Nothing happened.

She tried again. Not even a flicker. Maybe their goal was too far away. She concentrated on the spot just outside the protection spell around the house, just outside the curtain. From there they could find their way home. She concentrated.

Still nothing.

Jake looked up at her. "Is something wrong?"

"I'm thinking." She focused on the other side of the door. Surely she could transport ten feet away.

Nothing.

Think, Kristin. Think. Magic worked in this room. She had brought Jake breakfast. She had transformed back into her normal self. So why couldn't she transport? Tennyson and Zack had transported away. She was tired, but she knew she had the strength to transport. Maybe because she was trying to transport two people?

She released Jake's shoulder and concentrated on the room outside the door. She didn't move an inch. Time for Plan B. Too bad she didn't have a Plan B.

Jake and Tennyson had transported away when they were outside the house. Maybe Lucas had done something after she left. Maybe if they could get outside, they could disappear. With those thoughts, she cobbled together a new idea. Getting outside would be a lot harder, though.

Her wand nestled in her palm. She pointed at the door and realized she didn't know a spell to unlock doors. She did know one way to open the door. "Troll."

The wood exploded outward, leaving little more than a sprinkling of sawdust. So much for surprise.

"Awesome," Jake said, sounding so much like Zack.

"Come on." She grabbed Jake's hand and ran through the opening. She pointed her wand again.

At that moment, the hidden door sprang open. Lucas stood in the opening. When he saw her, he lifted his hands in the clichéd sign for surrender. "Don't shoot." And then he smiled.

Her hand trembled. She knew she should act, move, anything, but she couldn't blast him. He was evil, power hungry, corrupt, but she couldn't use magic to harm him. She pushed Jake behind her and stepped into the magic room.

"Do you like my library?" Lucas asked as he stalked her into the room. "Here I do my research and testing. Here is where I keep my most valuable pieces. Beautiful, aren't they?" He ran his fingers over the glass covering the tapestry.

"Sick, you mean." She kept the wand pointed at him.

"Put that away. We both know you won't use it." Lucas took another step.

"Don't try me." Her voice never wavered.

Three men followed Lucas into the library and awaited his orders.

"You can't escape. These rooms are especially well protected. No one can transport in or out of here. Not even me." Lucas continued to circle.

That explained why she hadn't succeeded. Her mind grasped at any new idea, anything, to save Jake. "Let the boy go. You don't want him."

"You're right I don't. Shall I kill him now?" In the next moment, Lucas aimed his wand at Jake and lunged.

"No," she screamed, shoving Jake firmly behind her. Jake whimpered. She braced herself for the blow.

Lucas's laugh filled the room. "I can't be bothered with such insignificance. It's you I want."

She couldn't circle any farther. The three men in the arch could almost reach her from this side. Lucas closed in from the other. She backed up until Jake bumped against the wall.

Lucas indicated her dress with a sweeping gesture. "Your attire suits you. Even now in your toga, you are a goddess."

Lucas's calm tone was more irritating than if he were shouting at her. And more frightening.

One of the three men dove at her. Jake cried and moved away. From the niche behind her, she grabbed the ruby sphere. She lifted it above her head to throw it.

"No!" cried Lucas.

The man backed away. She glanced at Lucas. He had taken a step back. She looked down at the sphere. The glow she had noticed earlier was back and growing bigger.

"What is this thing?" she asked Lucas.

"A pretty bauble, nothing more." Lucas had regained his calm tone.

"You're lying." Heat radiated into her palm from the orb. The orb blazed brighter, casting a ruddy brilliance over the area around her. The sheet she wore showed no sign of whiteness any longer. It shone red.

"Kristin, it's nothing. A toy." His words were too casual, too forced.

"Really?" She tossed it into the air and caught it again. Lucas flinched.

Now she laughed. Confidence flowed through her. Energy infused her body. Her mind focused. And she saw the answer. She could do magic here; she just couldn't transport. If she could *bring* breakfast for Jake, then she could *send* him away. "Give me your cell phone."

"What?" Lucas said.

"Give me your cell phone. Don't make me repeat myself."

He tossed it to her, and she let it fall to the ground. "Jake, pick it up and place it on that shelf behind me."

Jake darted out and snatched up the phone. He had to tiptoe to put it in the niche.

Without taking her gaze from Lucas or his three goons in the doorway, she bent down to speak to Jake. "When you get back to your father, tell Tennyson to use my cell phone and call Lucas's number. Can you remember that?"

Jake nodded

"It's important, Jake. Tell him to call Lucas from my cell phone."

"I won't forget."

"Good boy. Are you ready?"

Lucas smiled again. "You can't transport from here, remember?"

"Ah, but I won't." She pointed her wand at Jake and winked. "Time to go home, Jake."

She flicked her wand. A wind gusted through the room, and in a flash of red light, Jake vanished.

"Impossible," cried Lucas. "I've blocked all transport spells—"

"Ah, but I didn't transport. I just sent Jake home." She felt glorious, but her arms were tired. She checked the orb. It wasn't burning as brightly. It pulsed softly now, but its strength no longer poured into her. She focused and the glow flared up for a moment, then flickered away, leaving her weaker than before.

"Now what?" asked Lucas.

"We wait for a phone call." She stumbled backward.

Lucas saw her weakness and inched toward her.

"Not yet, Lucas. You can't have me yet." She lifted the sphere higher as if to smash it. Lucas froze.

The phone rang. "Sanctum," she said, and her wand disappeared. She grabbed the cell. "Hello?"

"Kristin, is that you?" Tennyson spoke on the other end.

"It's me. Is Jake back?"

"He's here. He's safe. Where are you?"

"Lucas's." She could feel the strength ebbing away. "I love you."

"Kristin, wait—"

She dropped the phone and pivoted woozily to Lucas. "I believe you can have this now." She tossed the globe as darkness engulfed her.

26

HOW TO BE A FAIRY GODMOTHER:

•

Sometimes Bending *the Rules Is Necessary.*

"KRISTIN!" TENNYSON YELLED into the phone. "Kristin!"

He heard her speak, then a rush of voices, then nothing.

With a growl of rage, he hurled the phone at the wall. "He has her."

Jake looked up from his father's arms. "Is Uncle Tennis all right?"

"He's worried about Kristin," Zack said.

Tennyson paced the room. He was glad Jake was back and safe, but Kristin should have been here as well. Fear ate into Tennyson's gut. "Reynard knows you're here. You'll have to move." Tennyson paced the room. "Callie, can you take care of them?"

"Of course." She looked almost insulted at the question.

"Dad?" Jake tugged on Zack's sleeve. "Did you know Callie is a fairy?"

Zack nodded.

"Why didn't you tell me?" Jake pushed out his lower lip. "And Kristin too. She was great, Dad. Really strong. And magical. You should've seen her with that red ball."

Tennyson looked up, then knelt in front of Jake. "What red ball?"

Jake drew his mouth to the side, thought for a moment, then nodded. "I don't know. Kristin grabbed a red ball from a shelf. It was cool. It glowed."

Impossible. The sphere was a myth. But so had been the *Lagabóc*. "A red ball? Did it look like it was made of glass?"

"Yeah, and the bad guy looked scared when she picked it up. That was pretty funny."

Merlin's Gifts. Tennyson hadn't reviewed the section of the *Lagabóc* that dealt with the Gifts. But if the sphere was real and Lucas had it, the Council needed to know. "What happened next?"

"She glowed red too. It was awesome. Then she said it was time for me to go home and then I was here." Jake nestled into his father's arms again. "She was brave, Dad."

"I know, little dude, I know." Zack looked at Tennyson. "What's our next step?"

"You guys have to leave." Tennyson rubbed his forehead.

"But Kristin—"

"You can't help me with this." Tennyson's voice was harsher than he intended. He expelled a breath of air. "Take Jake somewhere safe."

Zack said nothing for a moment, then nodded. He set Jake on his feet and led him from the room by the hand. "We have to pack."

Tennyson paced again. "I have to find the aunts. Maybe they can help."

Callie gave him a look of sympathy. "You can't get back to Lucas's house?"

"It was all Kristin. Don't you see? She's alone, and I can't help her." Frustration boiled in him. Lucas posed a greater threat than any of them had realized. Tennyson faced the wall and punched it. Callie yelped in surprise. When he drew his fist back, blood covered the knuckles.

Callie crossed to him. She reached for his hand. "Let me clean—"

"Leave it. I want to feel the pain." He was being stupid. And stubborn, but he couldn't prevent it. Helplessness gnawed at him. Nothing in his education or store of knowledge had prepared him for this situation. Kristin shouldn't have been able to find Lucas's house, yet she had. She shouldn't have to face Lucas alone, yet she did. She shouldn't be risking her life, yet she was. It was all well and good that he had discovered the *Lagabóc*, but what use was an ancient book now? The laws couldn't help him. He had failed her, and if he couldn't save her now, it would kill him.

He faced Callie and gripped her shoulders. "Take care of them."

She laid her hand on his arm. "Don't worry about Zack and Jake. I'll keep them safe. Find Kristin."

Tennyson couldn't even promise Callie he would. Without a word, he vanished.

AN HOUR LATER Tennyson stood in the marble foyer of the Council hall. He had believed he couldn't become angrier than he already was. He had been wrong.

They had rejected his ideas. No, not just rejected, but ridiculed him for wasting their time with fairy tales. They had found Ivan Dimitrov living a quiet life in northern England. He showed no propensity for evil or even anything more than chagrin for his mother's actions. He wanted to be left alone, and the Council was willing to grant his request. As for this Lucas Reynard, the Council had no record of him, and if he, Tennyson, persisted in furthering his theories, he would be declared a malcontent and accorded the restrictions of such a status.

In addition, this episode had shown that Kristin Montgomery had failed to prove herself capable of the honor bestowed upon her. She would be declared incompetent at once, and Tennyson must turn her over to the Council immediately for confinement. She was a Rare One after all and needed to be curtailed before she realized the full extent of her powers. They had already sent for the aunts to inform them of their decision.

So not only was Kristin alone and in danger, now she was a fugitive as well. Tennyson paced the floor outside the chambers. Arguing would prove nothing now. He hadn't believed the Council could be so pigheaded and shortsighted. With Aldous's death he could count on no friendly ear.

The aunts materialized in the forechamber. "Tennyson," Lily said and went to give him a hug. Then she noticed his expression. "What's wrong?"

"What isn't?" he countered. "The Council just declared Kristin incompetent."

"What!" cried Hyacinth. "Are they insane?"

"You tell me. They dismissed all the information about Lucas as lies, and gave me a warning as well."

"Those idiots," Rose said. "They've always had trouble facing the truth."

"The same thing happened when we chased Elenka." Lily clicked her tongue. "They don't want to believe they are so out of touch with the Arcani world. They forget their duty is to serve and protect us, not to buy into their elevated positions."

"Thus the need for change," Rose said. "I remember—"

"Forgive me," Tennyson said, "but we don't have time to discuss politics. Lucas has Kristin."

The three women fell silent. "Where?" asked Rose finally.

"At his house," Tennyson said. "But I can't get there. It's cloaked. Kristin broke through somehow, but I can't."

"That's our girl," said Hyacinth.

"Ladies, I think the Council can wait, don't you?" said Lily. She took Tennyson's hand. "We have more important things to do."

WHEN KRISTIN OPENED her eyes, she lay on the bed in the room where Jake had been held. The memories of this morning's rescue filtered back into her consciousness. She was in Lucas's house and Jake was safe. As she regained her bearings, she heard someone clear his throat.

"Good. You're awake."

With a gasp, she bolted up on the bed. The sheet she wore was tangled in her limbs. Lucas sat in a straight-back chair, watching her. She pulled down the sheet to cover herself.

"I've brought some of the things Ilse acquired for you." He pointed to a stack of clothes on the floor beside her.

She pulled the entire pile to her as if building a wall against him.

"It seems petty to make you wear that rag any longer." He shrugged. "Besides, it wouldn't do any good for you to distract my men any further."

"Your generosity is overwhelming," she said in a dry tone.

Lucas stood. "I'll let you change now, and then we'll chat." He started for the door, then stopped. "And don't be tempted to try to escape. You'll find it more difficult to do magic now." He left the room.

His words aroused a streak of contrariness. Kristin opened her palm and summoned her wand. It didn't appear. A second try brought a second failure. She focused on herself. No hint of magic thrummed through her. She pressed outward with her senses and she found a footprint. But it came across as a heavy barrier, a throbbing rather than a tingling. The magic was heavy on this room. Was it possible to cast a spell preventing all magic?

She sorted through the clothes and found tailored shorts with a matching linen blouse. A little more formal than she'd like, but at least it was a summer suit. The pile also included silk underwear and leather gladiator sandals. She had to admit that Lucas and company understood luxury.

Just as she finished strapping the sandals to her feet, a knock came at the door. "Are you dressed?" asked Lucas.

"Yes." She sat on the edge of the bed.

Lucas walked in. He shook his head. "What am I going to do with you?" He clicked his tongue as if chastising a small child.

"Let me go?"

"I'm happy to see you haven't lost your sense of humor." He sat beside her on the bed. "This was to be my home, my sanctuary, my castle. You've ruined that. How did you find me? No one could find me here unless I allowed them to. Even my men don't know where they are. No one can break through the spells."

"Good thing I don't know the rules then." If he thought she'd feel sympathy for him, he was mistaken.

"I have to find a new place because of you. I endured weeks among the Groundlings while I waited for this house to be built. All for nothing. Now my time must be wasted finding a new home for myself. I've already given the order to move. I can't forgive you for that." He traced a finger over her jaw. "A pity. We would have been quite a remarkable team."

She jerked her head away. "Do you have something to say?"

"I still haven't decided what to do with you. Perhaps I'll let you live. If I can find a way to control you. Because you know you aren't leaving here again." He stood.

She didn't let his words elicit a reaction from her. At least not outwardly. Inside cold fear sent its brittle fingers scratching along her nerves. But she wouldn't beg. And she doubted he'd fall for her playacting again. "Let me know when you've reached your decision." Pillowing her head on her arms, she stretched across the bed as if she hadn't a care in the world.

Lucas laughed. "You are magnificent. It would be a waste to kill such greatness." He left.

Her facade vanished as soon as the door closed. He'd have to kill her, since she'd never cooperate with him. She stood and tried to summon her wand again. Nothing. It was as if the past weeks had never happened. As if she never knew a magical world existed and she was a mere Groundling. As if she had never loved Tennyson.

And the loss left her bereft. She fell on the bed and hid her sobs in the pillow.

"WELL, THAT DIDN'T work either," said Hyacinth. She tossed her wand aside and stretched her arms over her head.

They had been working for two hours. Tennyson had fetched books, tried spells, and drank more tea than would fill a bathtub. A large one. With jets.

"There's nothing in here that will help us," said Lily as she closed the book and added it to the top of the stack in front of her.

Tennyson held his tongue. It wouldn't help to add his mounting frustration to theirs.

"Oh dear, we can't give up," said Rose with alarm in her voice.

"We're not giving up. We're just discouraged," said Hyacinth.

"I don't think you can speak for us all," said Rose.

"Oh? You're having a *good* time?" said Hyacinth.

Tennyson scarcely paid attention to their bickering. Nothing they tried, nothing they found, would help Kristin. God knew what Lucas was doing to her right at this moment. His insides clenched at the thought. Kristin needed his help and he couldn't give it. He wanted to punch another wall.

"The magic is just too strong," Lily said, flipping the last book onto the pile. "The protection spells are powerful magic for a reason, and we just can't get through them."

"What's the use of having magic when we can't use it?" Hyacinth said in disgust.

"Now dear, you don't mean that—"

But Tennyson wasn't listening any longer. "What if we didn't use magic?"

The three women stopped. "Don't be silly, Tennyson," Lily said. "The house is protected from Groundlings as well."

"From Groundlings stumbling upon it, yes. But what if we use a machine?" Tennyson was starting to get excited.

"What do you mean?" Rose narrowed her gaze.

"Neither Groundlings nor Arcani can find the house. But if we use a tracking device, a Groundling-built tracking device, why couldn't we locate him?" Tennyson eyed the women eagerly. "He expects us to use magic. So we won't. Lucas believes himself so above the Groundlings, he won't consider anything Groundling-made a threat."

"But what do we know about Groundling machines?"

"Nothing. But we can find out." He waited for their reactions.

"It's so crazy it might work," Hyacinth said. "I say we go for it."

Tennyson grabbed his cell phone and punched in Zack's number. "Zack, I need help."

"I'm there for you. Let me drop Jake and Callie off—"

"No, what I really need is information. Where would I purchase a tracking device?"

"Whoa. Who are you trying to track?"

"Lucas."

Zack let out a low whistle. "Well, he's got a cell phone, which means it's got GPS. But figuring out how to pinpoint him is outta my league, man. And probably illegal."

The joy deflated in Tennyson. Then Zack continued. "But I have a friend from college. He's into gadgets. Let me make a call or two and I'll get back to you." Zack hung up.

Hope rekindled. The three women questioned Tennyson with their expectant gazes. He shrugged. "He's calling me back."

Seconds ticked by like minutes, minutes like hours, and in the hour and a half they waited, Tennyson thought he'd go gray. Finally the phone rang.

"I got him, dude. This guy's a genius, but it's highly illegal. You need, like, subpoenas and warrants and stuff. He wouldn't do it until I promised I'd be there too."

"That's fine. When can he come?"

"Give me your address. We'll be there yesterday."

Tennyson rattled off the address of the house the aunts were staying in.

"Be right there, dude." Zack rang off.

Tennyson looked at the aunts. "They're on their way." *More waiting* was what he thought.

An hour later a bespectacled man wearing a rumpled white button-down shirt, no tie, was setting up a third laptop on the coffee table in the living room. Zack had introduced him as Kyle, but before he could give the last name, Kyle had stopped him. Kyle was nervous. "How do I know you aren't going to stalk someone with this information?" He pushed the glasses up on his nose.

Lily's laugh tinkled brightly. "Do we look like we're stalkers?"

"No," said Kyle. "But this is—"

"Highly illegal. Yes, you've told us." Tennyson couldn't prevent the impatience in his tone.

"Dude, trust me," said Zack with a grin and a slap on Kyle's back. "These guys can keep a secret. And I trust Tennyson with my life."

Rose walked into the room with a tray. "I made double espresso lattes for us all. And cookies."

Kyle's eyes glanced at the tray, then back. "Madeleines? My grandmother used to make these for me." He grabbed a mug and smashed a cookie into his mouth. "These are better than hers."

"The way to a man's heart . . . ," Hyacinth whispered to Tennyson.

Kyle sat on the couch in front of his impromptu techno array, a plate of the madeleines within easy reach. "We're set. You just have to call the guy and keep him on the line until I triangulate his position."

Tennyson picked up Kristin's cell. Luckily it hadn't broken when he tossed it. He scrolled down for Lucas's number and dialed. For a moment he feared Lucas wouldn't answer, but then Lucas spoke into the phone.

"I'm assuming this is Ritter."

"Can't trick you. No, wait; we already did." Tennyson made the okay sign with his thumb and forefinger.

Kyle shoved another cookie in his mouth and entered Lucas's phone number into the first computer. He gave a thumbs-up to Tennyson.

"And yet I have Kristin," Lucas said. "You aren't quite as victorious as you would like to think."

"That's why I called." Tennyson walked around to see

the monitors. All three screens were busy with oscillations, numbers, letters, passing by at speeds Tennyson couldn't follow. He shook himself and concentrated on the conversation. "What are you going to do with her?"

"That's entirely up to her. Well, not entirely." Lucas chuckled, and Tennyson's annoyance grew. Pompous bastard.

Tennyson drew in a deep breath. Now to entice Lucas. "I have some information you might like."

"Really? Why should you want to give me information?" Lucas's disbelief was palpable through the phone.

"Call it an act of good faith. Something I can bank on when we discuss Kristin's terms of release."

"Ah, but you see, I won't release Kristin."

Kyle held up one finger. The first point was identified.

"Which is one of our points of negotiation. Aren't you curious about the information?" Tennyson watched the screen again. The rapid exchange of data on the two remaining monitors hadn't slowed.

"Not particularly." Lucas sounded bored. "I don't have time for this, Ritter."

"The Council has found Ivan Dimitrov."

For a moment Tennyson thought Lucas might have hung up, but the numbers still cycled on the computers.

"I've never heard that name," Lucas said finally. "Why should I care about this man?"

"No reason. The Council has decided the man has suffered from his past enough, and they will no longer trouble him." Tennyson waited.

"Again I have no idea why I should care about some

stranger to me," Lucas said. "Now if there is nothing more . . ."

Kyle held up two fingers.

Tennyson hurried into speech. "Kristin has been found incompetent."

Lucas snorted in derision. "Fools."

"They have charged me to turn her in to them." Tennyson felt the stares of the aunts on him. He knew they thought he had revealed too much, but he didn't care if Lucas knew. He needed to find Kristin.

"And will you?" Lucas's question brought Tennyson's focus back.

"I haven't decided yet. I have to think about my future. Either way I want Kristin back." He held his breath. Would Lucas believe him?

"Thank you for the interesting stories, but I'm not sure why you concerned me with them. I have Kristin, the Council doesn't want her, and you, well, you have some thinking to do. Call me later if you can make up your mind."

"Reynard—"

The phone went dead.

Tennyson turned to Kyle.

"Got him."

27

HOW TO BE A FAIRY GODMOTHER:

•

Don't Mourn Endings; They Often Bring New Beginnings.

WHEN KRISTIN FINISHED feeling sorry for herself, she sat up on the bed and used the thoroughly rumpled sheet to dry her eyes and blow her nose. She didn't care if it was uncouth. Besides, she had more pressing issues. She was starved. Water wouldn't be amiss either.

She crossed to the door and tried the knob. Not that she had expected it to open, but she had to try. Fisting her hands, she started pounding on the door. "Hey, anybody out there? I'm hungry." Just because she was a captive didn't mean she had to be patient and polite. "Hey, dirtbags. I want some food."

She wouldn't be able to keep up the noise for long, but until she tired she had nothing better to do. Continuing to bang on the door, she now added stamping on the floor as well. Might as well give them the whole treatment.

No more than a minute could have passed before the knob rattled. She backed away from the door as it swung inward. Lucas walked in followed by a woman carrying a tray.

"Really, Kristin, such behavior is beneath you," said Lucas. He stepped to the side to let the woman pass. "Put it on the chair."

The woman did as she was told and then left the room. Lucas picked up the chair and placed it next to the bed. "Well, go ahead and eat. You clamored for it enough."

Kristin sat on the edge of the bed and scrutinized the tray. A neatly trimmed sandwich, slices of peaches and strawberries, and cheese and crackers sat on china plates. A bottle of water accompanied the meal. "You didn't do anything to it, did you?"

"And if I had, what choice would you have?" Lucas's polished voice slipped a little.

"Just asking." She picked up the sandwich. Chicken salad. Not her favorite, but it would suffice. She bit into it.

"I had an interesting phone conversation with Mr. Ritter."

She choked on the sandwich. Coughing, she said, "You called Tennyson?"

"He called me." Leaning against the opposite wall, Lucas observed her. "He passed along some information that I found very intriguing."

She furrowed her brow. "Why does this concern me?"

"But it does, you see."

No, she didn't see, but she'd let him talk. She took another bite.

"Of course I had to check the verity of his statements.

Turns out he was telling the truth." Lucas clasped his hands behind his back.

Clearly he wanted her to ask what the news was, so she was determined not to. "He usually does." She gave her attention to her food.

"The Council seems to think you are a liability. They want to incarcerate you."

She choked again. Grabbing the bottle, she gulped down a mouthful of water. It slid painfully down her throat. "Me? *I'm* a criminal? What did I do?"

A smile of delighted irony slid across Lucas's face. "They have found your actions alarmist and destructive to the state of the Arcani world."

Words failed her. This was insane. She had been plucked from her world without any say in the matter, and now the Council thought she was a disruptive element? Here she was, risking her own safety to stop Lucas, and the Council believed she was dangerous? She wasn't the one trying to take over the world. She eyed him. "I don't believe you."

"That's your prerogative, of course. Tennyson himself has been reprimanded and ordered to turn you in to them."

She wanted to wipe the glee from Lucas's face. "He wouldn't do that."

Lucas shrugged. "He said he hadn't decided yet. He has his status to consider."

No, it wasn't possible. Tennyson wouldn't abandon her to the Council. He loved her. He wouldn't betray her. Would he?

Suddenly her appetite wasn't what she thought.

"Now you can understand my disgust with the Council. They shouldn't set our rules, pass laws over us. They are ineffectual, bungling. *They* are the incompetents." Lucas sauntered toward her. "Maybe you should reconsider your position on my offer. No one has a better one for you."

A loud commotion interrupted her brooding. She lifted her head. "What was that?"

Lucas frowned. He crossed to the window and lifted the shade. "Impossible. You told me they had died." He threw her an accusatory glare, then ran from the room, slamming the door behind him.

She darted to the door, hoping he had forgotten to lock it. He hadn't. What had upset him? She went to the window and peered out. Her jaw dropped. Her aunts were here. She sought the latch to the window, but to her disappointment it had none. It was sealed shut.

The three women stood abreast of one another and watched with smiles on their faces as a line of magicals rushed outside to confront them. Smiles? From here, they looked like harmless old women. Kristin hoped they knew what they were doing.

In the next instant, her worries vanished as the entire row of men fell to the stone driveway. Kristin gasped in horror until she saw that the men were still breathing. They were curling up against one another, pillowing their heads on their neighbors' body parts. One had even stuck his thumb in his mouth. If she wasn't mistaken, the men were asleep.

Aunt Hyacinth appeared entirely too pleased with herself, and acknowledged the comments of the other two women with comments of her own. Oh, how Kristin wished she could hear what they were saying. Aunt Hyacinth always had such a wicked sense of humor.

Lucas appeared on the driveway. His face was almost purple with rage. He kicked at the men asleep on the ground until he stood in front of the aunts. He raised his wand. The women faced him calmly, brandishing their wands as one.

Deep beneath Kristin's feet, a vibration rumbled. A moment later she lost her balance and was thrown from the window to the floor. The window cracked as the house undulated. Bangs, pops, and groans erupted as the wood protested its movement, creating a cacophony of disharmony and unnatural rhythms. A jagged break opened above the doorway. She tried to get to her feet, but her progress toward the door resembled a drunk's walk as the floor rolled beneath her.

The door blasted open. Tennyson stood in the opening, pointing his wand inside. "Kristin." He lurched inside.

With a glad cry she threw herself into his arms. For now she didn't care if he was going to turn her over to the Council. She was just too happy to see him.

"We have to get out of here before he brings down the house around us." Tennyson took her by the hand and waved his wand. Nothing happened.

"No magic," she said. "Not in this room. We have to make it out." She pulled him through the doorway as another loud crack ripped the light fixture from the ceiling and brought down a beam of wood.

They stumbled into Lucas's magical library. The parchment had fallen to the ground, its case broken. The tapestry hung by one corner, as the wall had cracked behind it. As they tried to walk into the room, the floor buckled under their feet. A fissure opened. One side thrust itself up, folding over the other.

Tennyson glanced at the magical items strewn about the room. "No time," he whispered.

Kristin summoned her wand and it arrived in her hand as if finding its way home after a long absence. Relief sparked through her. She shouted above the noise, "We can't transport from here. We have to get out of this room."

A violent jolt shook the house. Tennyson was slammed against a wall as she fell to the floor. The skylight shattered above her. Screaming, she tucked into a ball. The glass rained down over her, but no shard impaled her. She looked at Tennyson. His fierce gaze stole her breath. With his wand pointed at her, he had created a sort of magical umbrella. The glass settled around her, but the house continued to sway.

Tennyson pushed toward her. "Let's get out of here before we're buried." He grabbed her arm and pulled her to her feet. They started for the arch, but another tremor sent them both to their knees.

"The house won't last much longer." She pushed to her feet again, but the quaking didn't stop. The ruby globe knocked into her sandals. She grabbed it, and power flowed into her. The sphere flared in her hand.

Somehow she knew she had to save this relic. But how? She couldn't escape carrying it with her. "Sanctum," she whispered, and to her surprise it vanished.

Tennyson pulled her up. "Move!" They dove through the arch into the main part of the house.

The ceiling crumbled around them. She ducked as Tennyson threw his arms around her to shield her from the debris. A huge hole appeared above them.

"That's convenient." Tennyson blasted a jet of colorful sparks through the hole high into the sky.

"Fireworks?"

"A signal to tell your aunts I have you." He tightened his grip on her. "Hang on."

The air squeezed out of her lungs and her vision went dark. And then they were in a bright living room. The ground still moved beneath them, but with none of the violence of the earthquake at Lucas's house. The tremor stopped a few seconds later.

Tennyson held her. She looked up at him and didn't know what to say. She hated the doubt that Lucas had planted in her.

Tennyson stared at her for an instant, then with a groan he lowered his mouth to hers and kissed her as if he couldn't bear not to touch her, as if he couldn't stand to be an inch away from her.

She melted into him and drank of him as if he were one of life's necessities. For this moment, for now, she didn't care that he might betray her.

"A-hem." A polite cough interrupted their reunion.

Kristin stepped back and saw the three aunts.

"We saw your signal," Lily said.

"So we knew you had her," Rose said.

"Even if our timing stinks," said Hyacinth.

They held their arms open. A happy cry burst from Kristin as she ran to them and they all embraced.

With an indulgent smile, Tennyson flicked on the television. Already the channels were reporting an earthquake in San Diego with its epicenter just north of the city. "He didn't control this one. The entire city felt it." Tennyson turned off the television.

"He'll be drained for days." Lily took a seat on the sofa. "He used up a lot of power this time."

Rose giggled. "Well, we weren't very nice. Inciting his anger that way."

"His house is uninhabitable, that's for sure," said Hyacinth. "Talk about cutting off your nose."

"No, he already planned to abandon the house. Since I breached the barriers. It was supposed to be his fortress." Kristin looked at the four of them. "So how *did* you find me?"

"GPS," said Tennyson.

"What?" She looked at them in disbelief.

"Let's just say that Lucas really underestimates the power of Groundlings." Tennyson settled into an armchair and watched her.

Unease stirred in her. Was he waiting to see if she'd try to bolt?

"I'll fix some snacks for us," said Rose, starting for the kitchen. "All that magic has made me hungry. You all just keep talking."

In the next minutes, Tennyson and the aunts filled Kristin in on their actions, how they found Lucas's house, how the aunts led the frontal assault, and how Tennyson broke in through the back. How the aunts had subdued Lucas's guards, how Lucas had completely flipped out when he saw the aunts and tried to exact his revenge on them with the earthquake.

"He confirmed that Elenka was his mother," said Lily. "He blamed the three of us for her imprisonment. I guess that part's true," she said with a sigh.

Rose reentered with a plateful of sandwiches and another of cookies. "Poor misguided boy. If only he could've been saved from her influence."

"Don't tell me you feel sorry for him," Hyacinth said incredulously.

"Not for him now, but for the child he was. No child

should suffer as he did." Rose bit into a sandwich. "If the Council had handled that situation better, we wouldn't be fighting this battle now."

"He would've killed us," Hyacinth persisted.

"If he could have, but he wasn't prepared for the three of us. The earthquake was a manifestation of his anger. One can't help but feel a little sympathy for him," Rose said.

"I can." Hyacinth folded her arms over her chest. "We're just lucky we got out of there before he could try anything else."

"I'm afraid we're not done with him yet." Lily shook her head.

"He has Merlin's Gifts," Tennyson said quietly.

The three women froze. The question-filled silence lasted a moment. Then Lily spoke. "Are you sure?"

"I didn't get to examine them, but I saw the tapestry, and the staff. And Jake spoke of a red ball."

"Good heavens." Rose grew pale.

The red ball. Did he mean the ruby sphere? Kristin studied the four magicals. "What are the Gifts?"

"A legend, but now I'm not so sure." Tennyson shook his head. "Merlin supposedly left three Gifts with the first fairy godmothers. Three powerful objects that when used together can change the course of history. I don't know the details. The *Lagabóc* can tell me more. If they ever let me back to it."

"But if Lucas has all three . . ." Rose's voice trailed off.

"He doesn't," Kristin said. She held out her hand and focused. Glowing softly, the ruby sphere appeared in her hand.

They stood in silence staring at the orb. Then Hyacinth spoke. "I think the Council is right to be afraid of you."

Kristin glanced at Tennyson. "Lucas said the Council thinks I'm a criminal."

"I'm afraid so, my dear," said Rose. "They've decided—"

"Shortsighted idiots," interjected Hyacinth.

"—that you are incompetent for the position of fairy godmother."

Kristin stopped and turned to Tennyson. "You're supposed to turn me in to them."

He scrutinized her. "Did you think I would?"

"Well, Lucas said you had an important position, and any association with me—"

He jumped from his chair, strode to her, and pulled her into his arms. His kiss silenced her. He pulled on her lips, coaxing trust from them, sending love into her.

The aunts sighed in unison.

Tennyson broke off the kiss with a laugh. "I'll show you more when we don't have our audience." He shook his head. "I will admit I gave Lucas the impression that I hadn't decided yet, but I already knew where my place was. Fighting beside you. The Council be damned."

Tears filled her eyes. "I've turned you into a criminal."

"No, just a rogue." He grinned at her.

"Count us in as well. We're rogues too," said Hyacinth.

"Now have a sandwich, dear." Rose passed her a sandwich. "Here try this one. It's turkey and Swiss. Your favorite."

Kristin stared at the sandwich. Her stomach flipped. "How can I eat if I'm an outlaw?"

"You need to keep your strength up for the fight against Lucas," said Lily. "All we've done is destroy his house. He's still out there planning his revolution, and from the number of men at his house, he's not alone in the endeavor."

"And we have an army of five." Kristin laughed at the futility of the situation.

"You forgot Callie and Zack. That's seven," Tennyson added with a grin.

"No, we have nine," said Rose.

"With the other two godmothers," Lily said.

"Assuming we can count on them," Hyacinth said.

"We can," Lily said. "That's why they're chosen ones. They won't fall for the Council's idiocy."

Hyacinth nodded. "True. I always did like Reggie and Stormy."

"Who are you talking about?" Kristin asked.

"The other two fairy godmothers, of course. The three of you," said Lily.

Kristin held up her hand. "Hold it. Three of us? What other fairy godmothers?"

"Didn't you look at the list we left you?" Hyacinth asked.

"Uh . . . what list?"

"On the back page of the rules we printed for you. We told you that two more will be chosen soon. So you wouldn't feel so alone as you figured out your powers," Lily said.

"She wasn't alone." Tennyson tightened his arms around her.

"We know that, dear, but there's a certain bond between fairy godmothers," Rose said.

"Um, you never left the list," Kristin said.

"Of course we did." Lily waved her hand dismissively. "Rose typed it up—"

"No, I baked her favorite cookies. We discussed what should go in it and I came up with the title, but I never typed it. Hyacinth was going to."

"Not me. I can only hunt and peck. It would've taken me weeks. I thought Lily was doing it."

"Oh dear," Lily said. "We didn't leave her the rules?"

"So it would seem." Hyacinth chewed a fingernail.

The three women looked at one another in chagrin, then faced Kristin with wide, apologetic gazes.

"It doesn't matter now," Kristin said. "We need to make a list. Does anyone have any paper?"

Tennyson laughed and with a flick of his wand he summoned a legal pad and a pen.

Her hands were full. She looked at the sphere. "Sanctum." It vanished.

"Amazing," Rose said.

"Well, she is a Rare One," Tennyson said with nothing but pride in his voice.

"Okay, we need to find out more about these gifts; we need to figure out where Lucas might be hiding." She started scribbling. "And I need the names of the other two godmothers. What else?"

Tennyson said, "If Lucas is Elenka's son, who is the Ivan Dimitrov the Council found in England?"

"We don't know." Lily's eyes twinkled. "But England would make a fabulous trip for a honeymoon."

Kristin's cheeks glowed with heat, but a smile curved her lips as she continued to make notes. "Don't push it, Lily. This is not some fairy tale."

* * *

SEVERAL HOURS LATER, having made their initial plans, Kristin and Tennyson said good-bye to the aunts. They would be vagabonds for a while, trying to elude both Lucas and the Council. Time would give her a stronger understanding of her magic, which she would need when they faced Lucas again. Tonight she and Tennyson were staying at a cozy B and B up the coast, but first he needed some things from home. His home. He transported her to his house.

"I can't believe I've never brought you here." Tennyson flicked on the lights. He walked to the bookshelves and pulled down two volumes. He glanced through the first and then the second, and threw them into a suitcase that materialized at his side at the flick of his wand.

Kristin walked around the living room. She knew this place. She had been here twice before. Only then she hadn't known it was his house. "Why can't we stay here?"

"Too many people know where I live. Unlike Lucas, I did allow visitors." He headed up the stairs.

She looked up as he disappeared into a room. The master bedroom she knew. With its wide window that overlooked the backyard and beyond it the ocean. She didn't need to follow him. She had seen it twice.

Home. Twice she had transported focusing on that word and twice she had ended up here. She brushed her fingers along the balustrade while she waited for him. Home. This was home.

"Do you want to see the rest of the house?" he called from upstairs. "You're moving in as soon as this mess is behind us."

And she would too, she promised herself. Someday

they would move in here together and it really would be home. But for now it was enough to know that home waited for her. Not just here, but anywhere that Tennyson was.

"Sure," she said, and she climbed the staircase.